Praise for Mark Alder's Banners of Blood:

'*SFX* five star recommendation . . . smart, gripping historical fantasy'   *SFX*

'A triumphant combination of great characters and an epic – yet not too sprawling – plot . . . a vivid and realistic story that, once you're in, you'll find it hard to leave'
Fantasy Faction

'What the author has accomplished here is nothing short of emarkable, providing a rich window into an alternative history that hits all the right notes and doesn't alienate those without a deep knowledge of historical happenings'   SF BOOK

'It is a novel that demands to be read'
Fantasy Book Review

'Expertly written, highly detailed and vividly imagined, this is an outstanding work of historical fiction/alternate history which pulled me in with its prose and story from page 1'   Grim Dark Fantasy Reader

Also by Mark Alder from Gollancz:

Son of the Morning

SON
of the
NIGHT

Banners of Blood: Book Two

Mark Alder

This edition first published in Great Britain in 2018 by Gollancz

First published in Great Britain in 2017 by Gollancz
an imprint of the Orion Publishing Group Ltd
Carmelite House, 50 Victoria Embankment
London EC4Y 0DZ

An Hachette UK Company

1 3 5 7 9 10 8 6 4 2

A CIP catalogue record for this book is
available from the British Library.

ISBN 978 0 575 11521 7

Printed in Great Britain by Clays Ltd, St Ives plc

www.gollancz.co.uk

PART 1

1346

The eve of the Battle of Crécy

Fowles in the frith,
The fishes in the flood,
And I must go mad
Much sorrow I walk with
For beast of boon and blood.

Traditional song

I

The count of Gâtinais was leaving, going to answer King Philip's call to arms. The count was not a warlike man, and he was old – though his sons who sat mounted at his side were strong boys, good in the jousts, better in the mêlée.

The late summer morning was pleasant, the dew still on the grass outside the great church, the sun calling light from the wet land. He did not want to go. This was a blessed land, its people's fingers stained yellow with the saffron they picked, the bees ambling among the flowers that grew from the turfed roofs of the cottages, the children fat and bonny.

'Why must kings want things?' Gâtinais asked his son Michel. 'Why must they move and change? Why not doze through life, by the sun in summer, by the fire in winter?'

'The English king wants our lands.'

'Not our lands. Aquitaine, a little around Calais.'

'Granted those, he will look for more.'

'I suppose you're right.'

He patted his horse's neck. It was a good horse, a courser he'd ridden on many a pleasant ride through the gentle fields around his castle. He didn't want it shot, spiked by English arrows, blown to bits by their guns or, worse, devoured by devils or demons or whatever strange infernal creatures the English had struck bargains with now.

'We have displeased God by allowing the English to prosper in France,' said Michel.

'How do you know? Wouldn't it please God more just to make a truce? Turn the other cheek and all that.'

'Those that turn the other cheek get kicked twice in the arse.' Robert, big burly Robert who'd nearly killed his mother coming into the world, smiled down at him, a head taller than his father. The boy was a credit, it had to be said. He favoured the war axe over the sword and was famous for his skill.

'Blasphemy, boy, blasphemy.'

'Less blasphemous than to allow the English and their devils to burn our churches, steal the relics of our saints.'

'Indeed. You've had your axe blessed?'

'And my armour, my dagger, my shield and my cock.'

'You're going to kill a devil, not swive one, brother,' said Michel.

'It's the bit I'd like least to lose.'

'Why?' said Gâtinais. 'You have four fine boys. One of them will make it to succeed you. Why do you need it more than your arm?'

'For fun, Father.'

'Oh, that,' said Gâtinais. 'All sounds rather tiring to me.'

'My Lord Gâtinais!'

Pushing through the crowd that surrounded the war party, through the villeins at the back, the merchants in front of them, through the wealthier peasants in front of them, the clergy in front of them and the wives and young children of the nobility at the very front, were two men. The first was tall and gangling and wore a paint-spattered felt cap. The second could only just be seen behind him. A short, squat man who looked as though a giant had pressed a thumb on top of his head before his face was quite set.

For an instant Gâtinais thought the short man might be a devil. He'd had the borders of his land blessed but they covered a huge area and he was aware there was only so much blessing even the most hard-working priests could achieve. Then he recognised the tall one. A man who had been doing a little business for him.

'Gâtinais! Noble Gâtinais!' said the tall man.

'Do not address yourself to the lord so boldly!' A man-at-arms pointed towards the man.

'Tancré?' said Gâtinais.

'It's me, Lord, Tancré, at your service.'

'Approach me, approach me.'

The crowd parted and the man came forward. He was dressed in a tunic that might once have been quite fine but now looked as though it had lain a while on the floor of a chicken house. The fellow beside him, he led by the hand. He was barelegged

4

and barefooted, just a long tunic to cover him – a piece of rough cloth with a hole for the head, no more. A few in the crowd threw insults and made jokes as Tancré raised the man's hand to display him to the lord. The people loved a simpleton and this man clearly appeared to be one.

'I have him, sir – Jean the Idiot.'

'We already have a fool, father,' Robert spoke.

'This man isn't a fool, he's a simpleton.'

'There's a difference?'

'Yes – what kind of idiot are you?'

'I thought the question was "What kind of idiot is he?"' Robert laughed. He liked jokes like that.

'A useful one. Try to copy his example.' Gâtinais gave his son a wink and then dismounted.

'Hold a while,' he said. 'I have an hour's business to attend to.'

'I can never guess summer hours. How long are they?' asked Michel.

'Long enough to have a drink,' said Robert.

'You might want to come with me,' said Gâtinais.

Gâtinais led the two low men to the entrance of the great church. His sons followed on, with country folk's easy disregard for the privileges of rank that said they should enter the church before the paupers.

'This is the man?'

'Yes, sir. He restored the windows at Lafage after the mob smashed the church.'

'When did that happen?' said Robert.

'A while ago,' said Gâtinais. 'The low men in that area had an outbreak of the Luciferian disease. They set themselves about their masters!'

Robert crossed himself. 'God save us from that.'

'He has done,' said Gâtinais. 'Good masters need not fear men trying to upend God's order. I am your protection.' He turned to Tancré. 'Didn't the men of Lucifer burn half that church?'

'They did, sir. But he rebuilt the window out of the heat-cracked pieces. He has a gift for it, sir. He is blessed by God to do His work.'

'Another one?' said Gâtinais. 'Him and half the world nowadays, it seems, if you believe them.'

5

'You can believe him, sir.'

From the darkness of the church porch a figure took form, black against the summer light. A priest.

'Ah, Father,' said Gâtinais. 'I have a present for you.'

The priest, a man who had done his best to bring severity and penance to the jolly county of Gâtinais but had largely given up owing to the abundance of very good mead, smiled.

'Sir?'

'Explain, Tancré.'

The priest gave Tancré the sort of look he normally reserved for peasants caught shitting in the apse – a look he had to employ far too often for his liking – but inclined an ear anyway out of deference to his count.

'My great Lord,' said Tancré. 'This is the man who can fix your window.'

The priest looked around him, at something of a loss.

'What window?'

'I thought you'd ask that,' said Gâtinais.

'You were correct, My Lord. Our windows seem to be in an excellent state of repair.'

'Not the bricked-in one behind the altar.'

'I feel that was bricked in for a reason. The church sits with the altar facing west. It's confusing for the parishioners to see the evening light behind it.'

'It was bricked in because a devil flew through it!' said Gâtinais. 'The count of Anjou's wife, mother of the Plantagenets!'

'That is an old legend spread by the enemies of England to discredit its royal line.'

'I'm an enemy of England, and I don't remember spreading it,' said Robert.

'Did it not perform miracles, this window, before that?' said Gâtinais.

'So it is said.' The priest gave an exaggerated shrug. 'The glass fragments certainly work none.'

'No, but they might were they restored.'

'No one even knows what it looked like.'

'The idiot doesn't need to know, sir,' said Tancré. 'He has a feel for it. He's your man to repair anything broken.'

'Set him to repair France,' said the priest. 'We have had enough of miracles. There are Devils abroad. The English army bristles with them, so it's said.'

'We will raise our angels,' said Gâtinais. 'And that will be the end of English devils. Let him see the remnants of this window, priest. I may not be long for this world and I would like to leave something to it. The miracle window restored would be a fitting monument, I think.'

'As you instruct, sire.' The priest didn't roll his eyes but only, suspected Gâtinais, because he was making the effort not to.

They followed the priest down the long apse of the church to a door by the side of a shrine to Mary.

The priest, rather sacrilegiously in the view of Gâtinais, took a small votive candle from the shrine and opened the door. They progressed down a dark and winding stair, the light bobbing before them.

'The crypt?' said Gâtinais, who had never been in this part of the church before.

'A store,' said the priest.

At the bottom of the stair was a short corridor with three doors coming off it.

'Look away, common men,' said the priest. Tancré and Jacques did as they were bid and the priest reached his hand into a crack in the wall to pull out a key. He used it to open the door to their right.

There was a waft of damp and the smell of long disuse as the door scraped open. The priest went within with the light.

'Follow, follow,' said Gâtinais, to the two common men, who were still looking away.

Inside was a large box, as long as a coffin but as wide again. It had a rough wooden lid on it, which the priest lifted away. It seemed to Gâtinais that the box was full of sparkling jewels, blue and amber in the candlelight. But among them he saw bigger pieces of what he knew to be glass.

'This is no place to keep a holy window,' said Gâtinais.

'The remains of one,' said the priest. 'It's said an angel stepped from this window and shattered it. God sundered it.'

'I thought a devil flew through it.'

'It was a long time ago,' said the priest. 'You believe what you like. As you can see it's some way beyond repair.'

So it seemed. Though the odd larger piece remained, most of the window was in tiny bits, dust some of it. Perhaps it had been ambitious. He should have looked at the window as soon as Tancré had suggested restoring it. He'd been so busy, though, organising the response to the king's call.

'Not beyond repair, sir. I promised you.'

'You are a miracle worker?' The priest raised a doubtful eyebrow.

'No, sir, but the idiot is. You watch. He can repair anything.'

'Beautiful,' said Jean. His voice was thick and guttural, a peasant to his core.

'Anything beautiful,' said Tancré. 'Let him show you.'

'No,' said the priest, as Gâtinais said 'Yes'.

'If it pleases you,' said the priest, adjusting his opinion to match that of his lord.

Tancré gestured for Jean to take up a piece of the glass. Jean put his hand over the box, as if uncertain which to choose. Then he withdrew one of the larger fragments, a sliver of blue the length of a finger. He held it up to the candle.

'What's he doing?' said the priest.

'Looking at it,' said Tancré.

'I can see that.'

Jean reached into the box again. Once more his hand hovered and then he withdrew a piece the size of a thumbnail. He studied that too, holding it to the candle.

'I don't think we can let this fool go heating up this glass,' said the priest. 'In some senses it might be seen as a holy relic. In some senses—'

He stopped short. The idiot drew a line with the glass across the back of his hand, drawing blood. Gâtinais exchanged glances with the priest.

'Is this devilry? Blood magic?' said the priest.

'No more than the Communion,' said Tancré.

'Blasphemy,' said the priest, without any great outrage.

The idiot smeared the blood across the edge of the bigger piece of glass. Then he put the smaller piece to it, as if expecting to use the blood as glue. He folded his hand over the two pieces and said:

'At times the enormity of my sins overcame me, and I sighed with confusion and wondered at the long-suffering patience and goodness of God. It seemed to me that I saw Him depute some good guardian to defend me from the attacks of the evil demons . . . Meditating often about this, I desired greatly to know the name of my guardian, so that I could, when possible, honour his memory with some act of devotion. One night I fell asleep with this thought and behold, someone stood by me saying my prayer was heard, and that I might know without doubt that the name I desired to know was Gabriel.'

'God's knees, what a mouthful!' said Gâtinais.

A very strange thing happened. Gâtinais only had eyes for the poor man's hands. The candle, the glitter of the glass in the box, the eyes and teeth of his companions, no longer seemed to shine from the darkness. Only the hands cupped a glow, as if concealing a taper, as if all the light in the little space had condensed into Jean's hands. Jean opened his grip and the light expanded to fill the room again. The two pieces of glass were whole.

'Swipe me!' said Gâtinais.

'It's a marketplace conjurer's trick, no more,' said the priest.

'Well if it is, it's a blessed good one. Where did he learn to talk like that? I've never known anyone outside a monastery gabble on so.'

'How did you do it?' said the priest. 'You could be tried for witchcraft.'

'Not by me,' said Gâtinais, 'so not at all.' The Church was always trying to encroach on the rights of the nobility, and trials for witchcraft were strictly a secular affair.

'It's the light, sir, he can use the light,' said Tancré.

'The light wants,' said Jean.

'What's that supposed to mean?' said the priest.

'He knows what the light wants, sir, he always says so.'

'More trickery. Mark me, Count, these men learn a few mystical lines that ensnare the credulous and use it to try to gull their way to fortunes. This is a trick, like the nut that vanishes.'

Gâtinais took the piece and studied it. It was whole, no line, no fracture, just a deep and perfect blue glittering in the candlelight.

'Well, we'll soon see, won't we?' he said. 'Allow him to begin the repair. If he can't do it, it will soon become obvious.'

'And then?'

'He's either rewarded or—'

'Cut off his hands?' said the priest.

'Let's taste the ale before deciding it's spoiled. Give the man a chance.'

'You can't let him go unpunished if he's a fraud.'

'No, no. But we think too much on harshness nowadays. Let us try to do a good thing.'

'Is it a good thing to allow a fool to sully holy relics?'

'Is he a fool?'

'A man who has been taught to ape a few lines of his betters. You will suffer, man, when your tricks are exposed.'

Jean spoke:

Et in misericordia tua disperdes inimicos meos et perdes omnes qui tribulant animam meam quoniam ego servus tuus sum.

'What, what?' said Gâtinais.

The priest crossed himself.

'A psalm,' he said.

'What the devil does it mean?'

'Do you not know Latin?'

'About as well as you know the use of lance and sword. Of course I don't know Latin – what's the use of you lot if the nobility are going to stick their heads into books?'

'"And in thy loving kindness cut off mine enemies, And destroy all them that afflict my soul; For I am thy servant."'

The idiot nodded and pointed. Clearly he didn't mind making enemies of churchmen, which marked him out as an idiot indeed.

'He has learned these things for the benefit of clergy,' said the priest. 'He seeks to be tried by a Church court rather than face the punishment due to him as a common man.'

'Well, that alone means he's not as green as he is cabbage-looking,' said Gâtinais. 'Let him try, priest. The country is full of devils, called by kings. Then there are the demons that whisper treachery in the ears of the poor. We have been lucky not to see these things amongst us. The window is a blessed object and would provide protection. Even word that it was being restored might keep dark forces away.'

The priest took up the piece of glass. 'How long would this take?'

'No more than five years, sir,' said Tancré. 'He is a marvellous fast worker.'

'A blink,' said Gâtinais, 'a blink in the life of this great church. Let him try.'

'How much does this rogue want paying?'

'Food only, sir. I have come to a financial arrangement with the count. Food only. He will sleep in the church or where you tell him, it's a more comfortable spot than any he has known.'

'We'll have to move good brick.'

'He will screen the gap, sir.'

'Come on,' said Gâtinais. 'If an angel dwelt in that window once, perhaps it could again.'

The priest handed the glass back to Gâtinais.

'Very well, though it's against my best instincts. I've seen enough marketplace conjurers and charlatans in my time. But if it's only going to cost me some bread and ale, then let's try. And if he doesn't restore it, I have your permission to punish him?'

'You churchmen are zealots for pruning a fellow, aren't you?. Yes. Clip away if you must but give him a fair chance. Nothing before I return from the wars.'

'And if you do not return?'

'Then it shall fall to my sons to take my place.'

'And if they do not return?'

'Then God is gone from the world and we are all damned. Now let's get back into the light. I have a useless king to follow.'

So saying, he turned to the steps, to lead his sons to war and all of their deaths on Crécy field.

2

The count of Eu pulled up the visor on his pig-faced helmet, wiped the smoke from his eyes and surveyed the disaster unfolding before him at Caen.

The English were massing all around the island town. He steadied his horse as a flight of ympes, tiny winged men no bigger than crows, swept over him, their swords and arrows like a glint of rain. By God, he was facing a strange alliance. The English, with their angel Chamuel, their hordes of devils under God and their swooping demons, the damned of Hell, servants of Lucifer. He thanked Christ he was French. Their army only contained angels and devils, who bowed the knee to God on high. But where were they? King Philip had to send an angel or a flight of stoneskins or something to help him. It was the king who had engineered this catastrophe in waiting.

Eu's footmen massed against the barricade on the bridge, mail clashing against mail, lances bristling. Behind them priests sang blessings, swung incense burners, flicked holy water over the troops. A formidable force, but the bridge would not hold. None of the bridges would hold. The barricades had been built too hastily, too few and not substantial enough. He had two hundred men on every barricade and a further nine hundred spread along the banks of Caen. Not enough, not enough.

Over the broken body of a cart on top of the barricade rose a grinning skull atop a man's body. The body was waving a sword. Later, he would know this to be one of the bone-faced men, 3rd Legion of the Devils of Gehenna. One of the many. His men jeered and jabbed at it but it was safely above their spears.

Soon, though, the barricades would be rendered useless. They'd had no time to remove the boats from the river banks. The English archers and men-at-arms were swarming into them, loosing arrows as they went, ducking beneath shields to avoid the returning fire. This was going to be a test.

He drew his own sword, Joyeuse, letting the blessed weapon's light shine out. The sacred king Charlemagne had wielded that sword to build the empire of the Franks and to wet the desert with unbelievers' blood and every Constable of France had borne it since. That gave the bone-faced man pause for thought and he ducked back behind the cart.

Robert Bertrand drew up beside Eu, magnificent on his white horse, his armour polished to brilliance, his surcoat embroidered with golden stars – almost an angel himself, he appeared.

'Not good, Raoul,' he said.

'Not good,' said Eu. 'How many of them?'

'Nine, ten thousand, excluding the *diaboliques*.'

'Six to one.'

'In the castle we could have held them.'

'If my aunt had a dick, she'd be my uncle.'

'We shouldn't be on this island. Are we throwing away France to protect the plate of a few hundred grubby buyers and sellers? Men of trade? My God, what a pass we have come to?'

'Apparently it's God's will.'

'The will of Prince John!'

'Same thing,' said Eu.

He meant it, too. Given his choice Eu would have knocked down a few of the city's houses and used the rubble to block the way. But no, strings had been pulled, favours called in. The town was to be defended unscathed. So instead of bogging the English down in a protracted siege, thumbing his nose at them from the island castle walls, that idiot Prince John had insisted he defend the second island of the town, to protect the merchants and their houses. He had told the messenger that he could protect the merchants but could not protect their houses. The prince had said that he could. Still, the prince was divinely appointed, his army backed by angels. To disobey him was to disobey God. So do and be damned, don't do and actually be damned. The castle was now crammed with the rich and influential of Caen, while anyone who had any idea at all about how to actually conduct a siege was out in the streets waiting for the English to destroy them.

As constable, he had the right to be in the tower. He had given it up. If his men were to stand any chance at all he needed to be with them. The English angel had recognised his royal blood, agreed to hold back its fire until God made His will known in the direction of the battle. It was strange indeed to talk to that thing, an enormous shining man, armoured and shielded, floating above the parapets, its voice intoxicating, sending Eu's head spinning. Eu had done his job, though, convinced it of his piety, or the sacrifices and godliness of the people of Caen, had asked it to look at the churches they had built, the art they had commissioned to God's glory. It had lost interest in raining fire down on his men.

Where were his angels? Where were his devils? All with the main army. Couldn't angels be anywhere? He'd heard it said. Well, if they could, they chose not to be at Caen.

An awful roar and the warhorse beneath him shivered. The English were discharging their cannon. Good. Those things were more of a peril to the men operating them than to his troops.

'If I should die . . .' said Bertrand.

'What?'

Bertrand shrugged, his armour so well made that it moved on his shoulders as easy as a cloak.

'It's a possibility. Devils. These low men, these servants of Lucifer who travel with the English king. They cannot be relied upon.'

'You're not going to die, Robert, my God, you're a marshal of France. Do you think the English have taken leave of their senses?'

'I think some of them may never have had any. These are new times, Raoul. The old certainties of battle do not apply.'

A great cry from the bank. Their troops were showering arrows on the English, the English returning fire from the bank. A thud as an arrow glanced off Eu's breastplate. He paid it no notice. There was no way an English bodkin would get through his armour at ten paces. At a hundred the arrows were but summer midges.

A great cry and a bristling mass of men came streaming into the barricade.

'There's one certainty,' said Eu. 'French knights fight harder than any devil. Your sword is blessed?'

'Of course.'

14

'Then let's cry havoc and stain these streets with our enemies' blood!'

Bertrand smiled. 'I'll see you in Heaven.'

'More likely England,' said Eu. 'Though we may be in irons. Squires, attend me!'

His young knights closed in, his page Marcel running behind carrying a teeter-tottering lance so much bigger than him it was a wonder the boy could lift it. He was no more than nine years old.

'Cheaper to get killed than pay your ransom!' said Bertrand.

'I'll remember that when the English come for me! Hold the barricades! Hold them!'

Swarms of devils hit the bridges. Giant beetles winging in, bone-faced men crawling over the piled barricades, streams of stoneskins dropping boulders and logs. A volley of blessed arrows from his own men saw the flight of gargoyles turn. Over the river he could hear a terrible roaring. That was no cannon. He told his squires to stand where they were. He wheeled his horse down to the waterfront to see on the other bank a monstrous lion, erect like a man on its back paws. It wore dull grey armour and its mane was like a brush of steel rods. Lord Sloth, Satan's ambassador. Eu had heard that good servant of God had thrown his lot in with the English.

His men were exchanging bow fire with the enemy, so he left his horse behind a house. Its caparison was thick but, at such range, the arrows might get through. He, however, was impervious in his armour.

He held up Joyeuse for the lion to see. Sloth roared again, its breath almost palpable across the river.

'God's sword!' shouted Eu. 'God's wrath for you, Sloth!'

'I serve Satan, and he serves God.'

'We all say we serve God nowadays. Perhaps this battle will see who the Almighty favours.'

Arrows peppered the bank. 'Your angel hasn't engaged, Sloth. It seems it thinks the day is in question.'

'I'll give you question!' roared the lion. 'I'll—'

A mighty noise, like a great sigh from behind him. 'The East Bridge is lost!' came a cry.

The lion turned away and ran along the riverbank.

Eu ran back, mounted and spurred his horse towards the fray.

His men were in flight, the low bowmen of Lucifer at their backs. The town was falling. He felt a delicious shiver go through him, like the first kiss of wine on a summer's afternoon. Men like him were born for days like these. He held high his sword and trotted towards the foe, his knights falling in beside him, the fleur-de-lys fluttering from their pennants.

'France! France!' he screamed.

Men stopped, turned, their courage renewed by the sight of such a leader. How many English? It didn't matter. The bridge was narrow, packed like a marketplace, the invaders disordered, bowmen, bone-faces and men-at-arms, not a lance among them. He levelled his sword and charged, six knights behind him, lances fixed.

Panic, utter and complete, as they hit the English line at the trot. Such a crush, such a glorious crush. My God, he caused his share of havoc but the English did the rest themselves, panicking, turning, trying to run over the barricade they had so recently overwhelmed, stamping down the fallen, tripping and being stamped. Such terror gripped them that they forgot to fight. His horse reared, but not in panic. Like him, it was trained for this. Its hoof came crashing down on a bone face's skull, reducing it to powder. He'd had the animal's shoes rubbed with the blood of St Cuthbert, an anathema to things of Hell.

Men hit the water, leaping for their lives. He cut and slashed, not really seeing who he hit, registering success by the judder of his sword. The charge had done its job, numbed minds, broken wills. The enemy didn't even bother to fight. Yes, you can kill a warhorse if you hold your nerve and present your sword, but say your prayers, for they will be your last. The mind may cry hold but the heart screams run. Weapons were flung down, shields cast aside in the panic to be away.

'To me, France! To me!'

His men followed his standard into the rabble, casting the English down, forcing them scrambling back across the barricades.

'Reform the picket!' shouted Eu. 'They'll not come so boldly again!'

Screams from behind. He wheeled. The shiny black beetle devils were engaging his men on the West Bridge, Bertrand's white horse among them, death in a circle around it. Another roar from the

East Bridge. Oh God, Sloth! He'd forgotten about him. And then a sound he had heard before but hoped never to hear again. People shut in burning buildings screamed like that, men on sinking ships. Something was coming across the North Bridge and his men, veterans of the English wars, were crying like children.

He spurred his horse towards the noise to find his troops in a mad flight. A noise like a monstrous drum. The shaking of the earth. A cry in an English voice:

'"He moveth his tail like a cedar: the sinews of his stones are wrapped together. His bones are as strong pieces of brass; his bones are like bars of iron."'

Eu lifted his visor to address the fleeing men.

'What? What?'

No sense, just panic. Why were they running? There was nowhere to run to.

He rode on to the North Bridge. A shiny black beetle flew before him, big as a dog, flapping and biting but Joyeuse cut it down, its body smacking to the stones.

And then there it was, lumbering on, accompanied by priests, who chanted and sang. It was like an enormous man, four times taller than the biggest knight, fat as the elephant of legend and wielding a headsman's sword, a long triangle, thick at the end. What strength did it need to swing that as a weapon? Its belly was huge and distended but ridged with muscle and a monstrous cock swung beneath its legs. Its upper body was bloated too – long arms as thick as trees. Its head was like a turnip, purple and yellow, a wide mouth full of cruel teeth. Behind it, cautious and creeping, was a mass of men-at-arms. Eu guessed the devil might not be too careful about who it swiped with that great sword.

'Behemoth!' it shrieked, its voice like the scream of a thousand birds. 'Behemoth! I am sin's reward!'

There were no defenders around it, all had fled.

Eu's throat went dry; he steadied himself on his horse, though he did not need steadying. It was as if he stood alone on a mummers' stage, he the knight, it the monster, acting out the old story. He crossed himself. The thing stank of sulphur and in one hand it carried the body of a knight. It bit off his head like a man might bite the top off a carrot.

He wanted to turn his horse and run but that was not part of the bargain. Serfs toil, churchmen pray, nobles fight. That was the deal and the higher the noble, the bigger the fight. He felt a tap at his leg. Marcel, his little page, had his lance. He took it.

'Thank you, Marcel. Retreat to the castle if you can.'

'My place is with you, sir.'

'Not here, boy. Tell my story.'

'I can't if I don't watch.'

'Make it up. That's what you do with knights' stories.'

'I must fetch more lances.'

'That won't be necessary.'

'They'll make you a saint for this.'

'No. They'll make me a saint for the deeds I do after I've killed it.'

'Then you will live to tell your own story!'

'That's not the way it's done. I would be compelled to be honest. Go. Now!'

'Behemoth! Sinners beware! Lord Satan punishes those who break God's law!'

The priests before the creature stopped as they saw Eu. They crossed themselves, one dropping his incense burner. A fully armoured knight on a warhorse could do that to an unwarlike man – scare him so much he couldn't think. Eu had done it to a few warlike men in his time, too. In his plumes and his surcoat, his great shield and his shining armour, he knew what he looked like. Death. Good. He was creating the intended impression.

A moment of silence, as sometimes happens even among the fury of battle. In an instant Eu was somewhere else – at home in his lands in Champagne, the summer evening and the honey bee lazy on the violets.

A wet smack on the stones next to him. The creature had thrown the corpse of the knight at him.

'Behemoth! Behemoth! Behemoth!'

'For God, St Denis and for France!' shouted Eu. He fixed his lance and charged, swiping in at an angle.

The creature screamed and raised its great sword, but Eu drove the lance into its armpit, releasing it as he went. The point stuck and went in but the creature seemed unfazed, wheeling to strike Eu's horse across the rump with the headsman's sword.

The animal didn't even cry out, though Eu felt it stagger and collapse. He'd had enough horses killed under him to know when it was time to dismount and he stepped neatly out of the saddle, light as a dancer, as the horse collapsed to the floor, its back legs severed. He drew Joyeuse, and turned to face Behemoth, the horse's blood washing over his ankles.

Two English men-at-arms had rounded the great devil, leaping in with spears to stab at him but one slipped in the horse's blood and fell, Joyeuse dispatching him quickly. But Eu too slipped and the other man jabbed his spear into him. It bounced uselessly off his breastplate and Eu cut his opponent down at the leg from his position on his arse. On his feet again, quick! A shadow like a bird above him and he threw up his shield. The blow was so hard it collapsed him to his knees. Again, that boiling shriek, like pigs in a barn fire but incomparably louder. Eu rolled, turned. The sword came down once more, sparking off the cobbles beside him. A third time. He threw up his shield and straight away knew his arm was broken. He vomited into his mouth with the pain of it.

Behemoth was above him, its great paunch rubbing the floor, the stink of its tree of a cock in his nostrils. He stabbed up with Joyeuse and the creature screamed, wobbled and, oh no, sat down like a landslide. Oh God, his legs were trapped, his sword arm too, though he would not release his sword. He pulled and pulled on the holy weapon, tearing at the thing's belly, engulfed in a tide of blood, hot entrails dropping around him like serpents. Behemoth howled and struck down with its sword, catching his helmet a glancing blow and skittling his senses.

He'd taken worse blows in tournaments or in the mêlée, been thrown from horses, smashed by maces, and all that good practice came to bear. Another man might have ceased to fight; another man might have been rendered stone by the force of the blow. Eu shook it off. Why do knights bash each other's brains out in tournaments? So, come the real fight, they have no more brains to bash. Tear, rip. He thought he would pass out with the pain but he couldn't afford to do that. A footman was above him, grinning, a cruel dagger in his hand. He drew a finger across his throat and split in two, from the centre of his skull down to his waist as Behemoth swiped at Eu and missed.

A beetle devil landed, clicking its mandibles. He twisted to get his sword free but the bulk of the devil would not allow him. The beetle approached, fitted its jaws around his helm, and bit. The steel creaked and groaned. Behemoth stood up. Eu tried to pull out his sword but it was still stuck in the creature's belly. He found his misericord and drove it into the beetle's eye, but the weapon bounced away. He'd forgotten to have it blessed! His vision blurred; his head felt as though it would burst as the beetle's crushing jaws clamped down. The giant teetered above him, ready to fall.

'Goodbye, Marie, goodbye, Celeste, goodbye—' He was halfway through his farewell to his family when something struck Behemoth like a stone from a siege engine. A warhorse had come in at the charge. The giant fell back onto the cowards who still hid at its back, expiring with a great sigh echoed by the men beneath it. He felt the pressure on his head release. More agony as he was dragged across the cobbles.

'Robert!'

It was Bertrand and a party of his men, the men-at-arms driving around the monster to force the English back with cries and jabs.

'Can you move?'

Eu shook his legs and then stood. He had to get to his feet. His men could not see their leader down.

'Very well, very good,' said Eu. 'Well, don't just stand there looking as though you've been stuffed, Robert, get my sword! It's in the creature.'

'You killed it, sir, you killed it.' It was his page Marcel.

'I told you to go.'

Bertrand ran to the fallen Behemoth and grabbed Joyeuse. 'Give it, give it,' said Eu. 'Boy, unstrap my shield.'

The page did as he was bid while more French poured in around them. The death of the giant had renewed the courage of his men and made that of the English falter. Fighting was all around them, the clash of arms, cries of exultation and of pain rending the air. Englishmen were already robbing the houses, emerging with fine carpets, clothes and what other plunder they could get while not ten paces away other men fought mortal duels.

'And fetch a horse,' said Eu. 'A horse, now. Get one!' The boy ran away into the mêlée.

Eu had been prepared for this. His old tutor Chevalier De Tares had specialised in running him into the ground, beating him with a stave and pulling such tricks as tying an arm behind his back or putting a patch across one eye in his schooling with the sword and lance. Hard in the yard, easy in the fight was the way of it. He recalled the old man's words: 'One eye, one arm, one leg. A knight will always be better than ten ordinary men'. He took a breath and looked around. The bridge was holding but men were pouring over the river now, some wading, some in boats.

The town was lost – no point in denying it. The castle on the other island was the only choice. The houses were forfeit and they had been idiots to try to defend them with so little preparation. He should have burned the lot of them to deny the English shelter.

The page arrived with a horse. He recognised it – Chevalier Malpré's. Very likely dead.

'Help me up!'

The boy knelt, offering himself as a mounting stool, and Eu winced as he scissored his legs over the high cantle of the saddle. The pain in his arm was great but he was secure, propped back and front.

'Get on!' he told Marcel. 'Get on!'

The page put up his hand, so Eu had to sheathe his sword and pull him up behind the saddle. The boy was light enough.

'The keep! The keep!'

His men poured backwards and he and Bertrand, knowing their duty, drove into the English on their horses, smashing them backwards, buying time for their men. Not too much, though; they could only hold the English for so long, blows bouncing off their greaves, off the horses' caparisons.

The little page stood on the horse's back, grasping the back of the saddle to avoid the stabbing English.

'Now!'

With a great whoop they turned their horses, his warhorse throwing up its back hooves as it had been trained to do, smashing an Englishman to the floor. Then they were barrelling through the streets, the English in full cry behind them. He ran down one man who was emerging from a house with a big mirror under his arm. God, what sport!

Over the bridge to the second island. The great gate of the curtain wall was still open, men pouring through. The English were behind them, though, or worse than the English. Lord Sloth, bounding on in a rattle of iron mane, chasing as quick as a horse. Fifty paces to go and his horse slipped, pitching the page from its back. There was no stopping the animal as it careered towards the gate. He brought it under control just below the portcullis and spun it around.

Sloth was on the bridge, the page on the ground between them.

'Get the gate down, this is no time to be a hero, sir!' shouted a man-at-arms.

'Then when is the time?' Eu spurred his horse towards the fallen boy, towards the roaring lion and the English hordes at its back.

PART 2

1346

Aftermath

I

The battle of Crécy was done and Charles of Navarre lay in the barn, burnt, though not bloody. The impressions of the day shook his sleep – the shudder of the French charge, the scalding hiss of the English arrows, the angels dispensing fire from on high and then . . . And then, the dragon. A dragon as big as the sky.

He had not slept, hardly could sleep, still in his armour but afraid to take it off in case he had to run quickly. He needed to be recognised as a noble, to be worthy of ransom rather than death. He was thirteen years old, nearly fourteen. The hope of the south, the hope of Normandy where his vassal lords lay. You'd have to be mad to kill him if you knew who he was. And yet at Crécy the low men had killed the nobles where they lay fallen. It had been as if they were tipping pots of gold into a bottomless pit. Did they know what they were doing, the riches they were destroying? Who knew? The cult of Lucifer had seized them and all the old certainties were gone.

No sleep, then, but some blurry, restless cousin of sleep. The morning after the battle dawned grey, like the last moments of a winter dusk. The light, it seemed, had fled when the angels had been torn from the sky by that blazing dragon banner.

At first, he thought it was a demon, trapped in the web where the roof beam met the wall. But Charles now saw that it was only a fly – fat and black, its legs moving hopelessly against its fate.

It was not yet dead and he wondered if he could unravel the web that snared it. Charles took the fly carefully from the web. It was not too badly caught and he felt its quick buzz against his cupped hands. He released it.

He had some fellow feeling with flies. Like him, they fed on rot and disorder, bloated themselves on misery. Ever since the angel at La Sainte-Chapelle had told him he would never be king of France, he had dedicated himself to the country's ruin, reasoning that if he could not rule then all rule should be impossible. He had sparked the too hasty charge at Crécy that had led to such calamity for the great houses of France.

Not that Charles delighted in the misery of everyone – just the royals who called him 'cousin' and stood between him and the French throne.

He could smile and laugh with the best of them; men thought him great company and he'd had already one or two sweethearts among the serving girls. He made them presents of sugar and lace – though nothing so fine as invoke the displeasure of the Almighty who, it was known, disliked seeing those he had appointed to low stations dressed up in the clothes of their betters.

He breathed in. A terrible smell. He realised it was his own sweat. He had become awfully sensitive to bad odours of late. He took out a little vial of perfume and dabbed it on himself. He loved perfumes of all sorts and this was a fine musk scented with cloves. The sharp, pungent smell comforted him. Ordinary men did not smell like that – only the best.

Charles went to his horse and untied it. It was skittish and nervous, still, spooked by the death of so many of its kind, spooked by the rattle of devils that fled from the whipping tail of the strange banner flying on the hill, spooked by the light-drained day but, above all, spooked by Charles.

Horses had never liked him much and, since his misfortunes flying with the angel feather cloak, his devilish nature had begun to leak more from his human skin. He struggled to control the beast, though it was only a plodder – all the finer, fiercer animals dead beneath the English arrows on the field of Crécy. Charles's face was burnt – the English sorcerer had thrown something at him and he felt mightily sick and weak. Angel's blood, no doubt. It had burnt his fingers even as he wiped it away.

He mounted and set off. He was no horseman, never having had much practice, but now his life depended on it – or at least his freedom. God, to get out of that armour – he'd had to sleep in it – to ditch the colours of Navarre, the red and gold chains quartered with the fleur-de-lys an incitement to any ransom-hungry knight or, worse, low man. If he should be captured by a mere soldier, the infamy would follow him for years.

However, the armour and colours brought protection. No one would dream of killing a youth whose war kit was the price of a decent-sized town.

Around his neck, his cats clung and mewed. He had brought only three with him, a fine black mouser, a lean tortoiseshell, and a puffy white thing that looked like a frozen explosion. Though they clawed and bit at his surcoat, he found them comforting. He was a magical creature, or half of one. It would take more than a peasant with a pike to capture him. And the dark was to his advantage, his eyes, those of an enormous cat, seeing better than any human could hope to.

There was nowhere to run to, though, or at least nowhere he knew. No one had thought the battle could be lost and the very suggestion of making a plan of rendezvous after a defeat would have been considered traitorous. Along the hedgerows men who had escaped the fury of the English lay collapsed or dying. Two nobles screamed from the back of a cart – the low man who had rescued them doubtless rushing them to a doctor in hope of reward. The poorer men cried out or wheezed from the roadside. No help for such as they, and rightly. Charles thought of the spawning mountains of his homeland in Navarre – a hundred peasants to a sheep, or so it seemed. The poor were too many, he thought, a burden on the nobility, robbers, cheats and liars. A winnowing like this was welcome, as long as he got back to safety.

He trembled when he looked up at the dark sky, seeing ympes – demons of Hell, the tiny prisoners escaped from their captive devils – like another swarm of arrows shooting past above his head. They turned and danced like starlings. What were they doing? A celebration?

Not far away, the English were moving through the country, howling out their victory cries. 'The boar, the boar!' – Edward's battle name. Other shouts too. 'Eden! Eden!' Torches flashed in the gloom on the hill. Those horrible bowmen, stinking of shit and rebellion, calling out to Lucifer, friend of the many, when they should have been calling out to God. Charles should have had their leader eviscerated when he had the chance back at Paris.

Too late now, too late. The country was in chaos and the poor had a place at the bargaining table. Were that to happen in his own country of Navarre or in one of his Norman provinces he would suppress it with vigour. Here in France, however . . . He smiled to think of the difficulties the mob might cause the kings of France and England.

He glimpsed movement on the horizon and kicked the animal on, away from it. Two hours' riding and he felt safer. The cries had died down and he allowed the animal to rest.

The horse slowed through a wood, its flanks lathering, its breath sawing. Charles could now strip off his armour. Although, of course, he couldn't. If he met up with the remainder of the French forces, he had to look like a king – a juvenile, sweating, battered king. He let the horse drink at a stream, looking behind him. The sun was a silver disc in a black sky, so faint he could look at it directly.

He had seen the dragon eat the French angels. *My God, what was that? Something from Hell?* Charles was not a youth given to panic and before long, he had calmed himself. Night had fallen on France, literally and metaphorically. The English were triumphant, King Philip humiliated, the flower of French chivalry dead in the mud of Crécy. If he could just get back to safety, he might account this a good day. An angel might have told him he, doubly royal, born of the fleur-de-lys on both sides, would never be king, but he was determined that whatever Valois imposter did sit on the throne would be king of ashes. The French crown was in a terrible position but he needed to be near to the king and his idiot son John to make sure it did not by some miracle recover. The French prince doted on him and acted as his protector, though Charles felt nothing for him. The man was a dolt, albeit a mightily useful one.

A party of crossbowmen, by their livery the Genoese who had taken such a battering in the opening exchanges of the battle, came panting through the gloom of the trees. Good – mercenaries, therefore buyable. He mounted his horse and kicked it towards them.

'You, men of Genoa! You, men!'

The mercenaries were nervous, several of them still with the white shafts of arrows poking from their thick coats. They all brandished weapons. My God, not a sword between them – a collection of picks, long knives and clubs. These men were not fit to even look at Charles, let alone accompany him. Still, needs must.

'You. I am the king of Navarre, get me to a place of safety.'

'*Inglis*,' said one.

'No, not English, you common clod, king of Navarre. Much gold, much reward if you get me back to— Whoa!'

One of the soldiers leapt towards his horse and the animal, which had suffered enough frights for one lifetime, simply died underneath him.

The horse wilted to the ground and the men were on him. Charles was a nimble and fast young man, but the obligation to wear armour meant he had no hope of outrunning the Genoese. Combined with the sickening effects of the angel's blood, he was easy meat.

They had him down and tied in only a few breaths.

'I'm on your side, you idiots. Navarre. Charles of Navarre. Personal friend of France and paymaster of your captains. Don't you recognise my colours? Charles of—'

The next word was hampered by the presence of a tooth in it, the crossbowman having punched it out. Charles appeared to be sitting on the ground. They fell upon him, stripping his purse, his sword, his dagger, swatting off his cats. Annoyingly, they didn't remove his armour.

They got him to his feet and shoved Charles on through the unnatural dark. The armour chafed him; his underclothes were all but boiling him alive. He marched until the faint sun vanished and an iridescent dusk, crushed blue and purple, the colour of dying angels, and then the real night came down. Then they tied him, lit a fire.

All through the dark, other fires were burning – the English army celebrating in the only way it knew how: rape and arson. The one consolation for a noble, he thought, is that virtually whatever is happening to you, something worse is happening to the peasants. He breathed in the smoke smell. His leg was numb and, if he didn't get out of his armour, he feared the sores at the top of his thighs, and on his shoulders, would turn into life-threatening wounds. He had to piss where he was tied, which did his sores no favours.

The men watched him. One pointed at him. They had seen his eyes, slit like a cat's. One made the sign of the Cross. Charles would nail him to one as soon as he got the chance.

His captors were divided between nervous chatter and brooding silence. They'd taken a pounding, first from the English bows – somehow the crossbowmen's protective shields had been stuck in the baggage train – and then from the charge of the French knights who came through them as they fled.

He had no sympathy. None, specifically for the plight of the crossbowmen or, for that matter, sympathy for anyone in general. They were paid to suffer and, in fleeing the field, had defrauded their masters.

'Where are we going?'

His Navarrese was not really near to the Genoese tongue, but he thought one of them might recognise it as neither French nor English and at least make an attempt to find out who he was. He took another kick in the guts. His gambeson and mail meant it was not painful, though it was demeaning. Other, more tolerant nobles would have made a particular note of the man who did that. Charles did not bother. They were all in for deaths that made Christ's look like a blessing.

The next morning they checked his armour was on securely. He was under no illusions why – first it would protect him if they were attacked, for he was after all a vulnerable prisoner. Secondly, they wouldn't have to carry it.

It was as if the dawn's light had drained from it, the sky turning a begrudging grey, the summer sun sick and pallid.

He was not cold, jolted along in his heavy armour, but he was in pain. Fires were on the wind. He guessed they were going south. Where would the English army go? Paris? He hoped so. It would be good to see the city burn. He could even stage a putsch in the south under the pretence of liberating the country while the nobles of the north took care of England. 'Never king of France,' the angel had said. Maybe king of most of it, though.

The country was almost deserted – the people having fled their own troops on their return. At a farmhouse they encountered five battle-torn French men-at-arms in the livery of Prince John. There was much jabbering and pointing.

'They're trying to tell you you've got a prisoner of the royal line of France,' said Charles to the crossbowmen. 'As you surely must know by looking at my colours.' He gestured to his caparison. 'You five – liberate me from these fools.'

'They are twenty, sir, we are but five.'

'You'll be but nought if you don't.'

The men looked very nervous.

'King, king,' said the French, but the Genoese looked at them blankly.

'Argent!' said one, slowly.

A man-at-arms pointed south. 'The king is there, sir,' he said. 'We saw his banners not an hour ago.'

'He's still got his banners?'

'Some of them, sir.'

'The Oriflamme?'

'I don't know. We saw its light. We should have won, shouldn't we; that's what they say. The Archangel Michael promises victory if it shines.'

'Seems someone else promised something else.'

'What was the dragon, sir?'

'Something from Hell, I suppose.' Charles shrugged.

'These days are full of devils. I don't like them, sir.'

'No? Better get used to them, I suggest.'

'The devils fight for us, the devils against us. I don't know whose side we're supposed to be on any more.'

Charles looked down at the bonds on his hands.

'Mine is always a good bet, I find.'

'They're saying it's your fault, sir.'

'What's my fault?'

'Navarre started the charge. The king wanted to wait until the next day.'

'Who's saying this?' It was true he'd given the order to attack. A delay of a day might have seen a sensible battle plan emerge. The English could quite easily have been surrounded and annihilated. Such a victory would have made for a stable and prosperous France – the last thing he wanted. However, he hoped he hadn't gone too far the other way. King Edward was a model king, 'fulle mighty' as the poets rather tiresomely attested, even the ones who weren't paid to. France might come together under him and prosper. *No, no, no.*

The Frenchman looked at his boots.

'I don't know, sir. I just heard it.'

'On the wind, no doubt.' He smiled and the man smiled back.

'You are made of tough stuff, sir. These men have used you cruelly.'

'Well, I shall make some use of them when we get back to my troops.' He smiled his cat's smile.

The French laughed and the Genoese glanced warily among themselves to hear it.

What a pretty pass when he was talking to a common soldier almost as if he was an equal. Still, he found that easy to do. His mother told him he had the common touch and meant it to needle him, but Charles saw no shame in making the common people love him, though he despised them. Men will do more for love than they will out of fear.

'Take me to the king,' he said.

'That lot won't like that, sir, they'll think we're going to pinch their ransom.'

'And what do you think their ransom will be? Go to the king yourself, then, and tell him I'm here.'

'Yes, sir.'

A big Genoese came up to Charles, a thumb's width from his face. He said something unintelligible and no doubt base.

Charles returned his stare, though he had to crane his neck upwards to do so.

'Best kill me now, old chap,' he said. 'Because I will certainly kill you and in an inventive way. I spend a long time thinking about that sort of thing.'

The man shoved him in the centre of the chest and Charles fell back onto his arse. He looked up and smiled. 'Enjoy yourself while you can,' he said.

It took them another two days to come within sight of the king's banners. The English, it seemed, were not chasing them but the bedraggled army moved as quickly as if the breath of Edward's warhorses was on their necks. The crossbowmen had taken the

31

precaution of stripping Charles of his colours and gagging him, lest their expensively dressed prisoner make any other opportunist think it was worth fighting them to capture him. Now he received all sorts of abuse as he passed – largely from the low men, who mistook him for an English nobleman.

The higher sort were too cowed to confront him. They had been beaten and they knew it, all their boasts and pride turned to dust.

They made the king's standard before he was recognised.

'My Lord!' It was Noyles, one of Prince John's closest men. 'Do you handle a prince of the blood so roughly, fellows?' The crossbowmen did not understand the language but they understood the sentiment well enough. Noyles's hand was on his sword.

Charles bit on the gag. He was tired and thirsty but that could wait.

Consternation among the crossbowmen. Shouting. One man fell to his knees. Quickly two others untied Charles, ungagged him. They too knelt, the rest of the troop prostrating themselves in the mud.

Charles wanted to collapse, to tear off his stinking armour, but he kept standing. No one would see him beaten or bowed.

He fixed his cat's eyes on the crossbowmen. Ducking from the farmhouse came the dolt Prince John, ridiculously dressed in the latest fashion of short jerkin, the tightest of hose, and a codpiece in the shape of a rooster's head. Well, at least he hadn't let a mortal blow to his kingdom affect his sense of style. You had to admire that about the man.

'Charles! You're alive!'

'By the grace of God, cousin.'

Charles widened his arms to embrace John but the prince did not approach him.

'You are cold, cousin?'

'Bring the lord wine, bring wine!'

'And bread,' said Charles.

Charles really fancied a nice wriggly mouse, all flip and flop on the tongue, but he disguised his more feline habits from the rabble to avoid kindling rumours.

'Cousin, will you not embrace me?'

'It is not politic just now.' John looked scared. For all his idiocy, his love of poetry above politics or the tournament, he was not a coward. He'd fought valiantly at Crécy. So to see him scared was unsettling to Charles.

'Is that Navarre?' He recognised the voice from within the house. The king – Philip; a useless bastard if ever there was one.

Charles would decline to bow – his claim to the French throne was better than the old man's, even if it was through a woman. He could never look at the Valois upstart without thinking the word 'interloper'.

King Philip emerged. He was a tall man and had to stoop as he came through the low door, almost as if he were bowing, which by rights he should have been. Charles sucked at his teeth, trying not to think of the pain of the sore on his thigh, nor of that in his mouth.

'Are you happy with what you wrought?' The king was white as a forepined ghost, his jaw firm with anger.

'I'm sorry, sir, you have me at a disadvantage.' As he grew up, Charles leant more and more to pronouncing the word 'sir' to Philip as he might to a dog whose manners he was seeking to correct.

'We were going to wait. We were going to form into battle order. Your men charged the English without my command.'

'Are we to be criticised for valour?' Charles put out his arms wide, speaking loudly.

'Is that what you call it?'

'The English were raining arrows on these low men of Genoa. They ran, turncoats. My men were incensed and rode them down on their way to the English.' God's nuts, Charles's leg hurt. He had to get out of his stinking armour.

'It turned the army into a rabble.'

'My men sought honour. The angels had not engaged. It was our bravery that showed God we were worthy of His help. The angels blew their fire at the English. It was sorcery and devilry that undid us, not the courage of Navarre.'

Prince John spoke. 'No one doubts your courage, cousin, we are simply questioning your wisdom.'

Charles felt his mouth go dry. John had been his champion since he was a small boy. John had hardly ever said a word against him, protected him from his father's justifiable suspicion like the idiot he was. The prince always sided with him. And 'we'! He had never heard John link himself to his father in that way before. Always it was 'he and I', mostly 'he, whereas I'.

'Where did that dragon thing come from?' said John.

'Hell, at a guess. Have you interrogated your devils?'

'They fled before that monstrosity. What was it?'

'A dragon that filled the sky,' said Charles. 'I am no Bible scholar, sir, but I would say it was the Dragon of Revelation. That would make these the last days, so we can prepare for the coming of Christ in no fear of the English, for we are His true servants. Let's hope the Lord returns before the news of the loss reaches the Paris mob. They'll be hanging nobles from the bridges.'

'Do you think so?' John crossed himself.

'No, sir. A dragon fills the sky, tears angels from their clouds, shatters them to rainbows. What are we to make of it? More to the point, what will the people make of it if we cannot protect them?'

'Doesn't Michael kill the Dragon in Revelation? Where is he now?' said John.

'It chases after a woman who has eagle's wings, in my recollection,' said Charles. The pain in his leg was very great but he kept a smile on his face. 'Perhaps you should ask one of the whispering ympes who speak to the poor. They maintain the Bible is a lie. Or at least, a very partial telling of a story. Perhaps they might have some wisdom to add.'

'That is a filthy blasphemy.' Another voice spoke, heavily accented. It was Charles de la Cerda, of Spain: an upstart who had hung around the court like an ugly younger sister, waiting for a marriage that would never happen. A pious fool, as far as Charles recalled, though he had endeavoured to have little to do with him. Some rural nobility from Castile, still with the stink of dead Moor on him from all those battles in the south.

Charles turned his slow eyes upon him.

'You are?' He knew perfectly well, of course.

'La Cerda, of the free kingdom of Castile.'

'Free because men like my father died defending it for you. And how does your king fat Alfonso reward us? By courting the English who have caused such misery in this country.'

'Come on, boys, don't squabble,' said John.

La Cerda bowed deeply. Charles saw the look he exchanged with the prince. It was as if Charles was looking into a mirror. He was ingratiating himself with the dolt. What had La Cerda been saying?

'You two should talk, you would get along. The good lord La Cerda came to our aid when we were sorest pressed by the English, he killed three of them in my defence.'

He looked the sort – well-muscled, tall and dark with a reasonable black eye puffing up the right side of his face. Spent all his time in the tilting yard or shifting hay bales with the peasants, no doubt. He could see La Cerda working on a farm. There was no end to Castilian depravity.

'Well,' smiled Charles. 'We are indebted. Prince John is a sun who shines on us all. France would never see day again were that flame extinguished.'

'And it would have cost us a small fortune in ransom had he been captured,' said the king.

'Another blessing.'

La Cerda bowed. 'I am France's servant.'

What did he mean by that? Charles didn't like his tone. The man was clearly an idiot to declare himself an open enemy of the king of Navarre, favourite of Prince John. Philip had survived the battle but couldn't have long now. He was old and must die soon. Then Charles would be Constable of France and have not just influence but power. La Cerda would be wise to make him his friend. So why confront him? Because his star was on the wane, however briefly, the king angry with him, and ambitious men like that must seize their chances when they present themselves. It was a gamble, a sudden rush into the tide of court opinion, courtiers' minds raw and vengeful with the shock of defeat. La Cerda hoped it would sweep him to the land of plenty. Charles simply noted La Cerda's ambition. He would do nothing about it for now. The court was full of ambitious men looking to pick the right enemies at the right time. Charles was, always and for ever, the wrong enemy. He prided himself on it. However, something about the Castilian disturbed him. Charles, with his cat's eyes and quick wit, scared most men. He did not scare La Cerda. Yet.

'What to do with these men of Genoa?' said Charles.

'I have hanged those I've found for cowardice,' said Philip. 'We should do the same with these.'

'No, no, My Lord, I beg you,' said Charles, 'after all, they did rescue me.'

'You would let them go, though they brought you here in bonds?' Philip was a wise monarch, if an indecisive one. One of his more unpleasant qualities, Charles thought, was that he was a good judge of character. He knew Charles and mercy were not even on nodding acquaintance.

'You are too stern, uncle. Release them, yes. Please. I beg you,' said Charles.

'Are you so weak, Navarre?' said La Cerda. The man's gall was astounding.

'You deal with it, John,' said Philip. 'Navarre – keep out of my sight. All is lost and it is lost because of you.' He went back inside the house. Was no one going to bring Charles so much as a cup of wine?

Charles said nothing. He didn't agree with the assessment. What were the English going to do now? Attack Paris? Then they would have to hold it, even if they were successful. Their angel had been chased off by the dragon along with everyone else's. No, he had no doubt they'd go home if they were sensible or just nicely roll out their brand of chaos across the country.

'We should punish these men and make an example of them,' said La Cerda. 'Prince, do not give in to soft counsel.'

'We should at least hang some of them,' said John. 'For the sake of form, as much as anything.'

'No,' said Charles. 'I would see them live.'

'No wonder you can't control your men,' said La Cerda.

'I am tender and known for it. I suggest we have half of them cut the hands off the other half, and then we blind those still with hands. That way there are only ten whole men among them and your sternness and my mercy are both satisfied. I need refreshment and to climb out of my armour but after that we can watch the events while we dine. Will you join me for dinner and mutilation, La Cerda?'

La Cerda coloured, looked to John. Charles knew the nobility well enough to know the Castilian would be unlikely to find the maiming of the Genoese difficult to stomach and guessed he had been more discomfited by the invitation to dinner from a man he had thought to profit from by making his enemy. Also, he had been made to look weak by offering the men death.

'I think it would be politic if you kept your distance for a while, Charles,' said John. 'There is another house not far from here. You may take your leisure and rally your troops there.'

'Cousin, the nobility are here with you.'

'The nobility is on the field of Crécy, dead in numbers never seen in France, and we must ask who is to blame,' said La Cerda.

'Yes,' said Charles. 'Was it Navarre, or was it the enormous, sky-eating dragon that tore down the angels of God as if they were pigeons and it the hawk?'

'It was of Hell,' said La Cerda. 'And where are you from, my mountain king, with your eyes so green and appetites so rare? You are not fourteen years old but speak like a man who has seen thirty. I heard a devil say you were one of theirs.'

Charles smiled, light and urbane. La Cerda had signed his own death warrant with his words.

'Anyone who governs unflinchingly is called a devil. We have all heard that accusation against us. If you haven't, then I suggest you press your subjects more. It's good for poor men to suffer. It is one of their talents.' Charles liked to be seen to keep his temper, particularly when he was losing it.

'Everyone knows Charles was cursed by the English sorcerer Montagu,' said John. 'But I will hear no more about it. Charles, you will find lodgings elsewhere and stay away until I call you in Paris. You need to do a little time out of the light of the sun, Charles, but you will soon enough again feel its glow.'

The light of France is out, the sun has gone from these lands but a new sun will rise in the south and burn these lands to ashes. Charles's face was stone, though his thoughts bubbled like the scalding water of a spring.

'I will give you a man to show you the way,' said La Cerda.

Charles swallowed down the pain of his leg. 'You are too kind,' he said. 'I hope to extend my largesse to you one day. Fetch me a horse.'

'I am not your servant.'

No, thought Charles, *for if you were you would face the same fate as these wretches of Genoa. But one day, you will be. And then you will know what it is to have your honour insulted.*

A palfrey was brought and Charles helped up. Charles nodded to John.

'I'll leave you to arrange the punishment, cousin.'

'My men will see it enacted forthwith.'

'Good.' Charles raised a hand to the crossbowmen.

A Genoese, not understanding a word, bowed his head to Charles.

'*Scusate.*' He gestured to his mouth to apologise for Charles's tooth. Charles put his tongue to the little gap.

'What's it say in the Bible?'

'Turn the other cheek,' said La Cerda.

'An eye for an eye appeals more to me. Or two eyes for a tooth.'

The crossbowman spoke in French.

'Thank you,' he said.

Charles smiled. '*De nada.* He turned to La Cerda. 'That's Castilian, isn't it? It means "of nothing".'

2

The Sire d'Ambret was drunk, as usual, but more than usually drunk.

If there's one thing the sire could do it was hold his beer. But his talents did not stop there. He could also hold his wine, sack, mead, and whatever other alcoholic concoction the rich country of France had to offer. However, having drunk roughly the weight of his horse since accepting the villagers' entreaty to fight for them the night before, he was a little unsteady in his saddle. Three men who had entered the drinking contest with him were now missing – flat unconscious in two cases, hiding in a barn in another for fear the sire would find him and make him continue the competition.

The village evening was pleasant; a low southern sun lingered on fields of gold, casting long shadows in front of him. *No better season to be drunk in than autumn*, he thought. The harvest in, the people in a mood for fun. Spring was good too. And summer, even the hungry month of July. Drinking warmed the bones in winter too. In fact, the sire had difficulty envisaging a situation, weather condition or time of day that could not be improved by inebriation. His horse moved gingerly, as if its short association with its rider had been enough to make it realise that any faster movement would result in a painful grab on the reins.

'Where is the varlet?' said the sire in French that owed more to Hackney in London than it did to anywhere in France. He smiled, burped, and effortlessly fell from his saddle.

'Varlets, not varlet. You are defending us against three of them and you're drunk!'

At the head of a small band of rough and shoeless serfs, stood a tall and beefy young woman. This was Angry Aude, a woman who had come lately to the village, bringing outside manners and ideas. Though she said her prayers and was godly, some of her views would not have been out of place spoken by a Luciferian preacher. The aristocrats, she said, had a duty to the toilers of the fields and, if they did not fulfil it, they should be called to account.

The sire looked up from the mud. 'I take that as an insult, madam. I am always drunk but today I have surpassed myself. I am royally lashed. I'd have drunk the angel off his perch in St Denis. I've seen that angel, you know. At the side of the king.' He raised a cup that wasn't there and shouted, 'I wager there have not been three men in history this plastered and standing.'

'You're not standing.'

'As ever, the devil is in the detail. Keep me from devils, I am sick of their company. Years I laboured to raise them but I would gladly never see another one. Sorcerer no more. Knight valiant! Knight pure. Knight errant, a champion to all who will pay him or swive him!'

'You took all our money!'

'And I shall repay you by knocking this knight on the nut. I am the model of chivalry. After that, we may dally a while in your chamber, my lady. I'm sure you will grant me that indulgence once I have avenged the wrong, the details of which escape me.'

'It's not very chivalric turning up in this state to a matter of honour.'

'I suggest, then, you have little experience of knightly combat. Most of the knights I've ever met make it a point of honour to turn up sozzled. It gives the other bastard a chance. And quells the fear. They are great ones for fear, knights, its summoning and conquering. Fear is a devil that lives in our breast seeking to master us.' He smiled and was sick.

'You can't even sit on your horse. Lord Richard has been fighting since the day he was born.'

'I am a master of modern warfare, lady. We do not charge on our horses no more, for fear of the English bows. The perfect gentle knight now fights afoot where the piercing shafts of the low men cannot make it through our armour.'

'Well, Chevalier Richard fights on horse and you'll have no chance against him one on one.'

The sire tried to stand, leaning heavily on his scabbarded sword. He got as far as his knees.

'I take that as a challenge,' he said.

'I'm behind you,' said the woman.

'So you are,' said the sire, turning slowly, as if he feared the ground tipping if he moved too quickly.

A commotion from the top of the village. Through the mean little huts a flash of coloured cloth brighter than ever a poor man could afford. Nobles.

'Can you stand, even?'

'Don't let that bother you. Don't fuss. When I best him, we'll sell his armour back to him, along with his horse and you can . . . I've lost my thread. What was I saying?'

'Oh no, here he comes. You'll die too.'

'I fought Hugh Despenser at Crécy,' said the sire. 'He was nine feet tall and had possessed the body of an angel and he's dead now. I think I can manage one mortal knight.'

'Three mortal knights.'

'Three sets of armour and three horses to carry them. What ho, my lords, what ho! Fetch my shield from my mount, Aude, dear, do.'

The woman went to his horse and unstrapped a fine shield. It was made of a light metal and bore the symbol of a Sacred Heart.

Three good warhorses, fully caparisoned in colours of blue, red and gold, clopped to a halt ten yards in front of the sire, their breath heavy in the dying afternoon light. Behind them, on lighter horses, were six younger nobles, carrying the lances and helms of their masters. A party of servants, some armed, followed them on foot.

The lead knight spoke. He was fully armoured and wore a surcoat of yellow chains surrounding a portcullis. This was the Chevalier Richard – a man who had come late to Crécy, seen the destruction, and gone quickly back to his lands.

His voice was relaxed, nonchalant. He was used to such challenges – or was trying to show that he was.

'You're here, d'Ambret. I thought you might have the good sense to run away.'

'Nah,' said the sire. 'Trust on anything, sir, anything, but my good sense.'

'Have you come to apologise and retract your insult?'

'To be honest, I find that I've forgotten exactly what I said. Something about you being a clapper-clawed son of shit, by the look of you.'

The Chevalier bit his top lip, clicked his teeth and said, 'You said I was a brute for enforcing my ancient *droit de seigneur* when my serf Aveline married.'

'Ah yes, you got first go on her, so to speak.'

'As I am allowed in law.'

'Christ's sweaty cock, I'm in the wrong game,' said d'Ambret.

'What is your "game"?'

'Champion. Available to the rich, and to the good-looking poor such as my lady here. These serfs have paid me a sou to act revenge upon you. Two sous and a serving girl's bed for the night and we'll forget all about it. Three, and I'll hold your horses while you serve revenge up on them.'

'Revenge?' said Aude, 'after what he did to Aveline? He murdered her husband afterwards too!'

D'Ambret was only slightly sick into his hand and considered that he had got away without anyone noticing.

'I murdered no one. That thief robbed one of my noble guests!' said Richard.

'Liar!' shouted Aude.

'You robbed him!' shouted another serf.

Richard looked wary. Serfs did not speak like this to their masters.

'So say I,' said d'Ambret. 'And invite you to prove me wrong on the field of combat or give us three sous.'

'I won't kill a drunk,' said Richard. 'Where's the honour in that? Give him the money, Gerald.'

'Sire, this man has insulted your honour!'

'Don't worry about it, boy,' said d'Ambret. 'I have met his sort in many taverns. They talk a good fight but when the fists fly, so do they.'

'You have to respond to that, sire!' The young knight next to Richard looked as if his eyes would pop out of his head if his lord didn't offer violence to d'Ambret forthwith.

Richard sucked at his teeth.

'Give him the money. We can be generous. These serfs are angrier than I thought but a few sous will buy their temper. Three sous – it is the price of their honour.'

The young man flung three sous into the mud.

'That's a good price!' shouted a serf.

'Thanks,' said d'Ambret. 'But now I'm calling you a pelican-buggering, pribbling, rump-renting, bear-biting flap dragon, a nut hook and a basket-cockle.'

'I have never been insulted like that in all my life!' said D'Ambret.

'Not to your face, I expect. I bet you think your servants never piss in your soup either. Four sous to retract the first insult, five the second.'

'The second wasn't actually an insult,' said one of the squires.

'Swive yourselves, the set of you. How's that?' said d'Ambret, lifting up his long coat of fine mail to scratch at his balls.

'You are a low man, d'Ambret, as I can tell by your words. You may have stolen arms from some sick knight but you will find it takes more than a fine shield and coat of mail to best me. Prepare yourself for Hell.'

'Already been there. I'm not planning on returning.'

'Get to your horse,' said Richard, 'I want to be back at my keep by nightfall.'

'I won't bother with the horse,' said d'Ambret. 'To be honest, I'm not much of a rider and I find using him in combat risks damaging him . . .'

'This is a low man who has robbed one of his betters,' said the knight to Richard's right. 'He deserves no respect of chivalry. Let me ride him down now.'

Richard shook his head.

'This pleasure shall be mine. As was that of Aveline. Know, serfs who live upon your masters' generosity, you have gone too far in employing this low man. We do not allow you to till our fields and care for our cattle for nothing. Yes, you take an ample portion to feed yourselves but it is too much. When we ask for something back, your ingratitude bursts forth like the pus from a boil. When I have bested your "champion" here, I shall teach you a lesson you won't forget.'

D'Ambret wobbled to his feet as Richard took a lance from his squire and turned his horse away.

'Hey, you're not taking a run up are you?' said d'Ambret.

Richard did not reply.

'That's hardly fair,' said d'Ambret. 'Last chance for four sous. Actually, a total of four and five, that's, er . . .' He counted on his fingers. 'Nine. I think.'

The knight pulled down his visor, levelled his lance and charged.

D'Ambret staggered slightly and drew his sword. It shone with the light of the dawn, though he held it limply, scraping it on the ground in front of him.

Richard was undeterred, his horse bearing down at speed on his unsteady opponent.

Aude screamed as the lance smashed into d'Ambret's shield. His shield? Where had that been a heartbeat before? On the ground next to his feet. The lance shattered but the horse charged into d'Ambret, its pummelling hooves making the ground shake, its great chest hitting d'Ambret square at the gallop, its harness ripping a great gash in the knight's plain surcoat. But it was as if the horse had run into a solid wall.

The animal cried out and fell, throwing Richard hard to the ground.

D'Ambert belched and weighed his sword in his hand.

Then he walked over to the stunned knight and beheaded him.

The other two knights and the men-at-arms cried out. 'You gave him no chance to yield!'

Another knight charged, the yellow billow of the horse's caparison bright in the dying sun, its hooves making the firm summer turf a drum. D'Ambret, who had rather overbalanced when cutting off Chevalier Richard's head, was facing the wrong way, disorientated from his stumble.

The lance could have been no more than the length of a forearm from d'Ambret's back when the shield spun him around, blocking the blow. The bright sword carved a crescent through the air, trailing sparks like a comet's tail behind it, and the knight lost a leg, his armour providing no protection at all. The last knight drew up and ordered the men-at-arms to charge. There were six of them, armed with spears and maces. They advanced nervously towards d'Ambret.

'Lads,' he said, 'my beef was with the nobles. You've no need to die here too.'

'We are six,' said one man.

D'Ambret looked puzzled for an instant – he had counted at least twelve.

'Go back to your wives.'

'Advance!' the remaining knight cried, and the men plucked up the courage to move, prodding forward with their spears.

The bright sword was at d'Ambret's side, the shield now on his arm. His mail lit up like gold in the dying sun. He would have struck an impressive figure if he had not been sitting down panting like a deerhound.

'I'm blowing after that one fight,' he said.

The men came on. Again d'Ambret sat mooning at them, gazing up like a man waking from sleep.

A spear prodded, a mace struck, but the shield was everywhere. When a lance did get through, it bounced off d'Ambret's mail and broke. The drunken knight's bright sword carved trails of sparks through the dusk, though the sire did not bother to stir himself from his sitting position.

Two men-at-arms lay dead before the rest broke, jingling back to reform behind their knight.

D'Ambret stood unsteadily.

'Know this, men of wherever this is! I am the knight errant d'Ambret, wandering the land in search of truth, justice, money and a damn good seeing to. Send word to your neighbours, particularly the well-off ones, that I am available to hire or to fight. You will do one or the other with me.'

'It's beneath our dignity to trade with you,' said the knight.

'Then send your best fellows, caparisoned in their best armour, riding their finest horses, if there is any manhood in these lands. But tell them, for God's sake, to fight on foot.'

'Why?'

'I don't want to risk damaging the horses. There's two dead here and they could have been worth half a good farm each.'

'You are a bandit,' said the knight.

'All men are bandits. Kings the worst.'

'You defy holy God,' said the knight.

'Oh, I wouldn't worry about that.' D'Ambret stood up tall. 'No, actually, I have been His champion.'

'And now?'

'Only my own.'

The knight spurred his horse forward as if to charge again, but thought better of it.

'Take your dead,' said d'Ambret. 'But leave their armour and weapons. I have won them by right.'

'Strip them,' said the knight. 'And know that I will be back here with men who can defeat you. Champion, you call yourself. I call you sorcerer, for no man could do what you did here.'

'You've clearly never met Montagu. He wouldn't have been so kind as to let you leave.'

'The Englishman?'

'The same.'

'He is dead.'

'Is he? I'll tell him next time I see him.'

The men removed the armour of the corpses, while d'Ambret called for a drink.

Angry Aude kissed him and hugged him. 'You shall have the rest of your reward.'

'Well, let's go to. The sun is setting, though I know a curious cock who wakes to crow at the hour of dusk. I am talking about . . .'

'I take your meaning, sir. Let's go to. I hope you will not mind that I keep a fire until late, because the people will be in the mood to cheer your victory and buy my ale. My boy can serve while you and I indulge our sport.'

'Lead on.'

D'Ambret followed Aude into the dark interior of her house, where the bed lay in between the barrels of beer, so that she might keep an eye on them by night.

The villagers came to drink and to talk and toast d'Ambret, while Aude's boy served and the children of the village pawed at the magic shield. D'Ambret was a little too drunk – even for him – to persist beyond his first round of pleasure, and the celebrations were still in full flow by the time he fell asleep.

By the time he opened his bleary eyes again most of the guests were gone – those who had not fallen asleep by the fire – and Aude's son lay asleep across the bottom of the bed.

'One more?' said Aude. 'I have never lain with a champion before.'

D'Ambret yawned. He was still deeply tired, groggy from the smoke of the house, warm in the glow of drink and the delicious idea, the suggestion, the mad dream that another erection might be possible.

'I am not a champion.'

'You fought like a champion.'

'I once summoned devils like a sorcerer but I am not a sorcerer. Well, maybe I am. More a sorcerer than a champion.'

He felt content. He was never as happy as when drunk in the arms of a woman, particularly one of Aude's comfortable figure.

'A sorcerer?'

He didn't really know if he was waking or dreaming now but he spoke anyway, seduced by the yeasty smell of Aude, the warmth of the house, the pleasant sensation of being drunk yet not plastered. He breathed in and smelled the ale of the barrel next to him. He loved ale, though he had drunk wine when at the court of King Philip. He'd never been happy there. They called ale 'the lord of the soil' and the soil was where he felt happiness, here among the snores of the peasants, Aude's hand on his semi-interested prick.

'Not a sorcerer.' He felt the need to confide, to put aside pretence and be himself. 'I am Osbert, pardoner of the Leadenhall Market, sorcerer to the French King through luck both good and bad. I tire of devils, though. I tire. It's easier to be a fighter and be free of the influence of great men. There's a living as a wandering knight and it's a good one with such as you as the prize.'

'Not easy to best the likes of Richard,' said Aude.

His dick was awaking from its torpor. He awaited, the delicious moment he would feel it change from Jack-Lazy-Abed to Tom-Ready-Sire.

'You are a great fighter,' she said.

'Just a wayward and a trickster, really,' said Osbert. 'It's the armour and the shield. They belong to an angel. Anyone could do it if they had the equipment.'

'Even me?' said Aude.'

'Or anyone.' He kissed her. 'Be ready, my love. I have a lance that would enter your lists. By lance, I mean . . .'

'I know what you mean,' she said, returning his kiss.

3

The road to Coventry was cluttered with merchants coming to the harvest fair, the canopies of their wagons, their hats and their coats like so many bright flowers in a meadow dazzling beneath the sun.

The crowd was such that the royal party could not have travelled quickly, even flying its banners. Isabella came to Coventry to give thanks for the victory at Crécy. And where better than Coventry, where the arm of St Augustine, who showed how just war can be in the name of Christ and peace, resided in the cathedral?

She rode for much of the way, loving to let the people see her and to be loved. No devil accompanied her for the fear that might occasion in the people. When she grew tired she took to her litter but, in truth, its motion made her sick and she preferred to ride one horse than be carried by two.

'Stay in the litter, ma'am, I beg you. We have many enemies,' said her lady-in-waiting, Alice. 'What if one of the French devils comes for you?'

'A devil would not dare strike down an anointed queen,' said Isabella.

'But what about your retinue? Us?'

Isabella put her hand on the girl's arm.

'It's a risk I am prepared to take.'

Still, Alice, nervous, shrew-eyed, said she was afraid. The queen was the summoner of all the English devils, along with the long-bowmen the strength of the nation. What of assassins? What of traitors? Where would England be then?

'It's hardly likely to endear us to the people if we come in breathing fire and stinking of sulphur,' said Isabella. 'My ordinary guard will serve me very well. We have no need for *diaboliques*.'

She was glad to leave the capital and travel north. London was in ferment. The preachers of the Luciferian heresy – that all men were made equal and would one day return to being equal – stalked the markets, risking attack by devils and the loyal poor. The little whispering demons, the ympes, still pitter-pattered in their batty flight through the air of evening, whispering dissent.

Coventry was different. There was no revolution in Coventry, no rumblings of discontent. It was such a wealthy, well-favoured city. Its blue cloth was known throughout the world for the depth and fastness of its colour, its glass works were marvels and, miles before they neared the city, the royal party saw the three spires of Christ's Church, St Mary's Cathedral and Holy Trinity shimmer into view. Verdant fields with too many sheep to count straddled the road, the shepherds running to see her litter as she passed and cry out 'God Bless You!' Well, she'd long given up hope of that. God would have to wait to cast her soul into eternal fire, though, and wait a long time. She dabbed a little angel's blood on her tongue. It kept her looking younger than her own daughters.

The city had no walls and this lent to its charm. It was like Arcadia, Eden, a place that knew no strife. That was why she had chosen to bury her lover Mortimer there, when her son had killed him. Gentle Mortimer. He would look on those fields and love them. He'd also clear the road better than the clod she had leading the way. She withdrew the curtain of the litter. God, it was hot in there.

'What is the delay?' She spoke to the leading horseman, a tall, commanding young man, at least by appearance. He didn't seem to be doing much commanding here.

'They won't budge, ma'am.'

'Cut off a couple of heads to encourage them.'

'Ma'am?'

'Not seriously, not seriously. Kick a few arses, though. Hard.'

'Ma'am.'

She let down the curtain. She didn't know if she wanted to remain in the shade and roast, or open the curtain to the sun and fry.

She tried to doze, but the rocking of the horses and the sound of villeins being slapped off the road made it impossible. For what must have been the hundredth time on the trip she burrowed down into the cushions of her litter to pull out a small enamelled casket. She examined it in the dim light. It was a chasse, a container for relics with a sloping roof like a church, inlaid with blue and gold, three golden orbs adorning its central spine. The motif showed the murder of St Thomas Becket, the four knights stabbing him as he lay on the altar. She'd wondered if King Henry, who had 'accidentally' ordered his murder, had planned the whole thing. Becket was worth much more as a saint, his blood healing ills, his bones providing fragments for the hilts of blessed swords, his teeth making brooches to defend against evil, than he ever was alive as an interfering churchman. The king all but commands the death, repents and shrives himself before the altar, Canterbury gains a saint, the king some relics, God a helper, Becket Heaven, and everyone is happy. Well, almost everyone. She doubted the knights had prospered.

She wondered how many of her entourage were her son's spies. None of the men, for sure. Edward knew very well that she was adept at swaying their loyalties. The women? Most of them, she guessed. She didn't really object. Such surveillance was the least she could expect.

The litter came to a halt.

'Now what?'

'A cart has shed a wheel, ma'am.'

'Oh, by St Fremund's severed head, how long is this going to take?'

'Only the saints know, ma'am.'

'Get my horse. We'll take to the fields. The rest can catch us later.'

'The people of Coventry will expect you to arrive in pomp, ma'am.'

'The people of Coventry will expect me to arrive. If we carry on like this, I won't.'

She stepped from the litter. God's teeth it was hot. Her horse was brought – a white palfrey. The ladies-in-waiting came from their own litters in a great cluck, begging her to wait. They hadn't got horses of their own. Well, there was an interesting point.

'You, what's your name?'

'Mowbray, ma'am,' said the knight.

'Accompany me.' She clicked her fingers at the two knights who guarded the rear of her litter.

'You two. No one comes in and out of my litter, not even my ladies.'

The casket would be safe there.

She swung a leg over the saddle's high cantle and the ladies ran around her, smoothing her skirt, begging her not to go, in case she might fall.

'I can out hunt any man,' she said.

'My Lady, that is blasphemy.' A tall, freckled thing spoke to her. What was the girl's name? Anna? The daughter of someone her husband was seeking to please.

'God is not so easily offended.'

She squeezed her legs and the horse stepped forward. Forget the road, she'd see how Mowbray could ride. With a turn and a kick, she was over a ditch that ran down the side of the road and into the sheep fields.

'Come on! Come on!'

The knight spurred his horse forwards and they were off, charging across the fields as if in pursuit of a deer.

'If you break your neck, your son will blame us!' shouted Mowbray.

'God will know you are innocent after Edward sends you to see Him!' she shouted back.

Would Edward be angry if she died? Whatever their differences, whatever their competing ambitions, they had always loved each other. Her son would be sad, perhaps, but relieved. Perhaps they'd turn her into a saint and use her hair to cure the ague. And perhaps not. And if Edward died? That would be necessary once the business at Coventry was done. It was regrettable and sad, yet impossible to avoid.

The sheep scattered from the charging horses, the crowds of merchants cheering her on. She looked so fine, felt so alive.

With the horse lathering and blowing, she made the suburbs. Here she found the source of some of the delay, never mind wagons shedding their wheels. The idiots had cleared the roads to greet her, meaning no one could get into the town. Their attempts to speed her way had all but nailed her to the spot. A great knot of dignitaries, as well as a gaggle of the curious townsmen and poor, blocked the way, held back only by some stout men at the front of the crowd. She should have some of these local potentates thrown from their offices – her grandson, after all, held sway in that city by right of his title of Earl of Chester. Her grandson. Rather, she should say, the devil she had bargained with when she had overthrown her husband. Her real grandson was gone. Regrettable, but unavoidable. She was thinking of having those words translated into Latin and using them as her motto.

'Ma'am! Ma'am!' The mayor scraped towards her, clanking in his gold chains, rings on his fingers, a fine beaver hat on his head and a staff topped with walrus ivory in his hand. Such finery. They had taxed this place too lightly, clearly.

'Lord Mayor,' she smiled, raising an expectant eyebrow. He caught her meaning.

'The gifts, ma'am, the gifts.'

He clapped his hands, the bugles sounded and sixteen pages trotted out to lay the city's bounty before her – great rolls of sky-blue cloth, glasswear, gloves, a fine sword and a psalter. All very pleasing, made to the highest standards by the best craftsmen. Coventry's workshops produced the finest goods in England. Still, it wasn't enough. She dismounted, dropping lightly to the ground.

'My leg chafes me,' said Isabella. 'Good mayor, lend me your staff.'

The mayor pushed out his fat tongue with the puzzled look of a mastiff who had been asked a question on astronomy

'That is my staff of office, ma'am.'

'Would you make your queen hobble?'

'We have a carriage waiting for you.' He smiled a broad grin.

Indeed, there was a fine carriage equipped with a painted blue cover in the quartered arms of the fleur-de-lys and English leopards.

'Only a few paces, but I find that hobble I but once in a day and it is quite ruined for me. Would you begrudge me support?'

'No, ma'am, of course not.' The mayor's smile remained, though his eyes died. He unpeeled his fingers from the staff and handed it over.

It really was a fine thing, stained a deep black with a gold claw holding a ball of walrus ivory at the top. He wouldn't be getting that back.

She walked to the carriage and waved to the people.

'We'll be staying at Cheylesmore Manor?' she asked the mayor, who bobbed alongside her like a gilded fool, though she had taken his tickling stick.

'We will, ma'am.'

She had stayed there before. Her son Edward – the supposed puppet she and her lover Mortimer had used to govern the country – had grown up quicker than she realised. He had kidnapped Mortimer in front of her, hanged him and cut him at Tyburn. She had buried Mortimer at Greyfriars, on her way to prison at Castle Rising. Her son had allowed her that. Why Greyfriars? She had made several bequests there in the past. Also, the monastery housed certain men who knew certain things.

'We?'

'The aldermen of the town will accompany you to see to your every need.'

'My first need is to have no aldermen. I am one for isolation. The park is as abundant as ever?'

'It is a haven for stag and doe.'

'Good. We will hunt the day after tomorrow. For now, we will observe the formalities of greeting and then be left alone.'

'Ma'am, a huge feast is prepared at the Guildhall.'

'Prepare another for the day after tomorrow. Give the present one to the poor.'

'It cost fifty pounds!'

Isabella smiled her perfect smile.

'Were you planning on entertaining some merchant? Some wife of a country knight? I am Isabella Plantagenet, née Capet, queen of England, rightful queen of France, mother to the greatest king this country has ever seen. Fifty pounds? That is not a feast fit for a miller!'

'There are few millers who eat for—' The mayor caught himself. 'A feast worthy of your magnificence will be prepared for the date you indicated, ma'am.'

'Yes, it will,' she said. 'Now take me to Cheylesmore. It's been so long since I stayed there and I long to see it again. Send my men and litter there immediately to follow me.'

*

That night, tired and stiff from the long journey, the queen dismissed her ladies from her room in the great manor. They were reluctant to go – as much because they would have to find a less comfortable perch than her bed to sleep on as from any annoyance at being unable to spy on her. She had them dress her before they went. Isabella normally bowed to the fashion for relative austerity in women's clothes, limiting herself to a few pearls in her hair, a simple emerald necklace, a cambric under-skirt and velvet mantle. Now, though, she dressed as she, and he – Mortimer – had liked.

Her blonde hair fell in a single plait from a velvet cap; her mantle was cloth of gold adorned with a constellation of diamonds, rubies and pearls. Her hands were heavy with rings and a sapphire necklace burned blue at her white throat. People had known how to dress when Mortimer was alive. The ladies had not asked, dared not have asked, why she spent two hours dressing for bed. Perhaps they guessed she wanted to test her magnificence for the coming days of feasting. No, she wanted to dress in the old-fashioned way. The way that had pleased Mortimer, the way that pleased her.

The reliquary was on a little table. She put her hand to it. That evening she would weave two magics – a small one and a great one. The reliquary would be needed later. For now, she only touched it for comfort.

She drew the magic circle on the floor with practised ease. Her mother had showed her the art – a gift of the Capetian queens. She drew the protective triangle, wrote the names of God, the names of the angels of the north wind, the south wind, the east and the west winds.

She was to summon the spirits of the air, strange things that had been there since the world began. God had made them and set them free to give sinners a taste of the torments of Hell and to spur them to repentance. The candles were lit; the dried tongue of a cat and the claw of a scorpion burned within them. Now the candles were extinguished again, only one kept alight by her side. She unclipped the linen that covered the window, a rush of summer air welcome in her lungs.

A knock at the door.

'You are not required.'

'Very good, ma'am.' That silly girl with the freckles again. She was beginning to despise her.

She began the chant, low and soft to avoid detection.

> *Come nightmares*
> *Wet from swimming all the waters of the world*
> *Eyes wide from counting all the stars*
> *Come nightmares*
> *Born of breath*
> *Denying breath*
> *Cold-shoed,*
> *Moth-winged,*
> *There is no broom at the door*
> *There is no belt on the bed*
> *Come nightmares*
> *The horses of sleep are awaiting you.*

Nothing at first, nothing for a long time. She continued the chant, repeated it again and again until the words seemed to her like the stir of a breeze on a summer's day, lulling, indistinct, the sound of the sea, of the wind among trees, always moving, always in the same place, a swaying between this world and the next.

A cloud across the moon. The light in the window boiled and flickered and then moths, more moths than she had ever seen, poured in, a purr of felt wings filling the chamber all about her protective circle, trying to get to the candle.

'Alice!' she called.

The girl was right behind the door and opened it immediately.

Isabella blew out the candle and the moths swept over the girl, stopping her mouth, her nose. She collapsed to the floor and the great blanket of insects flew through the house to fall upon the inhabitants like snow upon a meadow, commanding sleep, deep and long.

Another shape across the moon. A stoneskin gargoyle, falling swift as a pebble into a well, followed by another. And another and another.

The creature clambered onto the outside of her window as she stepped out of the magic circle. She took up her casket and passed it to the devil. It pushed off like a swimmer from a bank to hover in the air. Another took its place. In its hands it had a long length of cloth, like a hammock. It offered a hand through the window and she took it, surprised at how cold it was. She climbed through the window and sat on its sill. The gargoyle wrapped the cloth around her and she shifted her weight to sit on it. They lifted her, as if she was on a swing.

She flew off, a fox peering up at her, its eyes sharp in the moonlight. She went over the sleeping city, towards Greyfriars Abbey. The little magic was done. Now she must ready herself for a bigger test. One gargoyle flew in front of her, clasping her casket. The air was warm, the air full of the night scents of summer. Isabella hummed to herself.

> *Westron Wind, when will thou blow?*
> *The small rain down can rain*
> *Christ, if my love were in my arms*
> *And I in my bed again.*

'Oh, Mortimer,' she said. 'I who have been loved by so many, only ever loved you. But I am near, my love. I will fetch you from Hell.'

The gargoyles landed softly in the courtyard of the abbey. It was quiet and still, long before Matins, though the first hour came early in summer.

A man stepped out of the darkness of the cloisters. He was tall and thin but with a good belly on him. She could have mistaken him for pregnant.

'Friar,' she said, 'you have made the preparations.'

'Yes, lady. You have the ingredients?'

She gestured to the casket.

'Then let us begin,' said the friar.

4

A memory, or a dream? Osbert could not recall.

'Shall I play the knight' she asked, 'and you be the horse? I shall ride you until you cry "neigh".'

'Mount, good lady, and I shall carry you where you wish, though you may find me a bumpy ride.'

'To be worthy of such a handsome stallion, I must be fittingly caparisoned,' said Aude. 'Let me wear your mail, my love.'

She was above him, her heavy breasts brushing his chest, her body smelling of ale and cinders.

'I would see you naked, my darling.'

'There's none so naked as them that are half-clothed.'

'If it please you.'

She lifted off the fine mail shirt, soft as cambric but a deep silver that intensified the firelight, sparkling like the heart of a jewel.

She put it on. It was too big for her. She let it fall over her body and Osbert slid his hands beneath it to hold her tits, his thumbs caressing her nipples.

'A knight must have a shield and sword,' she said.

The little house rocked like a boat on the sea, floating on the ocean of drink Osbert had guzzled.

'Take them and let us ride for the dawn.'

Aude picked up the Sacred Heart shield and the scabbarded sword.

Osbert remembered little after that – the sensation of her on top of him, her rocking back and forth, a feeling between sickness and wild delight.

*

He slept heavily and woke as if from a fall. Harsh voices rattled his head. The morning was warm.

'D'Ambret! D'Ambret!'

He stood. He appeared to have become more drunk during the night. He leant to support himself against a wall, but it cruelly withdrew and he fell to the floor, a winding, stomach-heaving blow . . .

'D'Ambret! D'Ambret!'

He looked up to ask for a cup of beer to straighten his head. The hearth was cold and no one was around. Only one suit of the armour he had captured lay before him and with it a sword. Where was his mail? Where were the villagers? Where his shield and sword?

'There's no one here, Lord!'

Osbert turned his head.

There was one there. Him.

'D'Ambret! D'Ambret! Come out and face us, you ill-nurtured maltworm!'

Osbert clawed his way up the wall and stood again.

'The whole place has fled, sir.' A young voice from outside.

'The serfs are cowards and their champion too, it seems.' He heard the whicker of a horse, the jingle of mail.

No mail, no sword, no shield – just the armour he had won. That might not even fit him and he wouldn't know what to do in it, even if it did. He was in a fever of dithering.

'Look inside. Root them out.'

'Lord above! Preserve me. Preserve me!' He took up the sword. What, exactly, was he going to do with that? With the angel's sword he had just held it loosely while it tugged his arm about. The ordinary blade seemed heavy in his hand.

The door of the hut opened and there stood a blond young knight in armour, a surcoat of red checks on a black background.

'Aha!' He drew his sword.

'Have you come to die, young man?' said Osbert. 'I am d'Ambret, a sorcerer and warrior without compare.' He was sick a little in his mouth, the taste of stale booze retching up into his nostrils in a way that was not entirely displeasing.

'We'll see who's the better man!' The young knight leapt at Osbert, but had not seen a low beam in the darkness of the hut. He smashed his head into it and fell back onto his arse, dazed. Osbert planted a big kick into his face, knocking him cold to the floor.

Another, bigger, man was in the doorway, rattling in mail.

'So rude of you to call before I had a chance to dress,' said Osbert. 'Will you be the second man I slay this morning?'

The man-at-arms stepped back.

'My Lord, he's in here. I suggest we pull him into the open where he can't work his tricks.'

He couldn't outrun horses. He couldn't get out the back. All he could do was wait in the hut and hope they'd all be too scared to come in.

'Burn him out.'

That path no longer open, it seemed.

He took up a shield. He had been a cozener and a deceiver all his life. No time to change that now.

He stepped from the hut. He had a thundering sound in his head, like the drumming of great hooves.

'I apologise, gentlemen, that I was not awake to greet you but I am at your disposal now. Which among you shall I send to Hell first?' The thundering really was awful, almost unbearable. 'Come, I—'

He caught a movement from the corner of his eye and turned.

He only actually discovered that he'd been struck by a lance, and then a warhorse, later. Reconstructing the event from his place in the Château Richard dungeons, he realised he had, in some ways been lucky. He'd deflected the lance with his shield – by pure accident – and that had pushed him out of the direct path of the warhorse. That had struck him a glancing blow, knocking him cold but only breaking most of his ribs on the left side.

It was pitch-black but he knew the smell of cells well enough – piss, shit and whatever else comes out of the human body. He feared that he might very well have been a contributor to that stench himself. Damp and cold. He breathed in and it was as if someone was thrusting knives into him. His ribs! Manacles were at his hands and feet. He tried to move but he was secured to the wall on a short chain.

Having spent many years in one form of prison or another, the idea of being confined again filled him with dread. The mad priest Edwin had imprisoned him – or refused to release him – in a magic circle for years; the insane Hugh Despenser had kept him slaving to summon devils to stock his army for years more. He wondered what brand of insanity he was likely to encounter here. He felt around his cell. A damp floor, tight walls, a door. Lord, the pain. Did Christ suffer such torments?

'Don't forgive them, Father,' he said, 'they know exactly what they're doing.' His ribs hurt as he coughed out a laugh.

He thought of Aude. She'd taken his armour – or rather, he'd let her. Why had she betrayed him? What had he done to her? Had he not treated her kindly?

He put his hand to his belly, where the dreadful Despenser had burnt a magic circle. Not that, not even in his darkest hour, not even if he could. That circle had been activated by angel's blood, and he had used his last curing hangovers. There were other ways to conjure devils but he knew none and was grateful for it. He'd rather die in the dark than face any again. He'd had too much of them.

He lay there for a long time. He was parched, his head ached. As he got used to the pain in his ribs he realised that other areas were aching – his shoulder, for instance, had taken a fearful bash. Was it broken?

A voice in the darkness.

'What damned soul lies in here?'

That made his ears prick up. *Oh dear. Oh dear, oh dear, oh deary dear. Oh dear with a dear on top.*

'Are you ready for your torments, you mocker of great men? Are you ready to answer for your crimes at the Lake of Fire?'

Osbert crossed himself, painfully. He was in Hell. He had travelled there once before, or rather been sent there. But then he had been alive. Now, the evidence strongly seemed to suggest, he was dead. Remembering his Aristotle and trying to look at things logically, he had been struck by a charging warhorse. That, it was generally accepted, did nothing for the health. His experience of Hell had taught him one thing, however. With a little ingenuity, making oneself useful to the right people, then an eternity of torment could at least be made bearable.

'I know people here,' said Osbert. 'The merchant De la Pole is my friend. I'm sure if you lead me to him, he would handsomely reward you.'

'There is no De la Pole here. I am de Baux, lord of this castle since you killed my uncle.'

Still, Osbert did not quite understand.

'Then what part of Hell is this? If it is Free Hell, then know I died as poor as any man alive. If you ask Lucifer, I'm sure he would see that I'm one of you. Is Sariel here, the fallen angel? She would protect me.'

The door opened and Osbert's eyes were starred by a blaze of torchlight.

'There is no one here to help you. This is not Hell, but you will soon wish you were there. Take him. Let's stretch him on the wall a bit and see how he likes it.'

Oh God, it was the knight who had run from him. A coward's revenge is a terrible thing, he thought.

Rough hands grabbed him, his chain unlocked and he was kicked and punched and dragged from the cell.

5

The stone saints in the church sang to welcome her – high, soaring plainsong. She smiled to herself. A mark of royalty; those statues didn't sing for just anyone. The friar, bobbing along beside her with his lantern, could not hear them. For all his scraping before God, all his studies and prayer, he was not so favoured. Her gargoyles stood next to her, squat little things no higher than her waist. It was a miracle they had the power to fly at all, let alone lift her.

'There is a small matter to attend to before we commence,' said the friar. One of those vain men who affected a slight Italian accent to suggest time spent in Rome. Well, the Pope was now in Avignon, Rome a festering sore on the banks of the Tiber, its people returning to tilling the soil rather than the city trades that had sustained them in the days of the popes' excess.

They proceeded through the great church, the gorgoyles nervously waiting for her permission to enter. In the religion she had been brought up in, she might have expected her devils to have shrunk from such a holy place. Now she knew the truth – the devils were the jailers of God, keeping the upstart Lucifer locked in Hell, beneath the command of the jailer-in-chief – Satan. Devils, though God had made them hideous to terrify the souls of the damned, were His servants too. Like all servants, they were despised but useful.

'We are going beyond this world. We must do so with a clear conscience. Have you been confessed?'

'My confessor is not here.'

'I can fulfil the office.'

She stopped on the stair down. This man would have her in his power, know her secrets. Did he imagine that if he knew them he would live beyond morning?

She needed no confession. Other women might have trembled at the thought of their sins. Isabella had thrown down a king, arranged for his murder; she had opened the gates of Hell to allow devils into the world; she had drunk the blood of angels to keep her young and beautiful, cast spells, bewitched men. Still God loved her. How did she know?

'I am a queen,' she said.

If her husband Edward had been so loved by God, he would still be a king. But Edward had offended Him. She had been His instrument in removing him.

The friar bowed his head.

'Of course. I didn't mean to . . .'

Isabella studied him, slightly puzzled. Why was he telling her what he did or did not mean? Did he imagine she could be interested in his thoughts? Low men mean or do not mean whatever their betters decide.

To the lowest part of the crypt, where they'd buried him as if they feared he would rise again. They'd been right to be scared.

'The monastery is asleep?'

'Beneath the velvet wings of night,' said the friar.

Isabella regretted that men willing to sell their souls for gold and earthly power so often tended to the flamboyant. The abbot had proved unswayable. He had some sort of amulet, perhaps to save him from her magic, or perhaps he was as holy as they said. The friar had proved more pliable but she had swayed him with the offer of gold and knowledge, not bothering to employ her supernatural power of charm. It would demean her to use it on such a low man and besides, if the abbot was resistant to her magic, then it was not impossible he could recognise its effects in one of his monks.

'"Yes" would suffice,' she said. Mortimer had not been flamboyant, but that was right for a man of his birth.

Mortimer. She remembered him when he was young, at the court in France. He was not as tall as her husband Edward, didn't have the broad shoulders and the proud nose of the Plantagenet men. He was dark and compact, said little but watched her in a way that no man had ever looked at her before. She was beautiful, the beauty of beauties, and was used to inspiring desire, though more usually awe, in men. Mortimer, though – his eyes said something else, something between amusement and reproach. 'Did you ever think there could be anyone else?'

Importantly, Mortimer did things. He didn't dither like her husband, or listen to counsel or sit spooning with his favourites. Everything about him had been purposeful and direct. She recognised what he was immediately – the right arm she had been looking for. A hammer, to smash her enemies. She'd never wanted anyone else like she wanted him, before or since.

She could not charm him, use the strange – almost supernatural – power she had over men, because she didn't want to. She wanted him to love her as nearly an equal, not as the victim of a spell. He had loved her more fiercely than she had thought possible. He had thrown down her husband the king for her, controlled her son and made her ruler of England. That was before that night at Nottingham Castle, when the hated Montagu had led his men into the castle, stolen away her love and had him killed at her son's behest. She could not blame her son – he was a king and acting as a king – but she could blame Montagu. His instrument. She had done for him all right, seduced him and warped his mind, got him to bring her what was in her casket. He'd gone to damnation and gone gladly, for she who despised him.

She wished she'd been there to see his death – at Crécy, she heard, dressed in the rags of a pauper, speared through by her grandson. Or rather, the thing that had taken her grandson's place. Well, needs must. The Black Prince, as they were now calling young Edward, would be dealt with in time.

The crypt smelled damp, a hint of urine. What a place. There Mortimer was, in image on top of his tomb, as he'd been in life. He was a stone now. She touched the cold features, the strong chin, the sharp nose – far sharper than in life. Mortimer had been a warrior and he had fought too much in the mêlée and the tournament to have hoped for anything other than a squadge of dough for his nose. It was almost as if he was standing there at her side, his solid presence like a fortress, like a great ship. She hated to think of him in Hell, but that was where he had to be. She had been a queen, was still a queen. God had showed her He favoured her by overthrowing her husband. But God had favoured her son, helped him overthrow her lover. So, Hell. It was possible to slip through the cracks in its walls, with the right magic, the right connections, the right offerings.

'Unearth him.'

The gargoyles fluttered up to the tomb. Their nails drove into the concrete of the base, as loud as any mason's chisel. The friar flinched at the noise.

'Don't fear,' said Isabella. 'Your fellows are safely sleeping. And if they awake, then what? I am queen. Who here will question me?'

'None. But your son will discover what you are doing.'

'That would be a problem. Though not if I am successful.'

The gargoyles scraped and shook the base of the tomb, the muscles straining beneath their stony skins. What were they made of? The friar seemed to express her thoughts.

'Can God truly breathe life into stone?'

'God can do anything.'

'We all fear His power.'

She smiled.

'Even those of us he entrusts it to.'

The base came free and the gargoyles slid it aside. The smell of wet earth. There it was, a rectangular patch of soil – all Mortimer, who once ruled all England, now commanded.

'Dig,' she said, and the gargoyles plunged their nails into the soil, flapping and cawing as they burrowed down to where her great love was buried.

His corpse, of course, had suffered foul abuses. When they'd killed him at Tyburn, he'd died a traitor's death – his entrails cut out and burnt in front of him: hanged, drawn and quartered.

They cracked open the lead coffin. By the lantern's light she could see something very strange. He had lain in the dirt ten years but it was as if his body had been placed there yesterday – the ribs white and red, like something found on a butcher's hook, the arms flayed like hams, the head raw-jawed, the mouth having had a good deal of the flesh torn away. But he had not rotted; there was no smell, even as she had anticipated. She held his head in her hands. He was still handsome, despite his wounds, his black hair as shiny and shorn as the last night she had held him living in her arms.

'Lay him out,' she told the gargoyles, but they fluttered back from the coffin, crossing themselves. Beasts of the pit! They feared to touch such a noble man, so she did the work herself, assembling the jumble of bone, limbs and entrails as near to the shape of a man as they could. Her throat felt tight. How had that happened? How had she allowed it?

Montagu had dragged her love away, Montagu wrested England from her power. She almost wished she could damn him again. Perhaps she would be allowed to see him in Hell.

The friar chalked the magic circle on the flagstones around the ruined grave, scratching in the names of angels, of demons, of the spirits of the four winds. The gargoyles clattered, nervous, and Isabella put her hand on to the stony shoulder of one of them to calm it.

She placed the casket in between the sides of Mortimer's ribs. They had split his sternum in two when they quartered him. In a way, it was a compliment. Such a thorough punishment, the recognition of the level to which he had aspired. Ambition was a clear sin but she would argue that he had only supported her, a queen of France, not sought to set himself up as king. She knew that, in her heart, to be untrue.

'Should I open the casket now?'

'You will know when.'

'How?'

This was a saucy man. A fragment of the anger she felt towards Montagu fell towards the friar, as a seed flies from a mighty tree. One day she might call him to account for his presumption in asking questions of his betters.

For now she needed him.

'Begin,' she said.

The friar called the names of the angels of the north, south, east and west. He marked out the circle with holy water. He had access to the arm of St Augustine, and should have dipped the fingers in the water, if he had followed her instructions. He had. A gargoyle pressed at the edges of the circle, as if against an invisible wall. It could not enter, and let out a dry croak to express its unease. It was commanded by the names of the angels and respect for the sacrifice of the saint to stay where it was.

'The boundary is complete, ma'am.' He gave a flourishing little bow.

'Then let us prepare for our journey.'

She opened the casket. Within was her husband's heart, the heart of a king, tuberous, meaty, still wet with blood. The heart of a king. Carrying such a thing, they could not forbid her entrance. Such a sin against God that they must open the gates of Hell.

Isabella held the heart above the open grave.

'By the secret names of God, by the suffering of Christ, by my right as a queen of the holy line of Capet, who God blessed to call the spirits of the air and of the land and of the sea and of the ether, admit me to the lands of the damned.'

She squeezed the heart and its blood spilled into the open grave. Nothing happened. She glanced at the priest. He was fixed in his attention on her, his lips licking at his dry mouth.

'By the secret names of God, by . . .'

A sensation of standing at a great height overcame her. The mouth of the grave seemed darker.

'Admit me to the plains of Gehenna, to the starless chambers of Caïna, the brass city of Dis, the island of Judecca and the valley of the Wailing River, admit me. Recognise my sin.'

A sound, a deep bell. Then the buzzing of a fly, the cold metal sound of a drop of water and the hissing of a snake. A smell like burning hair filled the circle. The air was heavy and a gust of heat and cinders blew from the mouth of the grave.

The friar sank to his knees and vomited into his hands. The gargoyles chattered and squawked like caged birds at feeding time.

'What sinner do you bring, brothers?' A strange voice, sweet and melodious.

More cheeping and flapping from the gargoyles.

'Admit her.'

Isabella knew what to do. She stepped forward into the grave and then she was falling fast, from a brass sky towards a land of fire. Tiny claws seized her, bit at her. She was engulfed by a swarm of tiny devils, each no bigger than a bee, all stabbing at her, hissing like water on a fire.

'I am a queen! I am a queen!'

They fell away from her, swarming down through the burning air. So hot, so intolerably hot. Even the wind of her fall did not cool her but Isabella steeled herself, forced herself to breathe and be calm. She was falling towards a wide land of fire. Hell was beautiful, burning with colours she had never seen in life, or only in the heart of a jewel – emeralds, rubies, shifting plains of flame, amber smoke drifting towards mountains of steel.

She might die, might well die. What would happen to her then? A shape drifted in front of her, fell with her. One of her gargoyles? No. It was a great figure, twice her height, shadows flickering around it. A burnt angel with ragged wings, its body fireblack, withered like burnt wood.

'I would speak to the Lord of Hell,' she shouted. 'Take me to Satan!'

The creature extended a finger to the bloody heart she grasped to her chest. It smiled a bone-white grin.

'Yes,' it said, and caught her.

6

They dragged Osbert up towards the light with slaps and kicks, his eyes burning as they adjusted in turn to the flaring torches that spun dancing shadows on the stairwell and then to the dawn pouring through a great open window. His head hurt, his mouth was parched, his belly was rumbling, his hose were heavy with shit. All in all, he felt better than he did most mornings, the presence of the manacles at hand and foot excepted.

He was up high, on a rampart, hurried along beneath a wooden canopy. Cheers from down below in the courtyard, a mob just glimpsed – dowdy browns and greys shot through with flashes of scarlets and blues. All ranks of society had turned out for this one. This did not bode well – the combination of a mob and an accused man being, in Osbert's experience, bad news for the accused man. Baying masses generally did not demand that scrupulous justice be done.

At the end of the rampart, where the walls and the canopy ended, stood de Baux, a knot of four squires in full armour behind him. Osbert's guards shoved him on towards the lord.

'This is illegal!' shouted Osbert. 'I am a man of the Church and have the right to be tried in a Church court!'

'Try this for a learned point of view,' said a voice behind him. A splitting pain went through his head, the flash of a white light. His ears rang and his vision swam. He sank to his knees but was pulled quickly back to standing.

'Here is the champion of the poor!' shouted a guard. 'Here is the King of Shit in his filthy rags!'

A thump caught Osbert in the middle of the back and he fell forwards onto his face.

'See how he grovels!'

Osbert gave up. There was no point in standing just to be knocked down again, no point in doing anything. His fate was set.

'Who are you?' De Baux spoke, loudly to be heard by the crowd.

'I am Osbert of Paris.'

'You don't sound of Paris.'

'Sorry.'

Another kick to the guts. That one really hurt.

'Tell us the truth. Who did you rob to take the weapons by which you defeated us?'

No point in lying here.

'An angel.'

'Liar!'

Smack, a kick right on the tail. It set his spine humming.

'I killed the angel at the Sainte-Chapelle. I used its armour and sword for profit, monetary and carnal.'

'What?'

'Gold and whores.'

'How did a man like you kill an angel?'

'I was with some others. They stuck the Lance of Christ through it. The sky went black.'

The mob caught its breath to hear such blasphemy.

De Baux coughed.

'I have heard such rumours, which is all you have managed. A low man like you couldn't kill an angel.'

'A low man like me couldn't kill your knights either, but I did.'

'Through sorcery.'

'No. Though I am a sorcerer.'

Again the crowd sighed.

'So you admit it.'

'Look, mate,' said Osbert. 'That may be seen as a bad thing down here but up in Paris I serve the king. Where do you think the devils that strengthen our armies against the enemies of God came from? From me.'

'Hugh Despenser summoned those.'

'He summoned nothing. I summoned him and all his helpers.'

'If this is the case, why aren't you the head of a mighty army of devils?'

Osbert didn't really have an answer for that. 'It's not my station. I do not command, I follow. I am a loyal servant of the king. I . . .'

Why wasn't he the head of a mighty army of devils? It had never occurred to him.

'Is that so?'

'Yes, I was court sorcerer to Philip.'

De Baux smiled. 'So you are a lucky man. All you need to do is to summon a devil here and it will rescue you.'

'I haven't the ingredients.'

'How very convenient. The trial is over – throw this fool into the moat.'

They dragged him down to the unwalled section of parapet. He had always had a fear of drowning but, as they pushed him nearer the edge, he saw his fears were unfounded. The moat was dry. They planned to kill him with the fall. This did not concern him, as he was fairly sure he had the means to survive a drop on to a dry landing. It was what happened when he hit the ground he was worried about. How long would it take de Baux's men to find a crossbow? Not long, he guessed, and he was in no fit state to run after such rough treatment in the dungeon.

'Will you not save me? People of this castle, will you not save me, protect me as I protected you from your masters? Protect me—'

A horn sounded in the distance. Osbert lifted his eyes. Dust rose above a copse, halfway to the horizon. A ribbon of riders flowed from the wood.

'Strangers!' a shout went up.

'Banners!' Another.

Momentarily they forget about Osbert.

'Friend or foe?' said de Baux.

'Not the English!' A peasant voice, full of panic.

'If it is, then you should know I have acted as their spy!' shouted Osbert. 'I have traded court secrets with Edward himself. They will pay handsomely for me!'

'It's not the English!' A guard had his hand to his eyes shielding the sun. 'Those are royal banners!'

Osbert's knees trembled. The drop beneath him was steep, the expanse of land in front of the walls vast and with no cover if he tried to run. If anyone had paid attention to what he had said, he would do well to jump. The fate of spies was not a pleasant one – torture.

'Who is it?'

'The king's constable's banner. And a white stag on a blue field!'

'Who the hell is that?' said de Baux.

'La Cerda,' said Osbert. 'Favourite of the king. A friend of mine.'

'A friend of yours, you shit-soiled Saracen?'

'Even a king stinks if you don't let him take off his hose for a week! I told you, I'm the court sorcerer. I killed Hugh Despenser! He hated La Cerda.' This did not put La Cerda in a very exclusive club, as Despenser had tended to hate anyone who vied with him for royal favour.

'You struck down an God-appointed lord.'

'Believe me, mate, Despenser was far from that by the time I killed him.'

De Baux looked at Osbert with new eyes.

The riders from the copse trotted on and two knights from the castle rode out to meet them.

Banners were dipped, vows exchanged and the riders wheeled back to the keep, the throng behind them.

'Charles de la Cerda, appointed by God-blessed King John!' shouted a knight.

'Told you,' said Osbert. 'Refer me to him, they must fear me lost at Crécy. I will reward you when I return to the king.'

'*You* will reward *me*?'

'Yes. Handsomely.' *Handsomely* meaning by intimating to King Philip that de Baux had received English emissaries and should be hanged.

Two trumpets blew.

'Open your gates in the name of the king of France.'

'You truly can summon devils?'

'Yes, given the right ingredients.'

'What are the right ingredients?'

'Angels' blood. The relics of saints.'

'We don't have any of those.'

'Then the dragon?'

'What?'

'The dragon, that tore the angels at Crécy. I have it. I have it.'

'Where?'

'It's in a box!'

'Oh, be quiet, you wretch!' De Baux put his boot into the middle of Osbert's back, shoving him from the parapet.

7

She had expected that she would be able to fly over the walls of Hell, but no. They extended ever upwards, harsh red clay the colour of old blood towering into invisibility. The angel soared along the length of the wall, and she saw that it was not as solid as she had thought but had the consistency of a wet river-bank, oozing mud. Within it she saw what she had first taken for worms writhing along its surface, but she now recognised them for human arms, reaching out, imploring. As wide as the wall stretched, which was very wide, and as high as it grew, which was for ever, faces and hands broke free of the towering slime, as if on the edge of freedom before being sucked back into the mire.

'The ambitious,' said the angel. 'Those who sought to rise above the place God had granted them.'

Isabella, who was one of the long line of Capetian queens so noted for their skill with devils, who had ordered her husband's heart torn living from his body to work the magic to be admitted to Hell, who had gazed upon a thousand horrors fondly, now blanched.

'Mortimer.' How high had he tried to rise?

'Is he there?' She had to shout, the wind roaring in her ears from the speed of the angel's flight.

'I do not keep the records,' said the angel.

It hugged her tightly, though its claws were gentle on her flesh. She did not fear it would drop her but she felt a mild bite of anxiety that it could deliver what it promised. If it was some wandering fiend simply looking to torment her then everything might come to nothing. No. It would not dare to move against a queen.

It flew her to where an enormous flow like a waterfall of blood plunged down the wall, falling into nothing, a slope of drier clay on the approach to the flood. The slope bubbled with life, a slaughterhouse cacophony rising up from it. The forms of flayed men pushed against giant wingless flies, bald horses dragged ropes to which were fastened the twitching bodies of broken-winged bird men, of pig-faced men, their throats cut, twitching in the throes of death, though not – as she could see – dying.

'The wall is ever building,' said the angel, as they dropped towards the bubbling gate.

Isabella clutched the heart.

Above the Falls of Blood was a stone lintel, with an inscription: *Hic Ego Non*. Isabella translated tentatively. Latin had never been a joy to her. 'I am not here'.

'Who is "I"?'

'Death,' said the angel.

'Is Death in the rest of Hell?'

'I do not know.'

'If you don't, then who does?'

'No one. Or perhaps Satan. In the outer circles of Hell there is always hope. It is the tree to which the fungus of despair can cling. Beyond this gate lie terrors unimagined by men. There is no hope of them ending.'

Isabella swallowed. Would they release Mortimer for the price she was offering?

They fluttered down to the ground.

'This is the Martyrs' Gate,' said the angel. 'It is made from the blood of those who have died for God.'

'So many,' said Isabella.

'It is but a splash. We could build a thousand such gates, such has been the suffering of God's people.'

The angel released her. The gate towered above her, twenty times her height. The heat was horrid and sweat soaked her.

'New souls for Hell, new souls for Hell!' the flayed men cried out. 'Open the inner gate.'

This was too much for Isabella.

'I am Isabella, queen of the English, daughter of France, of royal blood, appointed by God. Bow to my superiority. I enter first.'

The ragged angel spread wide its wings. 'And I am Gader'el, who brought the instruments of war to man, so kings may be kings and those beneath them learn to serve. Open the gate!'

'Only the damned may pass through here. A queen cannot be easily damned.' A disembodied voice, high and pompous.

'I have killed my husband the king, God's representative. I have his heart, bloody in my hands. The heart of a king, crowned at Westminster in the sight of God and His angels.'

'Then you have sought damnation,' said the voice. 'And the heart of a king is powerful in magic.'

'I have sought it. I bring this bloody gift for Satan. Let me through.'

'Once you have entered there is no guarantee that you can leave.'

'I accept that. There is no worse torment than life without my love.'

'Oh, there is, yes there is. Step through. Take the road to the inmost gate.'

Isabella didn't know what to do. She had expected the bloody bloodfall to part or for some road to open but the blood continued its tumult, the damned souls screamed and the angel stood at her side, its wings jittering, insecty and ragged.

Have faith, Isabella. Have faith in yourself, in your royalty, in your strength and the strength of your love.

She made her way up the slope, peering through the crashing waters. She could see nothing but the foaming blood, hear nothing but its roar as it fell away into nothing.

She stepped within.

This time she did not fall. It was as if a veil of blood passed over her eyes, a flash of scarlet light. Before her was a tiny door within a huge gate, wet with blood. She bent and squeezed herself through it. As she wriggled through, she saw she was emerging into a sunny glade of cool oaks. Sunlight turned the leaves to filigree. She was in a sort of walled garden, roses all around. She walked through the glade towards a clearing. Here a table was set with a magnificent feast. Stuffed swans, gaping boars' heads, shiny in their gravy, a striped horse, more fruit and vegetables than she had ever seen, gaudy in greens, yellows and reds swamped the table.

On top of the table squatted a monstrous ape, pot-bellied and bigger than she was by far. It had patchy, mottled fur. On its head it wore a crown and in its hand it carried a splendid sceptre. It watched her with suspicious eyes before letting out a plaintive caw. With its free hand it picked up a hock of ham and bit in.

Isabella approached the table. She had expected to see the food crawling with maggots but it looked wholesome and good. The ape gnawed at the ham.

'I am looking for the jailer of Hell,' she said.

The ape just gave another great caw, its sharp teeth flashing yellow in its mouth.

She walked on around the garden. There were eight more tiny doors, as if built to amuse a child, all in weathered wood but strong and solid. Should she take one? She put her ear to a door. She could hear nothing.

The ape watched her with its slow eyes. She did not know what to do so she sat at the table. Should she wait to be served? Even in Hell they could not expect a queen to carry food from one end of a table to another. It grew dark, the sky above her lit at the furthest extremity of her vision by shining, stormy clouds. No stars but a purple glow in the sky. The ape munched on.

She got hungry. If no servant appeared soon she would have to take some of the food herself. She feared it, though. What foul tastes, what poisons were steeped in that appealing flesh? Dawn came, her hands wrinkled from holding the blood-slick heart, as if they had been in water too long. Her stomach rumbled. Poison or not, she was going to have to eat the food.

She reached for an apple. The ape gave a great cry and leapt across the table, shoving her back into her seat, raining blows hard upon her. She shrank down, covering her husband's heart, fearful the creature might snatch it.

It retreated and went back to sitting on the table, stuffing itself.

Is this the extent of Hell? She thought. To outwit an ape for your supper? It seemed a much lesser punishment than being sentenced to the living wall or the Lake of Fire.

'I am as hungry as I can be,' she said to the ape. 'I hunger for my love and can bear any torment to free him.'

The ape farted and belched.

'I would have dealings with your master.'

The ape smiled at her and burst into a chattering, knee-slapping laugh.

'I don't see what's so funny,' said Isabella.

The ape seemed to find this even funnier.

Isabella was not used to being mocked and did not like it much.

'I am a queen. You are bound by God to obey me.'

Again the ape screamed and hollered, throwing fruit and meat to the ground, banging its feet, thrashing its hands.

It scampered across the table to face her again.

'I am a queen!'

The ape waved its sceptre in her face, took off its crown and waved that too, hissing and baring its teeth.

Now, Isabella understood.

'Satan,' she said.

The ape grinned.

She held out the heart.

'This is for you.'

The ape evaluated her for a second, craned its head. Then it snatched the heart from her and thrust it into its mouth, guzzling and guzzling until it was all gone. It grinned at her with bloody lips.

'You,' it said. 'You have defied God to bring me a voice.'

'I have completed the great magic. I have damned myself living so my love may escape Hell.'

'You offer yourself to eternal torment?'

'Yes. If it will free Mortimer. But I have not finished living yet.'

'You brought me the heart of a king. It will be but a short time before you are back.'

So it thought. She would live a very long time. There were enough angels in heaven to keep her in angels' blood for eternity.

'I have not yet struck the bargain.'

'By being here you strike it!'

'I think not. Swear to let him out of your jurisdiction. Swear to open the gates of Hell for him!'

'All the gates? I cannot get through the third gate to release myself, Lady. I will not open the fourth for then my great prisoner Lucifer may break free.'

'I got here, didn't I?'

'Things are allowed to the souls of men and to princes royal that are not allowed to devils nor other spirits. The gate is made small for a reason.'

'Is Mortimer behind the fourth gate?'

'You are canny, Lady. No, he is not.'

'Then open the third. Devils might not get through but a man can, as I got in.'

Satan grinned. 'Yes, a man can be released. Ah, Lady, you see through all my subterfuges and evasions. I could allow a man through, give him passage through a postern gate. Ah, you see how the lesser devils enjoy freedoms their masters do not. I have never walked in the world, never set foot in God's higher creation. All I have is this dry replica . . .' He waved a great hand at the sunlit garden.

'Let Mortimer through!'

'What God has ordained cannot be lightly bargained away.'

'I have given you the heart of an anointed king, that is no small gift.'

'You have given me the heart of an anointed king, you have worked odd magics. And yet, and yet, you are still a queen. You may not be certain to be damned. God is mysterious. I need your soul, Lady. We are constructing a magic here. A queen who has chosen damnation will add powerfully to that. God has given you the right to command. So command your own damnation and I will give my order that Mortimer should be allowed through the postern gates of Hell. I will not hold Mortimer once you have made your oath. Command yourself damned!'

'I so command it. I damn myself to Hell.'

'To the Lake of Fire, if I so choose?'

'Yes.'

'To the living walls of Akash?'

'Yes.'

'To the Hungry Chamber?'

'Yes.'

'Then I accept,' said Satan. 'Your magic is complete.'

'Then release Mortimer!'

The great ape picked at his ear.

'Oh, Lady, I cannot.'

'You swore so to do.'

'I swore to let him out of my jurisdiction. I swore to open the gates of Hell for him.'

'So do so, or my oath counts for nothing.'

'It is binding,' said Satan. 'I release Mortimer from my power. If he approaches the gates of Hell then I will open them for him. But he will not approach.'

'Why not?'

'Because he never came here.'

'I buried him myself. I . . .'

Isabella felt the words like sand in her throat. His body had not rotted. She had thought it because of the powers he had invoked in life. But why had those powers not come to his defence when her son had overthrown him? Why had no devil plucked him from the gallows at Tyburn when one had rescued him from the Tower of London years before? But Mortimer had been freed from the Tower on the feast of St Barnabas in Chains. He . . .

Satan smiled his ape's grin.

'Mortimer is in Heaven.'

Her heart thumped at her chest like a cat in a bag.

'He rose up against an anointed king.'

Satan licked the blood from his fingers.

'God is mad,' he said. 'When He threw the usurper Lucifer from Heaven the dark one stuck a sword in Him. He cannot remove it. The pain drives Him to insanities.'

'In supporting Mortimer?'

'In supporting Edward. The line is corrupted by devils.'

'I corrupted it. I will make amends.'

'No, Lady, it was corrupted years before you were born.'

'That is a lie. Then how can God support them?'

'God is many things. And He is stricken. Perhaps He does not even know His will. Those of us who follow Him do what we must to interpret His desires. We seek to obey. But obey what? I am a poor devil and must do my best.'

'Your best favouring your interests.'

'The interests of order.'

'So how did Mortimer win his place in Heaven?'

'It was not part of the bargain for me to tell you.'

She saw it now. It was obvious to her.

'I will tell you then, what I guess. The Plantagenet line is both cursed and blessed. And it has succeeded in mixing its blood with that of the pure streams of France. The picture is smudged. God was in pain, not knowing how to impose the law He had set down. Mortimer sought to bring order to the situation, to cleanse the line and start again. By his boldness he won God's heart. You have no claim on him here.'

'That is some of it. Though the rot goes deeper than you know.'

'How deep?'

The ape sneered. 'Not in the bargain.'

'Then what of me?'

'You are damned. And for nothing. There are magics brewing in Hell. The soul of a damned queen might speed them nicely.'

Isabella took an apple from the table. Satan drew back his teeth but she stared him down.

'I am not yours yet. I am still blessed of God. I will find a way to redeem myself.'

'How will you do that?'

She smiled.

'I will undo all the wrong I have done. Like Saul, like Magdalene, like Augustine and St Francis, I will turn to God. You cannot keep a saint in Hell.'

The ape shat massively on the table, wriggling as it squatted.

'The third door,' it said, pointing. 'You will leave by it, and by it you will return.'

8

La Cerda's host were used to shocking sights. They had seen the angels torn, seen the sky black with the wings of devils and demons, watched the flower of French nobility wither under the bows of common men. However, the spectacle of a manacled wretch falling from a parapet as slowly as if through water was a new one to them.

It was not entirely a surprise to Osbert, he having taken the precaution of sewing an angel's feather into his hose. This was chiefly so that, when he tumbled over drunk, he did so slowly. But he knew well angels' feathers were also marvellous openers of portals in all sorts of structures, from doors to stone keeps, and so he kept it secreted in case he ever had to escape from imprisonment. In other men this might have been seen as an unjustifiable fear bordering on cowardice, but Osbert was no stranger to confinement and the hiding of the feather had been a wise precaution.

However, he had sewn it into his hose so tightly and positioned it so inconveniently that he had been unable to unpick it when manacled. It had done him no good at all in de Baux's dungeon, though he had attempted to employ its powers of making walls disappear by waggling his arse at the stonework. Now, though, it enabled him to float serenely to the floor. A brief wave of elation rose in him. He was free! Apart from the manacles, all that stood between him and open country were fifty men-at-arms, all of whom were watching open-mouthed as his considerable bulk floated gently to the floor like a leaf on a breeze.

Osbert landed, fell over, and quickly evaluated his options. He had none. That certainly made things easier. His confinement had reduced his legs to solid bits of wood; he had enemies behind, and a large number of men whose chief hobby was chasing things that ran away in front of him. Doing nothing was always Osbert's preferred course, though one that had rarely presented itself to him in a life of scratching a living from deceit and fraud. Here, though, it seemed very apt. He didn't even bother to get up but just lay back looking up at the fragile blue of the summer's day like a lazy man on a riverbank.

Before long, the fragile blue was replaced by the sturdy brown of a horseman's face.

'Who are you?'

Osbert didn't really see the point in lying any more. He knew that knights tended to divide their conquests into high value captives and dead people. He would place himself in the former group.

'Osbert of Paris, magician of the French court, summoner of the king's most holy devils.'

'If you are such a great magician, how come you're dressed in rags?'

'I have been cruelly imprisoned. Do you doubt my magic? Did you not see how I floated from these walls? Tell me how I did that?'

'You are a magician?'

Someone kicked him, quite hard.

'What was that for?'

'I've never kicked a magician before. I wanted to see what it was like.'

'What is it like?' said someone else.

'Just like kicking a shitty peasant. Give it a go.'

Another boot in the side and Osbert cried out again.

'Shouldn't he have turned you into a frog by now, Hubert?'

Osbert stood up and he saw he was surrounded by four dismounted knights. As he rose, one drew a sword.

'You're not my idea of a magician.'

'Is that sorcerer still alive?'

De Baux leant down from the battlements.

'Yes, My Lord, he is.'

'He obviously is a sorcerer if the noble says he is,' said one of the horsemen, younger than the others.

The other men nodded.

'Worth taking to the boss?'

'It's sorcerers we're here for.'

'Listen, fellow,' said the oldest of the horsemen. 'We've already fetched every drooling idiot between here and Crécy field to the lord and none have pleased him. If you are not a sorcerer, it would be better you said so now rather than risk his wrath.'

'Kill him!' shouted de Baux.

'I'm a sorcerer,' said Osbert. 'I'm the king's sorcerer.'

'What is he saying? He killed my lord and a clutch of our men even while drunk. He is a sorcerer. Kill him!'

The horsemen glanced at each other.

'Drunk, ugly, fat and coarse. He certainly fits the description.'

'I'm not drunk!' said Osbert. 'Not any more.'

'Take him to La Cerda.'

'Kill him!' shouted de Baux.

'Afraid not, dear chap, he's the property of royalty now. If I were you I'd prepare a feast and open your gates. The most important men in France beside the king and his son are coming to visit you.'

'He is a slayer of nobility. He is a champion of the poor. Kill him!'

'Everything you're saying just makes us more convinced to keep him. Now look to your cooks and your cellar-master. We've ridden a long way and expect some quality entertainment.'

The knight struck Osbert's leg irons a heavy blow with the pommel of his dagger. The lock sprang open and Osbert kicked them away.

Osbert was grabbed and pulled away from the castle walls towards the distant ranks of horsemen. His legs were agony and his lower back hurt dreadfully from his confinement but he was glad to be free, however briefly. He had thought for an instant that he would be offered a horse, but there was a dispute among the riders about allowing him to soil a saddle. Also, there was no proof yet that Osbert was indeed the court sorcerer and it would be improper for a churl to be allowed to ride a well-bred horse. And, yet more, allowing Osbert to ride alongside them might imply to anyone watching that they considered him their equal, which they certainly did not. Better, then, to drive him like an exhausted animal.

Mercifully, it was not too long a trot to the trees as Osbert feared he would be able to go no further. Already a camp was being established, doubtless to give de Baux the time to prepare properly for the arrival of the almost-royal troupe. Bright pavilions of blue, red and yellow billowed to sudden attention under the restraining ropes; pages chopped wood from the forest – something a poor man might lose his hand for.

'We can't present him to the lord like this, he stinks of shit,' said a horseman.

'In my defence, Lord, not all of it is my own,' said Osbert.

'Strip him,' said a horseman, 'that'll drop off half the stink.'

'I will not be stripped!' said Osbert. Even though his hose were foul they contained the sewn-in angel feather. That could be sold in times of extremity or used to pilfer and rob from any house or castle. He had not used it before since, being clothed in the riches of Heaven, he'd had no real need to. And he had found he loved to strike down the noble men, to bring them into the gutter with him. Much better to make a living as a hero than a thief.

The horsemen nodded to each other and dismounted. Rough hands seized him; he was kicked, forced to the floor, his tunic cut off him with the quick movement of a knife.

'Oh my God, those hose,' said one. 'Who's going to take those off?'

'Not me,' said another. 'Send for a low man.'

'They're all trailing behind, with the baggage,' said someone else

'A page, then.'

'A page can't be expected to face that.'

'Halt!'

The nobles were quiet.

From his place on the floor Osbert could see a tall and imposing man, his clothes sparkling as the afternoon sun caught his jewels of blue and red. He wore a tall feather in his hat and his riding boots shone like the back of a chestnut mare.

'I'm sorry to present this man to you in this state, sir. He says he's the sorcerer.'

'He doesn't look like a court sorcerer.'

'He's been in a dungeon, sir. I'm trying to strip him to make him more presentable.'

'I've seen shitty peasants before,' said La Cerda.

'Not this shitty, sir,' said the rider. 'He is truly a paragon of shittiness. He is a shitehawk nonpareil.'

A spotty page attempted to pass La Cerda a posy, but he brushed the flowers away.

'So what makes you think he is the sorcerer?'

'One of the locals shoved him off his walls, sir and he just floated to the ground.'

'How far a fall?'

'Ten man heights, sir.'

'Tell me of the court,' said La Cerda to Osbert. 'Give me its description, the things you might see there.'

'What would you like to know? Of the angel that sparkles above the Oriflamme in St Denis? St Michael himself. Or Jegudiel who dwelt in the Saint-Chapelle where the glass turns the light to butterfly colours and the holy Crown of Thorns sits upon the altar?'

'All things you could have heard.'

'When the angel died they wrapped him in two carpets,' said Osbert. 'Those two should be missing.'

'I never heard that.'

'There's plenty else you probably haven't heard either. What would you like to know?'

'What was the role of Charles of Navarre? He was a child then, wasn't he? The gang who killed the angel kidnapped him and let him go.'

Osbert didn't know what to say.

'Well?'

'I fear to offend powerful men.'

'You will not offend me. Know that I openly state Navarre is my enemy. He has betrayed the king, led the prince down wrong paths.'

'Oh, he was a bugger for that.' Osbert made a gesture with his hand and grimaced to indicate someone taking a wrong turn.

'So what happened to him? He was cursed by the English sorcerer Montagu, was he not?'

'I was with them. The gang had captured me and sought to use my powers. I was there when they killed the angel.It was me who worked with the king to call Despenser back from Hell, to equip his armies with devils, to drive the English back into the sea.'

'None of that worked.'

'The devils came, they served the king. The victory or not was in God's hands.'

'But what was Navarre's role? Was he using devils too?'

'He had his own devil called Nergal but he was dissatisfied with him and threw him out.' Osbert felt La Cerda needed to know no more about how he had helped Nergal possess the body of the fallen angel Sariel – something he still felt guilty about.

'How dissatisfied?'

'I believe the devil had told him he was going to ruin France and then failed to deliver on the promise.'

'Why would Navarre want to ruin France?'

'It's well known the angel told him he would never be king of France. "If I cannot play, then I will ruin the game," said the boy with the spiteful face. So goes the adage. And Navarre has a mightily spiteful face.'

'He does that.'

'Nergal said the boy was half a devil himself,' said Osbert, 'though you can only believe so much devils tell you, for though they follow God, they hate sinners and will mislead us how they may.'

La Cerda gestured to Osbert's belly.

'What's that?' he said. Osbert looked down at the scarred circle.

'A devil put it there. Despenser had him burn it on to me. It is a magic circle.'

'What for?'

'For the summoning of devils.'

La Cerda leant forward, pinching his nose to avoid the smell.

'That is indeed what it looks like.'

'You have seen many?'

'I have seen enough. These things pretend to be holy, of God, but they are not of God. Devils, demons, they are all the same to me. Hell is full of lies, and because a devil says he is a jailer and a demon speaks to the poor telling him that one day he will rule, it does not make either of them truthful. They are things of the pit and must be removed from France, and from the world. God has punished us for invoking such forces. Only when the land is rid of all of them will we see angels here again, will the dragon that beset us at Crécy be banished from the world and God's order restored.'

'Yup,' said Osbert. 'Reckon that's about right.'

He wondered if he should tell La Cerda what he had done with the box with the dragon banner in it. Probably not. Always good to keep some grain back for winter.

'I am God's avenging sword,' said La Cerda.

Osbert would have laughed if he hadn't been in such pain, and so acutely aware of how little nobles liked being laughed at. If La Cerda was God's sword, what was Osbert? *God's fool*, he thought. He imagined the clouds parting and the face of God looking down at him, laughing at his antics and capers, wondering what stupid predicament to place him in next.

'But first, to excise the rot of Hell from the land we must use its ways against it.'

'Seems wise,' said Osbert.

'Can you summon me a devil?'

'If you can get me the ingredients.'

'I can.'

'And I'll need a base to work from, somewhere I can be undisturbed.'

'Where?'

'That castle looks good. No one will ever notice you taking over such an insignificant pile, and you can get its master to provide my needs. You could set him to gather the ingredients.'

'No. We don't want word of this leaking beyond these, my trusted brothers.'

'Best kill him, then.'

'No need for flamboyant gestures.'

'Yes, Lord. But how will we prevent the lord of this manor spreading word of it?' said a horseman.

'He will not be allowed to leave until our work is done.'

'He won't like that, sir.'

'I'm not expecting him to like it. We'll clap him in his own dungeon if we have to.'

Osbert suppressed a smile, crushing it down into a simple ingratiating smirk.

La Cerda put his hand on the hilt of his sword.

'You'll get what you require,' he said. 'And we'll see if your claims are true.'

'I have spoken only the truth to you, Lord.'

'Good. Then I want you to rid me of a devil. A particular devil. I want you to dismiss it. Send it to Hell.'

'Name it.'

'Charles of Navarre,' said La Cerda. 'He is the fount of all corruption in France and I will show it to be so.'

'He's only half a devil,' said Osbert.

'Then send half of him to Hell. That would suit me down to the ground.'

Osbert wanted to cry out that it was an impossible task. Things could be called through the cracks in the walls of Hell, but you couldn't push a living man through them. And why not kill him? Wouldn't that be the quickest way of sending him to Hell? It was a question Osbert might ask later. For the moment, he was under La Cerda's considerable power and would not yet dare to question such a great lord.

'Clean him, feed him, and then we'll take Mass,' said La Cerda. 'Get him out of those irons.'

The horsemen fell upon him, pulling down his hose, cursing him as a filthy sack-a-shit and a dabbler in devilry.

'Don't take my breeches,' said Osbert. 'Don't take my breeches!'

A squelch as the hose, the precious feather in them were thrown into his arms. He was prodded and kicked through the woods.

'Is there water this way?' he cried out.

'I don't know,' said a horseman.

'You're not going to kick me until we find some?'

'Aren't we,' said the horseman, booting Osbert in the back and then wiping his shoe on the grass.

'Better find some quick then,' said Osbert, as he broke into a hobbling run.

9

The ape had opened a door for her and she was back in the circle, her jewels and taffeta filthy with the muck of the grave.

The friar lay curled upon the flagstones, gibbering of a stink of sulphur, a blast of heat, of dark wings and the face of death.

She stood up. The first light of dawn was splintering the dark of the crypt, lighting up the stairs as if they led to Heaven. Her gargoyles clacked and chirped outside the circle. Her head spun and she felt the powerful need to vomit.

'I am damned,' she said, in an underbreath. 'A queen, anointed by God, a royal among royals, damned.'

The church, though not cold, chilled her after the heat of Hell. She felt tricked, angry, though she had only tricked herself. How had God taken Mortimer, a usurper, to His Heaven? It was not possible, right or reasonable. God hated usurpers. Yet Mortimer's remains had not rotted. How had she not seen it? He was a saint. Had the Church announced him so? The Pope at Avignon had been a Frenchman. Had they canonised Mortimer without her knowing? But was it even possible to canonise a usurper? She glanced back into the grave. If she ever went there, she had seen a glimpse of the torments waiting. And what lay behind those other doors that led from the Hungry Garden?

Isabella felt a tear roll down her cheek. She wiped it away. Hell, for ever. That terrible wall, that stinking, crapping ape.

Most of all she felt the loss of Mortimer. She was separate from him now, finally. It was one thing to open the gates of Hell, another entirely to open those of Heaven. Isabella kicked a gap in the magic circle. She felt dislocated, uncertain. Could she live for ever? Were there enough angels to bleed for her to live so long?

The gargoyles chattered and cheeped.

Isabella gestured to her lover's remains.

'Gather them up, put them in the coffin,' she said. 'I command you as queen.'

But the gargoyles would not obey. Of course, they were things of the Pit and God had made them and put them in the Pit. They could not touch holy relics – not out of fear but out of reverence. A door opened above. The moth magic had worn off. The monastery was awaking, the bell-ringers coming in to announce what? Terce? It must be already.

She paid them no mind, scooping up the remains of her lover and transferring them back into the casket. She had held him so tight when he lived, his kisses like wine to her. Now, this offal, this holy offal, was all that connected her to him. Isabella wept as she returned the head, the legs, the lights.

'I have glimpsed my own damnation.' The friar moaned to himself, still curled in, grasping his knees.

'Be quiet. Your damnation is nothing. You are a low man. How much worse for a queen?'

'Who's there?' A voice from above.

'Fiends and devils. I had not expected the smell. Such rot,' said the friar.

A monk appeared at the top of the crypt stairs, framed by the light. If Isabella had never seen an angel she might have imagined he looked like one. He did not. He was a shadow. Angels were made of light.

'Lady, what has happened here?'

'Who are you?'

'Monks of the abbey.'

'And what are you doing here?'

'We've come to ring the bells.'

'Then ring them. I'm not stopping you.'

'Hell is wide and vast. The men there have no skin!' said the friar. The men did not move, just stood gaping.

'The grave. She opened the grave and the grave was the gateway,' said the raving friar.

'Oh, shut up. I put him in there, I can take him out.'

'You are Queen Isabella?' said a monk.

'Your queen. Your mistress.'

The monk bowed.

Still the friar rattled and gibbered. He had seen a glimpse of his own damnation. She, though made of sterner stuff, trembled within. She had cast her soul away, denied her right as queen to Heaven and for nothing. If Mortimer had been there she would rule, search the world for the blood of angels and live with him for ever. Mortimer was not there. He was untouchable. And yet . . . There, in his relics, was the way to commune with him. She did not want some light presence in her mind, or some song no matter how heavenly. She wanted him there, her fingers in his thick hair, his mouth on hers. She wanted his children, to be free of the devilish Plantagenets, to start a dynasty that would live for ever. Never, never, only damnation. She needed to think.

'What has happened here? Is that Friar Talbot? And what are these creatures? Has he raised the fiends of Hell?' said the monk.

The sun was strong in the summer morning, stained glass casting frozen ripples of blue and crimson on the stairs, like light through water, like the light of angels. She felt like some night-bred hag, shrinking from the rising light.

The monks hovered in the doorway, uncertain before her. Her son would hear of this, no doubt.

'Get to the bells,' she said. 'Are you so easily shaken from your duties?'

'Lady, I must report this to the abbot.'

Had Isabella been less shaken by her journey to Hell, had she been thinking straight, she would have never given her order.

'Kill them,' said Isabella to the gargoyles.

Clatters, screams – the gargoyles leapt upon the monks, grabbing two at a time and smashing them into the wall of the crypt before falling upon them to rip and tear. The deaths were swift and merciful, she thought, for those who had thought to question a queen. No bell for Terce yet; perhaps the rest of the monastery would still be asleep.

'I have seen fire and fiends and heard the cries of the tormented. I have known His wrath,' said Friar Talbot.

'Kill him too,' said Isabella. This was no time for half measures.

The gargoyles fell on the friar. The man screamed, torn and battered by the monsters of stone. Isabella crossed herself. It was nothing to the damnation that awaited him.

'Put the casket back in the earth and rebury it,' she said.

The doors flew open. Ten – maybe more – monks, armed with spears, two with swords. She had recovered her wits.

'You arrive too late,' she said. 'I have discovered a foul sacrilege here.'

The abbot pushed to the front of the throng.

'What has happened?'

'You have happened, Abbot. Your friar here is not content to remain a friar but would open the gates of Hell and pull fiends from the pit to do his bidding.' A taste like burnt hair was in her mouth. The wall of flesh. Oh God, the living wall.

'Are these the fiends?'

The abbot looked terrified at the sight of the gargoyles.

'They are, but they bow to my majesty, as all such must. Your fellows have paid the price for their unholy curiosity.'

'They disinterred Mortimer?' He had a look of suspicion about him she did not much like.

'Do you think I did it?'

The abbot's pink little tongue flicked at his lips.

'I, er. No.'

'Bring your monkish priest. Say the Mass. Bury him again with the full honours of Christ, for I tell you that is a sainted man. And remove these fellows who stain God's house with their blood.'

'These were good brothers,' said the abbot. 'Is it true that London now seethes with these devils?'

'God made devils to guard the fallen souls and angels He cast into Hell. They are servants of God, servants of Edward and friends of all true Englishmen.'

'Then why ever did they kill these good monks?'

'They are not good monks. They are the ambitious, the grasping, those who seek forbidden knowledge. They have mixed the names of God with those of demons, they have taken upon themselves authority that rightly belongs only to kings. Now send for my men, send for my ladies. You will entertain me here until this wrong has been righted.'

She crossed herself and knelt before Mortimer's casket. She could sense him there, present in his remains. His quiet, strong voice seemed to speak to her, though she could not tell what it said. She prayed to God, to Mortimer himself as a saint. The monks now crowded the crypt, some wailing, some praying.

Isabella closed her eyes and put her hand on the coffin, calling out in her mind to God to recognise her queenly right and allow Mortimer to speak to her. There were mumblings, there was song but the song was cracked, the voice not quite carrying the tune.

The monks saw her praying and all knelt too, praying to God to take the souls of their brothers, asking forgiveness for whatever sins they had committed.

'Mortimer, Mortimer, is there redemption? If you cannot join me on earth, how can I join you in Heaven?'

Her vision swam, the babble of the monks' voices like a stream washing away the sand of her thoughts. Someone had lit incense, sweet in her nostrils. His voice was indistinct, far off.

'I love you,' it said. 'Come to God.'

Isabella crossed herself again. His voice was like the sound of rain after so long a draught to her. Yes, she would go back to God, not by right but by deed. And Satan, though he thought he might have a claim on her soul, would find her harder to capture than he imagined.

'Fetch me a carriage,' she said. 'I am going to take confession at St Michael's in the Bailey.'

'You can take it here,' said the abbot.

Isabella smiled. She was aiming to become a saint, not an idiot.

IO

The world reduced to a box of light, impossibly hot in two padded gambesons beneath his mail, Eu shouldered his lance, feeling the sweat slick inside his gauntlets. He shifted his weight in the saddle. Before him at the end of the run was a shadow that packed the punch of a giant – his opponent – who, as soon as King Edward gave the signal, would charge towards him, attempting to put his weight, Eu's weight and the combined weights of their horses and armour through the tip of a blunted lance no bigger than a child's fist.

He had the urge to check the chinstrap on his great helm once again but dismissed it as nerves. Still, he pulled at his mail coif to make it scratch an itch on the top of his head and fiddled with the toggle that secured the helm to his shoulders.

He never saw the point of that in a joust – if your helm was knocked from your head then your page could just pick it up again – not like in a battle when you'd want it tied to you so you could put it back on again, provided your head wasn't still inside it. Through the coif and the long-eared cap beneath it, the cries of the crowd were muted. The horse was restless beneath him, a proper charger waiting for his command to explode.

No matter how many times he jousted, Eu would never get used to this: every sense overloaded; the lance light in his hand, the shield secure on his arm; the smell of the horse mingling with cooking fires, roasting pork and onions from the tournament field kitchens; the taste of sweat on his lips. His shield-arm still ached, though it was largely mended, thanks to the skill of the English chirurgeons. He was in no hurry to break it again, though, that was for sure. He felt more vulnerable in the joust than he ever did on a battlefield.

Everywhere, the banners of Castile flew. Edward's daughter – Princess Joan, pretty and young as spring itself – was to be married to Peter of Castile. The alliance would be a formidable one and a problem for France. Here he was, like a monkey performing at a celebration of his own country's misfortune. Well, what was Edward's motto? It is as it is. It is as it is.

He needed to return to France, to take up the reins as constable again, but bad news came weekly. The boy Navarre told him that La Cerda had taken over the administration of his lands in Champagne, was acting as constable in all but name under the favour of Prince John. If John's man had the King's ear, where might that lead? The man was an idiot, a God-appointed idiot. The ransom was not forthcoming, though, and he feared dark forces at work in the court.

The tilt barrier separating him from his opponent was insubstantial cloth, and head-on collisions were unusual but not unheard of. There was some sort of lesson for life there, he thought, separated by a nail's width of cloth from onrushing calamity. Like life, though, there was no opting out of it with honour. He thought of his daughters, of his wife. Coward thoughts, he cursed them. Though not too hard. He would charge, he would strike, he would uphold the honour of France even if it meant dying a less than entirely useful death.

He closed his eyes for a breath and imagined the wider day around him: the round table flags; the gaudily dressed courtiers who had come as Lancelot, Gawain or Perceval; Edward himself watching from his bench, dressed splendidly as King Arthur, a crown of burnished gold upon his head; the monolith of Windsor Castle rising in the early summer haze before Eu. Ladies had come all dressed as knights, riding coursers. The old people had called it unnatural. As if that was something that even meant anything in these days of devils and demons.

Time to go. He could not see the king and would have to wait for the page at the centre of the joust to drop his flag after the king had given the signal. There was a job – the flagman. Best be nimble. You wouldn't want to trip and end up under a horse.

The flagman waved and dropped the flag.

He squeezed his legs into the horse's side and it leapt forward like a tiger. Relax, relax, relax, tension in the arm. A breeze, a flash at his left side and it was over. Both had missed. Two passes to go. Eu was not a cruel man but he earnestly hoped to knock his opponent down so heavily he would be unable to get up for the contest of axe and dagger.

He wheeled his horse, his breath hot on the inside of his helm. No flag now, just 'feel' for when to go. Straight away. Another pass and the tip of his opponent's lance shattered against his helm in a flash of white light. He leant forward, grabbed the cantle of the saddle, dropping his own lance – which had missed badly. A glancing blow, but enough to temporarily scramble his senses. On reflex his hand came out and an unseen page put a lance into it. He'd turned his horse without even thinking of it. A box of light with a shadow inside it. The crowd's roar dull in his ears. Go! *Budda dum, budda dum, budda dum, budda dum.* Bang! An immense jolt in his shoulder, the crunch of splintering wood. *Budda dum, budda budda dum.* He wheeled his horse, tore off his helm, leaving it clattering on its toggle across the mail on his shoulders, threw down his broken lance, sat up in his stirrups and raised his fist to the crowd, not in exultation but relief. His opponent lay flat on the floor, suddenly a knight again, a colourfully dressed man in blue and yellow, not a shadow at all. For an instant Eu thought the man was dead, but no. Thanks be to God; he tried to sit up, though he was clearly stunned and fell back again.

Eu kicked his horse on to where Prince Edward and Queen Philippa sat, bowing before them in his saddle.

Edward stood, clapping, laughing.

'He thought he'd do the same thing to you twice, Raoul! A very bad idea with a knight of your experience!' The knight he had unhorsed was helped to his feet, but sank to his knees again.

'You're kind, sir. A fortunate strike.'

'You have a lot of good fortune in the lists, Eu. Have you ever been unhorsed?'

Eu bowed his head. 'Badly rattled a few times, sir, but the angels watch over me.'

That wiped the grin off Edward's face.

'Do they now. Though not at Caen, it seemed.'

'That day they favoured you, sir.'

'They did indeed. And continue to do so. You know my son has never been bested in a joust?'

'His skill is famous in every kingdom of Europe.'

Edward nodded grimly. 'If he comes through to the end of the day in one piece we'll square you up. What do you say?'

Eu extended a hand to Philippa. 'What does the lady say? It's her son. I . . .'

'My God, you're that confident!' The king turned to the nobles behind him. 'You see, that should be a lesson to our English knights. I tell Eu I want him to face the most formidable man in the lists across twenty kingdoms, and his only concern is that he will hurt him so he asks his mother's permission. You can't go into these things with an instant of doubt in your mind. If you do – bang!' He drove his fist into his hand. Then that look on his face again, *like a goodwife inspecting a marketplace fish*, thought Eu. 'Do you look to my wife to get you out of it – are you wily, sir? Do I misjudge your valour?'

Eu would have challenged any other man to back his words on the field of combat after such an insult, but kings are granted more licence than ordinary men.

'If the lady agrees.'

Philippa stood. 'I would gladly see it. Gladly. Why do we queens raise our sons if not to fight?'

Eu bowed and then Philippa did something extraordinary. She took the scarf from the top of her headdress and offered it to him. What did that mean? A gesture of extraordinary courtesy and welcome to an honoured prisoner? He bowed in his saddle.

Edward seemed mildly irked.

'Lance, axe and dagger. Three passes with each. You'll test my son at close of play and then we'll feast and tell our stories, what?'

'Should I survive,' said Eu with a smile.

'Don't be gloomy, Eu. Of course you'll survive.'

'Didn't the prince take the Count of Hasselt's head off his shoulders at Ghent?'

'Little Edward was only a boy then and suffered from an excess of enthusiasm. His skill has increased in the intervening years.'

'Glad to hear it.' Eu looked into Edward's eyes. Was the king really handing a sworn enemy the chance to kill his son? Deaths were far from uncommon in tournaments. And why endanger Eu himself, and with him a potentially enormous ransom?

'I'll ready myself,' he said.

'Do,' said Edward.

II

Dowzabel of Cornwall, so-called Antichrist and would-be down-thrower of kings and rulers, trod the streets of the new town. They were better made than any he had known. The streets were wide and laid with timbers to stop the boggy ground yielding to the wheels of the carts, the hooves of the horses, the feet of the great army it was built to house.

It was not easy coming here, a siege within a siege. Edward had invested in Calais, building a whole city outside its walls to accommodate his men and to send a message to the burghers of the town – we are here for as long it takes. Do not think that the winter will send us home, do not pray for rain or for disease among our army. Here we are well supplied, our water assured, our streets clean and our filth carried away. Siege fever will claim you before it claims us. Your bowels will revolt, your teeth drop out. You will feast upon the corpses of your dogs and then your kinsmen and then your children before we move. Do not yield now. The moment for mercy passed when this temporary city sprang up outside your walls.

And do not, above all, do not, pray for the rescue of your beaten master – Philip of Valois, who pretends to be king of France. He parades his army at the neck of the marshes, he threatens to break through by sea, he sounds his horns and his drums by night and by day. It is all he will do. The way to Calais is too narrow, we English too well defended for him to dream of victory. He could not beat us on the open fields of Crécy. How will he fare on the road through the marshes, four horses abreast, the white arrows of Wales and Cornwall and Romsey straining at the bow like hounds on a leash?

Dow was called from his tent by his ympe Murmur, the little winged man, blue as a berry, with his horns and trident, flying in through the untied flap.

Though the bowmen of Lucifer were well housed in the new dwellings, better than any had ever known in their lives, Dow had sworn never to sleep in a bed again until Eden was returned to the earth – Lucifer's garden, before God crept in disguised as a snake and offered humanity not knowledge, but order, one above another, kings and paupers. So, for the last year, he had stayed in his rotting tent while his army enjoyed the luxury of timber-built houses.

The demon sat on Dow's outstretched hand. It was Wymund, he said, come back to camp again.

An exiled thief, sent away from the company of Luciferians. He had returned six times before.

'Must I banish him again?' Dow smiled at the ympe.

'You must save him.'

'From what?'

'Our men are going to hang him.'

'We don't do that.' Dow stepped out into the morning. Already the heat of the August day had risen, burning off the dew. He breathed in the scent of the warm grass, felt the sun on his face.

'It's good to be alive in the morning light,' he said to the little demon fluttering at his side. 'Come on, let's rescue Wymund.'

He touched himself on the right shoulder with his left hand, then on the breast bone and then on the left – once for each of the prongs of Lucifer's pitchfork. Such gestures had become common since the army had assembled and it felt good to display his faith openly to his men. *His men*? He should not allow himself such thoughts.

Was he the leader of the boiling, angry, revolutionary poor? The thought made him uncomfortable. He was their counsellor, their adviser, their friend. But he knew well what they called him – or rather what his enemies did. AntiChrist. Demon, God's enemy. His friends placed a greater burden on him. They said he was the Second Coming. The Messiah.

His people believed that Jesus, who is called Lucifer, lightbringer, in the Bible, had come back to bargain with the old god to do away with ideas of sin and kingship. Jesus agreed to call God 'Father' if he would release humanity from the yoke of oppression. But the old god had tricked him and nailed him to a tree. Now the new Christ would come and restore Paradise on earth. He believed it with all his heart. But he was not sure he was that Christ. Surely Lucifer should come. Surely he should break free of Hell, where God had thrown him, overthrow God's jailer Satan and come back to set men as equals again.

But Lucifer had not come so that left him, trying to show people how to break the habits of knee-bending, order-following and cap-doffing their forefathers had handed to them in the same way the nobles' fathers had bequeathed their lands, cattle and servants to them.

Three men of Cornwall fell in beside him as he moved through the town – big tin miners, skin etched grey like demons themselves. He was known in the camp, of course, and it would not have been impossible for someone to try to kill him. The king would not move against him – he needed his bows too much – but some proud slave of God, a low man or even an impetuous noble, might strike him down out of fear of what he was. He greeted the men in their own language, his native tongue.

'*Cuthman*,' he said, with a nod: Friend.

Among the bowmen and the Luciferian camp this was becoming the way of address – his influence. He wasn't sure that was a good thing. But what if you release people from slavery and their first impulse is to begin looking for another master? What if, when you remove the shackles, you find yourself holding them?

He glanced over at the town, its walls pale and pretty in the sunlight, the sea a shimmer behind them. Beneath the walls was another camp, poorer than his own. These were the poor people of Calais, expelled by their masters to save food and prevent disease. King Edward had refused to allow them passage; the burghers of Calais had refused to allow them back in. So they sat beneath the walls – the old, young, sick and dying – their skin peeling in the summer sun.

Dow had tried to insist they be moved on, but Edward had told him he would not be dictated to. The starving poor were a drain on the resolve of the besieged, they needed to stay where they were to sap the nerves of the defenders. The Luciferians had given up some of their own rations to feed them but it was perilous to approach too close to the walls, for fear of crossbow bolts, hurled bricks, or just catching the diseases stewing among the expelled. Something needed to be done, though. Edward might use words like 'English' and talk of standing up for the nation, but that was just a trick to make the poor think they had common interests with their king. The people beneath the walls were Dow's nation – the dispossessed.

In the bowmen's quarter he could hear shouting, so he hurried along, his heavy falchion – the great cleaving sword he had stolen from a devil – at his side.

Six or seven men stood around two figures. One was the familiar shape of Wymund the thief, hunched forward over his knees. He was not difficult to recognise as his nose had been cut off, along with his ears, giving him the appearance of a weather-beaten gargoyle. The other was a girl so thin she might be mistaken for one of the bone-faced men, the skeleton army of devils Philip had employed at Crécy. She lay curled up on the floor, her hands over her head.

'Friends!' Dow called.

The men turned to him, making the three touches of Lucifer as they did so, a couple bowing their heads.

Stomping in from the opposite direction to Dow came the rotund Joanna Greatbelly, wife of the next person to appear – Edwin, the so called 'Black Priest', a priest of the Roman Church but a late and zealous convert to Luciferianism. The priest was a spare and bony man but he carried in his arms a stubby-limbed, squat-nosed little demon. This was Know-Much, his familiar. He was accompanied by a third figure, a tall and imposing man in the tattered clothing of a wandering fighting man. His hair was long, his beard unkempt. You would say he was around twenty-three if you did not know him to be over forty. He had drunk of angel's blood and appeared to be in his prime.

'Lord,' said one to Dow.

'*Cuthman*,' said Dow. 'No lords here, brother.'

Not strictly true, of course. The fighting man was Montagu, former Lord Marschall of England and now a Luciferian too, though for reasons that were entirely personal rather than ones concerned with the fate of the world.

'Yes, Lord,' said the man. 'Will you settle this for us? I say this Wymund should hang.'

'And I say he should not,' said another man. 'There are no hanging trees in Eden.'

'We are not yet in Eden, brother,' said Edwin, nodding in acknowledgement to Dow.

'What has he done?' asked Greatbelly. Instead of the yellow hood of a whore, she now wore the padded coat of a warrior. The Luciferians had agreed the rule that anyone who was of age should be allowed to fight, and anyone who was of age could decline to do so. Each would give the service they could, and a lifetime running a brothel in Southwark had given Greatbelly more fighting experience than most men of her age.

'He brought this girl to the camp.'

'I took her bravely from beneath the walls of Calais,' said Wymund. 'I risked spear and rock and buckets of shit to fetch her. And I paid for her – she's mine!'

'That is brave,' said Dow.

'He was looking to sell her here,' said the man.

'Sell her?'

'To make her work as a whore.'

Dow studied the girl. Her eyes seemed unnaturally large in her hunger-wasted face. She lay on the ground curled in on herself, staring into nothing but quite unmoving.

'He's banished from the camp as well,' said the man. 'Under pain of death.'

'We didn't say that,' said Dow.

'Then, Lord, what is to prevent him coming back here all the time?'

'Has he used you?' said Edwin to the girl.

Greatbelly knelt at the girl's side and put her hand to her cheek.

'Beer,' she said. 'Bring this girl beer, for her sustenance.'

Dow scratched his head. Wymund was the most difficult sort of poor person – made dishonest and unpleasant by his upbringing and circumstance. All he had ever got in life, he had to steal or lie to get, from his earliest years.

Montagu walked up to Dow and said, in the French-tinged voice of an English nobleman:

'If you do not deal with this, then how are the people of Calais to have faith in our promise to treat them kindly? What example does it give to the others of our camp who might consider the same, or worse? Our men may expect to do similar as the right of the conqueror. They will need strong deterrence.'

Dow said nothing. If Calais could be treated well in surrender, if the Luciferians could gain a reputation for mercy, then the poor of other towns might throw open their gates to them and the days of the kings might be at an end. If not – if his troops ran wild in the traditional way of victorious armies – they might not even establish Eden in one town, never mind in every town of the world. And yet it would betray everything to punish this man too severely. And then it begged the question of what could be done to him. He had lost his nose and ears to the laws of the lords. Cutting off a hand might kill him. Dow ran his tongue along the inside of his lip. The tongue was split where a priest had cut it as a punishment when Dow had been just a boy.

Beer was brought for the girl while Dow pondered, staring out to Calais.

Fires on the ramparts, four of them lit in beacons.

A great sigh came out from the new town, then cheers and celebrations.

'They're signalling surrender!' said Montagu.

So it was over. The year of waiting. Edward would fulfil his bargain to give the Luciferians the town and Eden might be restored. It had to be a sign. Good things were around the corner.

'Let Wymund go,' said Dow.

'He's committed a master's sin,' said Edwin. 'He has owned another person.'

'Thank Lucifer for this forgiveness, Wymund.' Dow gestured to the sun. 'Try to live your life in the morning light from now on.'

'Do I get to keep the girl?' said Wymund.

Montagu kicked him in the guts and Wymund fell forward with a great cry.

'No,' said Dow. 'No one gets to keep anyone. That's the point of why we're here.'

'I paid for her!'

'Be thankful the lord doesn't pay you what you deserve,' said a man.

'I am not a lord,' said Dow.

'You might need to be!' said Montagu. All around them, men were up carrying bags, baskets and even pushing handcarts in a rush to get in to plunder the city.

'No slaughter!' shouted Dow. 'No slaughter!'

From the gate six skeletal men walked, their heads in nooses, stooping in submission, or fatigue. Dow's heart went out to them for an instant. All order shaken, all certainties gone, putting themselves at the disposal of the English king as a sacrifice to save their people.

'They are a poor sight,' said Montagu. Dow's sympathy cooled.

'They are well enough dressed. Every day, all over creation, the poor are under siege by the rich. There are children living in the streets of London who would regard these good burghers as fat men. The siege is over for them. For us it never ends.'

'You cannot feel pity for them? It is one thing to be born a low man. To fall into it is quite another.'

'Lucifer fell from Heaven,' said Dow. 'He seeks to regain it but to bring all men with him. These men would tread on their fellows to regain their former state. I spit on them.'

A thick file of English men-at-arms came out to surround the burghers. Dow saw the banners of Edward hoisted and making their way towards them, though he could not pick out the king.

Then Wymund got to his feet and ran hard for the open gate of the city. It sparked a riot. His captors sped after him but everyone else in the camp assumed they were heading to the town for easy pickings and charged to follow. The men-at-arms saw the poor coming and, not wanting to lose out on the advantage their nearness to the walls gave them in being first to the plunder, surged forwards to the gates.

The six good burghers who had emerged with their heads in nooses were swamped, men-at-arms leading the way into the city, the bowmen and the lesser poor streaming in behind them. Dow saw the Earl of Warwick, his red surcoat marked with the bear and ragged staff, his sword drawn, trying to protect the men in nooses, calling his pages about him. Some cheeky fellow gave a sharp pull on one of the nooses and its wearer was tugged off his feet. The dispossessed at the foot of the walls took their chance, some running for the open countryside, some towards the sea, others back into the town. More people fell in the stampede; fights broke out between bowmen and men-at-arms.

'These men are for the king's justice!' shouted Warwick. 'The men of Calais are the king's property!'

But it was useless and eventually Warwick gave a big shrug and turned into the city itself. The men who had emerged from the town to face the king's mercy stood bewildered, wide-eyed, with the expressions of deer at the moment they are struck by the hunter's arrow, before they realise they are dead. But they weren't dead. They were ignored. Dow saw them turn to each other. They had expected anything but this.

Dow ran past them, into the city, to try to prevent the slaughter.

12

The first blow from the prince's lance struck Eu's horse and sent it staggering sideways into the throng of spectators who had gathered to see the show. Eu struggled to bring the stricken animal under control as a thick gaggle of townsfolk dived out of its way.

Some booing from the lower sort present, but the prince raised his hand in apology and Eu, once he had mastered the horse again, raised his in acknowledgement, though he had to swap mounts.

The sun was lower in the sky, spreading pink over the blue, the shadows longer. On the second pass it would be at Eu's back, not in his face as it had been before. The prince looked magnificent. He had spent the spoils of his Crécy campaign on impressive new armour – a large breastplate in the German style, a springing leopard in gold atop his great helm and the whole kit lacquered in black. His surcoat was emblazoned with his new symbol – the three ostrich feathers of Bohemia, which he wore in honour of blind King John who had so nobly and suicidally charged the English arrows at Crécy.

Eu lifted himself into the saddle of the fresh horse, his jousting armour so heavy and stiff compared to his battle kit. Still, better that than be smashed to pieces. The second pass, the horse throwing its head before leaping forward. A thump, a splinter and he was twisted violently in his saddle. The prince had hit him hard on his left shoulder, all but unhorsing him. His arm felt like a struck gong, all a-tremble, and he thought he might have broken something again. Never mind, get the horse about, put out the right hand and feel the lance placed within it. The crowd's roar was loud now even to his muffled ears. Their prince was about to fell an enemy – and not just any enemy: France's chief cockerel, the constable himself, never bested in a joust.

'We'll see.' This time he would make it stick.

His horse careered forward and then everything slowed down. In his eagerness to strike the prince, he had not paid any heed to the incoming lance. Eu was ripped from his saddle, on impulse flinging his feet from the stirrups. It was as if he flew, as if he could refuse the ground's invitation to join it and simply keep going in the air until he settled on a branch like a bird. He hit the sawdust hard, all the wind driven from him, his head snapping back and taking a heavy blow.

People were all around him – pages, doctors, onlookers, well-wishers, ill-wishers. He vomited inside his helm. It was taken from his head. Blood in his mouth. Was this it? 'God receive me,' he said to himself. A smiling figure above him, offering him his hand. An angel? No, a man.

'Well done, Eu, well done.' It was the prince himself, a hole in his breastplate like it had been made by a pavilion stake, the stuffing of the gambeson bursting forth like a mushroom growth.

Someone sat him up, unstrapped his shield. The prince crouched in front of him, tapping his own breastplate.

'Send this one back to the armourer's, eh? Your lance went through it like a finger through the crust of pie!'

'Did I unhorse you?' The question seemed stupid, childish, even. But he'd asked it, head spinning, thoughts jumbled.

'Not quite,' he said.

'You'd have done for any other knight in the kingdom, sir,' said the page Marcel. 'It's the lord's first time on the sawdust ever.'

'Can't say I like it much,' said Eu. A tooth felt loose, his head ringing like an Easter bell.

'Still got the axe and the dagger to come yet, Eu,' said the prince. 'Plenty of time for your revenge.'

Eu vomited again, a mess of blood and snot exploding from his nose.

'Of course,' he said. 'Of course.'

They got him to his feet, put an axe in his hand. The ground shifted sideways, tilted like the deck of a ship in a storm, and he fell again.

The crowd were baying 'England! England! England!' He had never heard such a strange cry. Men chanted the name of their lords, they sang the names of their home towns or their king. But England? Was that not a seditious cry, a shout against the Norman yoke, inherited from the rebels of yore? Was Edward, who claimed to be King of France, now calling himself an Englishman? The old kings of England would have seen that as an admission of common birth.

He got up under his own power.

'Take off my helm and bring my basinet,' he said.

The prince beckoned his page and his jousting helm was taken from where it dangled at his shoulder too. The modern basinet that replaced it had a tilting visor and Eu, still reeling, was bizarrely reminded of a duck. Strange thoughts came and went. The prince's armour, pierced. How? An image of the collision came back to him, the shattering of the lance. A flash of brightness. The feel had been different and odd. His own basinet was strapped on, lighter and with greater vision than the great helm it replaced. It was marked with a golden circle to represent a crown and topped with a fleur-de-lys-De-Lys. A gift from Edward to mark the exalted status of his captive. Eu knew who would end up paying for it – himself, through his ransom. Why did such banal thoughts come easily to him, when he might be about to die?

Little Marcel, his page, knew his business, fumbling with the knots to tie the helm on, buying his master precious seconds of recovery. Now the light of the day was filtered through tiny holes, like sunlight through trees. Eu felt strangely relaxed, as if lying by a river on a summer afternoon. Then he thought the points of light were stars. He fought to clear his head. If you focused on the inside of a basinet it would indeed be like a night sky with stars in it. You focused beyond it, pretending it wasn't there, and it afforded a good view of your opponent.

Like any trained knight, Eu was used to taking blows and to shaking them off but he had been hit very hard. He could not make himself concentrate on the potentially mortal combat that was to follow. The axe in his hand seemed unfamiliar, just a shape divorced from its function.

The pages were clearing the debris from the track. Why? They never did that – the shards of lances, the broken hilts were normally left on the field for curious boys to collect. Or to rot. Whatever, pages did not scavenge the field for shattered wood. The thought was like a leaf on the wind, here and then gone. He coughed. More blood.

His head cleared a little and the prince helped him to his feet.

'I've no wish to take advantage,' he said. 'If you would rather retire . . .'

'I'm fine. I'm fine.' In his everyday condition, Eu might have wondered about the wisdom of allowing a man who had just had all sense knocked from him to make decisions concerning his fitness to continue. His brain reduced to the consistency of blancmange, he felt ready to go, though his body seemed to vibrate like a struck bell. A small footsoldier's shield had arrived on his arm.

The jousting partition was lowered and wound in, flopping over the sawdust like a wounded snake.

They would fight before the king. The great trembling inside Eu rose up and for a moment he could hear nothing. The prince was speaking to him? What was he saying?

'Let's make this look good?' No one wants to be hit with an axe. Three good, well-signalled swipes, easily blocked with the shield and then likewise for the daggers; that was the way sensible men went about things, particularly when they had reached Eu's age and prominence in one piece.

No, the prince was not saying that. Eu inclined his head forward.

'I always play to win, Eu.'

'Very good.'

A trumpet sounded. Was it that of Heaven? No. The start of the foot contest. His page spoke to him, lips moving, sound issuing. No sense. The king waved a flag – a golden round table motif upon it. Oh yes, we're all meant to be at the court of the new Arthur, aren't we? How did thoughts like that come so easily, when the reality of what he was facing appeared as if through a fog, something seen only in a distorted reflection, not of its true self?

'England, England!'

A white light sparked in front of him, the herald of pain. Lying with his back on the ground, the events of the previous twenty heartbeats came back to him. The prince had advanced and struck him hard with the axe at the side of his head. He saw him coming. Was he still coming? No. Eu had been struck.

Either good workmanship or good luck meant the count had not been killed. Eu had an intense ringing in his ears and his vision was momentarily blurred. Eu saw the prince extending his hand towards him, pulling him upwards. The page guided him back to his mark. The basinet had been deformed by the blow and now the breathing holes were too close to his nostrils, restricting his breathing, making the helmet impossibly hot. He pulled up his visor. It was sheared away at one side and he had to bend it to clear his line of vision. Now it stuck out from his head like a metal wing.

He didn't see the flag drop this time but the prince came on again. A big cut down onto his head, the same as before. This time Eu threw up his shield and returned a blow of his own – a weakling's strike that clattered off the prince's shield without him even having to move it. Both strikes having missed, they went directly to the third. The prince cut down at Eu's leg, smashing into his greave. Eu, in desperation, had both hands on his axe and took a falling swipe at his opponent, catching him squarely on his helm and knocking it clean from his shoulders.

The prince was unfazed, smiling at him.

'A good strike, cousin. And now daggers!'

A page – not Marcel – pressed a dagger into Eu's hand. It was an ornate, jewelled affair more suited to ceremony than the field of combat.

He looked at its rubies glinting in the sun, little blood drops sparkling from their field of gold.

'Again!' King Edward cried out.

Eu's leg was numb from where the axe had struck, but it seemed his armour had saved him worse injury. The prince came at him and in an instant Eu's head was clear. His rattled brain emerged from its fog as if into a clear dawn, everything brighter and sharper than it had been. He had heard tales of knights, sore pressed, gaining this instant of calm among chaos and now it settled upon him.

The prince was careful in his advance, the blade of his dagger bright as a sun flash on a summer lake. They circled. One strike from the prince was just an exploration, Eu's reply the same. The second was more serious as the men engaged shields. Eu's arm was blocked out but the prince slid his dagger down and into Eu's leg, though it did not penetrate the armour. Three more circles and then the prince went for him, trying to smash his dagger hand with a stab from the side of his shield. Eu got his shoulder into the prince's shield, turning it aside and exposing his inner arm to an angled thrust. The prince cried out as the dagger found the unarmoured inside of his forearm.

Eu fell back onto his arse but the prince had dropped his dagger, blood all over his hands as he tried to stem the flow of bleeding from his arm. Pages surrounded him, bringing bandages. The great lion Sloth roared out – in approval or disapproval, Eu could not tell. Then the crowd went quiet, silent, or so it seemed. He unlaced his helmet and blood poured down his neck. The force of the prince's strike on his helm had cut him.

Eu tried to stand, but his strength was gone.

'You did it, sir, you did it!' Marcel was close at his ear.

'Bring me the lance heads,' said Eu. 'All of them from my broken lances. As soon as the people disperse, find them. And for God's sake someone bring me a cup of wine!'

13

The city was in a poor state. Habits die hard and the invaders, drunk with success and much wine, had set fire to a grain store and three rich houses before the king was able to restore order. Only the presence of a detachment of wreckers – men employed for their skills in destroying the enemy's property – saved the city from burning. They quickly demolished the burning buildings, ripping them down with great hooks on ropes pulled by horses.

Dow ran through the tight streets, barrelling over the siege debris, the smashed timbers, the rubble of houses caved in by war engines, the piled bones of dogs, cats, horses and rats, stripped of their meat.

Everywhere he went he saw horrors – senseless murders: a boy of ten with his throat cut, bled white on the crimson ground; a husband trying to defend his wife and daughters against the mob; a rope-maker who had used the last of his wares to hang himself.

'Stop! Stop!' he shouted. 'This is to be our Eden, it cannot be built on the bones of our brothers!'

No one paid him any heed. The frenzy was on them. A year's worth of bad feeling had fermented in the invaders' guts as they shivered in the snow and the rain and the mud before the implacable city walls, and now it vomited forth, carrying all before it. Dow came to a big guildhall, that of merchants, announced by the sign of scales at the door. The door was wide open and inside he heard screams. He went within into a big meeting chamber surrounded with the arms of the merchant companies.

A gaggle of the poor huddled in the far corner while Wyland, his ravaged face drunk with delight, poked a dagger at an old man he was forcing to dance for the entertainment of five or six bowmen – one of whom played a small pipe. Dow recognised the very people who had been looking to hang Wyland not a summer hour before. Now, one wore a rich cloak, another was weighed down with silver plate, while one more pulled at a terrified, thin girl, trying to rip open her ragged gown.

Dow felt a dry anger rise in his throat.

'Brothers,' he said, 'these are our kin.' The piping stopped.

'They're merchants!' said Wyland.

'No, they're poor people like us who have taken refuge in here. We should be their protectors.'

'They're church-blinded fools,' said Wyland. 'See!' He jabbed the dagger towards the old man, who shrieked and crossed himself.

'Then they will be converted, not killed.'

'Send them to their God or ours!'

'Lucifer is not a god. He holds this life as important as the one to come.'

'Well, if he's not a god, who gives a Saracen's ball-sack what he thinks?' said Wyland. 'Look, your Antichristness, or whoever you are, you've helped me out before so I'm going to give you a chance. Leave now.'

'What do you say?' said Dow to the other men.

'Such freedom is allowed to the followers of God – why not to those of Lucifer? We do no more than any Christian army.'

A voice from the gallery above:

'Wahey, fellows! Look what I've found. More gold than I can carry!'

A stout Londoner had emerged, clad in a great gold chain. He showered coins on those below. The men scrambled for the loot as the Londoner cascaded down more and more coins.

'This truly is Eden!' said Wyland. 'It rains gold from the heavens! And look, there are rubies in this treasure!'

He drove his dagger into the old man's heart. The man fell, bright blood spurting out over the coins.

A woman screamed and leapt on Wyland. Two of the Frenchmen, driven to desperation, threw themselves weakly at the bowmen.

Wyland stabbed the woman, kicking her legs from beneath her and sending her sprawling down. He bowed extravagantly to Dow.

'All in the service of the new Eden!' he said. 'Though we don't mind making a few coins on the side, eh, boys?'

Dow freed his falchion from his belt and split Wyland's skull. It seemed everyone was on him then – the bowmen and the French. A dagger stabbed at him but he cut off the hand that held it; he was grabbed from behind but Dow was trained as well as any knight. He swayed his hips to one side and struck back at his attacker's groin with the pommel of the falchion. The man held on but Dow pulled out his own misericord in his left hand and stabbed back. The grip loosened but his troubles were not yet over. A Frenchman had picked up Wyland's dagger and came lunging for Dow. He stepped aside.

'I am trying to help you,' he said, but it was no good. The man came on and Dow had no choice but to kill him, taking him underneath his arm with a cut from the falchion.

Two bowmen ran out of the door, one clanking with plate, the other holding his surplice like an apron, full of chinking coins. All the French were dead and a bowman sat with his back against the wall, a livid wound at his chest.

Only the man with the pipe remained. He, it seemed, had avoided the mayhem. Was he simple? He stood with both hands on the pipe, as if ready to play, staring at Dow as if enchanted. The Londoner in the gallery had disappeared. To Dow it seemed that only he and the piper existed, that all the noise and chaos of the city's sacking was so much birdsong.

'Brother,' said Dow, dropping his misericord and extending his hand. 'Brother, we cannot build Eden this way. Help me hold the building until wiser heads arrive. This money should be shared to help us in our new life here.'

The piper pursed his lips. He looked at Dow sideways like a dog trying to work out a strange squeak. He laughed, a high, idiot giggle.

Dow killed him too, taking his head straight from his shoulders with a swing of the heavy falchion. Only afterwards did the rage that had risen in him register in his mind. As the weapon swung he was only an observer of his own actions.

He sank to his knees among the blood and the gold, the bodies of the French poor and the English poor. No, not the bodies. One bowman was still alive, the one with the severed hand. Dow went to him.

'I am sorry, brother. Let me tend to you!'

He knelt beside him. The man was whispering and Dow leant in to hear his words.

'Gold,' said the man. 'Give me gold.'

Other voices, more men of Lucifer coming in from the street.

'Help me,' said Dow. 'Help me here.'

But they ignored him, diving in among the gore to pick out the fallen coins.

14

This, thought Osbert, *could be quite a comfortable little nook*.

Back in the castle, he was shown to a little room in the main keep overlooking the courtyard. He saw how it would all pan out. In the morning he would close the door, burn incense, intone meaninglessly for a while, draw circles in chalk on the floor and pretend, loudly, to be trying to summon Charles of Navarre. He didn't even know if that was possible, but he was fairly sure it wasn't possible for him – particularly given the materials at his disposal which amounted to chalk, candles, incense and not a lot else. After an hour or so of chanting, he'd put a chair against the door, wrap himself in a rug and return to sleep.

This happy fantasy had seemed like reality until the first night. He'd even managed to find a bottle of brandy. Drinking alone with only the light of the moon cutting through the slit windows to see by, there had been an attempt to open the door. As he had wedged a chair against it, it was impossible to open. A knock followed.

'Who is it?'

'Open the door.' It was La Cerda's voice, thick and low.

Osbert hurriedly removed the chair and did as he was bid.

In the gloom of the keep, La Cerda's olive skin almost shone gold. There was a radiance to him and Osbert would have sworn the chamber was lighter for his presence.

The lord was unaccompanied. He came in and closed the door behind him.

Osbert made the sign of the Cross and bowed his knee.

'What are you, Lord?'

'A lover of God,' said La Cerda.

'You are surely a saint.'

'Not yet. It's said my line is holy and I hope to be one.'

'Offspring of angels!'

'Of Abel, who was Adam and Eve's son, slain by the hand of his brother, the first martyr.'

'Oh, bad luck!' said Osbert, for want of anything else to say. That story had always confused him. God made Adam and Eve, yes. They begot, or begat – he couldn't remember which – Cain and Abel. The next thing you know humanity is all over the place begging the question of what went on in the Garden of Eden. On the other hand, did it not say in the Bible that God made a whole lot of humans on day six? It was a long time ago; things got confused.

La Cerda said nothing. He simply reached inside his coat to produce a small box.

He passed it to Osbert. 'You want me to . . . open it?' asked Osbert.

'Well, I don't want you to swallow it, by Christ's cullions. Open it.'

The box was good dark wood, perhaps walnut, inlaid with silver clasps, finely worked. Osbert undid the clasp and tipped back the lid. He gasped. Inside was a key, but a key the like of which he had never seen. It seemed to hover above the cushion of the box. It was made of fragments of tiny emeralds, all hanging in a little cloud. Then, in a breath, the emeralds turned like starlings and were a mist of blood, still in the shape of the key.

'The Key of Emerald and Ruby,' said La Cerda.

'What strange door does this fit?'

'It is a key to Hell. I want you to use it to lock Navarre away where he belongs.'

Osbert felt a chill come over him. He had been to Hell before, stood before the first gate when Dow had opened it. He had no wish to go back there or to open a gate himself.

'Where did you come by such a thing?'

'I told you that my line is descended of Abel, the first martyr. We have custody of the Cave of Treasures where his body was laid. This key, God himself made from his blood.'

Osbert trembled. 'That's Abel's blood swimming about there?'

'Yes.'

'And you would simply pass it to me?'

'You must use it.'

'But the key for which gate?' He knew the Antichrist Dow had the key to the first gate. Montagu had another which he had taken at Caesar's Tower in the old Temple of the Hospitallers. So this was two, three or four. Whatever, it couldn't be used without at least Dow's key. And, from what he knew of that miserable, slightly crazy boy, he was unlikely just to hand it over with a 'God bless you, Lordling.'

'Why trust me with it?'

La Cerda drew him close, far too close. He spoke no more than a span from nose to nose.

'I have consulted a thousand learned men. I have seen men call shapes from the air. I have heard the rattle of demons within magic circles. All these things. But you, you, with your drink and your coarse talk, you have raised armies of devils. I have heard it said you went to Hell yourself.'

'I have travelled there but, in truth, Lord, did not much like the weather.'

'You will do as I say, you will achieve what I want, or you will suffer under those skies eternally. You are as sure of damnation as any man I have known.'

'Why not just kill Navarre, Lord?'

'Not so easy. He still retains Prince John's favour, enough at least to protect him. If he could be banished to Hell then no one could complain that it was other than the will of God.'

'Why do you bear him malice, Lord, if I might make so bold? Which I just have.' Osbert watched the little key turning its colours, glowing in the dark of the room.

'I sense what he is.'

'A devil?'

'Worse. A devil who does not know his place. A thing out of nature. He should bow before kings but he plots against them.'

The key turned, dissolved and reformed in front of him. Osbert felt sick.

'This is great magic, Lord. This . . .' He ran out of words and then heard himself say,

'Do you have a right to use this?'

'You are impertinent,' said La Cerda. 'But I will answer you, hoping it will help you in your efforts. It has been in my family for generations after Abel. I am descended from Saint Louis, king of France. It's said he took it on crusade.'

'Louis was of the Capetian line of kings?' The inference was clear. So was Charles of Navarre. Shouldn't he be La Cerda's ally?

'And God willed that the Capetians fell. The Valois are God's appointed kings and I will serve them. But if God wills that they fall . . .'

Osbert did not need the rest explaining to him. If the Capetians staked a claim to the throne again, it would be through La Cerda, or his allies, not through the wild King of Navarre.

Carefully, Osbert closed the lid of the box.

'Will this help your magic?' said La Cerda.

Osbert wanted to reply honestly, 'I haven't the foggiest idea.' However, great men don't wish to hear such things. 'Yes, Lord,' he said. 'Yes. One other thing might help, though.'

'Yes?'

'You have angel's blood in your veins, however weak. It might . . .'

La Cerda snatched the brandy cup from Osbert's hand and emptied the little liquid that still remained in it onto the floor.

He drew his knife, rolled up his sleeve and cut into his forearm, just where the barber makes his cut. When he had squeezed out half a cupful, he held his arm up.

'There,' he said. 'For what good it might do you.' He tore a strip off his shirt sleeve and, before Osbert could stop him, reached over to take the bottle of brandy from the table. He doused the wound in the precious liquid, then applied what remained to the cloth and bound it about his arm, enlisting Osbert to tie it off.

'Brandy for wounds?'

'My physician recommends it and we've found it stops swelling and putrefaction.'

'Modern times!' said Osbert, looking at the empty bottle, secretly wishing this wasteful practice would not catch on.

When La Cerda had gone, Osbert sat looking at the little box on his table. He had seen Dow use such a thing but he doubted he could. First, to know the way to proceed, he would have to summon his familiar.

The next morning, he set about the task, drawing a magic circle in imitation of the one carved on his belly, marking it with La Cerda's blood. Whatever the nobleman had in his veins, it was not angel's blood or, if it was, then a very weak imitation of it. It did not tingle on his fingers nor did it alleviate his hangover when he licked at it.

Still, he drew the circle, called the names of the spirits of the compass, invoked the archangel and called out the name of his familiar – Gressil.

The creature popped up, wriggling through the slit of the window. It was like a rat only much larger.

'Ah, my familiar,' said Osbert, as the little creature appeared at his window.

'Ah, my familiar,' it said, hopping into his room.

'We've had this before,' said Osbert. 'You are my familiar, not I yours.'

'I called you here.'

'No you didn't, I was dragged here in chains.'

The creature raised its eyebrows. 'Almost as if you were summoned.'

'I summoned you! Look – the circle, the candles, the blood.'

The creature shrugged. 'I was on my way here anyway.'

'You were on your way here! Look. I need your help. But first I need to bind you to silence.'

He went to the circle and hummed a spell of control. 'By the four humours of man, by the power of the Holy Spirit, by Christ's blood which . . .'

'You could just ask me to keep a secret,' said Gressil.

'Can you keep a secret?'

The rat said nothing, illustrating, thought Osbert, his remarkable powers of silence.

'All right. You will promise on Christ's blood not to divulge what I am about to tell you.'

'I promise,' said Gressil.

Osbert picked up the little box and opened it in front of the rat. Its eyes bulged in its head.

'How do I use this?'

The rat visibly gulped. 'Is that what I think it is?'

'I'm a magician, not a mind-reader. How do I know what you think it is?'

'It's a key to Hell. The Key of Emerald and Ruby.'

'Then it is what you think it is. I need it to open the gates of Hell. To throw someone in.'

'Well,' said Gressil. 'That will be a problem.'

'Why?'

'Because to use that key, you'll need to already be in Hell.'

'How so? I have seen such keys used.'

'You have seen one such key used. The key to the first gate. That is the key to the third. And who knows what terrors await in there?'

'So who has the key to the second gate?' wondered Osbert.

Actually, that was pretty much his second thought, after *I wonder how long I can stall La Cerda on this one.* La Cerda was descended from a line of saints but he doubted the nobleman possessed their patience. High men didn't like to be burdened with details such as 'There are two gates, erected and sanctioned by God himself, between me and using the key you have so generously bestowed upon me. That, and an army of fiends, tormented souls and God knows what.'

If Osbert obtained the first key from Dow then he could lock Navarre in the first layer. But would that be enough? He would not at all put it past the king of Navarre to bargain his way·out. And he knew there were little cracks in the walls of the first two layers, as well as postern gates to release the lesser devils. The fact that he had never encountered anything from the third told him that such gates and cracks were fewer there.

However, there were problems. He would need the key from Dow and then he would have to find who had the second key. He had his plan.

'You can talk to the ympes of the air,' said Osbert, flapping back his arms and suddenly feeling rather important.

'No. I'm a devil, not a demon,' said Gressil.

'Oh, that's that plan swived then. I need to find the Antichrist.'

'He was at Calais the last I heard.'

'Then find him. Get that key to Hell. If you can't steal it, bargain for it.'

'What shall I tell him?'

Osbert thought for an instant.

'Oh, I don't know. Some old cullions. Tell him I have the third key. If he gets me the first and second, he'll only need the fourth and he can let Lucifer out.'

The rat ducked, as if someone had taken aim at his head.

'Well, go on,' said Osbert.

The rat pulled back its lips over its teeth, crossed itself and squeezed out through the slit of the window.

'Now,' said Osbert, rubbing his hands. 'On to another ritual. This one, I think, requires wine and a harlot.'

15

Eu lay on a couch in his pavilion, Marcel the page before him, two shards of Eu's lances under his arm. It was night and a beeswax candle cast its uncertain, wavering light against the cloth of the tent, making Eu wonder if he was still suffering the effects of the knocks the prince had dealt him. His whole body hummed with the force of the blows he had taken. Still, the Black Prince was in a worse condition, it was said. His wound had bled heavily and, though it had been bound, he had lost consciousness.

If this had happened at Crécy, Eu would have been delighted. However, it was simply not the form to deal your hosts a mortal blow – even if those hosts would not let him leave.

'You have scoured the entire ground?'

'Yes, sir.'

'Lay out the shards before me.'

The shards were blue, tipped with black.

'And the lances I was provided with were just like this?'

'Yes, sir. What difference would it make if they were not? A lance is a lance, isn't it?'

Eu smiled. He liked this boy for his boldness. Some men expected their pages to be no more than mute servants, but Eu thought that boys who would grow to lead armies in war needed to learn to question and reason, rather than unthinkingly obey.

'There are essentially only two sorts of lance,' said Eu. 'Blunt and sharp. Blunt ones, on the whole, do not go through the best German armour like – as the Prince said – "a finger through the crust of a pie". In fact, it would take an uncommonly good sharp lance to do that.'

He thought about the prince's jousting armour. He had worn a breastplate with an extra layer of iron over the unshielded right side. There was a small lip where the plate protruded, exactly where the breach in the armour had occurred. A blunt lance would shatter against that. A good, sharp lance might stick. But that didn't matter, because the armour wasn't designed to be used against sharp lances.

The page looked pale.

'What is it, Marcel?'

'Sir, this was my first tournament, and in a foreign land.'

'Yes?'

The boy drew in a deep breath.

'Another page approached me and tried to offer me help.'

'What other page?'

'I don't know. Everyone here is strange to me.'

'Did he bear the livery of any great house?'

'He bore a fleur-de-lys on his tunic. I thought it strange. An English boy – real English, I mean, not from the court, I think. He did not speak well in French.'

A fleur-de-lys? The royal sign of France. That didn't mean much – Edward had added the symbol to his arms as a statement of his claim to France. Eu's own arms, as constable, bore it. The two countries were so entwined that it could belong to anyone. And would someone seeking to provide him with a sharp lance really be so bold as to announce who they were?

'How did he help you?'

'He didn't. I wouldn't let him. You are my responsibility, no one else's. I have that honour.'

'So you told him to be on his way?'

'Yes, but he wouldn't go.'

'So you fought?' Eu knew what happened when pages disagreed. Boys being schooled for battle were rarely shy with their fists.

'Of course.'

'And?'

'Another page called me "Frenchy" and ran away with your lances. You were about to enter the lists! I thought I would die.'

'So you chased him and retrieved them?'

'Yes, by our pavilion. The trumpets were sounding.'

Eu saw easily what had happened now. The lances had been swapped. Marcel had been distracted and a sharp lance substituted for his blunt one. How had anyone not noticed? Perhaps the sharp point was coloured black. Perhaps it was cleverly disguised with a light foil of wood, a bung of wood with a core of metal. Anything could be done; he had heard of such tricks played before – or rather, he'd heard rumours of them. But, if the lance had been sharp enough and strong enough to pierce the prince's breastplate, surely it would not have broken. It would have gone straight through his chest and come out the other side. Eu had felt lances torn from his hand in battle in just such a way. If you were going to go to the trouble of providing a lance with a sharp point, surely you would bother to make sure the lance was a proper, solid war lance and not a weakened jousting weapon.

He tasted blood in his mouth. His head ached. He really needed to go to sleep. But what was going on? Had there been an attempt to have him murder the Prince of Wales? There were easier ways of killing the prince than that – though if you started assassinating the heirs of major European thrones, where would you end up? Italy, probably. The thought made him smile momentarily.

He saw the advantage of having the prince die in such a way – Eu would take the blame, an individual man, not a representative of the House of Valois. But the prince had not died, despite his armour having split like the skin of a grape. Yet pricked by a dagger, he had been wounded. Eu did not know how this could be.

'The prince is a devil,' said Eu, to himself. 'The rumours are true.'

16

'I have drunk of angel's blood.

'I have thrown down a king and torn out his heart.

'I have made a devil the prince of England.

'I have travelled to Hell and struck bargains with Satan.

'I am heartily sorry for these sins.'

Isabella had never cried in her life. She did not think she was capable of it. Even as a very young girl, friendless on her wedding night, when her husband left her to go and sport with Gaveston, even when her husband left her to the Scots, even when Mortimer met his fate at Tyburn, she had not cried. Now she did.

She had imagined she could do anything – outlive God, throw down kings, call her lover back from the prison of Hell. But with Mortimer in Heaven, the only way to get to him was to join him there. All her sins weighed in on her now – the murders and the deceptions, the deals with creatures of the Pit. Her soul was heavy, in need of redemption. If Heaven was where Mortimer was, then to Heaven she must go.

A gulp from the other side of the confession screen. Isabella did not include a list of the people she had killed in her life, largely because she had forgotten many of them but also because some of them had been great enemies of God. There could be no sin in killing them.

'I had expected something—'

'Less?'

'Yes. Less.'

'I am a queen. As our virtues are greater than those of ordinary men, so are our vices.'

Isabella had always liked the priest at St Michael's. He was that rare breed for a churchman – someone who not only believed in God but acted as if he did. He kept a simple house, had only one servant, and travelled on an unimpressive horse. Some priests and most bishops set themselves up as princes if they could. Could she rely on him? Probably. She felt his terror even through the screen.

The priest took in three large breaths.

'These sins took place since your last Holy Communion?'

'No.'

Another gulp. She knew what he was thinking: she had taken Communion in a state of unconfessed sin – itself a sin.

'Does God speak to you? As queen?'

'There have been no angels in England in a long time. Not that I could visit.'

The priest muttered some Latin under his breath.

'I am truly penitent. I have seen Hell, Father, and I do not wish to go there. And yet, I have bargained my soul with Satan.'

'For what?'

'For the return of Mortimer.'

'And Satan betrayed you?'

'He misled me. Mortimer is in Heaven.'

'Such a rebel?'

'Against men and devils, not God.' Even as she spoke, she felt a weight lifting from her. 'Father, when I threw down my husband, I was doing God's work. This much has been revealed to me.'

'How so?'

'The greatest devil told me, under a solemn vow before God. The Plantagenet line are all descended from devils. Mortimer was doing God's work.'

'Was not his grandmother a Plantagenet?' The priest almost seemed to suck the words back in as he spoke, fearing he had said too much.

'His grandmother was the bastard daughter of old King John. Or so it was said, and so John believed. But in truth who knows who she lay with?'

The priest moaned. 'Such sin. And among such great men.'

'I am here to atone for it. I am here to put things right.'

'How? By exterminating the entire Plantagenet line?'

Isabella's hands went to the nosegay about her neck.

'Would that please God?'

'Lady, I cannot say. I . . .'

She thought of Satan's words. By Mortimer's boldness, he had pleased God. She would do the same.

'There is a point,' she said, 'when a tree becomes so rotten, that it must be felled for the safety of all, no matter how long it has stood, no matter how venerable or loved.'

'I have not instructed you to do this.'

'So what should I do?'

'For such sin? Give away all your goods. Walk in sackcloth. Pray always. Go on a long pilgrimage. Fast often. Become a nun and pray day and night!'

That was easy. She had not eaten since she returned from Hell, could not eat. Food seemed repulsive to her now, along with the jewels which had been her delight. All her former life had been lived in error and she must put things right.

'I will do all these things,' said Isabella.

'Had you not feared for your soul before?'

'I had not thought to die.'

'And now?'

'It is my only wish. But I must be free of my sins.'

'I cannot grant this, Lady.'

'Who could?'

'The Pope. No one short of the Pope!'

'Then I will see him,' said Isabella.

'And what of the devils on the throne of England? Will you leave them there?'

'I will apply the old cure.'

'Which is?'

She did not reply. She would use the best resort of kings. Death. And then the Pope would grant her absolution. She would travel to see him in his court in Avignon. Pope Clement loved France, so he should love her – a queen of France by birth – and should love what she proposed to do. The English monarchy would be returned to its pure line. The house of Plantagenet must fall. They had used her like a brood mare. A true line must be put in its place. She had thought that she would be its founder, but now that plan had to wait. It was a sin to drink the blood of angels and sinners did not get into Heaven. She would age and die as a normal woman from now on.

But first she would rid England of its stain, or at least purge that which she could. The idea had been growing in her for some time. When she had ascended to the throne and overthrown her husband, she had bargained with devils to do so. She'd said only that she would make one of their number prince of England. It was no sin to kill such a presumptuous fiend. And her son? Yes, he too would need to be dealt with.

Isabella hesitated over Edward. They had been very close once and she had thought him the very perfect model of a prince – brave, strong, gifted at arms, and – above all – pliable. When he had rebelled against Mortimer, cast off all reasonable guidance and direction, she had thought her heart would break.

She concentrated on that – her outrage at what her son had done, breaking into Nottingham Castle, through whatever magical means he had used, to steal gentle Mortimer from her. All her hate had poured into Montagu, who had led the band which abducted her lover. Now she tried to direct that towards her son. It was he who had set up a special gibbet at Tyburn just for Mortimer, he who had ordered Mortimer's entrails burned in front of him.

God favoured Mortimer, that much was clear. How else had He welcomed him into his Heaven?

Yet still she could not quite feel comfortable doing it. Part devil he might be but Edward was an anointed king, his 'son' the anointed prince – no matter that he was a devil. She could not move against them lightly. But move against them she would.

Her first step would to be ensure they had some more formidable enemies in France than the vacillating Philip and his idiot son John. The Valois could not be trusted. House Capet would have to ascend again, one way or the other. Her nephew had made that argument when he had written to her in some writhing, odd ink telling her he planned to ally with Edward, help him in to France, and asking for magical help. *That* had too many dangers – Edward and Navarre together might conceivably win. And then, line of devils or not, angels might attend her son again, as a reward for his valour and recognition of the throne on which God had set him. No, that plot must fail, but she would have to offer Charles something to help him abandon it. She would have to pretend to help him.

Before absolution, then, further damnation. More magic would be required, more royal blood. Well, there were happy coincidences there. England should never be strengthened by an alliance with Castile. The marriage of Joanna and Peter must not take place. She took out her pen to write to Charles of Navarre. Then she sent for the count of Eu.

17

Navarre had written to Eu and suggested he try persuading the English royals to reduce his ransom. He should make promises, show himself of service, he said. Perhaps he should even hint they would remove the blockade on Calais at the neck of the marshes, now that the town had fallen. Calamity was occurring in France. La Cerda had been given control of all of the constable's lands. It was an outrage, said Navarre, an outrage, but he could do nothing about it. Eu's heart sank but a letter from his wife confirmed the truth of it.

Eu sensed he might have one potential ally at the English court, the lady who had given him her favour at the tournament. Was that an invitation to further contact? He would take it as one. He sent the lance head from the tournament field to Queen Philippa. He received an invitation to an audience within the week.

He might have been in France as he was called into Philippa's day room. All the wall hangings were in the French style, showing French scenes. Here there was a lady receiving a flower beneath a castle that could only be French, there a knight with the fleur-de-lys on his banners. But England was not France. Though it was only October, a fire burned beneath a brick chimney, the smoke hanging at the ceiling. Eu himself had worn furs – nothing extravagant, just a coat of camlet Edward had given to him, topped with a simple cap.

The difficulties in speaking privately to a queen are considerable, particularly for a man, and a prisoner at that. Queens are never alone. Their ladies attend them constantly from waking to sleeping and, when their ladies are not there, their husband inevitably is.

Even a queen as favoured as Philippa could not talk alone to someone like Eu without exciting comment. So there are ways and means of engineering privacy known to queens throughout Christendom. The first is to call a meeting late. Young ladies have their business and some of that business is best conducted in the night hours, when poems – and more – are received from certain gentlemen.

The older women are more inclined to stay with their queen, but she is able to let all but one or two go as an act of kindness. The one she kept by her side in her reception room in the Round Tower was a woman old enough to be the queen's mother – arguably anyone's mother. She was that most useful of attendants, largely deaf, sleepy, and apt to forget whatever it was she did manage to hear. However, there was one more person in the chamber – someone Eu had not expected to see. Joanna, princess of England, sat embroidering by the fire.

Philippa herself was at ease behind a table, plump, full-breasted, clearly pregnant. How many children now? This would be her twelfth. King Edward was a man of famous passions and it seemed that his wife devoted herself to slaking them.

Her lady pointed Eu to a seat

'You have brought the board, Count?' said Philippa. She spoke in her beautiful Northern French, her consonants tinged to a brittle hardness by a Flemish frost.

'Yes, lady. It was difficult to get. Our ambassador had one.' He produced the board of the Philosophers' Game from its velvet bag.

'Couldn't you have asked one of your spies?' said Joanna, smiling.

'They have not made themselves known to me, My Lady.'

'Then you should worry about your position at your court.'

She smiled, teasing. Her words bore a bitter truth, however. Why hadn't the spies contacted him? He had told himself that it would be too difficult for them, but difficulty was meat and drink to a spy. Had there been stirrings against him at home? Had his capture at Caen been blamed for the debacle at Crécy? He knew what his enemies would make of it. Or was spying just becoming too difficult in this age of devils and magic? Joanna collected her things, kissed her mother and left.

'You are accomplished at this game?' Philippa gestured to the board.

'There was a fashion for it in Paris a few years ago. I have played since I was a boy.'

'Then you must instruct me. We are so far behind here in England.'

'In everything but war.'

'In everything but that.'

Her lady gathered herself in her chair and tried to look interested.

Eu opened the board and laid the pieces out. The lady crossed herself.

'They are not devil signs, My Lady,' said Eu, 'simply numbers.'

'They don't look like numbers.'

'The game is more easily played this way. Using the Roman numbers taxes an old head like mine.'

'This is two, isn't it?' said Philippa, picking up a counter bearing a swan-like sigil.

'Yes, madame. I shall explain them all before we begin.'

The queen's lady made a queer shape with her mouth and then yawned deeply. Clearly mathematical board games were not to her liking. She put down her needlework and lay back, hands on her belly.

Eu passed the queen her reckoner and set out his own. He saw what was required. They didn't need to play. The heat of the fire, combined with a very detailed explanation of common victories, of grand victories or victories of excellence achieved by aligning mathematical progressions across the squares, would be enough to serve their purpose.

'Why is it "the philosopher's game"?' said Philippa. 'Why not the game of numbers?'

Eu smiled. 'It is indeed called the game of numbers, ma'am. But also, as it demonstrates the progressions of the great Pythagoras, it reveals to us the harmonies within nature, harmonies ordained by God. Unshakeable harmonies.'

The lady let out a breath like a post horse after a day's ride. She was asleep.

'This move would be safe?' said Eu. The queen caught his meaning.

'She never wakes,' she said. 'It is not her only charm, but it is chief among them.'

'Why am I here?'

'For the sake of harmony. I am afraid.'

'Of what?'

'You know the rumours that surround my son?'

Philippa moved a five back and forth across the board.

'That he is an uncommonly able warrior.'

'The lance head,' she said.

'Yes.'

'It . . .' She didn't say what she wanted to, but made a gesture with her fingers to show it the lance bouncing away.

'He could have been killed.'

'God would have protected him, had he not been . . . The dagger was blessed. That hurt him easy enough.'

Eu lowered his eyes. As he thought, the queen had tested her son. Now what?

The queen placed an eight next to the five. Now an eleven went next to the eight. A good sequence. Philippa had played this game before.

'If my son was abducted at birth and replaced with—'

'That is a wild supposition.'

'He would never suckle at my breast.' Her eyes avoided his.

Eu said nothing. She wanted to unburden herself. He wasn't going to stop her.

'He had a wet nurse?'

'Queen Isabella provided her. I was ill after the birth and could take no part in the selection.'

'It sounds like you regret it.'

'We all know now what that woman is capable of. I visited her at Nottingham. The skies around it were black with devils.'

'The devils do God's work. We know that.'

'Do they? What is God's work, Count, because I am not sure I know. Do you see His hand in the affairs of men? If He wants stability and order, where is it? He is all-powerful.'

'My philosophy is limited to that of this game, ma'am.'

The lady-in-waiting snuffled in her seat.

'I need your help, Raoul. My son is not close to me. He never has been. He scorns me, has never touched me. Even as a child.'

'You are of a royal line.'

'Yes. Appointed by God. A devil would not approach me. We need to test the prince. If he is a devil then he cannot cross a magic circle. I need a man who can draw one.'

She stacked the pieces of the game – two squares, two triangles, two rounds, number thirty-six at the base, twenty-five above it, sixteen above that, squares of three, two and one one above that. It made the white pyramid, the game's second most powerful piece. Eu saw in the pyramid the image of the world, the teeming multitudes below, the rare, the singular perched on top.

'Why are you asking me this? You put yourself in great danger. I could report all this to Philip.'

'It's no more than what half the marketplaces between here and Paris are saying. Your family has been friends of the Capetians and the Valois for generations. Because my husband quarrels with my cousin, it's no reason for us to forget old ties. You will not betray me because of our current little skirmish.'

'I am French and you are English. Or on the side of the English.'

'How modern of you, Count, the virtues of being "patriotic". It is a lie we tell the poor, is it not, and the more credulous of the nobility? Family first. Family always first.'

She gestured to the board, as if implying that the war – with its thousands of noble dead, with its burnings of valuable lands, animals, serfs and villeins – was of no more importance.

'Then what do you want from me?'

'You had a famous sorcerer at the French court. Could he be used?'

'Osbert, yes. He has gone, I think. I could write to Navarre and see if he can discover where he is.'

'Do. I would employ him. Do you think he would work for me?'

'If he moves against your son then he is doing the work of the court. He will not know the request comes from you. If it emerges the Black Prince is a devil?'

Philippa passed her hand over the stack of counters she had made, scattering them across the board.

Did she really mean . . .? Her face looked wan.

Well, a country's line could not be given over to devils. That was an inversion of an order set by God. Devils were servants, monstrosities created to torment the monstrous, the damned souls of Hell. The Black Prince was a formidable enemy, the fiery and reckless John of Gaunt the next in line to the throne. It would be good to have the English side of the family at each other's throats – honourable to rid the world of a usurping devil. It would be insupportable, as a guest of the prince, to kill him. But only if he were truly a prince and not something sent from Hell. To kill a prince on a battlefield was one thing. To intrigue and cast sorcery against him quite another.

'Your other children—' he said.

'There is no doubt about them.'

Eu picked up a counter and studied it in the firelight.

'All right. But I beg you write to your brother and have him remove La Cerda from my lands. You won't get your ransom any other way.'

"I will do it. I swear.'

'Then I will write to Navarre. He is suspected as he grows. He is intelligent and ambitious but he is close to the prince. He will be able to find Osbert.'

'Good. That is the holy sword Joyeuse, is it not?'

'Yes.' Eu was, of course, allowed his weapon at court as no noble of the blood would ever use it against his captors. Such would be a disgrace.

'Then let us use its power.'

'If God grants it to be so.'

'If God grants it.'

The two knelt together and Eu put the naked sword on the floor before them.

Philippa spoke:

'By this blessed sword that Thou hast ordained as the scourge of all wickedness, which is the protector of the Church, of widows and orphans against the works of evil, which is the terror and dread of all wickedness in both attack and defence, hear our prayer. Let Thy ears be attentive to the depths of our beseeching, Lord. Royal virtue, joy of the mind, recall the anguish and sorrow Thou didst endure at the approach of death, when filled with bitterness, insulted, and outraged. Thou didst cry out in a loud voice that Thou wert abandoned by Thy Father, saying: "My God, My God, why hast Thou forsaken me?" By this anguish, I beg of Thee, not to abandon us in our anguish, O Lord God. Amen. Set our anguish at an end and light us the path Thou wouldst have us tread.'

The sword shone its holy blue light and the two remained kneeling for a long time. A cry of 'Goodness!' and Philippa for an instant thought God had spoken – but it was not God, just the old lady-in-waiting, stirring from her sleep.

She sat up, tears streaming down her face.

'Forgive me, My Lady, My Lord, forgive me.'

'What is it, Goedelle?'

'I have an awful dream,' she said, 'an awful dream.'

'What dream?'

'I was in church, but no church I have ever known and you were beside me, My Lady. The window was all broken in, all smashed, but a horrible man like a devil was rebuilding it. And he had in his hand a piece of the glass and he gave it to you, Lady, saying blessings on you and telling you God wanted you to have it.'

She crossed herself.

'And then the window was nearly mended and in it shone an angel in the shape of a knight, all colours of the rainbow. Only one piece remained and the man, the evil little man, said, "Finish the window, as God intends," and you put in the piece of the window and the angel spoke. Lady, I fear to say what it said.'

'Speak, Goedelle, tell me.'

'It said that it had come to wipe away your son and all your line. It said he was cursed of God.'

Philippa went to Goedelle and hugged her.

'Just a dream. Just a dream.' Then she turned to Eu. 'Find this man Osbert. Something must be done.'

18

'The letter.' Charles of Navarre extended his hand to the messenger.

'You were not easy to find, sir,' said the young squire. 'The letter came to Champagne and I had the honour—'

'Get out!' The man stank. Everyone stank nowadays, Charles was finding. He took out a handkerchief dabbed with perfume and breathed in the deep, spicy smell.

The man bowed and retreated from the room. It was a day room beneath the keep that looked out on a grey moor beneath a grey Norman sky. Well, this was the nearest he could be to Paris and be safe. And Normandy, though another country, *was* safe so far. His banners flew there in a blustery breeze alongside those of the Norman lords. They had courted him a little since he had come to his Norman lands – his by ancestral right. His nobles knew which side their bread was buttered. Philip was old, John an idiot. Difficult to know who to ally with when the old king died. Charles and his mother, with their solid claim to the French throne, were a good outside bet for those lords who Paris held in contempt anyway. Well, one part of Paris, the occasional Paris that sometimes held the itinerant court. Another side might welcome them more.

Before him stood a ridiculously dressed man, all brocade and swirls of a sort no merchant should be able to afford, let alone dare to wear. This was Etienne Marcel, clothier, the head of the so called 'Third Estate' of Paris, part of the legislative assembly that advised Prince Philip, for all the notice he took. Charles indulged the outrageousness and pretended to lend a sympathetic ear to the merchant classes, for who knew what the future might bring? Other nobles were right to look down on such men, but not clever to dismiss them. He recognised their energy, their usefulness, even their power. And Philip was ignoring the estates, dismissing their problems. The country was racked by English 'routiers', rogue bands of men and devils who stalked the countryside, burning and killing wherever they went. The men were their own masters, the English king having no command or use for them, though disdaining to do anything to stop their plundering ways.

'Why will he not ban devils from his realm?' said the clothier.

'Too much use for them,' said Charles. 'He wants devils in his own court. He thinks of his own needs, not those of his people. I am different. Let me lend you two hundred men to help protect your trade.'

It was a gesture – some of the routier bands were three times that number each – but it was more than Philip seemed willing to commit. Since Crécy he had been paralysed, torn by indecision, advised by idiots. His nobles would not come to his command any more, particularly since he had mustered them to fight the English at Calais and turned back with a fit of the collywobbles at the neck of the marshes. His lords had gone home without drawing a sword, or getting a penny in recompense for the expense of the journey.

'My dear Marcel,' said Charles, 'would you now excuse us. I have family business to attend to. Do walk in our gardens here and it would be my delight to entertain you at dinner.'

'You are too kind.' Marcel bowed deeply.

Charles smiled. 'I am a prince for all men.'

Marcel left, one or two stupidly attired flunkies following him out.

'I don't know why you deal with those people,' said his mother when the merchant was gone. 'They are parasites, neither labouring nor fighting and most of them not even praying. Men of no honour or worth. A drain on the kingdom.'

Charles shrugged. 'I am a friend to all.'

There were more powers in France now than the nobility acknowledged. The low men had risen up for Lucifer and secured Calais, or a good bit of it. Merchants, thought Charles, might one day be a power to themselves, and so were at least worth trying to understand, or even cultivate.

'Pass the letter to me, son,' said Queen Joan. She dipped a little stick into a tiny bottle she held in her hand and dabbed it at her eye. Belladonna, to make the pupils grow larger and therefore to make the person seem more attractive. She blinked heavily.

'They have cut this with perfume. I'm not sure it altogether works.'

'You are thinking of entertaining, Mother?'

'No.' She blinked. 'Just trying this out. A present from ladies of the court.'

Charles opened the letter, resting it on the great tawny cat on his lap.

'It's in code,' he said.

'Let me see.'

She put her bottle to one side and came over to him. He gave her the letter begrudgingly. Always poking her nose in, that woman.

'It's the cypher of Champagne,' she said. 'Our ancestral lands.'

'Is it safe?'

'Not very – but it's something we share, or used to share, with the Count of Eu.'

'It's from him? In England?'

'That's his seal.'

'And?'

'His land has been taken over by the rogue La Cerda.'

'I hear of that man more often than I hear the bells of the hours.'

And that in Normandy. My God, were Charles in Paris his ears would no doubt be ringing with that detested name.

'Eu says Prince John must be separated from false friends.'

'That'd leave him rather lonely. He has a point, though, doesn't he? I've always liked the count of Eu.'

'We were once neighbours when we possessed our lands in Champagne. Before the Valois bastards robbed us.'

'Has he many friends?'

'Very many. The lords here love him more than they do us. As constable he has settled their differences well and favourably.'

'Interesting,' said Charles. 'He could be a useful ally.'

'Undoubtedly. And, by luck, he wants a favour.'

'Yes?'

'You know the sorcerer of the court? Osbert the Mage.'

'I know he threw poison in my face at Crécy.'

'No time to bear grudges,' said Joan. 'Or rather, small ones. The man is useful to us now. Eu wants him in England.'

'For what purpose?'

'To aid Queen Philippa.'

'No one knows where he is. But tell him we will find him. Though, if I do find him I will tear out his throat.'

'Do not harm a useful man.'

'He burnt my face,' said Charles, as if that trumped all arguments.

He surveyed the snapping chains of his banners. ' There is a cold wind blowing on the Valois if we make alliance with England.'

'She is Valois.'

'The Valois who have treated us so basely, not her side of the family. With him on our side . . . With the English on our side . . . Oh, Mother, war is a marvellous thing for the ways it opens, the new friends it finds. We could reclaim our birthright.'

His mother put her hand on his shoulder.

'Do not dream it. The angel said you would never be king of France.'

Charles's cat's eyes betrayed no emotion. 'Yes, mother, but as I have grown I have come to see there is one thing the angel overlooked.'

'What is that, son?'

'I disagree with it.'

Charles sat down. For a moment he seemed like the child he was, swinging his legs from the tall chair.

'I have pondered hard on what the angel said, and on my devil father. It means half my nature is base. Half is that of a servant, a mere jailer.'

'The baser blood is overwhelmed by the royal,' said his mother. 'You are wholly my son, my heir.'

'It is in a devil's nature to defer to royalty, to bow and be cowed. Why not in mine?'

'As one plant is grafted to another to strengthen it, the weak qualities of both disappearing, so you are made.'

'So I am stronger than a king?'

'The angel at Pamplona has acknowledged you. You do God's work, son, nothing could be clearer.'

'I do. I am a king, therefore my work is God's work. He has favoured me. I am marvellous agile, dainty on my feet, strong and fast, so much cleverer than any crowned head of Europe, an Aristotle among asses.'

'You are.'

'So how do I gain the power I seek? Isabella overthrew a king. She would know. Can you not use Isabella's magic? She used spells to turn herself into a powerful seductress. We could seduce La Cerda. How good it would be to use him.'

'It would not be possible.'

'Why not?'

'My son, do you not see? A man who has the strength to overthrow kings, to become a king, has the strength to resist all but the strongest enchantment.'

'So why don't we use the strongest enchantment? Why stop at La Cerda? Why not enchant Prince John and have La Cerda killed?'

'I have no idea how such a magic might be made.'

'But Aunt Isabella might. I will write to her for advice.'

'You would not want to go through with what she would recommend.'

They sat for a while, Charles looking at the letter, too proud to ask her what it said. Eventually, he said what was on his mind.

'The Valois cannot be allowed to reign for ever, Mother. You have raised me to think of nothing else.'

'And so I have.'

'Pay Eu's ransom,' he said.

'It's a fortune. We hardly have that much money.'

'You told me we were rich.'

'Not that rich. Edward's demands are outrageous. He doesn't want Eu back – he respects him too much and fears his cunning. Philip is an easier opponent without him.'

'Have I been lied to, Mother? He wants only 120,000 florins.'

'That is too great. It would leave us penniless.'

'We will reap the rewards. Philip would be sure to welcome us back for delivering his fine captain to him. Eu would be in our debt. We could attach conditions to his return to assure that.'

'Nothing can be assured. Instead of La Cerda in your way you have Eu.'

'But if Eu could be made to promise to recommend us for the constableship – or to give it away. He is a man of his word and very influential with the king.'

'You are dreaming, son.'

Charles blinked, his pink tongue flicking at his ivory teeth.

'My will, as king, is that we do this.'

'And mine as regent is that we do not.'

'We play for the highest stakes now, Mother. With Eu home, La Cerda's time will be harder and we may come back to favour with Prince John. Think what riches we will reap then. He must soon be king. And the count of Eu cannot live for ever.'

'I won't wager the family's fortunes on the whims of that idiot John. Son, you must think bigger. This is not about countries or who is and is not the king. It is what the Valois took from us when they forced my husband to swear fealty to them as kings. Remember, you swore calumny on all of France.'

'I did.'

'So forget intriguing with Eu. England must be our friend now. Let us invite them to Normandy. Let them no longer be bottled in Calais, but free to cause what havoc they may. Or, if the game plays differently, let us betray them to Philip.'

'You have a safe cypher?'

'The safest,' she said. 'I have a subtle ink indeed, made of tiny devils. Write what you will, but as you are a king and they respect your wishes, then a word and they vanish.'

'Show me.'

She went to her table and picked up a bottle, elaborately worked in a net of silver.

Charles took it and opened it. Inside a black shiny mass of tiny bodies writhed, each finer than a hair.

'These are devils?'

'They are. Left by Hugh Despenser at the Temple when he went to Crécy to die. Write to the English. To the Black Prince, if you will – he is incautious. We will ally with them and bring them here.'

Charles took the bottle to a table, cut a feather into a nib and dipped it in.

'Charles,' he wrote in a blotchy hand on the table. It looked exactly like ordinary ink.

'Tell it to be gone,' said his mother.

'Be gone,' he said.

The ink was suddenly a mass of tiny writhing bodies that slithered back into the bottle.

'This is marvellous safe, Mother.' He would write to Edward for sure but he would also, he thought, write to his aunt Isabella and to Eu. There was more than one path to power in France and he would see which one opened before deciding to tread it.

19

For three days the king struggled, and Dow struggled to control their men. By the 4 August, what could be looted had been looted, who could be raped had been raped, and the men were too drunk or too hungover for any more slaughter.

'We will go to every door,' said Dow to Montagu. 'We will reclaim what has been stolen and we will distribute to every man and woman exactly what they need. The rest of the money will be used to rebuild the town, our Eden.'

'You will provoke a riot,' said Montagu. 'Better to let what is be. The worst offences can be dealt with later.'

'We'll deal with them now. We will take them one at a time. Men who imagine themselves separate from others are weak. Come for one, and come by name – the others will think themselves safe. Only when we have dealt with the worst of them will the rest realise we mean to come for them too. They will hand over their gold.'

It felt as though there were a ferret gnawing at his guts; his hands trembled and his tongue was dry. Everything undone. Well, he would have to remake it. If that meant blood, it meant blood. As a temporary measure.

He had established a court in the guildhall and surrounded himself with Luciferian zealots – his own Cornish people. Cornwall had kept the light of Lucifer burning in even the darkest time. These men had lived as bandits on the moors for years, sharing everything, no thought of one man putting himself above another. They had no leader, though they recognised the wise from the foolish and they were bound by a common language. Come for one of them and you come for them all.

The guildhall seemed the best place for the trials. When you have killed a man for laughing at you, then it is easier to kill those who commit more grievous sins.

The first in was Thomas, a wrecker from Hull. He had killed four in a family of tanners – all but the mother, who he had raped on the corpses. He had become drunk and boasted about it to some men of Cornwall. They had brought him to the hall.

It did not seem difficult to establish that the facts were true. The wrecker's mates came in to plead for him – they said he was a man driven mad by war; that the family were fit to die of starvation anyway; that they would pay for his release. One showed Dow a jewelled communion goblet and offered it for his friend's release. Dow had the man of Hull hanged from the beam of a shattered house, and the goblet thief beside him.

'I thought we didn't do this,' said Greatbelly.

'I thought we didn't do this,' said Dow, holding up the goblet. 'It's one thing to rob a church. A good thing. It's another to conceal the plunder from your fellows, to put selfish desires above the common good. Our beliefs must be protected, even if it means doing things we would prefer not to do. I see that now.'

'You sound like a priest,' said Greatbelly. 'Do not be another magistrate, Dow.'

'Those I kill will return,' said Dow, 'when all the gates of Hell open and Lucifer emerges. When they stand in the morning light their souls will be purified.'

'Lucifer does not judge.'

'Though I do. It is a means to an end. We remind our people of their duties to themselves and to others.'

'You are on the side of the French!' shouted a wrecker, as he watched his friend kicking out his last.

'I am on the side of all the poor. Nations are but the conceits of kings. When Lucifer made the world, his light did not shine more on the English than the French, nor more on the Tartars than the Saracens.'

'Traitor!' shouted the man. A man of Cornwall struck him and the wreckers set on the man of Cornwall. In moments it was a riot, the Cornish and the Northern wreckers thumping lumps out of each other.

'Brothers! Brothers!' cried Dow.

But it was Montagu, wading in with the holy sword Arondight drawn, its cool blue light a smear in the gloom of the tight streets, who restored order, knocking down three men with the clever trips and pushes he had learned in his training as a knight.

'The next man who raises a hand dies!' he said.

'Then will our Antichrist kill you too?' said a man, picking himself up from the filth of the street. He spat.

Dow turned away from him. He knew he was losing his people. But were they his people? How could they turn on their fellows like this? How could they prey upon people just as poor as they, French or not?

More trouble as the next day dawned. Edward, it appeared, had granted his men free pardon and allowed them to keep any loot they had taken, short of houses, which were his to dispense. He had spared the burghers of Calais who had emerged in their nooses and taken only the houses of the rich for himself. All poorer dwellings were given to the Luciferians to dispose of as they saw fit. The people came to Dow, asking him to settle disputes of who owned which house, who had the right to stay where, to ask for pardon for the goods they had looted and for the right to keep them. He said that he alone could not rule on such matters, and that the whole body of the Luciferian people must decide or elect someone so to do.

He met them at dawn in the town's main square – the marketplace as was, when there had been provisions or anything else to sell.

The Luciferians crowded in under the rising golden light. At normal times, they would have had no leader. Those who felt compelled to speak would speak and those who wished to stay silent stayed silent. Dow never spoke unless asked for his opinion, which he invariably was. Even then, he tried to hold back from voicing his views. If the people naturally sought leaders, he thought, then their nature was their enemy and he would not help them surrender to it.

There was passion there. The Cornishmen all brought three-pronged pitchforks, Lucifer's sign – the tool of toil turned into the weapon of liberation. They held them proudly aloft, surrounding Dow. A woman in the crowd sang a high, joyful song of praise to the dawn, the morning light and to the morning star that accompanied it, and a deep drum sounded to open the meeting.

The first voice raised called for thanks to Lucifer for the deliverance in battle and the crowd raised up their faces to the sun to thank him. Dow felt glad to see so many standing tall, greeting Lucifer as equals, not bowed in submission to the God of the Church.

The second voice was not so grateful. A woman shouted out, in a heavy French accent, that the people of Lucifer were no more than hypocrites. They had promised to spare the poor but they had set on them like wolves. The crowd turned to see her and a London voice called her a French bitch. Horse shit flew and the woman was dragged into the crowd.

'Save her,' said Dow, to the stout Cornishmen at his side. Six of the tin miners waded into the crowd, their fists swinging to make way.

Discord and anger. 'He'd rather save the French than his own!' Another voice, this one of Wales.

'Why should Edward's men be given licence while we are kept on a chain?'

'We had more under God than Lucifer!'

'Friends!' Dow shouted.

Abuse came back; he was called 'scum' and 'a Frenchman' and then, worst of all, 'King'.

'King Dow!' shouted someone. 'Bow down – King Dowzabel wants to speak!'

There was a brief lull.

'I am no king!' he shouted.

'I wish you were – Edward's offering a better deal!' A scuffle.

'Lies!' shouted another voice. 'Dowzabel shines with the light of Lucifer.'

'Swive yourself!' said still one more.

The smack of fist against face, more scuffling, shouting. Dow climbed up onto the supporting pillar of a house to address the crowd, to prevent a riot.

'I am no king but, as one of you, equal and no different, I tell you this is wrong. We came here to build Eden, not on the backs of our fellows but alongside them. There has been a grievous slaughter here. There has been theft, not for the common good but for personal gain.'

'Not for your gain, you mean. You just want all the pie to yourself without leaving any for us.'

'We came here in the light of Lucifer. We must go on that way!. Everything will be shared to build our new Eden!'

'Shit!' shouted someone else, and a bottle crashed off the pillar above Dow.

'Brothers! Sisters!' shouted Greatbelly. 'Hear what Dowzabel has to say.'

'Put my dick in your mouth, you fat whore, maybe it'll shut you up!'

More shoving, someone fell. A scream and then the crowd erupted, men of Cornwall fighting men of Wales, fighting men of the North and those of Essex.

Three big men, one with an axe, came for Dowzabel but Montagu stood in their way. Two died before they had got within an arm's length of him, and the other lost his nerve and ran.

Smoke was in the air. A flash of fire. Someone was burning the houses.

'This is our inheritance!' shouted Dow. 'Do not burn your own homes!'

'It's a shithole!' shouted a voice. 'We're better off with the king!'

A great rush came forward at Dow – men brandishing swords and clubs.

He drew his falchion.

'Away!' said Greatbelly. 'Dow, get away.'

'I need to speak to them. They need to hear me.'

She shook him by the shoulder.

'Aren't you always talking about the will of the people?'

'Yes!'

'Well, what do you think the will of the people says now?'

'Go!' said Montagu 'Go! They're after you. We'll talk later.'

Dow had no choice now. Two men of Cornwall grabbed him by each arm and pulled him away from the throng.

He was bundled down alley after alley.

'Not the guildhall,' said Zepar – a Cornishman and one of the true Luciferians who took the names of demons.

'Then where?'

'Here!' It was a squat church Norman style, its windows smashed and its door broken in.

They took him inside, the sun cutting shadows across the stone. A dead priest sat against a pillar, as if weary from sweeping the floor.

A severed head, neatly bearded, sat on the altar. It watched them come in.

'The place has been looted, they'll not come here again,' said Zepar. They made their way through the church, to sit behind the altar.

'I'll find our friends,' whispered Murmur in his ear. The little man flapped out of the church, dancing through the sunbeams like a butterfly.

Dow breathed in. He'd failed. He had thought he had shone a light into the hearts of the poor but he had failed to see that, when the poor accounted themselves wealthy, with enough plunder to last them a month or a year, they no longer thought themselves poor. And what had Dow become? Here he was with a bodyguard, protected from his own people like a tyrant.

The town burned around him through the day. He tried to get up to leave, to stop the destruction, but Zepar, now joined by other men of Cornwall, would not let him. He couldn't command them; they were his equals. In truth, he didn't know what he would do if he did get out.

None of them spoke, just sat grim-faced, the taste of smoke in their mouths. Montagu arrived at sunset.

'I have failed,' said Dow.

'No,' said Montagu. He knelt beside Dow. 'You have been outmanoeuvred, that is all. I am sure Edward set agitators among the crowd.'

'Why not before? Why not after Crécy?'

'Because you were still useful to him, Dow. He's given you your Eden, as he promised, but it lies in ashes about you. He's demolished all the houses between here and his quarter of the town. He has the merchants' dwellings, you have a wasteland and are discredited in front of your men.'

'They are not my men. They are their own leaders.'

'But they have not been raised to think that way. You must appear to them as a hero and a warrior as you did when you unfurled the dragon banner.'

'I did not unfurl it.'

'They thought you did. That's all that matters. But you have shown weakness. These men were bred to know masters. It's their only way of thinking.'

'So Edward now presents himself and they will bow the knee?'

Montagu put his hand on Dow's shoulder. 'Yes. They want bread. That's all. They follow who feeds them, who lines their pockets with gold. You threatened to take that away'

'For the common good.'

'We,' said Montagu, tapping himself on the breast, 'the aristocracy, are interested in the common good. You plough the fields, you pay your taxes and our bond is to protect you. No one on my estates ever starved.'

'Though they ate gritted bread while you dined on swans.'

'It seemed natural to me. What other way could be imagined? Such was God's will, I thought. And so do these men, or many of them, though they make the sign of Lucifer, though they stand with their faces raised to the morning light. For every one who truly believes in the friendship of Lucifer, there is another who is here because he follows the crowd, who fears to say what is in his heart. Give him gold, or a stolen candlestick and he feels bolder.'

Dow cast his head into his hands. Edward had seen the weakness of his position and exploited it masterfully.

'At Crécy you made a promise,' said Montagu. 'If I advised your troops, if I advised you on your dealings with Edward, you would help me find the true Prince of Wales, the true heir to the English throne and help rid it of the devil who has usurped that name.'

'I did.'

'Then help me now. We can find him – we have the means of the angel feather cloaks. When he is found and returned here, Edward will be destroyed, utterly discredited. You can do to him what he did to you.'

Dow sat for a while more, his legs numb from sitting on the stone.

'The cloaks weaken those who travel by them.'

'Yes. But we are made of stern stuff, you and I, Dowzabel.'

'Why can't you go alone?'

'Without your say so I have no right to the cloaks. And you need the glory, just as I need your help. You are a rare magician.

You have seen God and faced him down, if you are to be believed, which I think you are. Whatever awaits me when I find the true young Edward, I want you at my side.'

Greatbelly came into the church, a meat cleaver in her hand.

'Is he in there?'

'He's here,' said Montagu.

She bustled towards him.

'You're all right. I'm glad. I'm sorry, Dow, we tried to make you something you're not.'

'How many men remain loyal?'

'How many remain alive? Cornwall is on your side, mostly, some of the men of Wales, but the new converts from London and the marshes have pledged faith to Edward if he allows them to keep their spoils to themselves.'

'I need to remain here,' said Dow. 'I need to be with Lucifer's friends.'

Greatbelly knelt and hugged him to her.

'No. You cannot be here for now.'

'Come with me,' said Montagu. 'There is more than one way to shake a king.'

'And who will speak with Lucifer's voice here? Who will establish Eden?'

Greatbelly kissed him on the top of his head.

'I will,' she said. 'Who better than a whore to haggle with powerful men?'

PART 3

1348-1350

The years of the Great Pestilence

I

Far below, far below, they saw a great port under a penny moon, white walls stark in the silver light.

The port was almost empty of ships and all around the walls, laid out for a league around the city, were the tents of what must have been a huge army. Siege engines and earthworks surrounded the walls, and a great herd of horses grazed beyond the limit of the tents. Out at sea, a string of ships sat bobbing like vultures waiting for a lion to drop.

Montagu and Dow spiralled downwards, ever downwards, caught in the angel-feather cloaks' cocoons of light. They spun as they fell and Dow felt the familiar surge of nausea brought on by their magic flight.

Montagu caught his breath as he saw they were tumbling towards a high tower. The windows were surely too narrow for them to pass through. But pass through they did, landing with a soft thump upon the floor of a deeply carpeted room. At first Dow thought he had stepped into a fire, but he saw that the room was decked in gold and carpets strewn with precious gems. One wall hanging showed the night sky, the swirl of the stars picked out in diamonds, and another Christ on the Cross, His blood rubies, His skin silver against cloth of gold.

A fine feast was set upon an altar – fruits and meats, a calf's head, the eyes vacant, the meat partly picked away so that the creature seemed to grin down at him.

Montagu retched. He was on all fours, his head spinning, his body weak. Dow, however, stood. There were men about them, swords and knives drawn. He smelled incense and felt the heat of a fire. Words were gabbled in a tongue Montagu half understood. Spanish? Italian.

They were seized, disarmed, the angel feather cloaks stripped. A blue light in the chamber. One of them had drawn Montagu's sword Arondight, that had been Lancelot's. Another held up Dow's heavy falchion. Montagu was bright red, sweating; he tried to stand but he was kicked to the floor by a heavily built man who wore a gem-studded surcoat in the Italian style. There was something odd about him. Montagu focused. The man's head was misshapen, formless, almost like a wax figure, made by a child who had then pushed its thumb into it. Were Montagu's eyes full of water? No, the man's head was really like that.

Montagu had a terrible urge to sink into sleep, as a drowning man might suddenly want to give in to the pull of the water.

'We are English, come for King Edward's true son!' said Montagu.

'Kill them,' said a voice, in English, as if for his benefit.

'No, no, no!' Something crossed his vision. A pair of rich red boots.

Montagu forced his eyes upwards to discover he was looking at Edward III, or rather, Edward as he had known him when he was young – sixteen or seventeen – when they'd conspired to wrest back power from the tyrant Mortimer. The voice was not Edward's, though, but a foreigner's, heavily accented. Italian almost certainly, Genoese at a guess. This young Edward was dressed in the Italian fashion – in a very short tunic, red embroidered with silver swallows. He was paler than his father, slimmer. There was one other in the room beside the young man and the creature with the smudged head, though the third was behind the other two and Montagu only got a sense of him when his sword had been stripped away.

'It's you,' said Montagu. 'True prince of England.'

The man took Montagu by the arm.

'Who are you?' he said.

'They are assassins, sir, sent by the Tartars to kill you.' The thing with the misshapen head spoke in English too, its mouth no more than a flap.

'Do Tartars send Englishmen?' said the prince. 'And such weaklings?'

'They send anyone.' From behind the prince and the devil a short, powerful man in a tunic bearing a white fluted cross emerged.

Montagu recognised it as the livery of the Knights Hospitaller. He knew well what they were – magical middle-men, who had absorbed the Order of the Templars and forced its magicians to do their bidding. He had fought with them and against them, but you could say that for a lot of people.

The Hospitaller held Arondight in his hand, the blue light of the sword's steel sharp even under the lamplight.

'Allow us to dispatch these rogues, sir,' said the devil.

'Why does this one call me a prince?'

'Because that is what you are,' said Montagu, 'taken from your cot in a bargain between Isabella, your grandmother, and the devils who backed her rise against her husband.'

'My grandmother?'

'And an enemy of God.'

Even as he said it, Montagu felt a tinge of betrayal. He had betrayed his best friend, the king, in lying with his mother, cuckolded the king's father – no matter everyone had believed him dead. In penance for his crime he had sought damnation, thrown himself in with these Luciferians.

The Hospitaller strode forward with Arondight raised, but the young man held up his hand to stop him.

'I am Giovanni Doria, Prince of Centola,' he said. 'My grandmother was Maria, and I should know because I sat at her knee. Why should I listen to beggars, even when they come clad in shining cloaks?'

Montagu still could not stand.

'I am William Montagu, Baron Montagu, right hand of Edward II, king of England and France. I am no beggar, sir.'

'Then why do you dress in rags?'

'In imitation of Christ.' Montagu found his grim sense of humour had not been weakened by the travel.

A great noise outside. The shouts and curses of many men. Giovanni, as he called himself, crossed himself.

'The horde at the gate, sir, no more. They won't attack in numbers at night,' said the Hospitaller.

Montagu had enough strength to move himself to sitting. *The horde? The Golden Horde of fearsome Tartars?* That meant they were in the east.

'Where are we?' he said.

The Hospitaller and Giovanni exchanged glances.

'You don't know?' said Giovanni.

'We travelled here by God's will,' he said.

'By Lucifer's.' Dow's voice was a whisper.

The Hospitaller lunged at the boy with Arondight, but Giovanni quickly and expertly tripped him as he advanced.

'I have not finished questioning these men,' he said.

'They are devil worshippers,' said the Hospitaller.

More noise at the gate – huge cries.

'I've told you to put down your sword,' said Giovanni. 'As prince and your God-appointed master, I command you.'

It had to be Edward's son. That temper, so quick to boil, the way he stepped forward to confront the Hospitaller as if he was on the verge of striking him.

'Let me fetch more men. We moved you here to protect you from the likes of these, sir!'

'And a fine job it's done,' he said. 'Look at them. Neither of these men can stand, let alone threaten me. Get your "more men". I will discourse with them in private. Allow none in until I say so.'

'You'll be on your own, sir.'

'On my own with a good sword against two invalids. If I can fight off four Tartars, I can deal with these. You, too, devil, go!'

So it was a devil, a servant of God. Montagu had concluded it seemed too stupid to be a demon.

They left the room as he commanded. Giovanni – Edward, as he should be known – went to the small window and gazed out.

'You are really the right hand of the king?'

'I was.'

'You speak like a man of breeding. It's good to talk to a near equal. These Templars are base men, low knights for the most part.'

'A man is more comfortable with those of his own station,' said Montagu.

'Indeed.' He peered harder out of the window. 'If they get in they'll kill me, which will be a pity.'

'And all of us,' said Montagu. 'Isn't that what Tartars do?'

'They do. As, to be fair, so do we to them. They are heathens, knowing not God nor the salvation of Heaven.'

He turned back to Montagu.

'It's because of me they are here.'

'They invade a town to get to one man?'

'I killed one of theirs.'

'A prince.'

'A holy man, or magician. He offended my honour.'

'In what way?'

'He said I would bring about the end of the world,' said Giovanni, lightly.

'They say that of many men.'

'Not of me,' said the prince. 'Not and live.'

'So you fled?'

'We did. We were lucky to have met them outside of their city. They would not let me in.'

'Why? You Genoese trade with the heathens.'

'We do. Again, I think it was this magician's insistence that I would cause their ruin.'

'Why did they not just strike you down?'

'At first they seemed afraid of me,' he said. 'Then the death of their holy fellow hardened them up. They demanded Caffa give me up. But this is my city – the Hospitallers who serve me have a garrison here. There was no chance of that.'

The sound of the battle outside floated over his words. Montagu couldn't help feeling that a prince should be at the front of his men, but he said nothing. He felt very ill still, the taste of vomit in his mouth. The youth Dow crouched, sweating. The blood was issuing from his mouth again.

Giovanni saw him glance at Dow. 'Why do two sick men invade my room by magic?'

'The magic itself weakens us.'

'These Hospitallers are attended by devils,' he said. 'That is something I hadn't realised before my journey to the east.'

'Why were you going there?'

'To enjoy the hospitality of their leader. The Hospitallers' oracles had predicted something was coming for me. Perhaps they meant you.'

'We haven't come to kill you.'

'No, but you will.'

Montagu was puzzled by that.

'Then why don't you have us killed?'

'And defy the will of God?' he said. 'I know what I am. I know why I am here. I come from a corrupted line. I am a corruption – so much has been revealed to me in prayer and fasting. The holy man was right. I am the end of the world and, though for years I sought to avoid that fate, I now see it is impossible to do so. When fate appears in a flash of light in a high, fortified tower in the middle of a siege, you know there is no way of running from it. God has had enough of man, it is time to start again. But my angel has revealed that.'

'If you have an angel, call it against this horde!' said Montagu. 'You are not of a corrupted line. You are the pure prince. The corruption takes your name and your honour.'

Giovanni smiled. 'I was six when the angel first appeared to me. It explained who I was. I have royal blood in me, true, or it would not have come. But the Plantagenets were founded on a union with a devil. This was not meant to be, for God says only men must rule over other men. Devils are servants and must not rise to greatness over his lower creations.'

'Your line is corrupt?'

'Geoffrey, who founded our line, lay with a devil. Every child since has carried the devil's blood.'

'That is against God's holy will!'

'Yes. But God does not control all those he commands.'

Montagu found he was shaking. *The whole line? King Edward too?* Well, he was the boy's father. *Yes.*

'Did your father know?'

'I don't know. The angel appeared to me. Perhaps it would appear to him.'

'Angels never appeared to him, I know that.'

'Then he may not have known.'

'So why not go to the woods and be a hermit? Give up all this.'

'I was afraid. Hard for a man to admit, but I was. But now I see that God has put me in an inescapable position. He thinks the time is right. I can flee him no longer.'

'For what?'

'He is sick of the people of the earth, disgusted by them. The last time he did for them by flood. This time he will let their inner corruption eat them alive. It requires only the magic to do it. A drop of angel's blood. Or rather, half-angel. Corruption will mix with corruption and multiply many times. "I heard a great voice out of the temple saying to the seven angels, Go your ways, and pour out the vials of the wrath of God upon the earth. And the first went, and poured out his vial upon the earth; and there fell a noisome and grievous sore upon the men." I will bring the angel to pour the first vial.'

'Is that God's will or your will?'

'I am but a vessel for the will of the Lord.'

Montagu had seen too much magic to doubt its effect but he could not sit by and see this man conjure a spell to destroy creation. Could it be done?

Dow let out a great cough and the blood burst from his nose again.

'The Lord has given us a sign,' said Giovanni.

He took a fine cloth from a table and wiped Dow's nose.

'He has done miraculous things?' he said.

'He has.'

'Then this is him. My mirror. The king's blood corrupted by angel and by devil. The angel told me he would come.'

A great crash and a roar from the horde. Giovanni went back to the window.

'The gates,' said Giovanni. 'They could not last for ever.'

Montagu tried to get up but he was still too weak.

'I will call the angel,' said Giovanni. 'And we will end this.'

'Those cloaks,' said Montagu, 'are of angels' feathers. Put one on and wish to be away. You will be there before you know.'

Giovanni glanced towards the cloaks.

'I wish to be in Heaven. And may get there if I serve the Lord.'

He locked the door to the tower and brought down a heavy bar.

'Can you stand?' he said.

'I am weak.'

Giovanni proffered him Arondight, hilt first.

'For yourself, then, if all goes wrong.'

'I will not kill myself.'

'You must have care for your soul.'

'I don't care for my soul, I care for my reputation. Let me be eaten by devils but I will not take a coward's way out.'

'Is the sword holy?'

'It was Lancelot's.'

'Then hold it close. You will need all the relics you can get.'

'What of him?' Montagu gestured to Dow.

'He is safest of all.'

A hammering at the door. A voice in Genoese. Montagu understood a little. 'Sir. Now.' – that was all.

'The head Hospitaller,' said Giovanni. 'I think they know my destiny and were seeking to keep me from it. As I too sought. Now no more.'

He bowed before the altar, crossed himself and sank to his knees.

'Malakh ha-Mavet, who gave Moses the soot to throw before Pharaoh. Destroying angel, who took the firstborn but passed by at the sign of the blood of the paschal lamb. Sword of God, holy abomination, come to me now. There is brightness here for you to extinguish, beauty to be annulled. You are God's vengeance who undoes all the works of man. Now undo man himself.'

Montagu felt the air thicken. His head swam and his guts contracted. He gripped Arondight and prayed to St Anne, whose tooth was in the pommel of his sword.

'Mother of the mother of God, be at my side now as you have been in my every battle.' Guilt bubbled up inside him. Hadn't he vowed to be damned? Here he was begging the saint for aid, like a child in the dark.

The air became grey. A smell of burning filled up the chamber. At the door, the Hospitallers hammered and shouted. Other voices were now close, harsh and alien. The horde had entered the keep? How? Bribery or cowardice, doubtless. Much easier to get through the doors of a great tower by targeting human weakness rather than that of iron and wood. Men offered their life can quickly forget their vows to their masters.

The boy Dow was on his knees. His front was covered in blood which still dripped from his nose and mouth.

Giovanni went on, 'Bearer of plagues, he who raised the flood the Ark floated upon, choking smoke, thing of night and the fogs, come now.'

Above the altar a smudge of smoke formed – an almost perfect circle, dark and turbulent.

'Ender of days, purifier, he who never knew Eden, come to me now. End the world!'

Montagu got to his feet, fighting nausea, fighting dizziness. He had to kill this madman before he could go through with such a foul magic. If this was God's will then Montagu was, as he had willed himself to be, God's enemy. He grasped Arondight. The saint's voice rang in his head, high and clear. She was still with him. Holy Mary's mother stood at his side. He saw her before him, in a shimmer of blue light. Giovanni was on his knees; it would only take one blow to kill him.

'Give me strength, Lady.' He staggered towards his man.

'Be healed,' said the saint. The lady stretched out her hand but not towards Montagu – towards Dow.

The boy got to his feet. The circle of smoke contracted to a black dot not bigger than a fist.

Montagu raised the sword and Dow charged him, dragging him down.

The circle exploded in an instant and all the gold and fine jewels were turned black, as if coated by a dark frost.

'What are you doing?' said Montagu.

'Beginning again,' said Dow.

'He wants to destroy humanity,' said Montagu.

'I can save it – those that deserve it,' said Dow.

Giovanni stood up, his arms wide.

'Purge the earth as you told me that you would. Destroy everything so God might deny Lucifer his second Eden!'

'He opposes you!' said Montagu. 'He intends to see you fail! Listen to him.'

'Intends,' said Dow, as if spitting something from his mouth. 'What did the mouse intend when it woke the cat?' He stood up.

'Bring your diseased angel!'

'Where is the seed for such a calamitous weed? Where the spark to light a fire to burn the world?' The voice was like the fall of earth on a coffin lid and it came from nowhere.

'Corruption on corruption, bad blood on bad blood, the man-angel and the devil man's blood mixed!' said Giovanni.

He held up the cloth he had soaked in Dow's blood and drew a knife.

'No!' Montagu summoned his last reserve of strength and leapt at Giovanni, swinging Arondight in a big circle. Giovanni's head fell from his shoulders, a fountain of blood hitting the ceiling of the room, splattering over Montagu and over Dow.

Dow put his fingers to his lips.

'You cannot fight the will of God, Montagu.'

'Though you do!'

'Yes, I do.'

Dow rubbed his fingers together, mixing his own blood with that of Giovanni.

The sounds of battle faded to nothing. Montagu felt as if turned to stone. Even Dow seemed paralysed. The only thing that moved was the blood trickling across the stone floor from the stump of Giovanni's neck. Something was wrong with the way the blood flowed, thought Montagu. His thoughts seemed unwieldy, slow to react, like an ill-trained horse. What was wrong with the blood? Oh no. It was flowing the wrong way, back into the body of Giovanni.

The sounds crashed back in. The first time he'd seen a shambles at the market, where they slaughtered the cattle in the street, he had fainted. He'd been four years old. His nurse had taken him back there again and again until he was inured to it. A Montagu couldn't quail at the sight of blood. It was that first feeling that seized him now – terror, incomprehension, pity even.

'Are you here?' shouted Dow. 'Are you here?'

A ram was at the door, battering and smashing, the wood splintering under the assault.

Giovanni's headless body got up to its hands and knees, searching for the head.

'I like you better blind,' said Dow.

He took up the eyeless calf's head and set it on the stump of the neck. The arms reached up to settle it, as if putting on a hat.

'Come,' said Dow. 'Earth is yours.'

The door went through and the horde were upon them, the little squat men with their sallow faces, their swords and their smiling eyes. A wild-haired man who bore a staff of skulls was at their front. He pointed to the monstrous thing Giovanni had become and said a word that could only mean 'Kill!'

They fell upon it. Its body fell apart under their blows, chopped to a carcass, limbs severed, torso split by seven or eight heavy blows. The men of the horde did not stop when it fell but carried on hacking, smashing and stamping. Dow dragged Montagu as far from the door as he could, picking up his falchion from where the Templar had left it.

The man with the staff pointed it at Dow and spoke, in Genoese, or what Montagu assumed was Genoese. One of the languages of the Holy Roman Empire. He bowed and put forward a big purse – the size of a small bag, though finely stitched in goatskin. Montagu opened it. It was full of gold. Montagu could not believe it. He was offering to pay for the damage that had been caused. My God, he had truly only wanted Giovanni and now he looked to restore normal trading relations with Genoa.

'Give it to my friend,' said Dow. 'It will be too heavy for me to carry.' He pointed at Montagu

The man shook his head. He put his hand into the air, his gesture indicating 'higher'. He was asking for the ruler of Caffa, or whoever was the ruler now that so much slaughter had been done.

Dow shrugged. The room was becoming colder. The black frost deepened on the gold and the jewels. The men of the horde glanced at each other. Their breath pushed plumes of steam into the air of the room. The man with the staff and the bag of gold put his hand to his throat, his companions too. They choked and spluttered, fumbled for support on the walls but they were dying, Montagu could see, great boils sprouting from them, their skin breaking in corruption. They fell, writhing and crying out.

From the floor, the ravaged remains of Giovanni's body reassembled themselves, each finding its brother but not quite in the order they had been. The ribs were inside out, exposed, the lungs and heart visible within – at first still, now twitching and glistening. The exposed bone of an arm found the joint of a shoulder, a bloody leg reunited with a hip but a skinless shin joined the wrong way round. The thing reached out and set the calf's head on its shoulders and stood uncertainly from the floor, as the calf that had given its head once had when born naturally from its mother.

It lifted its bloody nostrils to the air and sniffed. The thing was blind!

It craned its head, as if seeking advice.

'I will guide you.'

'Kill it!' said Montagu. 'Kill it! It's an abomination.'

Again, the creature craned its head.

Dow took his little pipe from his pocket and lifted it to his lips, playing a peasant's tune. Montagu recalled the words.

> Fowles in the frith,
> The fishes in the flood,
> And I must go mad
> Much sorrow I walk with
> For beast of boon and blood.

The creature turned to Dow and took a pace towards him.

'All of them,' said Dow, 'from the richest to the poorest. Humanity is corrupted. We'll have Eden again and we will start anew.'

The creature gave a slow nod. Then it opened its mouth and out poured a black multitude, a gushing, flowing river of hopping, biting fleas. Montagu gasped as he tried uselessly to stop the creatures pouring over him. He could not and, in a moment, he was dead.

2

The Pope, to Isabella's surprise, rejected her request for a meeting. No explanation, no elaboration, and she wondered if it had been wise to deliver the letter by a clanking stoneskin. It was well established now that devils served God, but perhaps the Pope was of an older outlook that uncharitably viewed anything with horns, wings and a tail as an enemy of the Almighty.

This was a setback, for sure, but Isabella had waited long enough for her Mortimer. She could wait a little longer.

She made preparations for the arrival of Eu, not least a brief correspondence with interested parties in France. She would go to a convent, bide her time and wait for the dice to fall. She would raise no more devils and live the life of a penitent until God recognised her plight and gave her an audience with the Pope. Yes, she saw what needed to be done. Charles of Navarre must be guided on his way to power, but not in a way that might strengthen her son's hand. He wrote back to her to thank her for the spells she had sent him and suggested that the Count of Eu might be the ideal man to further both their aims.

Eu arrived at the Cheylesmore Lodge a few days after the Feast of the Assumption, a long evening in August. He was received by her maids and given lodgings and food for the night. She had decided she would greet him the next morning as, though she was keen to get down to business, great ladies do not come scuttling downstairs to greet mere counts.

She received him in the morning room, the walls draped with the best tapestries requisitioned from the rich guilds of Coventry. Most of them had been acceptable scenes of hunting – one, pleasingly, of her marriage to old King Edward – but one, from the Dyers' Guild, was rather puzzling. It depicted two men taking a sheet from a barrel while another, richly dressed, held what must be an abacus and gazed into the distance, as if into the future.

After Eu had greeted her correctly, set a little vial of perfume in a silvered bottle before her as a gift, she dismissed her ladies and his men.

'What do you think of that?' she said, nodding at the tapestry.

Eu studied it with a look of mild surprise.

'Did you choose it?'

'No, I hung it here for its curiosity value. Odd, is it not?'

'Very odd,' said Eu.

'Who could think that a dyer, no matter how rich he had made himself, no matter that he be richer than a king, could be thought a suitable subject for a tapestry?'

'A dyer, presumably.'

'They have thoughts?'

'Thoughts cost nothing. They are available to rich and poor alike.'

'I shall have you marked for a man of Lucifer,' she said, smiling, leaning forward almost as if to touch him on the hand but then withdrawing slightly.

She saw she had his attention. Isabella had ridden at the head of an army and knew what it was like to face battle, though she had not been raised to it, like a knight. In this, though – this courtly dance of flirtation, teasing, suggestion of favours material or perhaps more that might be granted should the target of her art bend to her will – she was without equal. She saw Eu's eyes narrow. He knew what men had done for her – setting forward thinking they were fulfilling their destinies with spear and sword in their hands, when all the time they were simply fulfilling hers.

'What can we make of this?' she said. 'I have seen tapestries before that show the low people toiling but always in their place – harvesting, smithing, threshing or building under the eye of the nobleman, his hawk upon his arm. Can work – necessary, trifling, sweating, dirty work – be placed on a par with the acts of princes?'

'If no one works, the acts of princes do not get done. The smith that beats the sword, the cook that feeds the army are as necessary in their way as the paladin who strides the field, a bane to all his foes.'

Isabella puckered her lips and widened her eyes as if she had just been told a rather off-colour joke.

'You *are* a man of Lucifer!'

'Let's just say I have been in war, great Lady.'

'And I too. But I never imagined that the farmer who made the hay for my horse was as important as me, at the head of the battle.'

'Not as important, Lady, but important nevertheless – as the beetle gobbled by the goose is as important to its presence at table.'

Isabella waved her hand like a lady dealing with a midge.

'I did not bring you here to talk of the barbarities of the modern age.'

He inclined his head.

'I have certain communications in my possession,' she said. 'From the king of Navarre.'

'He has been a stalwart defender of mine at the Paris court.'

'Well, yes and no. More no, actually. You are aware he would see himself king?'

'Impossible. His family surrendered their right years ago.'

Isabella smiled, as if to a slow child who has produced an amusing, if wholly wrong, answer to a simple question.

Eu caught her meaning. 'There are other men in that position. King John. His son Charles. The Valois line is secure.'

'It would not be so if the English have another Crécy.'

'Hardly likely. Mistakes were made that day that will not be repeated.'

'My son, Edward, has not given up his claim to France.'

Eu sat up straight.

'He will find it harder to make his way this time.'

'He has Calais.'

'A city under the control of a whore, at the neck of marshes that may as well be the neck of a bag, so securely do they hold him. When Calais is France it is a valuable trading port. When it is English it may as well be under siege.'

Again, Isabella smiled.

'Do you imagine my son couldn't fight his way out if he pleased?'

'Yes I do, or he would not be in there. His bowmen are heretics and blasphemers. Many of them have never had a proper roof over their heads. They have no will to move from that town.'

'There are other bowmen. And other entrances.'

'Where?' She saw that Eu was rattled. He almost stood.

'Normandy.'

'I can think of ten good castles and as many good towns he would need to overthrow to get through there again. The Norman lords are safe under the command of the King of Navarre.' The words seemed to drop from his mouth like misfired gunstones.

Isabella widened her arms.

'Last time,' she said, 'we fought largely alone. Gascons, yes, and other men of wider Aquitaine. But with the Normans on side too—'

'Would Navarre be so treacherous?'

She opened a bag at her side and took out a document.

Eu picked it up and read. It was a letter from the king of Navarre. It promised access to his Norman lands for an English invading force, military help, and an understanding that Edward would be king of half of France, he the other half. The letters seemed to swim before his eyes. It was Navarre's hand, for sure, his big childish scrawl – Eu had seen it on enough official documents at the French court.

'How did you get this?'

'I am not without friends at Windsor.'

'Why are you showing me it?'

'Why do you think?'

'I have no idea.'

She leant forward, suddenly intense.

'You only need to know that I do not wish this escapade to succeed.'

Eu studied the letter again. Yes, it was Navarre's scrawly hand. It could not be mistaken. He read on. His benefactor, the man he had thought would help him, was secretly planning his country's downfall. So why offer to help Eu? Was Navarre playing a double game? Did he hope to betray the English, defeat them and then . . .

Of course. Eu would be back in France, beholden to Navarre, in his debt. This was Navarre's way of becoming constable. Were the

English too stupid to see that? Was Isabella? Or perhaps it was a truly subtle plan, one of hoped for outcomes and contingency positions. Maybe Navarre would betray the English; maybe he wouldn't. Eu bristled. Did Navarre think he could be bought like a market day pig? Did he think France could be bargained away in the same manner?

'With Navarre's help, with the Black Prince so much older, so much stronger than at Crécy, you cannot guarantee its failure, ma'am. Already Princess Joan travels to be wed at Castile. That will be a mighty alliance.'

'She will never make it,' said Isabella.

'She might, she . . .'

Isabella fixed him with her cold blue eyes. My God, what kind of monster was this woman, who would kill her own granddaughter?

She went on, as if discussing the price of spice on the Leadenhall market.

'What if the plot were exposed? What if, instead of a welcome party in Normandy, my son met with the flower of French chivalry, ready to defend their lands? Might such a victory not encourage a French angel to return?'

Eu puckered his lips, as if trying a new food and deciding if he liked it or not.

'It might. Or might not.'

'An angel needs to return. I have need of one.'

'You are English!'

'An Englishwoman, true,' she said in her perfect court French. 'I see no chance of an angel coming to England – we are in league with every kind of fiend. If one comes to France you may be sure I will speak to it. But you need it more. France needs the emissaries of God among it again, doing its bidding. Would not the slaying of a great imposter, a devil in the role that God set for man, please the angels?'

'Navarre?'

'Yes. But one even greater too. I could hand you my grandson. You could pick your time to remove him from the English ranks. His sudden disappearance on the morning of battle would affright the entire English army. And it would please God, I believe.'

Eu remained calm, though she saw the sheen of sweat on his brow.

'Then the rumours are true.'

'The true prince was taken as an infant and replaced with that thing.'

'Does Edward know?'

'I don't think he believed me.'

'At Crécy he let him be sorely tested.'

'And by you at the tournament, if my spies tell me true. He knows – he must.'

'I think he tried to have him killed. By me.'

'I doubt it. My son is direct, and if he wanted the creature dead he would be dead. More likely he was seeking to confirm what he already suspected.'

'To what end?'

'The Black Prince is a devil, and a very powerful one. If Satan has placed an emissary as heir to the throne of England, then Satan has a purpose. That means he wants something and can be bargained with.'

'More devils.'

'Directly obtained.'

Eu laughed. 'With you removed from the reckoning.'

'Indeed.' She smiled.

'So you have not moved against the prince?'

'I am moving against it. This is why you are here. Because God's interests and my interests no longer coincide with those of my son and this thing he has invented called England. My son has been my enemy since he dragged my love Mortimer from my arms and butchered him at Tyburn. I cannot have him stronger. I cannot have him independent.'

Eu looked ready to bolt for the door.

'I will pay your ransom,' she said.

'That . . .'

He did not want to say it, but surely Isabella didn't have the money to cover that. She had lands, yes, and more since her escape from her prison in the east, but the amount Edward wanted would test the French crown, let alone the little English one.

'You think I haven't the money?'

He said nothing.

She took off her rings and threw them towards him, undid the fine necklace at her neck.

'You will have to add a little,' she said. 'I can give Nottingham Castle back to my son, perhaps Castle Rising too. Beyond that, everything I own.'

'Leaving you with nothing.'

'Yes. Nothing. I am sorry for what I have done and intend to live the life of a nun.'

Eu could not have been more surprised if she had said she was going to sprout wings and fly him home personally. In fact, in these days of sorcery, he would have been much less surprised.

'And in return?'

'You will be the count of Eu. It's simple, is it not? I ask no more of you than to fight for your country, rid it of evil men and resist the invader. Keep the letter for when you return. And one thing more. The prince is a devil and can be summoned like a devil, though it will take great art to do so. You must find a cunning man in France. The Hospitallers might provide someone if they don't know your purpose, or one of the old Templars. Was there not a man at court who summoned many devils for Hugh Despenser when he fought with the French?'

'There was.'

'So seek him out.'

She took out another scroll.

'I am sworn not to harm this Black Prince. Not so you. Use the cunning man, the sorcerer, whoever you can find and take this, along with certain relics I have collected. Dust from Becket's tomb, the hair of St Joan. Summon the prince to Paris and kill him there. You still have the great Charles's sword?'

'I have. They have not taken it from me.'

'Do you wonder why not? Such devils are wary around blessed items such as that. Summon him to France and kill him with whatever blessed items you can find. Do it at the just moment, exactly when it will weaken our forces most.'

'And if your son, the king should be killed?'

'Then that is God's will. Go, dear Eu. Restore your France, save it from the grip of idiots and evil men. And bring back its angels, for I need to speak to one.'

'You would shake nations simply to speak to an angel?'

She found herself bowing her head, as if in prayer.

'For love and for Heaven, I would cast them into the sea.'

She dismissed Eu from her room and sat down to write to Navarre.

'Eu is coming. Give him a month before you act.' She included certain spells and with them the travel itinerary of Joan of England for her journey to her new life in Castile. Then she drew out the box that contained her poisons. How many of her ladies-in-waiting were spies? All of them, she guessed. She would kill them all to be sure before she left for Navarre in case one had managed by hook or crook to find out what she was doing. She would start with that simpering wretch Alice.

'Alice!' she called. 'Alice! Attend me.'

But Alice was nowhere to be found. Isabella called for a groom. She would ride for Dover immediately.

3

'I would have loved to have seen her in her wedding dress.'

Edward clasped Philippa to him. The great devil Sloth looked on, his head bowed onto his great mane of steel rods in respect.

The queen's face was wet with tears. She made no effort to brush them away.

Joanna was dead, their daughter, killed by the Great Plague on her way to be married at Castile. Not yet fifteen, she had been Edward's favourite, and he had put great faith in the value of the alliance her marriage to the great Spanish state would bring. Now? All ashes. All ashes.

Edward tightened his jaw. He was as near to weeping as Philippa had ever seen him, but tears were not for the king. They were for other, lesser, men, women and children. The king's grief ran to anger, to the smashing of chairs, sometimes of people. Now, though, he stood almost limply, dazed. Grief had come upon him too many times. He had punched and he had kicked and he had broken and torn and what good had it done him?

'What a spectacle she should have made,' said Edward. 'What a pleasure to man and to angels. Where are the angels? Where are the angels? Where is God? Why has He forsaken me?'

Philippa crossed herself. Was Edward comparing himself to Christ? If he was, then he was a poor Christ. The only time he turned the other cheek was to drive a fist into it.

Philippa had been at the fitting. The rakematiz alone had been 150 yards long – silk, imported at huge expense. Then all her lovely clothes for the feast. They had worked a way to build corsets into two of the dresses so they were almost invisible, one dress in green rakematiz embroidered all over with roses and wild men chasing wild animals, the other brown with a base of powdered gold, woven with lions as a sign of her royal birth. Then there were the velvet suits strewn with silver, the golden corsets of stars and diamonds, the diamond hairnet, the boar brooches in tribute to her father. All these riches in Joanna's train walled in at Bordeaux by the docks, which had then been burnt and levelled by the townspeople terrified of the Plague.

'You look like you have fallen from Heaven,' her mother had said to her. And now she had gone back to it.

'The alliance is gone,' said Edward, stating the obvious.

Philippa didn't mind that he turned from the personal tragedy to the political so quickly; she knew him to be a practical man who had suffered a great many deaths of those dear to him. He had his own ways of coping and she needed to respect those.

She held his hand.

'Where is God?' he said. 'Where is God? He has never helped me, never stood by my side. One minor angel He granted me – one. Philip filled the air with his angels. And where was God when the dragon came? What does it say in Revelation? That the dragon shall be cast down! And yet it tore the angels from the sky as the hawk tears the dove. Where is God? Where is God?'

He leant against the wall, thumped it with the butt of his fist. Other men might weep. Edward raged, but Philippa could see how hurt he was. Joan was his favourite.

Philippa said nothing, bowed her head, let her tears flow. She had another burden on her heart, more and even worse than this, and she could not tell him. She was sure their son had been taken and a devil put in his place. She had swapped Eu's lance for a sharp one and it had pierced Edward's armour but the prince had not even been unhorsed. In the contest of daggers things had been different, and Philippa knew why. She had arranged for Eu to be passed a blessed dagger. So the ordinary lance had failed to wound the prince but the blessed dagger had cut him. Only one conclusion could be drawn: he was a devil. Now, what to do about it? Eu had not yet found the sorceror, though he was sending letters discreetly.

Edward thumped the wall. 'It cannot be that the high lord in his castle is struck down by this Pestilence the same as the peasant or the thrall wallowing in his shit. God would not do that. He put me here! Why would he strike at me?'

'He strikes at all Europe. The great families have lost members everywhere – Valois and Capet, Plantagenet and Habsburg. It is an evil killer, without godly distinction.'

'We have no army. Those not dead of the Plague have gone to join the Luciferians in Calais. Those who abandoned Lucifer are going back to him for fear of the disease.'

'Rule against that. Prevent them from leaving.'

'I have. It makes no difference. Keep them here and we breed ferment at home or die like summer flies. And who can issue an edict against death? If I could, I would have banned Joan from ever dying. Where is the rightness? Where the proper respect for degree and royalty? This must be a thing of the Luciferians – by any standard of decency it should only strike low men!'

'Imagine how our Joanna would have shone beneath the sun of Castile.'

'Her glory would have matched that magnificent orb,' said Sloth.

Edward did not hear them, it seemed. He was doing what he always did: turning his mind to practical matters to avoid being overwhelmed by grief. He'd done so whenever a child of his had died, and there had been many. William, Thomas, and William of Windsor again within the last year, the little boy dead of Plague. Blanche too, dead before her first year. Each loss she felt keenly and she knew he did in his way but he was a man and a king. He did not dwell on grief but threw himself into action, to forget his pain.

'We rely on devils. They are all we have. So we are in my mother's power,' he said.

'They owe fealty to you.'

'We are still in her power. I do not like it.'

A messenger came in, a boy. He hesitated in front of the king but Edward waved for him to speak.

'The Lady Alice,' he said. 'Travelled from Coventry.'

'My mother's girl?'

'Not today,' said Philippa. 'Don't let's see her today.'

She had been a childhood companion of Joanna's – raised in the same household, along with Prince Edward. The reminder was too sharp.

Edward touched her arm. 'The state goes on. Our family goes on. England, whatever that means, goes on. My mother is our protection. We must discover what she is up to.'

'Then we are protected by a wolf.'

Edward took her other hand, looked into her eyes. 'The angels are gone. France has its sorcerer and its devils. We have my mother's sorceries and a handful of pacts with people who should be our sworn enemies, the stinking dogs of Lucifer. We cannot do without her.'

The girl Alice was shown into the room. She broke Philippa's heart. She was a lady from Cambridge, brought up with Joanna by Marie de De St Pol among books and scholars. They had been friends until the princess's duties had called her back to court and Philippa could not bear to see her now, expecting to see little Joan scurrying in behind her, still eight, still five, still twelve – still any age but dead.

The lady bowed.

'You know the news?' said Edward.

From the tears on the girl's face, Philippa knew that she did. Alice inclined her head.

'You have news of my mother?'

'She has met Eu's ransom price. I have the money and the deeds with me. He is on his way to France.'

'What? Why? Wait, I can't take this in. My mother has given me her castles?'

'Along with the county of Guisnes in France, which belonged to Eu.'

'For what purpose?'

'She is aiming to become a saint.'

Edward actually laughed, incredulous.

'Why?'

'She has not said, but her devils have gone. She has become a nun and seeks God's guidance. She will travel to see the Pope, when the Pope is a man who will see her. Clement has refused her request but she says popes do not live for ever.'

Edward shook his head. 'She must be stopped. No good will come of that.'

'She sailed yesterday.'

'For which convent?'

'She did not say.'

'And Eu?'

'Gone too. He has taken a boat from Dover.'

Edward looked to Lord Sloth.

'Can you catch him?'

'Where is he headed?'

'Calais is not available to him. He will not risk Flanders. Further south, then?'

'You should intercept your mother too,' said Philippa.

Edward turned to her. For the first time in her life she saw scorn on his face.

'She is a queen. No devil will raise its hand against her.' He softened. 'And she is on a pilgrimage. How would that weigh with God?'

'Then Eu?'

'He must die. Sloth, see to it.'

'People will say you took his ransom and betrayed him,' said Philippa.

'I will kill him off the coast of France. He will be released from my pleasure by the time he dies.'

'If he reaches France we cannot touch him. Philip is forbidding devils on the coast. He is the king,' said Sloth.

'I am the king of France!' screamed Edward. The lion bowed its great head.

'I recognise that,' said Sloth. 'But others may not. It will not make things easy.'

'So you go and kill him now, then!'

'Edward, if your lieutenant butchers him then people will call you betrayer again. No one will ever pay a ransom in future,' said Philippa.

This time, Edward kicked a chair, smashing straight through its back.

The Alice girl lowered her eyes. Philippa didn't quite like her. Too clever for her own good, like all the de Châtillon women. Her mother, they said, had been maid, wife and widow all on the same day when her first husband was killed during a joust at their wedding celebration. She had been left with a massive fortune and a taste in weak, rich husbands who died too young.

'And why did you not tell us of this as soon as it happened? Does not my husband furnish you with winged devils to relay information?'

'The queen placed a circle around the lodge in Coventry. No devil could approach. She refused to release me or any of her other ladies from her sight.'

The queen had a lump in her throat.

'But she didn't take you with her?'

'She has gone alone with only two knights for protection.'

'It's us that will need the protection!' said Philippa. 'What can this mean?'

Alice bowed her head. 'I heard her talking to Count Eu. I pressed my ear to the wall and heard what she would do.'

'Which is?'

'They will use magic to draw Prince Edward to Paris. There they will slaughter him.' Everyone in the room, the lion included, crossed themselves.

'What magic could compel a prince of the blood?' said Edward. 'If such were possible, half the crowned heads of Europe would be disappearing, their children with them.'

Philippa crossed herself. A prince could not be summoned by magic. But a devil? Yes. So Isabella knew. Had she always known?

'I cannot say, for fear,' said Alice, 'though I know it might be done. Let me tell you in a roundabout way, as befits one bearing bad news to a king and fearing their majesty. Let me show you by story and hint what I mean.'

'You can speak plainly here, child, no one will harm you.'

Alice's eyes went to the splintered chair. She dipped her knees.

'My lady Isabella has books.'

'What books?'

'Of contracts. With devils.'

'We know that certain queens of the great houses of Europe have always possessed certain magical arts. You know her ability with devils,' said Edward.

'I have no such art!' said Philippa.

'You're from Hainault,' said Edward. 'I married you for your beauty, not for sorcery.'

'Particularly of line Capet, which is tangled with your own. The Valois queens lack such art.'

'My mother is an accomplished sorceress,' said Edward. 'Only a fool would deny it.'

'Well, where did such powers come? Where did they strike bargains with devils in the first place?'

'There is the rumour about the count of Anjou. His wife was said to be a devil. She flew through the window of the church at Gâtinais when they tried to baptise her children.'

'Why would a devil fear such a thing? They are God's servants.'

'Not all devils are content to serve any more, it seems.' Alice opened the little bag she had with her.

'I took this from your mother's secret drawer. She has many such books and this is the littlest and least read of any of them, though she keeps it in her travelling chests. By night at Coventry she flew through the window, but first beguiled her ladies with a sleep magic. She had done it before and I, who suspected her, took the precaution of anointing my eyes with holy oil from the martyr's tomb at Canterbury that night. I did not sleep and I stole this from her.'

'Thou shalt not steal!' said Philippa.

'Thou shalt not do a hundred things,' said Edward.

'God lists but ten.'

'He lists far more than that, as you know, and men still do as they please.'

'Edward!' She had never seen him like this. He was often angry but this was something more. He looked as if he was boiling from the inside.

'What does the book say?' he cried out, as if in anguish.

'You need to read it yourself.' Alice pressed it into his arms. 'Read it and then decide if you can let its contents be known. The murder of the prince is not the limit of your mother's ambition.'

'What else does she want?'

Alice curtsied. 'My Lord, I fear to tell you.'

'Is it worse than the murder of our son?' said Edward.

Alice kept her eyes on the floor and said nothing.

'Speak, girl!' said Edward.

'I do not know how, but she seeks to bring Mortimer back from the dead, as the French brought back Despenser.'

Philippa looked to Edward. His face was white with fury. The meaning of that was clear. Isabella intended to be queen in her own right again, with Mortimer beside her as king.

'She was ever an unnatural woman,' said Philippa.

'Can she do it?' said Edward quietly.

'Ask the friars of Coventry or the priest at St Michael's of that town. There was some strange business there. Monks died, devils ran riot, and the queen hurried to make her confession,' said Alice.

Edward looked to Sloth. 'Bring the priest of St Michael's.'

'He won't break the vow of confession,' said Philippa.

'He will break it,' said Edward. 'The Lord Sloth will see to that.'

Philippa touched her husband's arm.

'What will you do?'

'What needs to be done,' he said.

'You cannot hurt a priest! Edward!'

He turned away from her. 'Call the prince – he needs to be warned about this attack upon his person,' he said to his retainers.

Philippa ran from the courtyard. She needed to get a message to St Michael's as soon as she could. The priest would have to hide.

4

New joys, or old joys experienced in new ways. Charles had always loved to prowl the rooftops, to look in on people in their most private moments, unseen. To watch a child sleeping in its bed, or an old man snoring hard enough to wake Heaven. To see a girl comb her hair, or even a grown man piss in a bowl, was to have something no one else had – to be like God, sharing in moments that his people imagined they shared with no one.

Now, at Pamplona, in the heat of the summer night, he felt restless. A storm had ambled in during the day – a half-hearted affair that had failed to clear the air and left big clouds obscuring the moon. It was dark – though his eyes were keen. Spatters of rain fell still. Charles was on the roof of the Plaza de Castillo– the central 'palace' of Pamplona. This was no true palace but in reality a sparsely furnished castle. Pamplona was a fighting town, clinging to the bowl of its valley like a burnt pastry to a pan as the Moors, the Castilians and God knew who else tried to chip it away. He had come south to avoid the Plague that was sweeping the country. Inaccessible little Navarre had so far avoided the worst of the carnage that was happening elsewhere. Charles took heart from the Pestilence, felt emboldened. Had he not vowed destruction on France? And now that destruction had come, turning the unforgiving, craggy landscape of his kingdom into a fortress against the disease that was sweeping the world.

Still, it offered no sort of luxury to one born in Paris. Thick walls, high towers. Charles was hot and stripped off his fine shirt, his boots too. His cats were restless, nervous of the weather but keen to seek out the pigeons and doves of the roofs, winding around his legs as if to push him on, hold him back, impel and impede him all in the same movement.

He had left his perfumed kerchiefs behind, for the world smelled clean up there. The wet smell of the rain thrilled him, the warm splat on his bare skin, even the mild breeze. It was an itchy night, a night that wanted things done.

He stretched, thin and lithe like a cat, or like the cat devil his mother had lain with rather than extend his father's weak and subservient line.

He ran across the roofs, almost silent, delighting to slip and regain his balance, teetering above the wet cobbles, so far below. Should he jump? Would he land? He knew he could leap from a high tree without hurting himself – as a boy, he'd dared the count of Amiens' son to follow him and the idiot had broken a leg. Charles had not associated with him so much after that. He wanted friends who were . . . springier.

His cats followed him along the rooftops. This pleased him. He had been working on a motto that he would adopt when he took full control of the kingdom from his mother: *Qui sequitur me non sequi.* Those who follow no one, follow me. Or something like that. He'd written it himself and all the scholars he'd asked to check it were too scared to correct him, even if it was wrong. That was pleasing. Charles was beginning to think that the threatened exercise of power was more appealing than to exercise it for real.

He stopped at a window. There a whole family of eight slept in a single bed, boiling each other up. They had cast back the shutters, careless of biting flies, in order to gain a little cool. It felt good to sit and know that he could step in, light a candle and burn them all to death; to know he had that power. He would never use it, but he could use it. It sat snug in his pocket, so to speak, a little secret he shared with no one.

He needed the release from tension. His aunt Isabella had given him the words by which a great magic might be done and the itinerary of Joan's progress to Castile. He had dispatched assassins to intercept her. But at Bordeaux, Joan, her entourage and his assassins had all been taken by the Plague, walled in to the port, and burnt before her heart could be taken. To Charles, this seemed a cruel waste.

Later, he would not remember when the idea to visit his mother occurred to him. It was by chance, if anything. The windows of the castle were designed for war, not comfort, and he had barely been able to wriggle out of the one to his chamber. His mother, however, had a more luxurious lodging, higher than his.

He stood on the edge of the highest parapet of the fortress, looking out over the night. A few lights still burned, the odd candle here and there, but the town largely lay grey like something undersea – the sea of Northern France, not the Ethiopic Ocean of the south. For the first time he felt like he had something in common with the place. It was like a dark flower, waiting to bloom, a wash of seaweed waiting to be beached and show its colours to the sun.

The rain grew stronger and he scaled down the outside of the keep, using the big stone waterspouts as platforms, hopping each to each.

He swung easily into his mother's room. It was only then he realised how wet from the rain he was and that he had left his shirt on the roof.

The room had a rich aroma of perfume and fart. One lady lay in the bed with his mother, the thin little girl – well, girl of his own age – sent down by the Norman lords. The other ladies lay on a broad pallet at the bottom of the bed. They were lightly clothed in their pale nightdresses. Charles studied their forms, the sweep of their torsos in a grand S, listened to their soft breathing. He had never cared much for women, nor for men, in the carnal sense. His mind had never run that way before. But now he wondered what it would be like to put his hands on the soft sweating form of Lady Escors or on that of Lady Aumale; to rearrange her dress so that her big breasts were visible; to strip and pose these women in their sleep, to see how their various curves fell together, in what patterns and what new shapes.

He padded to the side of his mother's bed. The Norman girl was dark and pretty, her mouth pursed as if she might whistle as she slept. She had a fine down on her top lip, red lips, olive skin, as smooth as an olive's as well. His mother, asleep, looked old. Her mouth was lined and her jaw slack. Her skin had darkened in the sun of the south, despite her best efforts, and now her startlingly blonde Capetian hair seemed even whiter by contrast. What was she capable of? Of calling a cat devil from the pit of Hell and fucking it right there on the bed.

He wondered how he had been conceived. What was the arrangement? Did it go behind her? Did she pleasure it in some other way and rub its seed into her? He wondered exactly what this devil had looked like. He had never asked. A great cat? A man cat? A man with a cat's head? Had it been Sloth, the English lion? No, she had specified cat. He laughed silently to himself. His mother should have asked for a lion, a mighty leopard. Perhaps he then would have turned out three yards tall like Sloth, with breath like a blow from a mace. He licked his teeth and pulled down the front of his mother's nightdress to expose the top of her chest. It was white, pale. Yes, she had darkened in the sun and no mistake.

He felt a great tenderness towards her. She had battled for him, raised him well, protected him from enemies and taught him to cultivate the right friends. She had made him subtle and thoughtful. But she had underestimated him. He could not be controlled. A cat cannot be herded, much less a king. A king needs to be cruel. He kissed her on the forehead.

If only she would submit to him. She stirred in her sleep, her lips parting. What had his father known? Had she enjoyed her time with the devil? He wanted to touch her but the feeling disturbed him. Instead he leant across and touched the Norman girl on the shoulder. She did not stir. He slid his hand down and touched her breast. He felt angry, violent, alive. Why?

Because he held the power. Silent, unobserved, looking in at a window, he controlled everything – to stay, to leave, to kill if he'd ever had the urge. But she, even asleep, commanded him, called his cock to attention, made him want to please her so she would say what an excellent fellow he was to satisfy her so.

He turned his attention back to his mother. She was a truly beautiful woman, or had been. She was thirty-five now. Dry forage, as the poets said, on the cusp of old age. She looked peaceful as she slept, one of those faces that seemed made to be rendered in stone on a tomb. She would wither, become like the dried out old hen who slept at the bottom of her bed. What had she to live for? The next two or three years, before men would trust him to run his own affairs? And was she not a saintly woman? She had built churches, gone on pilgrimages and now had protected the grave of a great king from desecration. She would go to Heaven, she had done penance for her sins.

He had strangled his mother before he had time to stop himself. Later he would try not to remember it, try not to enjoy it: the sensation of the pulse at her neck, racing and then fading; the sudden kick that almost woke the girl; his mother's eyes opening, calm. His mother was a royal lady until the end – she would show no dismay, no fear, as she faced death. The death throes were sweet to him, sweet as the surrender of the pigeon is to the cat. Her neck was already blooming into red welts as he crossed himself.

What I am now? What am I now? He flexed his muscles. The lady-in-waiting stirred. He would have to go.

He trembled, alive, the taste of salt in his mouth. He had killed a queen. No devil could do that, no snivelling jailer of the Pit. Royals killed royals and never without the blessing of God. He felt like the child he had never truly been, exultant and terrified all at once. His eyes filled and he crossed himself again. He thought to cut out her heart there and then. It would be a powerful relic. But he had no knife. He would leave that to other, lower, lesser men.

'Good night, Mama,' he mouthed, and kissed her on her red lips. Then he slipped from the window, swinging down to his own room and his snoring, drunken grooms to wait for the screams.

5

Through lowlands and highlands, fields and wood, Dow played his little pipe and the carcass creature followed, black with flies and fleas. Through crystal dawns and ruby sunsets, seasons of snow and seasons of sun, he walked and it followed – the fleas, and death in their wake. Dow gave his odd companion a name – Butcher, for it reminded him of the carcasses you see on a market stall.

He visited rich towns and laid them to waste, little villages and tiny farmsteads. When he walked in he found the bloom of life. When he walked away again the bloom was withered to the stem.

His ympe Murmur was long gone, appalled by the destruction. But Dow did not see destruction. He saw the corpses as seeds from which would grow the new Eden. Sometimes he lost his way, returned the way he had come. When he did so he saw wild flowers and brambles snaking over the farmers' tilled laines, walls crumbling, thatch fallen in. All this in just a year. Within ten years the earth would be as it was again when the first humans walked upon it. Those that survived would have learned Lucifer's lesson of justice and comradeship, learned to work together without greed or wish to better a neighbour, to be truly glad of the gift of breath the bright angel breathed into them at the first.

Champions came to face him – some, anyway. He knew what he was – a rumour, a story on the breeze, spread by penitents and frightened children, whoever Lucifer allowed to survive an encounter with him and his monster. He saw the whipping men, marching in lines down the old pilgrim routes, thrashing their backs raw. Man had sinned and must return to God, punish himself. Dow had smiled at that. As if corruption was a devil that could be thrashed out with a scourge.

When God had risen up against the creator Lucifer, he had offered to put some men above others, make some kings and and cast others down as beggars, if only they would worship him. Dow had imagined that only the kings had agreed to this bargain and worked to oppress other men. At Calais, and other places, he had seen that God may have offered all men a choice: I will raise some, lower others; you will not know where you stand until I say so. Men would accept that, he thought, the chance of rising up above their brothers enough to accept the risk of being cast down beneath them. That same impulse had not died when God set His order in place, the desire to rise on the backs of others, be it in ever such a small way. Humanity was irredeemable.

So start again. Kill the men and the women, the fathers and mothers, the child on the breast, the old man in his bed. Kill the pigs in the byre and the sheep in the fields. Kill the dogs who ate their corpses, if that is what it took to restore Eden.

Knights came to face him but died before they could fix a lance, spluttering from their horses, collapsing in a crash of mail.

'You are Death,' said one.

'No,' said Dow. 'I am life. I am rebirth. I am the winter that comes before the spring.'

'These are the final days,' he said. 'This is the apocalypse.'

'God is not coming. I am preparing the earth for one much greater than he.'

The knight spat at him and died.

No true war in the country now – the odd English band passing by with fire and rape, then dying among the piles of its own booty. Surely now, surely, man must learn his lesson. Surely his eyes must open. But no. Still he saw looting, scenes of depravity and murder where people had taken the power of death into their own hands as the bow wave of the Plague approached.

Over one village, he saw the flag of Lucifer flying, the three-pronged pitchfork, the symbol of oppression turned into one of liberation. Or so he had thought.

He approached at nightfall, for a moment leaving his pipe unplayed, Butcher standing beneath the dappled moonlight of a wood, a glistening horror in the silver beauty. He approached, walking in unchallenged. All the familiar sounds were about him – the weeping of women. No, not weeping. You could not call it that. It was a convulsion of grief, something beyond ordinary misery, the music of Hell.

It was summer, the air warm, fires dancing at the village centre, a tinge of smoke in the air. Bodies lined the main track between the houses; not the bloated victims of Plague but those of violence – red limbs, cracked skulls, entrails grey and wormy. It meant nothing to him now, or perhaps the sight pleased him. These bodies were the fertiliser for the shoots of the new world, the soil bed from which they would spring. All corruption purged, all weakness gone. He thought of the words of the Bible, spoken by Lucifer in his guise as Christ: 'The meek shall inherit the earth.' They would, indeed they would, because such a glut of violence would be visited on the earth that men could never think of violence or personal gain again.

Shadows across a bonfire. A woman was being chased – or rather shoved – from man to man, suffering the fate of women in war and its aftermath. A little boy was clinging to her, desperate.

Dow looked on with compassion but with no thought to intervene. A purge was happening, a letting of the world's blood, and he was the barber with the razor. Such things would continue to happen until they happened no more, and then they would never happen again.

'Hey!'

'Hold up! Who in the name of the devil's dick are you?'

He had been seen. Swords were drawn. The woman and her son were not where they were before. He couldn't tell where they were.

'A friend.'

'We've got no friends here, friend,' said a voice. He couldn't see the men; they were just shadows against the fire.

'Not your friend,' said Dow.

'Then whose?'

'Lucifer's. The original light.'

'Then you are a friend,' said the voice. 'Come and join us at our fire.'

Dow walked forward. He was surprised to see that the men he had been speaking to were no more than boys, really. Fourteen years old, maybe fifteen. They were dressed in the booty of war:

fine jackets, beaverskin hats. One wore a well-wrought silver bowl as a hat.

The woman had been caught again and recommenced her begging.

'Cut her throat,' said someone. The child, though it could not have spoken the English of its tormentors, caught the meaning and let out an enormous howl.

'You are men of Lucifer?' said Dow.

'We march under his banner. It brings terror,' said the boy in the silver bowl.

'Doesn't Lucifer preach love?'

'We're about to give her some love,' said the boy. 'Banners, flags. What of them? The lords have struck a truce so we must make our own war. We can do what we want.'

'And this is what you want?'

The boy opened his arms, shrugged deeply. 'Yes. What else is there?'

Dow felt enormous compassion for him. This boy could not imagine himself in a merchant's house, surrounded by servants. He could not imagine himself in Eden, giving and sharing companionship and love. He had been preyed upon, spat upon, trodden down by lords and masters. The only thing he could imagine was to tread and prey himself, to move through the world like a pestilence until physic cured him or there was nothing left to kill. *You have come from nothing, you offer nothing and you are going to nothing*, he thought. *My poor, vicious child.*

Dow watched the woman struggling against two youths.

'I'm hungry,' he said.

'Plenty of food here,' said the man-boy.

He offered Dow a small loaf. He took it, broke it. Someone killed the child, stabbed it, kicked it to the ground.

'The bread's fresh,' said Dow, under the screams of the woman.

'We were lucky here. The first in this village. Rich pickings! Though there are others behind us. They say there's plague to the east.'

'Yes. Do you have beer?'

They had the woman now, two holding, one on top of her.

The boy picked a bottle off the ground. It was sealed with wax and cloth. Dow broke it off. The yeast tasted good on his tongue.

This wasn't drinking beer, the everyday ale, but celebration beer – made to get you drunk.

'Will you kill her?' said Dow.

'You can have a go before we do, if you're worried.'

'I'm not worried. There is no tenderness to it.'

The boy looked at him oddly. 'You are a fighting man?'

'Yes.'

The woman bit one of the men and he cursed terribly.

'You have no band, no company?'

'I did but they betrayed me.'

'How so?'

'It doesn't matter,' said Dow. 'It's a sweet night. We have a fire, food and companionship. Let me play for you.'

'I would like that,' said the boy.

'So would I.'

He set his pipe to his lips and began his tune as someone beat the woman to death, fists thumping out a broken rhythm.

'That is a sad air,' said the boy.

Dow paused his playing. 'Yes. But we hope for better times, do we not?'

'What times could be better than these? We are lords of the earth.'

'I have played for lords before.' Again he played, the firelight dancing on the face of the boy. Two other youths came back, one nursing his hand.

'The bitch bit me,' he said. 'You have a minstrel here? You play well, friend.'

Dow carried on. One of the boys, drunk, danced a comic jig, his breeches still around his ankles from his moment of fun.

Then: 'There's something moving out there!' The boy in the bowl hat pointed back down the main track of the village.

'Who's there?' Another youth had an axe in his hand. 'If these are friends of yours, piper, say so. And be sure that if they bear us ill will I'll split your skull before ever you stand.'

Dow kept playing.

'Who's there?' The boy pulled up his breeches. He looked so young, thought Dow, so young.

'Who's there?' The boy with the axe had his hand on Dow's shoulder. Others emerged from the darkness. An older man.

'Raiders? French?' he said.

'Ah!' The boy with the axe smacked his neck with his hand.

Dow kept playing.

'Shut that pipe up,' said the older man. A big fly smacked into his forehead and he moved to swat it, too late.

'Something's moving, something—'

More flies thumped against the men. Other things too.

'Fleas! I'm lousy with fleas. Ah! Ah!'

Dow played on, the same simple tune repeating itself again and again.

'Are you doing this? Are you a sorcerer? Are you—' He never finished his sentence, his eyes rolling in his head as he fell.

Only the boy with the silver bowl for a hat survived the night and, Dow saw, he would not see midday. He was soaked in sweat, a great pustule under his chin, his eyes sunken, blood at his nose. He scrunched up his eyes, tried to turn away from the sight of Butcher.

'Who are you?' he said to Dow.

Dow did not answer him.

'Save me.'

Dow shook his head. 'I cannot. You were lost the day you were born. Be happy. We are starting the world anew. And when we have it new, we will empty Hell of those who deserve to be free. Perhaps you will be one of them.'

'Lucifer says all will be free.'

'That may no longer be possible. You came from Calais?'

'Yes.'

Dow pointed ahead of him.

'That road is the correct one?'

But the boy died before he could reply.

6

The cathedral itself could have been a fort – its sturdy square columns rising high into the afternoon sun, the arches of its windows small, looking better suited to keeping siege stones out than letting God in. Outside, the people of Pamplona thronged in the white sun, all the colours the poor little town could muster on display, like a field of fading flowers. The talk, of course, was of the queen's death, but also of the Pestilence. It had yet to touch Pamplona and people said it was the king's virtue that kept it away.

Charles's coronation was to be combined with his mother's funeral – emphasising the strength of his claim to the throne; no matter that the new king had the eyes of a cat and was attended by six prowling mousers.

Charles trembled, dabbed a vial of perfume on his handkerchief and breathed in, trying to lose himself in the smell of cloves. He could still feel the sensation of his mother's neck under the pressure of his fingers, the brief moment she had put her hands to his forearms to fend him away before relaxing. Had she welcomed death? Had she realised at the last that the future of her line was more important than her existence? He thought of her, and he thought of the Norman girl who had lain in the bed next to her, the softness that seemed to radiate from her in her sleep. He felt hot and confused. He should ask for her to be brought to him. Perhaps, though, he shouldn't. He didn't like the way she made him feel.

He had thought that when his mother had gone, all uncertainty would be removed from his life. But the manner of her death – her neck in his hands, that girl besides her, the female smell of rosewater, lavender and musk . . . Everything before had been clear, and everything after too. But it was as if the moment of his mother's death had a life beyond the instant it occurred. Ever since, he had always been in that chamber, the Norman girl's breath in his mind, the dim arch of the windows, shapes that would be unseen by ordinary eyes. He would never forget it. Would he ever want to? Charles flexed, stiffened every muscle in his body, and relaxed. It seemed something beyond his power to decide about, more like a lingering taste in the mouth than a thought.

His brother had come: solid Philip of Longueville, only thirteen years old, four younger than Charles, but so imposing physically – big, muscular, his forehead jutting low over suspicious eyes. He was dressed in blue and yellow, as fine as a peacock. Philip gave the impression of spoiling for a fight even asleep in a chair. Charles was pleased to see him after so long, and embraced him.

'I take it the restraint of our mother's years is now over,' said Longueville.

'We will tread carefully,' said Charles. 'But our enemies will sleep less easily in their beds tonight.'

'I'd help them sleep,' said Longueville, patting the big sword he wore on his hip.

'You will have every chance, brother.'

Longueville gripped Charles's arm. 'You have nothing to fear from my direction. I know well we are a small kingdom and stand or fall together. You are clever, brother. I would benefit from that. I am strong. You can benefit from that. Think of me as your instrument. I will be your sword.'

Charles wondered if his brother had been put up to that speech by an adviser. If so, it was a good one. Could he trust his brother? He'd see. There would be a task for him when he was old enough to perform it, something to bind them.

'Is my sister here?'

'I saw her train behind me.'

'She has arrived late,' said Charles.

'She fears you, brother.'

'A dutiful sister has nothing to fear from me.'

Longueville smiled. 'Perhaps it is the duty she fears.'

'She certainly hasn't done it with Peter of Castile.'

'He had a say in the matter.'

'Only because his father indulges him.'

'We should press him more greatly now the English girl has been dealt with.'

'I have bigger ambitions for her.'

Into the square before the cathedral came two tall outriders on coal-black horses, sporting the golden castle of Castile on their red surcoats. Clattering behind them, his sister's coach, accompanied by six more riders, red and gold pennants streaming from their lances. Behind that came the coaches of her ladies, pack mules and servants bringing up the rear.

Blanche had come from Castile, where she was at the court of Alfonso, trying to flutter her eyelashes at his oldest son, Peter. It had met with failure. Peter was not to Blanche's liking, nor, it seemed, she to his. He had developed an affection for blonde women, whereas her hair was as dark and deep as sable fur, like her father's. Beside that, he had the violent temper of many of the Burgundian kings. She had managed to wriggle free of her obligations by a combination of wit and charm, and then Joan of England had come along to save her. Blanche Sagesse – Blanche the Wise – was what her friends called her. Blanche the bloody awkward, Charles called her. With a little more effort, a little more willingness to get on her back, she could have won him, he was sure. He needed Castile on his side as leverage against La Cerda. She could have taken a few bruises and kicks up the arse for that. Still, now there were bigger fish to fry.

A knight opened the door of her carriage and she stepped down. The mob in the square would later say it was as if the sun had emerged from behind a cloud, as if a base cloth had been removed to reveal a priceless jewel beneath. The mob were never much for poetry but, when he looked back in future years, Charles would be forced to agree with them. All the women of his family were beautiful but some seemed possessed of a deeper allure. Like his aunt Isabella, here was a woman who could make a country fall in love with her. But unlike his aunt, she was his subject. She would be useful.

Blanche bowed to Charles. 'King. Brother. My dearest Charles.'

She was a vision – two years older than him at nineteen, dressed in a long blue cote-hardie tailored tight to her body in the latest style.

'Do you have Peter yet?' He, of course, knew that she did not.

She gave a little moué with her mouth. 'He's not interested in plain old me.'

'You don't look that plain to me. You are going to have to land me a king sooner or later, you know. If you need instruction in womanly tricks, half my mother's ladies were old sluts, I'm sure they could offer some pointers.'

'There are strumpets enough in Castile, if I should ever need such advice, which I'm sure I should not, being a lady of high virtue.'

'The point is to remain of high virtue while suggesting that, should he marry you, you will perform deeds to make the whore of Babylon blush.'

'Thank you for that, brother. You have developed the customary kingly bluntness rather quickly, I see.'

Charles smiled. He hardly knew his sister, really. She'd gone to Castile at twelve, and before that had largely been at the family estates in Normandy. Still, he liked her. No spaniel, to flip onto her back in submission. He looked hard at Blanche. Did he recognise something of himself in her? Her eyes, her manner of tilting her head. Catlike? Had his mother, who had lain with a devil to sire him, lain with one to beget her too? He hoped not. It would make his plans for her difficult. He concluded he was being overly worrisome. All the women of the family had a bit of bite about them. None more so than the one now arriving.

It was his aunt Isabella – dressed as a poor sister and carried on the back of a donkey. She was attended by five nuns and only one knight. Overdoing the penitent thing, he thought, but then there were always spies around. He'd seen a stoneskin flapping to the roof of the castle. At whose command? Perhaps the Pope or Edward would hear of her lowly state and do – what? Her motivations were opaque to him.

'Now here's a woman who gets what she wants.'

Isabella dismounted the donkey. No nun ever dismounted like that – more like a squire trying to show off at a tournament than a bride of Christ.

Charles kissed his aunt's hand. He felt no thrill like other men said they felt when they saw her, let alone touched her. His mouth was dry. Did his devilish nature help him resist her? Or was it something else?

'Your convent is comfortable?'

'No,' she said. 'But that's rather the point. Penitence and all that.'

She smiled briefly.

'I have what we need,' he whispered.

'I guessed you might. Did your mother pass by fortune or design?'

'God blesses me.'

'Well, we're about to see, aren't we?' She crossed herself. The gesture irritated Charles. There was a slight nervousness to it. He liked to think of her as bold and fearless.

'The angel has received me before.'

'In a half-hearted way, if the stories I heard were true. Things may be clearer now you are unambiguously the king.'

'I was unambiguously the king before!'

She put her hand on his shoulder.

'Then perhaps you should have dug old Richard's heart up and left your mother to her sewing,' she said quietly.

A stoneskin settled on the spire of the cathedral, black against the cerulean blue of the sky.

'Is that yours?' Charles asked.

'I need some protection.'

'I wish you would keep it away. It frightens the people. This is little Pamplona, not London where devils are everyday sights.'

'It is a servant of God.'

'A point that is largely lost on the mob.'

'What do you care what the mob think?'

'They are useful. Aunt, tell it to leave. No, don't. You cannot be seen to command it.'

'My stoneskins are useful too. I hear tell of La Cerda. Strange news from the south.'

'What news?'

'He has taken some southern fortress, no more than a pile of rocks, and is brewing foul sorceries there.' She sounded like a grand lady pretending to be shocked by some minor court scandal.

'Then let us brew a sorcery of our own.' The stoneskin flapped and readjusted itself. 'After the angel is summoned, I'll blast it to atoms.'

'It will appear when you are crowned?'

'It should.'

His aunt was disturbing to him now. So like his mother – blonde and pale, delicate hands. He had never seen Isabella's power to move men before. Now he understood it more. Her eyes were like a cat's, though not in the way his were. They had the slink and slide of a cat winding at your feet – pulling you on, pushing you away.

'You have the heart?'

'In a vase by her body.'

'You are truly a resourceful boy. I will need to watch you.'

'We will guard you from night prowlers, from demons and beasts, for as long as we are friends.'

'Then let us always be friends.'

Was that, thought Charles, *a declaration of war?* No. His aunt needed him.

They entered through the high doors, into the massive interior, cool after the sun of the hot day. Already priests were awaiting them, his mother's body laid out in front of the high altar, draped in a sparkling cloth of gold. The angel wasn't there, it seemed, though it could not fail to appear with so much royalty present. Could it? There were two people notably missing. His uncle John, prince of France. John's father too, Philip, the king. He had not expected him to come, but Charles had high hopes John would have made the effort. They had sent a message and he would have delayed the coronation, if only there had been a reply. But there was no reply.

The nobles filed in behind him, the gentry behind them, and the lower folk who could shove and squeeze their way through the doors behind them. Charles felt his eyes fill with tears as he approached his mother to kiss her. She smelled of frankincense and the bitter herbs she had been stuffed with to preserve her in the southern summer. If only she hadn't been so . . . So *there*. Always in the way.

He turned to the congregation.

'We know well who did this. The demons of the poor, flying by night. My mother was a good and kindly woman who did not deserve this fate. I pray to God that they send such a demon for me so I may send it back to Hell.'

He drew his sword.

'Too long has Navarre knelt, been bullied by Castile, gone begging when it might have gone armed for war with demands and threats. I will make this country great again. I will avenge, with my own hands, the death of my mother, the . . .'

The Norman girl was standing to his right, he noticed, her eyes red with tears.

He stalled, his breath catching. Then he said, 'We will cry no more. If there are to be tears in our lands they will be those of our enemies, brought here in chains. I am the end of tears. I am the beginning of light, of glory, of riches beyond imagining.'

As if on cue the angel inhabited the angled sunbeams of the church, turning them to the appearance of flowing silver water.

'We are blessed by God!' shouted Charles.

'Amen!' said the congregation

'Welcome, Asbeel!' said Charles. 'Come and dwell in the beauty of our church, of our crown.'

A shitty church, a shitty crown. No wonder the archangels dwelt in the beauty of St Denis or the Sainte-Chapelle. This scraggy little angel was the best they could attract in Navarre. And yet it was more than all of France and England had for the moment.

'There is blood.' The voice was like the shifting of sand in a rattle, like the stirring of the sea. The beams of light turned red. The congregation breathed in, as if in echo.

'The blood of kings that flows in my veins,' said Charles.

The light deepened to purple, as if his royalty had been respected by the angel and it had answered with the best of colours.

'Not all royal blood flows here.'

God's cobs, the thing had chosen the moment of his coronation to start making sense, and the worst sort.

'Respect us,' said Isabella. 'Respect me, scion of so many royal houses; respect Charles who God has raised to this position.'

Now the light split into glittering silver snowflakes that filled the church but never settled on the body. A beautiful chill came into the room, the sound of chimes and music.

'God has work for you,' said the angel.

Charles raised his sword again and the congregation applauded.

'God raises you up.'

Wild applause.

'High is the precipice. Would you throw yourself down?'

Isabella was on her knees, the congregation following suit. She mouthed prayers and crossed herself.

'Will you lead our armies?' Charles asked.

'We will deal with you. Lady, the leader is near. He is shaping the light. He is taking form.'

The thing had stopped making sense again. Charles liked it better like that.

'How shall we go on, how shall we proceed?'

'The poor,' said the angel. 'Use the poor. A time of trial. A time of darkness. You have something.'

'I have the heart of a queen,' said Charles, under his breath.

'And what would you have for that?'

'A weapon against my enemy.'

'A bribe to the jailers of Hell,' said the angel. 'For a time I would be free of the struggle, of the stink.'

What was it on about? This angel had long been perplexing.

Blanche walked out of the congregation, up to her brother.

Her eyes were on the shifting light, her hands raised.

'For a while. Friend, free me,' said the angel.

'You are mad and cannot be allowed through.' Where did that voice come from? Rasping, like a devil's.

This was not going the way Charles had expected.

'In here?' His sister pointed to the silver vase containing the heart.

'In there.'

'Sister!' Charles went to stop her, but she had picked up the vase.

'Free me!'

Why did an angel need freeing? They could be everywhere.

Blanche pulled the stopper from the vase and raised it up to the shifting light.

'Free me.'

She upended the vase and took out the heart.

'Here,' she said. 'Here.'

The blood coursed down her arm. Dark clouds boiled in the vault of the church. The people fell to the floor, abasing themselves. A voice, like the moan of the wind.

'You will undo all our schemes, sister, you will undo them all,' said Charles.

'I will fulfil them!' said Blanche.

The great cloud descended on her like a vortex. Lightning flashed and the air turned to ozone. Charles felt the hair stand up all over his body. Thunder, and his sister fell to the floor. The lower people panicked and ran, the nobles remained gawping. Only the Norman girl came forward to help his sister. Isabella seemed dumbstruck, staring up at the ceiling.

'All is beauty. All is beauty!' said Blanche.

'Blanche! Blanche!' said Charles.

'I am Asbeel,' said his sister. 'Trapped in Hell when the gates shut on the bright enemy Lucifer. I have been a long time shining in the darkness.'

Her beauty was the beauty of the heart of a jewel, and all men who saw her fell in love with her so they were as stone statues, rooted where they stood.

Isabella smiled.

'You will need,' she said to Charles, 'to keep her in a veil.'

7

Philippa stood from where she knelt, her knees stiff despite the prayer cushion. These days, she was hardly ever not at prayer and her knees were not thanking her for it. She looked out from her chamber window over the fields of Windsor, the river silver under a clipped coin moon. She had spent many such nights here since the death of Joanna, restless, tired, praying for an answer from God, fearing to receive one.

She felt cooped up at Windsor, though she was glad of the protection its walls gave from the blue sickness that was ravaging the country like the angel of death. Worse than the angel of death. In Egypt that had only taken the firstborn son. This affliction took everyone. They had suffered at Windsor, but nothing like what had gone on in the wider country. She heard tell of towns where everyone and everything died, down to the dogs in the street. Edward told her it had even hit Scotland now – the Scots swooping down over the border to plunder the dying English and laugh at God's judgement on them. Most of the clansmen hadn't even made it home, and those who had brought pestilence trailing with them. A grim loot indeed. This was the puzzling thing about the Pestilence – it made no distinction for rank, for country or family. If God had sent a plague to punish the English then why punish the Scots too?

She had thought that the Plague had visited those who had made pacts with devils – as England had done – but the Scots had no such pact. No devil had accompanied them on their raids; no demon either. It made no sense at all. She crossed herself. Was it true, what they said? God had made Satan to keep Lucifer, the rebellious angel, in Hell? That devils were the jailers of Hell, demons the lost souls and fallen angels that were imprisoned there.

It seemed to be so, and now the English court was thick with the creatures – most notably the hideous Lord Sloth, the Iron Lion. She had seen him eat a three year old bullock at one sitting, uncooked.

At her back, her ladies dozed. She crossed herself, said a prayer for the living and the dead. Old Goedelle, who had come with her when she had married Edward, snuffled and turned, her snores like someone dragging a table. She had thought many times to have her removed from her bedchamber, but Goedelle had been with her so long and served so loyally that it would seem too great a slight. And at least she had survived. So many had not.

Her daughter's costume from the Round Table Tourney still lay across a chair, as if it might stand and magically fill with the living Joanna. She kept that in her memory in favour of any more ladylike dress. She remembered her on that day, dressed as Lancelot. The older folk were scandalised to see women dressed as men, but surely a little colour and adventure was allowable. She wished the old folk were still alive to be scandalised, the young who had shocked them, too.

The night was warm for April and the smell of the fields and woods was sweet in her nose. Some old smell of fern suddenly recalled home – Hainault, all those years ago – and she had a longing for the foods of her youth. Her cooks had never got the hang of eels in green, nor rabbit in beer, nor any of the other dishes in which she had delighted as a girl.

Joanna would not leave her mind. It was as if she stood beside her, bright, lively, lovely Joanna. She had never liked Prince Edward, though she had been raised with him at Marie de St Pol's manor in Cambridge. She crossed herself again. That lady had been suggested by Queen Isabella, the king's sorcerous mother, and accepted without protest by her son. Was St Pol chosen for a reason? Such thoughts have a life at midnight and scuttle like rats in the attic of the brain.

She knelt to pray again. But she did not know what to pray.

The air was very still, she thought; even old Goedelle her maid had stopped her snoring.

'God Almighty, I am your servant Philippa. I . . .'

She thought of all the other people like her, pious souls on their knees for God, begging Him to relent in His persecution of the world. Kings and queens, priests and, no doubt, the Pope had prayed for remission of the Pestilence. And yet nothing.

She knelt for a long time, as if the pain in her knees would in some way please God and make Him take the Plague away. She felt hot tears on her face as she murmured her daughter's name. Even this felt selfish, full of pride. Why was her loss so much more important to her than that of the rest of humanity? England was a country of the dead and she, a royal, whose God-appointed task it was to protect the people, had been powerless.

'Forgive me, Lord. Forgive me. Forgive us.'

Goedelle stirred in her sleep. 'He's here,' she said. 'He's here.'

Her tone almost made Philippa laugh – indignant, as if someone doubted her. She thought hard, though, on what Goedelle had seen in her dream.

Eventually she stood and went back to the window, listening for the night birds, the call of the owl or the nightingale.

Down by the river she saw a flash of blue, like a piece of the day let in to the night. It came and went in a blink, so quickly she wasn't sure her eyes weren't playing tricks on her. But no, the flash again, only longer.

She crossed herself. What was it? Some devil? A will-o'-the-wisp? She thought to send word to her husband in the morning, to tell him to prevent his devils wandering the land at night, terrifying whoever remained alive. She thought to return to her bed but something stopped her. The light flashed again.

She felt drawn to it. The colour of blue was too lovely, too fascinating to be something of Hell, she thought. Behind her one of the ladies turned in her sleep. The room suddenly felt unbearably stuffy, the air too close and heavy. She would go for a walk, she thought, take in the night air. She knew, of course, what she planned to do but could not yet admit to herself she had in mind such boldness. The light, though, had ignited something in her. It had called and she felt compelled to answer.

She got out of her nightdress and pulled on a pair of hose that had been designed for a tourney – one that had been called off because of the Plague. It was a man's jacket, plain and green, too. By the day of the contest – whenever that came – it would be decked in glittering stones, but they had yet to be attached and lay in a pot by a chair. She took, too, one of the boys' swords that had been commandeered for the costumes, and stole out of the room.

France was in disarray and no threat, the land at peace, and no guards stalked the corridors of the castle nor set much of a watch at the walls. She moved down the stairs without encountering a soul.

She went out of the tower and across the courtyard to the first bailey. There was no guard there, or on the second. The whole castle looked in a state of ruin at present – Edward's mania for building sweeping the castle. A new chapel was to be erected in thanks for the Crécy victory. And, it was to be hoped, to entice the English angels back. One of Sloth's leopard men was asleep on top of the gatehouse but didn't wake as she passed through. The third gate was locked and the guards all asleep, so she lifted the latch on the postern gate and slipped through. She felt vulnerable now, the cold air of the river wafting up at her.

Another blue flash, and she made her way down the river bank towards it. In the dark of the trees she suddenly felt very foolish. What if this was some robber's trick?

Then, right next to her, his filthy face briefly illuminated by the blue – a broken man and a vagabond, hanging in rags. She wondered she hadn't smelled him. He was terribly thin, his head like a skull. It was all she could do not to cry out but she was in no danger. He fell immediately to his knees, his eyes very white in his sun-browned face.

'You are the one?'

He spoke thick French.

She didn't know what to say.

'I am.'

'He said you would come. Here, give me reward. I am starving. I am starving.'

He put out his hand. In it was a fragment of blue glass, as big as a fingernail. It shone with the light of a summer sky.

'Sir!' said the man. 'Sir, your *noblesse oblige*, sir!'

Tears streamed down his dirty face and he reached towards Philippa as if towards a vision, as if he could not quite believe her to be real.

'You are not of this country?'

'Not, sir, but I am . . .' He seemed to struggle to say what he was.

'You are?'

'I am come from there. From Gâtinais, and the church of Gâtinais. I am Tancré. All dead there, no food. This spoke to me and said come here. Do not punish me, sir, I only convey the truth.'

The light from the glass was enchanting, fascinating.

'Have you food, sir?'

She took the glass and looked closer. Inside the blue something was moving. A shadow, a fire . . . something. And then, unmistakably, the outline of a finger, pressed to the glass.

'He is trying to get out,' said Tancré. 'He is trying. An angel is coming back to France. At Gâtinais, in the church. He is coming. Have you food?'

Philippa crossed herself and stared into the glass. She saw a vision. It was her son, Edward, the Black Prince as they called him. He was himself, though horribly changed. On his head were horns, at his back a long and pointed tail. She nearly dropped the fragment, such was her shock.

'Give me reward,' said Tancré. 'I am starving.'

'Apply at the gate tomorrow. Tell them the queen orders you fed. There will be coin for you there.'

She crossed herself and ran back towards the castle, clasping the fragment of glass.

8

It was cold on the barge. The sky was an unseasonable grey, spitting with rain. Charles smelled corpse fires on the air. Paris was reeling beneath the Plague and people hurried past on the banks of the river, stooping and ducking as if expecting a bolt from Heaven. Another bolt, maybe. 1349 had proved no better than 1348, and in some ways a great deal worse.

The journey by cog to the mouth of the Seine had been perilous – English pirates were in the waters, Gascon pirates, Castilian pirates. Useless truces had been struck by Philip and Edward during the Plague but no one had told their men. The duke of Lancaster was scorching a black mark across the south, burning villages and castles to no apparent purpose; Philip dithered, refusing to send men from his attempted blockade of Calais. He spoke uselessly of a 'contagion' – not that of the Pestilence, but that of the Luciferians in their Calais slums. Paris would be next, he said, the poor and undeserving rising up against their masters in ungodly rebellion. He was more afraid of his own people than the English, it seemed. All in all, Charles concluded, things were looking up.

Charles had no fear of the common man. The people had always liked him and now those that were alive to see him had turned out to wave.

'Spare us from the affliction!' shouted a voice.

'I am here to cure you!' shouted Charles. 'I have brought with me an angel in the flesh.'

Blanche drew back her veil and the people gasped. On that grey day she did seem to glow slightly, or not exactly glow. It was as if the day had been painted by a poor artist using dull paints but she had been rendered separately, by a master using the finest, sharpest colours available.

Everyone bowed, crossed themselves, cried out to God for the mercy he was bringing. Blanche put down her veil and the barge sailed on.

'How are you going to deliver that one?' said Count Ramon at his side.

'It's a charlatan's trick,' said Charles. 'If the Plague stops, well, didn't I say it would?'

'And if it doesn't?'

'The dead won't remember I lied.'

'I wonder you bother so much about the opinion of the mob.'

'Where do we get our armies? Who do we need to suffer and sweat so we might live in luxury?'

'I despise them.' Ramon shivered at the thought of the common people.

'Of course, so do I. But it doesn't mean I can't use them.' He bowed extravagantly to the people on the bank. 'They may prove useful yet.'

Smeared on the walls of buildings, even on those of a ruined church, was the three-pronged cross of Lucifer. It seemed the people were turning to what comfort they could get.

'Would you meet with the Luciferians?'

'Not that class of mob,' said Charles. 'Traders, merchants, small craftsmen. These are the bricks on which palaces are built. If those bricks are removed, palaces can fall.'

'La Cerda's flag, Lord!' One of the pages had become rather excitable, pointing up at the formidable white walls of the City Palace.

Charles, who had been elated to come to Paris, felt a skip in his stomach.

There it was, the stinking yellow castle of Castile on its blood-red background, floating alongside the fleur-de-lys. His own flag, the chains of Navarre, was nowhere to be seen. If La Cerda actually had any influence left in Castile Charles could have understood John's love for him. But the man was an outcast. All he had, he had through John. All he had, he had taken from Charles, supplanting him as favourite.

Charles remembered when, ten years earlier, he'd travelled down this river with his mother. Then the flags of Navarre had been everywhere and a king and prince turned out to meet him. No longer. He had been raised to grow to influence in the French court, to learn what he could before overthrowing the idiot Prince John. And all had gone well, until Crécy. He'd been too confident, thought he could get away with anything.

He smiled to himself. Well, that was a mistake he intended not to make again. Lesser men might have found caution, lesser men might have backed down. Not Charles. If one roll of the dice went badly for him, he doubled his stake on the next. If that lost, double the next and the next after that, then stake your own life if needs be.

A decade before, the water had been bright as he'd passed under the last bridge before the palace. He recalled the reflection of the sunlight on its underside, like snapping mouths. He'd thought he would be the one snapping, but it seemed now as if Paris was a trap for him. A taint of poison ran through these waters and he knew who had put it there. La Cerda. If he was there, then Charles's access to Prince John might be limited. Charles adjusted the crown that sat on his head. It would be necessary to remind everyone exactly who had been set on high by God, and who below, when he arrived at court.

As they entered the city, scraggy gangs of people stood and stared, pointing at his colours, pointing at him, begging alms, forgiveness, curses, begging – he thought – for relief at having someone to beg to. Charles felt a shiver. Who did he have to beg to? Traditionally a king only had God but the king of Navarre wasn't even sure that option was open to him. Beg to yourself, he thought. At least you can be certain of a sympathetic hearing.

He'd written to tell Prince John he was coming but La Cerda might have got wind of it and come in from whichever of his rich lairs he was laid up in. Charles's spies had been able to find out very little. His enemy was away on his estates, hunting. Really? Was La Cerda the kind of man to work for an advantage so hard and then turn his back on it as soon as it arrived? Personally, he thought his aunt's tales of La Cerda's sorcery more believable. He expected to run into La Cerda sooner rather than later.

Still, perhaps he was skulking away in the countryside while the Plague raged in Paris. Charles himself had taken to the countryside of Navarre – the disease had finally torn through the crowded streets of Pamplona, killing so many. He wept for his people, for the service and taxes they brought him. The only consolation was that France had suffered as badly.

Every port they tried to dock at refused them entry, or was so stricken with the Plague that it would have been unwise to set down. Charles was unconcerned by the Great Pestilence – he felt the combination of royal and devilish blood would keep him from it. Blanche was possessed by some sort of angel, so should be all right.

While they had waited to return to Paris, he had kept Blanche in a nunnery. But then the nuns began dying and they moved her up into the mountains. She would sit for hours staring out at the moon, which gazed blankly down on her like the face of yet another, yellow-faced, pox-ridden corpse.

His petitions to be allowed into Paris had finally been successful three years after Crécy. The English had been swallowed by the Pestilence too, and truces were struck to leave killing to God for a little while. Of course, this left bands of soldiers unemployed in France and they still scoured the countryside bringing plague and war as before, but without the pretence of a kingly banner to hide beneath. Until they too succumbed. Death was everywhere, stalking the land.

Some blamed a conjunction of planets, others foul humours rising up from the earth, displaced by earthquakes in the east. Still others spoke of a living carcass that strode the land, a demon that resembled a side of beef on a butcher's hook and that breathed contagion wherever it went. Whatever had caused the Plague, Charles was warming to it, now he saw the handsome country of France reduced to wreck. He wondered if Philip could get the Plague. As a king, maybe not, but perhaps his son might contract it – or La Cerda. There was a thought. Maybe his enemy would fall to become part of the Great Mortality.

Sometimes Charles wondered if he himself had been responsible for the Pestilence, in a good way. He had wished ruin on France, hadn't he? Was God fulfilling his wish? It seemed possible and made him feel bolder. More than could be said for his retinue.

His men were a dishevelled looking bunch. Most of them were not the first choice for an elite guard but with so many dying, what could he do? He'd had to double their pay just to get them to come. All over the lands of Navarre and France, and other places too if he guessed right, the usurious poor were taking the opportunity to demand an increase in wages. With stonemasons or woodworkers dying by the hovel-full, those who remained were in high demand. By God, this was a good plague for some, a very good plague indeed. He did consider that he might be one of those lucky few. He had damned France to ruin when the angel told him he would never be its king. That had come to pass. If he had caused this devastation then he had reason to smile indeed never mind the list to the purse.

Here at the centre of the city, bodies bobbed in the water. The people just threw them in rather than bothering to bury them, it seemed.

The smell was far from pleasant.

They came to dock at the quay of the palais.

Ten years before a phalanx of minstrels had greeted him, the king and Prince John in their best clothes – in their better clothes, as in markedly and pointedly better than his.

Now the streets were almost deserted. In Pamplona, as the Plague had descended, all order had gone with it too. The merchants and the nobles couldn't sleep easy in their beds for fear the plundering poor would come in to steal their goods and rape their daughters. With all his enemies in disarray this did not concern Charles too much. He would wait out his time in France or in the countryside and then return to punish the perpetrators, or anyone who he thought looked like a perpetrator, and take the goods for himself. Yes, it was working out as a very good plague indeed.

There were three corpses on the steps of the palais. Two men and a little girl, paupers by the look of them. If he'd not helped kill the angel in the Sainte-Chapelle perhaps it would have come out and spared France. And perhaps not. The Dragon of Crécy might have driven it off, too.

He stepped from the barge and gave a tip to the tillerman. He felt like making a joke, saying, 'Thank you, Charon,' because the Seine really was like the river Styx now, truly a river of the dead. Still, he didn't. He didn't speak to lesser men unless it was strictly politic.

Blanche stood beside him in her veil. She was dressed in scarlet – to suggest sauciness – though Charles was certain she would sway John's heart had she been dressed in a serf's smock. There would be the impediment of John's current wife, but that could be seen to. So many deaths nowadays, one more would hardly be noticed.

It was September. Surely the Plague must soon be over. It had slowed in the winter the last year. Half of him hoped yes, half of him no. Typically, Paris enjoyed colder winters than Pamplona. Yet another advantage God had seen fit to bestow on it. It would be good to find that Philip's famous cooks at least had survived.

'This is a fine welcome,' said Ramon.

'The kingdom is weak,' said Charles. 'It needs a strong hand.'

'None stronger than yours, Lord.'

Charles smiled his cat's smile.

'But first the subtle paw, eh?'

His men assembled in front of him and they marched up the steps to the Palais. One young boy stood guarding it. My God, did the mob know what stood between them and the riches of the Sainte-Chapelle? Did the mob even exist any more?

'Announce the king of Navarre!' said one of his men.

The boy looked on uncomprehending.

'Announce the king of Navarre!'

Charles rolled his eyes to the grey heavens. 'He doesn't speak our language.'

My God, he was going to have to address this trembling child himself. In the days before the Plague his travelling companions had been knights, well versed in diplomacy and languages. Now he hovered at the door like a stinking debt collector. Which he was, in a way.

'Announce the king of Navarre,' said Charles, in French.

The boy gulped and nodded.

'To who?'

'To Prince John, or his footmen or . . . to the court.'

'I must stay here, that is my task. There's no one to announce it to.'

'The king isn't here?'

'I don't know. I was told to stand here, and raise the alarm if anything happened.'

'Who to?'

'The captain.'

'Then announce me to the—' Charles could hardly believe he was going to say such a thing. Announced to a captain! What next? A serving girl? A palace dog? His temper snapped.

'Get out of my way.'

'Gladly, Your Majesty.'

Charles pushed into the splendid interior. Christ's stones, it hadn't been cleaned for a month by the look of it. Discarded chicken bones lay on the floor and a rat ran down the corridor. Glass and jewels, gold and beautiful tiles, and in the middle of it all a pile of shit left by who knew what or whom. Charles had to smile to himself. *How well sits your crown, Philip, that you stole from my family? How well? Look around you and ask whose side God is on. He is on mine.*

He was surprised the interior had not been entirely stripped. But who was there to strip it? And did the people still think angels dwelt in there? Ah! He saw why. Standing next to an exquisitely rendered motif of a unicorn was a immaculately dressed young man. His tunic was of the finest green satin picked out with yellow swallows, his robe of fur magnificent and his trousers fashionably tight. Only when he bowed low was it clear that the back of his head was eaten away and writhing with bright white maggots. A devil, then.

'My Lord,' it said in a cultured Parisian accent.

'You are?'

'Simon Pastus, late of Hell,' he said, 'an ambassador sent to survey the state of the realm of men after so many summonings.'

'Sent by whom?'

'By Satan, Majesty. He whispers through the walls to me.' He bowed again, the maggots writhing foully. Charles's puffball mouser circled around his feet nervously.

Charles smiled a neat little smile.

'And what will you tell Him?'

The ambassador mirrored Charles's smile perfectly.

'What one always tells kings. Exactly what he wants to hear.'

'You are a wise creature.'

'I won my wisdom the way the true knight wins his spurs – in scars,' said Pastus.

'As all good servants must. Can you convey us to the king?'

'The king is at Vincennes,' he said, 'but John has braved the city and is upstairs. I was told to stay here, to deter any foolish pilferers. It's been quiet work, I tell you, none has come through.'

'My men will hold the hall, and you may convey me to the prince. Which of his nobles are with him?'

'Mainly lower men. Those of greater quality are staying out of the city. The younger and less favoured accompany John, the risk being worth the reward.' He coughed and struck a vaguely theatrical pose. *Odd things these devils*, thought Charles. *Odd thing I. One of them.* He would not ask about La Cerda, though he burned to do so.

'Lead,' said Charles. He told his men to stay.

They walked through the splendid but filthy palace. There were servants about, but not many, and they soon scuttled away as the royal party came through.

'New souls for Hell!' shouted Pastus as he went through the corridors. 'Who will come with me to the Lake of Fire where your sores and boils will seem as blessings?'

He smiled again at Charles. 'It alleviates the boredom.'

'The people are afraid.'

'There has been a mighty winnowing.'

'Is the Pestilence from Hell?'

'Good Lord no. Hell groans under the weight of souls who are coming to it. We of the infernal regions are a bureaucracy. We are not set up to deal with so many. Hell is becoming unbearable.'

'Isn't that rather the point?'

Pastus giggled and put his hand over his mouth, like a nun hearing a naughty secret.

'If not Hell, then where does it come from?' said Charles.

'Only God knows that.'

'Perhaps he does. Have you ever met God?'

'No. I, a low devil, no. Why do you ask, sir?'

'Oh, I was just wondering what he was like.'

The devil glanced left and right and said, as if conveying a naughty secret at a dance, 'Well, he knows how to handle a plague, doesn't he? We've seen that before. Blood magic. Ohhh!' He gave a shiver.

'Blood magic?'

'All that smearing the blood of the Paschal lamb on the door, the first plague too. "By this you will know that I am the Lord: With the staff that is in my hand I will strike the water of the Nile, and it will be changed into blood. The fish in the Nile will die, and the river will stink and the Egyptians will not be able to drink its water." It's all about blood with God – it holds a fascination for Him, I think.'

'Blood of the martyrs, blood of Christ.'

'Streaming in the heavens, as the good book says.'

Charles liked this devil. He was sophisticated, knew how to talk to high men in an interesting way without bowing and scraping or setting himself up as an equal. Much better than the country clod soldiers he'd endured during the journey down. If he hadn't needed them for appearance's sake, he'd wish them dead along with the other multitudes.

He remembered his childhood at this palace, when it had teemed with bustle and the urgency of servants and messengers about their business, aristocrats lounging against the splendid walls. Now he passed through as if in a dream, its familiar corridors altered and strange.

There were other devils there too – one with a hundred tiny human heads, another a lump with legs and no head at all. *That's luck for you*, thought Charles.

'These came with you?'

'No. They were left here when the late Hugh Despenser went to Crécy. They were to guard his treasure.'

'He has treasure?'

'Had. All taken by the crown, I'm afraid, that which wasn't lost to the English.'

'Is he in Hell again now?'

'I should say so. Much demoted, too.'

'Good.' Charles hadn't liked the arrogant Despenser, particularly after the English lord had inhabited the body of a dead angel and gone crawling all around the tower Charles lived in, in pursuit of the English killer Montagu.

Finally they came to the throne room.

A sweet gittern strummed and the smell of incense percolated under the doorway. Finally, thought Charles, civilisation.

There were guards at the door here, well dressed but unimposing. The ambassador immediately instructed them to knock and announce the king of Navarre. This they did in a thick-tongued, mumbling sort of way. What if the Plague went on? Could the servants and soldiers really get any worse? Any enemy who could muster a force to invade now would win with ease. But none could. Not in the whole disease-eaten world.

As his name was called he heard a shriek from the other side of the door which he recognised as John's voice. Then the doors flew open and there was the great lumbering John, the gittern in his hand. My God, he was playing it himself. Were all the minstrels dead?

'Cousin, you live!'

John threw his big, clumsy arms around Charles and the young man feared for an instant he might be crushed or battered by the gittern. It was as if the nightmare of the last three years had never happened and he was the prince's closest friend and confidant yet again.

'By the grace of God, sir, as I see you do too.'

'Yes, but it spares no one, this plague. It kills all, low and high, without discrimination. That I think is its most fearful aspect. It is no respecter of rank.'

'Doubtless an emanation of the Luciferians, those English vermin,' said Charles.

'Oh, quite,' said John. 'Come in, sit down. Wine! Bring my lord wine, he has been away too long and has been sorely missed.'

A dirty-looking – and to Charles's eyes rather drunk – servant stood and bowed, lolloping towards the door. Was this how the last days of Rome looked? No, no barbarians. The palais could be improved by a decent fire, he thought. Perhaps he'd start one. And perhaps not. Behind John the normal crew of musicians and poets sprawled, along with his wife Bonne. She looked promisingly pale. She would have to go, so Blanche could marry John and Charles's influence be secured for the future. With Blanche in the prince's bed, Charles would have an advantage La Cerda could only dream of.

'Your father is not here?'

'He will return in the morning. La Cerda has taken him hunting to get him out of the foul air of the city.'

'I wonder you all don't go,' said Charles.

John shrugged miserably. 'Everywhere's the same. You never know whether you're running towards or away from this plague. Might as well sit tight in the relative comfort you're used to, rather than face Nature in all her foulness. May as well die happy.' He raised his own glass. Charles's mouth watered. The cellars at the palais were famed throughout Christendom.

'I have brought my sister,' said Charles. Blanche, in her veil, curtsied behind.

'Charming,' said John. 'Have you met my wife Bonne?'

'I have not.' Blanche curtsied and Charles gave the queen an extravagant bow.

Bonne trotted over to meet them. She was still an attractive woman for her age – thirty-four, Charles calculated. He kept a mental note of the birthdays of most monarchs, the better to assess their chances of popping off any time soon. She was careworn, her face gaunt. That look had been quite fashionable until the Plague had taken hold.

Charles lowered his head.

'I saw your father die at Crécy,' he said. 'He fought like a lion.'

'It is good of you to say it,' said Bonne. 'He might be a live lion had the day been better accomplished.'

Charles nodded. 'The Genoese, ma'am. They carry the same flag as the English and may as well have been fighting for them, so knavishly did they conduct themselves.' He couldn't help but notice a slight waspishness to Bonne's comments. Still he was blamed! He was struck by a great sense of injustice. He was guilty as he had been accused, more guilty for he hadn't just been rash in leading the army forward but deliberately foolhardy. It was wrong they should think such a bad thing of a prince, though.

Bonne inclined her head.

'Let us see your face then, girl,' she said to Blanche.

The girl reached up and drew back her veil. Her beauty was unearthly, shocking, staggering.

John's jaw fell.

'Madame,' he said. 'You are beyond . . . Beyond . . .' The words choked in his throat.

Bonne put her hand to her neck. She was flushed, almost staggering.

She pointed at Blanche. 'You will have him,' she said, and dropped to the floor as if her bones had been turned to jelly.

John looked at her body, looked at Blanche.

'She is dead?'

Courtiers rushed over, felt for a pulse, pushed a tiny mirror beneath her nose.

'Dead!' said a foppish young man who knelt before her. 'Dead!'

'By God's bones,' said John, as if in a stupor. 'I must marry this lady, if she will have me.'

'I would be delighted, Most High Prince, appointed by God,' said Blanche.

Charles looked down at the corpse. *Well*, he said to himself, *That went better than I thought.*

9

Osbert had been colder, he was sure. In a life of great trials, he certainly must have been more uncomfortable. But he could not rightly recall exactly when.

The mule should have provided some warmth but it proved a begrudging animal in that way. Every time he put his numb hands into its mane it simply stopped, causing much shouting, abuse, and the occasional smack from the knights he travelled with.

He had not actually believed they were going to attempt to travel in that snowy country, but they had said it would be easier than autumn or spring. Frozen roads, frozen rivers were preferable to mud and ooze. Staying put in the cosy castle, fiddling about with magic sigils and demanding ingredients that included wine, bread and a good fire was preferable to him. Sorcery could be a marvellous warm practice.

He rarely took out the key to Hell but when he did, it exerted a great fascination for him. When he had first seen it, he had thought it changed between emerald and ruby, forming itself as if from a mist. Now it seemed both emerald and ruby at the same time. That is to say, if he'd have been asked the colour he would have said emerald, but then thought it was ruby. Or he might have said ruby and then thought it was emerald.

When he was not looking at the key he was sitting wrapped in blankets in his room in front of a little brazier he'd put by the window. It was a nice life – snow without, a glow within.

In fact, he had just been in the process of imagining himself as a hibernating bear when he had suddenly been banned all food. He didn't understand why, but he was used to being hungry and it was only three weeks into his denial when the knock had come from La Cerda's men telling him he was due to travel north.

'Why?'

The knight who had delivered the message replied by slapping him hard across the face and saying, 'Less of that! It's your duty!'

The journey north was horrible – over frozen rivers and fields, through towns so deserted they used the doors of houses for firewood. Everything dead, everything gone from the earth.

'Where are we going?' he asked, but he got no reply. They were travelling north, that was easy to see. Paris? Oh no, not Paris. He wondered what sort of reception he would get there – having killed the major ally of France, Hugh Despenser, albeit by accident and in self-defence, and having scalded the king of Navarre. Perhaps Navarre would not be there. And perhaps he would. Would La Cerda protect him?

Annoyingly, no one would let him eat on the journey and he had only water to drink; no beer, which risked a belly complaint.

At night, locked in some barn where the horses of the local people had died standing where they had been tethered for want of someone to free and feed them, he dreamt. In his dreams he reintroduced himself to King Philip, got his fine robes and quarters back. He toured the palaces, chasing the servant girls, eating, drinking, dealing with the odd devil, doing a little summoning if he could get the ingredients. But always in his dreams was the youth Navarre, stalking him like a great cat, looking for vengeance for the hurt Osbert had inflicted on him at Crécy.

He awoke to a blue dawn, hungry, cold and sober. The men called him 'sorcerer' and he did not stop them. It did not make them respect him but it made them fear him at least a little, though they would not let him eat.

They did not go to Paris. Instead they swerved north-east, to a little village tucked among hills. It was here that he encountered La Cerda.

His men had taken the village over completely. There were no French folk here, just Castilian soldiers extravagantly wrapped against the cold, beating their arms as they trotted between the houses.

La Cerda had set up court in a good-sized inn that it was the village's fortune – now its misfortune – to possess. It was ideal for billeting La Cerda's retainers. Osbert wondered what had happened to the former inhabitants. Paid off or bumped off? Dead of the Plague? Sent to freeze? Death held such a rich hand of cards now; so many to choose from. There were gangs of Englishmen on the roads now – or people calling themselves Englishmen for the terror it inspired. One more burnt village, one more slaughter among the slaughter of the bandits and the Plague; no one was going to notice.

Still, there was a good fire with something like a chimney, ale was served and there was bread on the table. These three things were, Osbert had often noted, the sole requirements of a happy life. His mouth watered – a long time without food now. His hose were slack at his belly, his head light.

The knights shoved him forward towards La Cerda. The lord sat with his feet on a stool near the fire – plainly dressed as any soldier. Only the fine sword that was propped against the table marked him as a man of quality.

'My Lord.' Osbert bowed, wiping snow from his scarf. His eyes stung slightly with the contrast between the cold outside and the smoky interior of the inn.

La Cerda hardly acknowledged him. For a while he sipped on his ale. Then he did turn his attention to Osbert, studying him as if he were a greyhound of uncertain parentage.

'You have the key?'

'My Lord, I do.' He bowed.

'You brought us nothing in the south,' said La Cerda.

Osbert thought it best to say nothing. In dealings with powerful men he had learned that any utterance at all could be misinterpreted so it was safer, when at all possible, to utter nothing. La Cerda jutted his chin towards him with an 'eh?' He took this as an instruction to reply.

'The conditions were not ideal, My Lord.'

'Well, the saints know, they're a lot less ideal now.'

Osbert bowed his head.

'The key will not work?'

'It is a matter of the right conditions – astrological, phenom-enological, flubbilogical and wubbilogical,' he said.

La Cerda gave him a long, unwavering look.

'Well, now things are flubbilogically, wubbilogically swived. Navarre grows in power.'

'I am sorry to hear that, Lord.'

'You should be, because if it goes on, I'll spill your entrails and try to read my future in them.'

Osbert grinned, nervously.

'Navarre has used his strumpet sister to enchant the prince. His influence grows daily.'

'Say it is not so, Lord!' Osbert sank to his knees. The grovelling may have been theatrical but theatrical grovelling was, in Osbert's experience, something demanded by great men.

'It is so. The enchantment must be broken. You will do it. My men are here at your disposal. Whatever you need, whatever unguent, bone of saint or tooth of martyr, we will obtain it.'

Osbert felt panic rising in him.

'And the . . .' He looked around him. 'Other thing?'

'That too needs attention. But first rid us of this damned succubus.'

'My Lord, it is not so simple. We do not know the nature of the enchantment, we do not know if it is demonic or diabolic. We know not if it takes its power from the spirits of north, south, east or west, we do not know—'

La Cerda held up his hand to silence Osbert.

'How would we know?'

'I would have to see the lady. Or rather approach her and construct a charm first to protect myself from enchantment. Then and only then might I get to the prince.'

'Very good. You'll ride for Paris at dawn. Infiltrate the court, see what needs to be done and do it.'

'But, My Lord, I am known to many there. I will be recognised. Navarre will kill me if he sees me.'

La Cerda's eyes were cold.

'I have thought of that. It's why I've been starving you. You need to be convincingly hungry. Go and offer yourself as a shit shoveller or a kitchen hand. No one ever looks at those. God knows there'll be vacancies with the Plague.'

'My Lord! That is beneath my dignity.'

For the first time in his acquaintance, Osbert saw La Cerda smile.

'You have some dignity? You are a stinking, grubbing man. Unfortunately you are a stinking, grubbing man I have to rely on.

My men will escort you as far as the woods of Vincennes and then we will proceed to the court. We will watch you go in. I have a man among the servants there who will give a certain signal when you've arrived. You can choose to run away if you want but we will hunt you like . . .' He searched for the right word. 'A fat drunk. I doubt you'll run for long.'

Osbert swallowed drily.

'And no food or ale tonight,' said La Cerda. 'You sleep in a stable. I want you cold, wet and starving by the time you arrive. Now thank me and get out of my sight. You ride at dawn.'

'Thank you, My Lord,' said Osbert, with a bow. 'You do me much honour with such patronage.'

Then he went to the stable, wondering how far he would get if he stole a horse and set off across the snow that night.

Not far, was his conclusion. He sniffed at his armpit. He did stink a bit. Well, at least he wasn't drunk. At least? He would give anything for a draught of wine. And here came one of La Cerda's men, swigging from a bottle.

'Brother!' said Osbert.

The man grunted. 'I'm here to watch you.' He tapped the bottle. 'This is for me.'

IO

Bonne, it was said, had died of the Plague. Such a blow so close to the royal personage of Prince John was too much to take. It was agreed the queen would be buried that day, with as much ceremony as could be mustered at such a difficult time, and then that the prince and his entourage would move to the hunting lodge at Vincennes outside the city to join with his father King Philip.

This would also give the monarch a chance to meet his new daughter-in-law Blanche. In other times it may have seemed unseemly that the prince should marry with such haste. However, with the country under the grip of the Pestilence, with the three-pronged fork of Lucifer openly daubed on churches and palaces, such niceties could be ignored for a while. In such shocking times, nothing from man could offend the conscience. Even murder, it was said, began to look reasonable as the killer spared his victim a lingering death. A story was told of a man who had gone to murder his cheating wife and her lover, only to find them dead in each other's arms and to die on the way home himself.

So Charles found himself at the great lodge at Vincennes. The hunt was still out when they arrived. Protocol would have seen them wait outside but John, at the beseechment of Blanche, agreed to take them inside to await his father.

Charles was very much looking forward to seeing La Cerda. The old king could not have much longer to live and, with Charles's enchanting sister betrothed to the prince, the tables, it might be said, had turned.

The great room of the lodge was well named – high mullioned windows shining golden light over a great table; a comfortable throne for the king; deeply padded couches for the courtiers. The place smelled pleasantly of sage and cooking meats, and the clatter from the kitchens and the movement of servants might have almost convinced you the land didn't lie under a curse. The ladies of the court kept themselves to themselves until the men returned from the hunt. It wouldn't do to be chatting with a foreign prince while your husband lay dead in a ditch. Besides, old Queen Joan the Lame was laid up in bed again, her left leg a torment. God could be cruel, he thought. A just deity would have made the right one just as bad. High-minded, holy bitch.

Charles bit upon a spiced apple. The fresh ones were on the trees but he preferred these, preserved in sugar and cinnamon. The French did them much better than the Navarrese. John had wasted no time in calling the king's minstrel – his own having died. The man was a saucy fellow and paused at the end of each air to take coins from the nobles. Charles was inclined to strike him but, in these days, that wasn't a wise course of action. The minstrel could play well and, more pertinently, was alive. Drive him off and you might not find another for months. He flicked him a coin of his own.

It was good to see John dancing with Blanche, spinning beneath the shafts of light. He imagined the shafts as strings, the dancers as marionettes, turning and bowing to his command.

Finally, the king's bugles. A little off-key. More deaths in the court musicians, clearly. In fact, when Charles came to look at it, there was death in every detail of modern life – in the new arrogance of low men, in the damp of a sheet that would have once been properly aired, in the garden that the great hall overlooked, overgrown, given over to mere nature. A satisfying state of affairs from his point of view. He had not won the game, not sat himself upon that comfy throne, but he had seen Philip's wine turn to gall in his cup.

Someone was cursing a groom – a heavy Castilian accent. La Cerda. Charles strained to hear. La Cerda was asking someone if he would have all the horses lame. The count was in a bad mood. Charles smiled. It was about to get worse. John bowed to Charles and took Blanche out of the room to greet the returning riders.

The hunt had a flavour all of its own: the smells of the summer evening, of sweating horses, of leather; the call of the grooms and the boasts of the noblemen, their ladies rushing to meet them.

Charles bit little chunks out of the apple. One for the high, chomp, one for the base, one for the beggar and one for his grace. Chomp. One for the lad who chases the maid, chomp, one for the father who'll see him well flayed.

A great cry from outside, wailing and shouting. Of course, John had not told anyone of the death of Bonne yet. At Vincennes, his father must be the first to know. At other times – the birth of a grandson, news of a victory – an enterprising nobleman or even a lower man might have run to the king to be the first to tell him the glad news. No one wanted to be the one to bring Philip the news of his daughter-in-law's death. He hadn't much time for his son, but Philip had loved Bonne.

Charles sat for a while drinking in the pleasant noises, saying to himself a little snippet of verse from the Bible: 'In that place there will be weeping and gnashing of teeth'. That was meant to come at the end of the world, wasn't it? What if this was the end of the world: France one big pit of corpses; devils and demons free on the earth; the dragon tearing angels from the sky at Crécy? Well, he had no cause for concern. All he had done was make life hard for the usurper Philip. God would smile on him.

The door flew back and into the room strode La Cerda. He came flying towards Charles, taking him completely by surprise and lifting him bodily off the floor. Charles's six cats went flying from him.

'You,' said La Cerda. 'You! I never thought you'd have the nuts to face me. You're going to wish you'd stayed out of my sight!'

'Hold on, old man!' said Charles, who feared his head might be shaken from his shoulders. Only when he saw La Cerda's hand go to his knife did he become worried.

'A blade drawn in the presence of the king?' said Charles. 'I think not, sir – that way lies the gallows!'

La Cerda threw Charles down onto his back. The cat-like king hopped to his feet again.

Now his sword was free.

'You think to strike a crowned head. Who are you, you base man?'

'I'm the one who's going to save France from you.'

'From me? Oh yes, the Pestilence, the English, the demands of the peasants – all those pale beside the threat posed by little Navarre.'

Charles bowed, sarcastically lowly.

'I think you plot against our prince and against our king. And now who has drawn before the king?'

'To defend myself against a ruffian!'

La Cerda didn't look much like a ruffian, it had to be conceded, in his cap of deep green velvet, matching coat embroidered with a stag shot by an arrow.

Philip came into the room. Slightly puzzlingly, from Charles's point of view, he was hand in hand with Blanche. That wasn't very seemly.

'What a daughter we shall have!' he said.

He wore a look of complete bliss, a radiant smile on his face. He was dressed identically to La Cerda. Well, the Castilian interloper had really got his feet under the table here, had he not? Until, of course, Charles cut them off.

Blanche smiled too – her hair the lustre of a panther's back, her olive skin as smooth as buttermilk, her dress of deep emerald seeming almost chosen to match the king's own. She looked, thought Charles, frightening. This was more than normal beauty, more even than his aunt Isabella possessed. This was something beyond and above nature, the dream of a supreme artist. Yes, she looked like the dream of God.

La Cerda crossed himself and touched a charm he wore at his neck, a curious scribbled circle on parchment worn like a bib. Charles had seen its like before in the scrolls of the Templars he had stolen from their former stronghold at Le Marais. A ward against enchantment. Well, he'd put it to the test here, for sure.

The whole court was dumbstruck by the sight of Blanche unveiled. Dukes and counts bent the knee, Prince John wore a look like a spaniel doting on a mutton chop, even the ladies of the court were enraptured.

'Is this sorcery?' said La Cerda.

'You have a refreshing directness, La Cerda. I understand it to be the mark of low men. This is simply my sister, Blanche. She is engaged to the prince.'

The words seemed to trouble Philip, though he had moments before announced Blanche as his new daughter. La Cerda saw the look on the old man's face.

'Sire,' he said. 'Great Lord. Your wife will expect to see you and hear your tales of valour from the hunt. Do not disappoint that invalid lady.'

'My place is here,' said Philip. 'This beautiful lady must enjoy our best hospitality. Bring wine, bring the most delicate meats, bring flowers, bring all the splendours our court can afford.'

'You honour me greatly, father,' said John.

'It's not to honour you but this wonderful creature of Navarre!' said Philip.

'Sir, your wife.' La Cerda was pleasantly desperate now. Charles wondered what it would take to make the Castilian beg? Not the threat of death, that wouldn't do it. The loss of loved ones? No, loved ones were being lost at a terrific rate anyway. He examined his rival carefully. My God, was he that rarest thing? A good and selfless man? Rare as a cockatrice.

'Yes, my king, your wife,' said Blanche. 'Go to her. No one can come between a king and his holy queen.'

Wait a moment, Blanche was acting on her own accord. She was possessed by his angel and owed fealty to him. She should be waiting for instruction.

'If I must part—' said Philip.

'I shall await you,' she said.

She gave a little wave as Philip allowed his grooms to escort him through the great hall. Prince John quickly came to her side and took her hand. She looked down at his hand as if she didn't quite know what it was.

'My betrothed,' said John.

'He is the king,' said Blanche, somewhat absently.

'Sister, dear,' said Charles, 'you're not making any sense.'

'The king is put there by God,' said Blanche. 'We seek always union with God.'

Charles drew her down to his level – he was still short, despite heading for manhood.

'That was not the plan, sister, dear.'

She smiled at him and patted him on the head.

'It's God's plan. Fear not, brother, I shall rule wisely and not trouble you in Navarre, which is your place and where you should stay. I shall be in my rooms until dinner. Do not disturb me there, for I shall be at prayer.'

She swept through the room, her maids scuttling after her, Prince John scuttling after them.

In all the confusion Charles had forgotten to ask her to expel La Cerda.

Charles jabbed his finger at the charm at La Cerda's neck.

'Where did you get that?'

'My own business.'

'Well make this your business. Saddle your horses and get back to your lands, for once I have spoken to my sister, you will find yourself safer there.'

'I ought to cut off your head!' said La Cerda.

'Presuming you could do it, I wonder what my sister would make of that.'

He smiled. The king of Navarre was beginning to enjoy himself properly for the first time since he'd strangled his mother.

II

The priest at St Michael's had finally been caught, betrayed by a farmer with whom he had taken refuge. His screams seemed to echo around the halls of Windsor for a week or more. That could not be so, because he had only been interviewed for a few hours before he died.

Sloth had roasted him over a fire in the courtyard of the upper keep. Edward had watched the torture in great anguish, almost weeping to see it.

'You will not take me, devil,' said the priest, 'for I know that, I will die now come what may. And what if I break my vow? An eternity of this! I will bear the pain and keep my hope of Heaven!'

Edward had stopped it there. He had, he said, an idea. The Bishop of London was brought, fat old Stratford, shining with gold and gems, half drunk as usual. He had excommunicated the priest. For what? For defying God's king. The priest wept and said he had no choice; his vow was greater. The Bishop pointed out to him that, since he was no longer a priest, his vow meant nothing. He could break it, be forgiven, reinstated to the Church and blessed. The lion would kill him quickly and Heaven would be his reward. Otherwise? They would make the fire smaller and return him to the spit. He would die outside the protection of the church, outside of the favour of God. The torments he would face would make the roasting look like soft treatment indeed.

Philippa had tried to intercede. This was too great a manipulation, surely an offence to God.

'Is it an offence to God?' said Edward to the bishop.

'No, sir.'

'Then there you are.'

The Black Prince had watched proceedings without blinking, splendid in his jerkin of sable picked out with silver leaves.

Did he know what might be said? Surely he could not remain so calm if he did. Philippa felt as though she would burst. She must reveal what the glass had shown her, remove this devil from their midst. What purpose had he been put there for? Where was her real son? Her heart ached to think of it. She had stared into that fragment of glass so many times now, and always seen the same vision. Was it a vision sent from Hell to trick her? She had prayed earnestly, sprinkled the glass with dust from Becket's tomb. No, she was sure it was a holy thing, from a sacred window.

The priest had cried and blubbered, wrung his hands and told how Isabella had travelled to Hell; how she had dealt with Satan but discovered Mortimer was not in Hell but in Heaven. The courtyard had fallen silent, barring the sobs of the priest. Finally, Edward broke it.

'That's a lie. How could such a traitor, a usurper, go to Heaven?'

Sloth struck the priest, slapping him with the back of his great grey paw.

'I swear, My Lord, I swear. And there is more. If you will reinstate me to the Church I will tell it and go to Heaven, for I fear you cannot let me live once I have revealed it. Please, send your courtiers away. This is for your ears only. Send away your wife too, please, Lord, I beg you.'

'Tell,' said Edward. 'Men are bound by secrets and those I have about me here are dear to me as any.'

Philippa glanced about her, her heart racing. Twenty, maybe thirty courtiers – numbers were thin since the Plague had bitten – stood around the courtyard. Three years before the king would have had a hundred in attendance, maybe more. There was Thomas Holland, who had captured Eu along with Sloth; there was Otho Holland, his brother, such a kind and gentle man but an ogre on the battle field; there was the paragon of chivalry Jean de Graily, Captal de Buch; there William Montacute – the traitor Montagu's son – a loyal boy whom the king had rewarded despite his father's sins; there was Roger Mortimer, the grandson of the greatest traitor, Mortimer himself, unmoved by the priest's claims. As a king, Edward's greatest strength was that he bore no grudges, and so disputes in one generation did not turn into vendettas for the next. Could he trust all of them? Could he trust Alice, the spy who had brought the priest to such a pass? There she was in her dress of pale yellow, hovering at the edge of the crowd of knights.

'My Lord, such is your mother's offence that I cannot say it in front of these men.'

'You are afraid of her? A lady?' said Edward. 'Afraid not of mail and armour or swords and lances but of embroidery needles, of skirts, and petticoats and garters!'

'I am afraid of she who wears them, afraid here and in the world to come.'

'I give you my word against her, here and in the world to come. Let us all swear. Let us swear to defend something greater than family, or friends or oaths or allegiance. Let us swear to defend England. For though we are men of many lands, this is what we fight for. This soil, defended against all.'

'She is the land's greatest enemy.'

'Then let us band together against her. You, here, you men who I trust with my life, now prove to me that you will face Hell, enchantment, angels' wrath and hellfire for this thing we will call England.' He switched from his court French into English to say his speech.

'My mother is my enemy and, though that may seem an offence against God, it is not. Evil be to he who thinks of evil! God is gone from the world, or unreachable. But that does not mean His order or holy laws must be abandoned. We fight for Him no matter what.'

The men drew as one.

'For England! We are Knights of . . .' He cast around for words.

'The garter?' Alice had spoken out of turn and it seemed she knew it. She put her hand to her mouth. Edward smiled. 'Yes,' he said, 'yes. Let us be knights of the garter! For any knight can defend his realm against the sword and the axe. These days we face pressures more subtle and diabolic. Knights of the Garter! Swear that what wrongs you hear today, you will put right. The angels are gone. God is sleeping in His Heaven! What must we vow to? To England!'

The priest wept.

'My Lord, your mother believes Mortimer was sent by God. Your father's line is corrupt. She would exterminate you all. She wants to cut off the Plantagenets at the stem.'

The men looked around at each other. Some let their swords fall, others held them up as if paralysed. As Edward had asked them to unite around a new idea – England – they had been reminded of their old ties. Many of them were cousins to the king, their families joined by blood. Devil blood.

'Can it be so?' said Philippa. This was far worse than ever she had imagined. Not just the prince as devil, but a whole line of devils!

'It is so,' said Edward. 'I read it in the book Alice took from my mother. It is something Mortimer said to me, that I never believed. We are the Devil's Brood. Our history is plain. King Richard tried to atone for his family's sins by crusading, seeking to know God's mind, overthrowing his father. King John tried to call Satan to save his skin, sacrificed his treasure to the sea and was excommunicated for his pains.

'The book bears the signature of Eleanor of Aquitaine, who some call the mother of the Plantagenet line. She promised that, given access to devils, she would mix her blood with the already devilish blood of the Angevins who we now call Plantagenet and would, for earthly power, work for the dominion of Satan on earth. *Satan Volutus Divina Absentem*. In Place of the Absent God.'

The Black Prince stepped forward.

'It is so,' he said. 'God is wounded, perhaps dead. The demons of the poor rise up and He will not raise His hand. But there is one who will.'

'Who?' said Philippa.

The Prince smiled. 'Satan Servant of God, of kings, of order. Ally with him and England will prevail! Spurn him and this Albion will crumble to the sea!'

'That will never do!' said Philippa.

'Oh, Mother,' said the prince, 'you know well that we are with him already. See Sloth here, see our devils. Why did they come so easily to us? Why were the angels held back for so long? What more can we bring out if we openly ally with Satan, God's servant? What if we work for his dominion on earth? He honours kings, he respects the rule of God. Then would the servants of Lucifer quail, even those who claim God Himself. Where is God? Where is He?'

'He would not reveal himself to you, devil!'

'Why do you call me that?'

'I have seen what you are! I know what Isabella did. In prayer and devotion, your nature has been revealed to me! You are a devil, it is true what men say! Edward, King, strike this thing from your court. Order it back to Hell to its master Satan. It is here to bewitch you!'

The prince bowed his head.

'If Satan is my master, then God is his, just as the man who serves the prince by proxy serves the king. Does it not, in the Bible, call Satan a son of God, a member of God's holy council? God has abandoned the world! Once it is returned to order, then He will think it fit for Him once again. Satan will come from Hell if he can and, if not, his laws will be enshrined here, enforced by tooth, claw and horn. Kings will be kings. The poor will be the poor! England will bring order to the world, flying under the banner of Satan – the burning whip!' He gestured to Sloth's surcoat, the emblem of Satan.

'God has not abandoned the world!' said Philippa. 'Did not an angel fly above our armies but a few years ago?'

'And where are the angels now?' said the Prince. 'Not here, not in France. I hear that they are not even in Rome or Avignon. Where are they?'

'Then must we give England over to devils?'

'It is our destiny. The destiny of our whole line.'

King Edward drew himself up. He pointed at young Mortimer, then at Montacute.

'What is my motto?'

'It is as it is,' they said together.

'Yes. Can we avoid having devils? When my mother is working her magics, doing who knows what for who knows who? They say Philip has a fallen angel on his side now. If the other side has such power, we must have it – and more. If they strike bargains we must strike the biggest bargain available to us. God would be my preference. He is not there. And so, his servant Satan.'

'How shall we even do this? How?' said Philippa. 'Without your mother, there are no devils to be had!'

Alice bowed a little bow. 'I grew up under my mother's tutelage. Lady St Pol was versed in such things, and I believe that may be why Queen Isabella recommended her to raise such . . .' She paused and gestured to the prince. 'Remarkable children. My mother sat me at Isabella's side, not for love but so I might learn. I have learned. I have seen her books. I have seen her practices. I have watched her. But you will need a key, for Satan himself is a prisoner.'

'Which key?'

'The first key brought the demons of Lucifer, the champions of the poor into the world. The second key is I know not where, nor the third. But find them, let me question devils and other men and we will have Satan here on earth, bound to our command. If God is gone then who better to replace Him, to command His devils, than a king and a king of England too?'

Edward looked to the ground, then to the sky. 'There can be no half measures,' he said. 'Let us bring what devils we can here. Let us strike the bargains that will see England triumph, all devils removed from France, all demons of Lucifer back in their rightful place in Hell. It is time to . . .'

Philippa knew he wanted to say 'atone', but could not in front of his courtiers.

'Remove all pretence,' he finally said. 'We are Plantagenet, the Devil's Brood. I believe God put devils' blood into us to strengthen us for the fight to come. Our blood makes us more, not less, holy. When we breed the warhorse, do we not mate a courser with a rouncy, the resulting foal so much hardier on the trail, faster in the charge and nobler in the gait than either who begot it? Each of us here has this blood. Look at us. Are we not stronger than ordinary men? Are we not quicker in the fight, lighter in the dance, more honest, more purposeful, better in every way? Are we not?'

Those around him replied as one, 'We are!'

'Then we will be Knights of Satan. Satan under God. Now swear fealty to England, to Satan and to God.'

'We swear!'

'You are bewitched!' Philippa pointed at her son. 'I know what you are! I know you for a devil!'

'And I too,' said Edward. 'And what if he is a devil? He is God's devil, England's devil, my devil! These are strange times. It is as it is!'

The Black Prince drew his sword, knelt and presented it to the king. 'This, I believe, was my destiny. Why I was sent to this court, to lead us to this moment! My father has spoken our motto already. We are where we are and we must do what we do. Evil be to him that evil thinks of it!'

He stood tall and addressed them in French, their language, the language of the English kings. '*Honi soit qui mal y pense!*'

The knights held up their swords, some boldly, some with shaking hands.

'*Honi soit qui mal y pense!* Satan! Satan! Satan!'

Philippa fled from the courtyard.

12

Blanche's wedding to Prince John had not come as quickly as Charles had hoped. There seemed to be some reluctance on the part of the lady herself. In the normal course of events this wouldn't have been a problem. Blanche could simply be told to do her duty and marry the oafish prince, as countless other beauties from little kingdoms had been told to marry oafish princes from large ones before. Charles had, indeed, tried such a tactic. However, Blanche had simply stood mooning into space, ignoring him completely. It occurred to him to have her beaten to snap her out of it, but her effect on his guards seemed pretty much the same as her effect on all men. He wasn't quite sure he could make them do it. He knew his aunt, who possessed much of this supernatural allure, hadn't felt a rod across her back since she had been old enough to make men notice her. But Isabella's charms did not work on royalty. Blanche seemed to enrapture all but him and those protected by holy charms, like La Cerda.

He wondered if he could somehow get that charm off La Cerda, and had been on a night-time excursion around the roofs of the hunting lodge to see if he could manage it – as a second best to strangling the Castilian fool in his bed. La Cerda, however, had either heard the rumours surrounding Joan of Navarre's death or he had a Castilian distaste for the cold. Whatever the reason, he had boarded his windows up solidly and there was no way in to his rooms.

All through the grand Christmas dinner, Blanche sat as if enraptured by the king. Angels, Charles recalled, were in love with royalty. Then why not him? Half-devil, did the angel shy from him? Or did the natural repugnance between sister and brother count still for something? Worse still, was this a slight? Was a king of Navarre not enough to inspire devotion in an angel, whereas a king of France was?

'What do you want from me?' he asked his sister. 'What can make you do your duty? Look at Prince John. Is he not a handsome man?'

'Who looks at the moon when the sun is in his splendour?'

'He is married. Lawfully married, under the eyes of God.'

'And for that reason I think only chaste thoughts when I regard him. But regard him still I must.'

Charles looked hard at Philip. He was tall, pinch-nosed; his eyes were rheumy. Did he have the Pestilence? God, let him have the Pestilence, please – Charles offered a prayer. No, God, don't let him have it. That way the whole court will have it and there'll be no one to administer the country. Might the king die of natural causes anyway? He offered an earnest prayer – though he knew not who to nor really what about.

The king's eyes were fixed on Blanche too, his wife Joan – a lady of great holiness and royal breeding – ill in her chamber and absent. She would not have interfered anyway, thought Charles. He admired her for that. A true queen must know when to oppose a concubine and when to simply stand aside, allow her husband to slake his passions and discard the strumpet.

He'd forced an audience with Queen Joan the night before. In truth, it had not been difficult. The whole court were enraptured by Blanche and stood to watch her dance with the king in the candlelight, his great tall, bent figure looming over her like a tree ready to fall. Prince John remained silent, seemingly stuck to his bench, not eating, not drinking, just watching.

Charles was at a loss to know what to do. He had assumed his sister would be easy to control. Now this. Well, he told himself, as an enthusiastic servant of chaos in the realm of France, is this not a good thing? Are not the Valois divided while their enemy the English establish a base in Calais?

He doubted the English would ever be able to use Calais as a bridgehead into France. The way over the marshes was too narrow, the town too small to really service a decent army. Still, as a trading base it was excellent and provided a key to Flanders and beyond. Things were going well there for the English, his spies told him. The insufferable youth who called himself the Antichrist had disappeared and now a whore was leading that weird sect of Lucifer in Calais, itself much diminished in the eyes of the poor.

He marvelled at the presumption of those people. As if they could have the wit to overthrow an anointed king.

La Cerda, he noticed, was glaring at him from a distant table where he sat with his retainers. Charles had his own good men around him and hoped to be soon joined by his brother Philip – something of a prodigy at arms. He had wondered what manner of devil his mother had lain with to conceive Philip. Charles was like a cat, Philip like a bull.

Charles got up and walked around to where his sister was sitting, eyes on the king.

'Do you think,' he said, 'that you might have La Cerda executed? You could suggest it to Philip.'

'La Cerda walks with the light of God.'

'Well, it doesn't stop you cutting off his head, does it? He won't be walking anywhere after that.'

'He says his prayers and builds great churches.'

'Laudable, I am sure,' said Charles. 'But, were I to be given his lands, I would build the biggest church anyone ever clapped eyes on in all of Christendom. I would build a church the size of Paris – subject to practicalities, of course.'

Blanche stared at La Cerda.

'Thou shalt not kill. That is God's law. I cannot disobey it. Not kill a man like that.'

A thought struck Charles. 'But I am your king and your brother. Shouldn't you obey me?'

She moved a napkin to her lips.

'I should. But do not ask me to kill, Charles.'

'I'm not asking you, I'm telling you.'

'Thou shalt not kill.'

This was a troublesome woman.

'Is there anything in the Bible about "thou shalt not exile"? I think not. Exile the ruffian. He offends our eyes.' Charles sniffed at his perfumed kerchief.

Blanche bowed her head slowly and leant across to whisper to Philip. The king nodded gravely but he put his hands on her arm, as if imploring her.

The bastard won't do it, thought Charles. *He isn't enchanted at all, he's just got a good old-fashioned marrow in his trousers.*

But Blanche merely inclined her head and smiled.

Philip raised a finger, a wonderful brilliant finger, and three of his men-of-arms came over. La Cerda, who missed nothing, stood. One of the men-at-arms left the room and Philip gestured for La Cerda to approach him.

La Cerda fairly stalked across the floor towards the king. Unarmed, not even possessing a dagger in the king's company, he had few options, thought Charles.

'You have displeased us,' said Philip.

La Cerda, white with rage, turned his eyes on Charles.

'You, or this enchanter?'

Charles put his hands to his chest in mock shock.

'That is Navarre, the good and loyal brother of the most favoured Blanche, betrothed of our son John.'

'What have I done, Lord?'

Philip seemed confused for a moment. He turned to Blanche and whispered.

'What has he done?' She, in turn, looked to her brother. 'What has he done?'

'This and that,' said Charles.

'You have done this and that,' said Philip. 'And for such offences will be banished from our kingdom.'

He seemed to run out of ideas of things to say.

'Get thee hence,' suggested Charles, helpfully.

'Get thee hence.'

'Father!' said John. 'La Cerda is my most valued servant!'

Well, thought Charles, *that hurts*.

'Might he not stay, Father?' said John.

'No. Off he hops,' said Charles.

'No. Off he hops,' said Blanche.

'Off you hop,' said King Philip.

More men-at-arms filed into the room – around twenty - most unarmoured, some in their underclothes as it was late, but all with swords or maces.

La Cerda's retinue was greater in number but their weapons were left in their lodgings where, Charles was confident, they were now being removed.

La Cerda pointed at Charles.

'You will come to no good. I curse you. I curse your stratagems and designs. May they all come back to soil you like piss in the wind!'

'When I piss in the wind I turn my back to it,' said Charles. 'That way I can be sure that whoever it blows on, it blows not on me!' He bowed.

La Cerda turned on his heel, his men sweeping out of the room behind him.

'I've counted the tapestries in your quarters!' shouted Charles. 'I'll know if they're gone!'

The next morning, Charles was chuckling to himself as he went through the weapons that had been collected from La Cerda's men. Thirty good swords, a variety of hammers, maces and axes. They'd let them keep the lances and bows – they had to eat on the road. He could still smell the wine and the ale drifting up from the hall below. He fancied a cup of wine. He had been too wary of an attack – armed or not – by La Cerda's men to drink much that night, and had spent some of a cold dawn on top of the lodge, watching La Cerda's men file away across the snow. What an insult. The low people would see them – knights without swords; men without cocks, in effect. He had gelded La Cerda, yes he had. Though he took care to remind himself that geldings can still kick.

The fire was not yet lit in his room and he guessed the maid might have died in the night. He stood looking at the chopped logs and the kindling. He certainly wasn't going to light it himself. Like any knight, he could knock up a fire in an instant if he had to – it was an essential skill he'd learned as squire to Prince John. But a king couldn't do that in a hunting lodge. His grooms were asleep all around him but they too were noble men and would not light a fire here. They needed a maid. How much, he wondered, would the next maid demand for her services? Since the Plague it was as if the low folk held the aristocracy to ransom.

The screams cut through the muggy interior of the hunting lodge. They sounded rather refined screams. The servants were more guttural, making more of a 'kwwwwoooooor!' noise than this one, high and sustained. Female, certainly. A lady-in-waiting? He wasn't even all that curious, he just wanted a fire. Everywhere you went nowadays, howls of grief were as common as the call of thrushes.

And, like thrushes, you heard them the most in the morning, when people awoke to find the dead at their side, when ladies awoke to find no maid answered their call, when horses fretted in the stables for want of a groom to clean and exercise them.

A knock on the door of his chamber. His grooms awoke; Charles drew himself up.

A groom opened the door to reveal a pale-faced servant.

'The queen!' was all he could manage. 'The queen!'

'The queen wants you to light my fire?'

'No, sir. No. The queen is unfortunately dead.'

Charles's eyes widened. *Unfortunate for whom?* he thought. Certainly for someone – everything nowadays was unfortunate for someone. He went through a mental list. Was it him? Possibly? Philip? Maybe. John.

'Oh my Lord! Take me ot the chamber!' The implications struck him like a cavalry charge.

Charles followed at the run, winding around the staircases of the great lodge to find the queen's chamber.

Within was a bloody sight. The queen had been butchered in her bed. Her murderer was not difficult to find. The king sat on the edge of her bed, his wet red dagger in his hand.

Prince John was not there – notoriously difficult to rouse.

'She died,' said King Philip. 'Taken in the night.'

Charles wondered if he should try to remove the dagger.

'What was the cause, Lord?' Charles was trying to be helpful. Philip was the highest authority in the land. His word would determine what killed Joan, not the sight of the dagger in his hand, nor even had someone seen him plunge it into her breast.

'She died of Plague. Is it not clear?' Philip's eyes were like those of a panicked horse, thought Charles. 'So many taken and now one close to us. Is it not horrible, my Lords, is it not horrible?'

'Horrible indeed, sir,' Charles turned to the servant. 'Announce to the rest of the court that the Great Pestilence has taken Queen Joan. We will make the provisions for a funeral.'

'She must have a funeral,' said Philip. 'Full of pomp and majesty. She was my queen and my love.'

'Yes, sir. Might I take the knife?' Charles removed it from Philip's hand and placed it on the table.

"But then,' said Philip, 'oh happy day. I am free to marry the darling Blanche.'

'She's betrothed to your son, sir,' said Charles.

'No longer. I broke it off last night. They weren't right for each other. She needs a king as a consort, no mere prince.'

Charles broke into a big smile.

'That is good news indeed, sir.'

A besotted king, an otherworldly sister. He would be de facto ruler of France. He could formalise his power in a way that would make his enemies fear him – and give him access to huge power and wealth.

'There is the question of the constableship, sir,' he said. The right hand of the king!

'We have no constable,' said Philip. 'Not until Eu returns.'

'He is coming to us as quick as he can, sir? No English captain would convey him, I am told and devils hunt him. I am sure he will be here when he can.' Edward, Charles had discovered, did not consider Eu's ransom paid in full. Eu, having sent certain letters of promise, did. At the moment Eu was hiding, having the moral right to leave England but not the opportunity.

'Send for Blanche,' said Philip.

Charles's mind was racing. In days of Plague all was uncertain – John might die. The little Prince Charles, his son, might die. Lots of the Valois might die, particularly if given a little bit of encouragement, clearing the path to the throne for his nephew – it would be a boy. He would be regent. 'Never king of France,' said the angel. But regent, up to his neck in gold and castles, restorer of the Capetian fortunes. Or would it have been better if she had married John? He did a quick calculation in his head. No, he would have to kill roughly the same number of people. This way he'd just be able to get on with it sooner.

'Well,' said Charles to the servant, 'send for my sister and then clear this corpse away. Come on, man, don't just stand there, there's a future out there waiting to happen.'

13

The lodge at Vincennes had received Osbert easily – the kitchen porter had come over feverish that day and had been booted out. He was surprised at the rate of pay he was offered – a small stipend on top of his food and board. The kitchens were warm, the work easy because of the reduced number of nobles and, in particular, attendent servants at the lodge, and there was plenty of opportunity to dip a finger into a meaty Parma tart or a pottage of rys, to take a pinch of powder douce as he passed or snaffle a salty rissole. Even the wine was not that well guarded. The chief cook – who had been a mere apprentice before the Plague took his master – said standards had slipped since the Great Pestilence had come. Was it possible to have a good plague, Osbert wondered? Here, he was sure it was.

In fact, for a short time he was as happy as he had ever been. There was no pressure on him that he could not answer, no demanding king or lord, just the smell of cinnamon and ginger, the taste of exquisite wines. The Plague had also very pleasantly loosened the morals of the scullery maids, one of whom had tugged him off in the pantry for a couple of silver deniers. This was Gilette – she had been a milkmaid until everyone on her farm had died and she had come into service rather than starve. Her skin was as pure and unblemished as that of milkmaids tended to be, and she had a gap in her teeth at the front which made her whistle pleasantly as she spoke. This meant it fell into that broad category of female traits that caused Osbert's codpiece to tighten.

'God seems gone from the world,' she'd said as she'd wiped the mess from her hand.

From where Osbert was standing, things seemed to be going along just fine without him.

'If He doesn't come back by Thursday, will you let me fuck you properly then?'

'For five deniers. Why not? Why not? If we are both still alive.' He saw she was crying and felt sad for her. He put his arm about her and hugged her.

'Everyone dead,' she said. 'Everyone.'

'You and I survive.'

'Why?'

'That is a troublesome and rather useless question, I have found,' said Osbert. 'I limit myself to what, who, how and, if pushed, when. Why is not for us.'

'But why?'

'I don't know. There will be a better world. One day. I met a boy once who said he could bring Eden to the earth. Can you imagine, you and I wandering around in a garden full of talking snakes, where we meet God coming the other way in the afternoon? As a person.'

'I would like to meet God,' said Gilette. 'I would like to ask Him why. Why bring life to bloom if it is to be cut down so cruelly? Why does He allow it?'

'Now you sound like a Luciferian,' said Osbert.

'Do they die of the Plague too?'

'I hear it has reached Calais.'

He thought of his friends there. Dow. That serious, scarred little boy would be nearly a man now. Could he shake the world, as he had said? Osbert did not doubt it. And Orsino, the Florentine killer. What had become of him? Even Montagu. He remembered him on the ship they had taken to France, looking as if the world was his to command. Well, the news said he had fallen from favour now but Osbert had seen him fight. Devils looked weak by comparison.

'You are crying too,' said Gilette.

'Five deniers is a lot of money. But I will find it.' She laughed, wiping her face.

'It seems right to fuck. All this death. Let us trip the dance of life, let us fuck before Heaven and say "This is what we say to your death."'

'For free?' said Osbert, brightening. This was a philosophy he could share.

'For free. But give me the money anyway.'

Osbert gave her a quizzical look but said nothing. Strange times, strange dealings. How might life have been different? What would it have been to have been born a simple man, unmarked out by God or Satan or whoever had marked him out (without so much as a by-your-leave); to have tended the same piece of unremitting earth from the time he could crawl to the time they put the earth over his head; to have married this woman and lived the life of toil, pain, happiness and tears that people had lived for generations?

He smiled to himself. His thinking was wrong. God had become a Luciferian, it seemed. No longer did He hold His special destinies back for the noble and the heroic. He handed them out to everyone – everyone who lived. Gilette had left her farm and had come to work in a palace. The palace had taken her in. Instead of knowing one loutish man her whole life, now she would know many loutish men. One of them might live in a town or take her far away to new destinies. If she ever went back to her farm, she could take what land she liked from her neighbours – the dead rarely complain. The Plague was good and bad, he thought, as all calamities are.

For instance, life at court was to his liking. The tone was very pleasantly set by the king himself. With his new wife Blanche – he'd married her two weeks after his wife had died – he spent every waking hour rutting like a man half his age. The sounds of his groans and her wails could be heard throughout the lodge, as the great chimney that served the oven also served the king's chamber.

'I'm surprised he's got it in him,' said the cook.

'I expect he won't have for long,' said Osbert. 'He has to run dry eventually.'

The cook laughed. He liked Osbert, it seemed, which was lucky because with so few staff – the kitchen was down to no more than twenty – there were few places to avoid people if you found them disagreeable.

But the king did not run dry, and there was a call for foods with chick peas, birds' brains, egg yolks, and cloves in milk. Osbert tried all these foods and found that they did, indeed provoke lust. But, there again, pretty much anything provoked lust in Osbert and he was obliged to spend more of his deniers in an attempt to discharge it.

The great advantage of his position was that he was not expected to leave the kitchen. He even slept there, warm by the ovens. He might venture into the servants' dining halls but never any further. He was not allowed there, never mind expected. The expulsion of La Cerda made his task more pressing but not so much that he couldn't lie low.

So it was that he spent a few good weeks, as happy as a louse on a sheep's back. No one could touch him here – he was safe from La Cerda and from Navarre. The porter who had been feverish returned, well again, but Osbert was kept on. The Plague did touch them at Vincennes, but not as badly as it had struck in Paris. The corpses threatened to swamp Notre Dame, it was said, though no one wanted to go in to test the claim.

Spring came and then summer. The Plague got even worse in Paris and the scullery maid Gilette, who so enlivened Osbert's days, went to visit her family and didn't come back. Had she died? He worried about her for a while, but then no more. Best not think on such things for those who want to stay sane. Often he thought he was coming down with a fever, felt for a lump at his throat, or was convinced there was a tightness in his armpit. He wasn't looking forward to his own death. Having had a taste of Hell when the boy Dow sent him there, he was in no hurry to return.

Autumn came around, the woods a glimmering copper. The kitchen was down to fifteen now and deliveries were difficult to get – they relied on the hunt and what could be gathered from the woods most of the time. The only constant was the groaning and shrieking that came down the chimney.

'He'll wear it away!' said the new cook.

'I reckon he must have two,' said Osbert.

'I'm surprised Navarre lets him keep us all awake like that.'

'Lets him?'

'He runs the show now – the young Prince Charles follows him around like a puppy and everyone's convinced he's going to be uncle to a new prince. Old John's taken to his rooms in pique since his dad nicked his bride. The footmen'll tell you what's what. You see how long John lasts!'

'Do you think Navarre will kill him?'

'He killed Queen Joan, didn't he?'

'I don't know.'

'That's what I heard. She was cut to ribbons, though no one talks of it.'

'No one talks of it' was kitchen code for 'everyone talks of it'. Who exactly had been responsible was a matter for debate. Many flatly refused to believe that the king had been capable of such a monstrous act. The servant who had discovered her body had died the same day – of Plague, said the king of Navarre. Some noted that it was unusual for the king to concern himself, let alone mention, the fate of servants.

The kitchen people died; new ones came and they died too. The cook died in May and was replaced by a new cook, who died in early September.

Osbert did what he could to bring the harvest in – cropping apples mainly – and the cook showed him how to lay down cider the day before he died. A new cook had been sent for, new hands too. By mid-September hardly anyone who had been there when Osbert arrived remained. But, happy day, Gilette returned. He found himself fond of her now. He had ceased giving her money for her favours and instead brought her nosegays and things he thought might please her. They went walking together and he found her good company. He hoped she wouldn't die. That was a bad thought because so many people did die.

Then, one soft blue dawn when he was out gathering mushrooms, he heard the hunt go by. Venison, at least, was in good supply with no one there to poach it.

He lay down on a grassy bank and watched the sun rise, thinking of Dowzabel, that strange, serious boy who seemed to turn any conversation you ever had to Lucifer, Son of the Morning, angel of the dawn. The morning star was up, a sharp twinkle. He could hear the hunt stirring away across the fields by the stables, a distant clamour of hounds. In his time at the palace he had encountered none of the nobility who might recognise him, but he wasn't too worried. La Cerda was right – no one looks at servants, especially one as ugly as he. He was, he supposed, much changed from his time as court magician. He was younger looking from all the angel's blood he had consumed to fight off his hangovers, and his hair was long and unkempt, his beard ragged.

What it would be, he thought, *to lie on this bank in the warm sun for ever.* To exist whole and complete, here in this moment – no demands of the body, none of great men to contend with, to enjoy an unthreatened repose for ever. Was that Heaven? Something like it, he supposed. He closed his eyes, drifting off a little. He thought of Gilette, but not in the way he was accustomed to think of women. He thought of her lying next to him, the kitchen spice smell of her hair, her rough hand in his.

She was away in the palace somewhere, doing God knew what. In these days of Plague the servants had to do tasks that would have been quite outside their remit normally. She was probably stitching something or maybe even tending a noble baby. When noble ladies die off, someone needs to take their place. From milkmaid to lady-in-waiting. What a topsy-turvy world. What a bumpsy-mumpsy, top-to-tail mimsy-momsy world, what a . . .

A shadow fell across his face and he was suddenly cold.

'The court magician. Yes, it's you, isn't it?'

He opened his eyes as if pricked by a dagger.

In front of him stood an exquisitely dressed gentleman of the court in blue brocade. His face looked familiar but Osbert couldn't quite place it.

'Who is Gilette? You spoke of her in your sleep.'

'No one to trouble great men. Just a country girl of my acquaintance.'

'I sense you love her!'

'Perhaps. I haven't had the pleasure.' Osbert felt very much as the worm must feel under the eye of a blackbird.

The man smiled.

'Oh, but you have, my lord mage. The pleasure, the pain and everything in between. You've had the lot! Pastus. Simon Pastus.'

Unusually for a nobleman, he extended his hand to help Osbert to his feet.

Osbert took it and it was as if every bone in his body had been turned funny, a sickly vibration humming through them.

Upright, Osbert released the hand.

'I am but a kitchen hand collecting mushrooms.'

'No, no,' said Pastus. 'I am quite sure of who you are. After all, it was you who summoned me. Do you not remember, in the

Temple of Paris, with the unfortunate Hugh Despenser? I should have thought it would be unlikely to slip your mind. Look!'

With a quick movement, he pulled up Osbert's smock to reveal a complicated pattern of scars on his belly. It was, as anyone with half an eye could see, a magic circle.

'Oh, that Simon Pastus, of the Screaming Towers of Maloch?' said Osbert. He'd summoned so many devils he forgot all their names but that one, for some reason, had stuck.

'The very same. I have a message for you.'

'From whom?'

'Satan.'

'The jailer of Hell?'

'No, Satan the costermonger who lives on the Quai d'Orsay,' said Pastus. 'Yes, Satan, Lord of Hell.'

'I've come to his notice, have I?'

'Very much so. You've been pulling devils through the cracks in the walls of Hell for a while now, haven't you? And you have something of interest in your possession. A certain key.'

'How does he know that?'

'You are in the service of a devil known as "Gressil"?'

'He's in my service!'

Pastus raised his eyebrows.

'That's as maybe. Whispers have come through the walls of Hell. Whispers have come back again. Satan wants you to do a little job for him.'

'He'll have to get in the queue,' said Osbert.

'He is not used to queuing.'

This would, as far as Osbert could determine, constitute quest number three he had been asked to fulfil. He considered his options.

One of Osbert's more surprising faculties was that of speed; he was a fast runner, and now he set off at a clip across the fields back towards the lodge. He jumped a stile, turned his ankle on a root, limped on, fell, stood, limped some more, glanced back and saw no devil, slowed to a hobble, and finally made the kitchen. Where the devil was waiting for him, picking his teeth with a straw.

'Keen to get on?' said Pastus.

'Not exactly,' panted Osbert.

'Well, you will be when I tell you what's on offer.'

'What?'

'Salvation. Hell will not take you when you die.'

'What will happen to me?'

'Well, who knows?' said the devil. 'Perhaps you'll wander the earth as a ghost. Perhaps you'll enter Heaven. Perhaps all sorts of things. One thing is certain. You won't be getting the special attentions of the Sisters of Suffocation in the sands of the Desert Perilous.'

'Best avoided,' Osbert nodded.

This was, maybe, a chance. He had never seen how he could avoid God sending him to Hell for his deeds but here was a way out that sidestepped God. What if Hell refused to take him? Life as a wandering ghost couldn't be all that bad. He could creep into ladies' chambers, lie under the summer moon on perfumed riverbanks, chat to other ghosts if they were amenable. Does every cup of wine, once drunk, become a cup of ghost wine? Were there ghost cellars waiting to be plundered?

'So you will do it?'

'Well, I can't say until you tell me what he wants.'

'You will find all the keys to Hell. And then you will let Satan out.'

Osbert smiled the smile of a man who did not feel like smiling.

'And where do I find these keys?'

'You've got one.'

'How do you know I've got one?'

Pastus twitched his nose.

'I can sniff it. It is the Key of Blood. It will open the door in Hell's third wall. Satan could be free.'

'If you could get the other two.'

'We've seen the Antichrist use one other. There's only one more to find.'

No secret about where that was, thought Osbert. He'd seen Montagu take it at Caesar's Tower in the Temple – the Knights Hospitallers' nook at Paris. He wasn't about to burden Pastus with that information.

'Surely two more. There are four gates of Hell.'

'Lucifer is beyond the final gate. We only wish to release Satan.'

'And you can't find this other key yourself?'

Pastus spread his hands wide. 'No.'

'Then what makes you think I can?'

'You have achieved many things. You have torn angels from the sky, you have killed a great devil, you have been to Hell and returned. Satan believes you may have God on your side. Or you may have been in God's plans. When He had plans.'

'Well if He does, He's got a funny way of showing it. Can't Satan get out himself?'

'Clearly not.'

'But his lower devils can.'

'So God deemed it. Satan is a mighty devil. God would not allow him into the world. He set him above the angels to keep Lucifer in Hell.'

'But if he gets out, doesn't Lucifer?'

'Let Satan handle that.'

'And what,' said the pardoner, in the manner of a goodwife returning faulty cloth to a market stall, 'has God to say about all this?'

Pastus looked around him and sniffed. Corpse fires were on the air. Osbert had not noticed them before.

'God is gone, it seems,' he said. 'Someone must restore order to this realm. Perhaps then He will return.'

'Someone like Satan?'

'Yes.' Pastus poked Osbert hard in the chest. His finger felt as sharp as a bodkin and Osbert glanced down to check he wasn't bleeding. 'And someone like you. I tell you this. God is absent. Perhaps the day of the Devil is coming. Is a devil king not a king as much as a human king? The day of the Devil is coming. God is gone. Man may follow. Who remains? Who remains?' Now Pastus thumped himself in the chest.

'And I am to be offered salvation?'

'Freedom from the torments of Hell.'

'I want more.'

'What?'

'Gilette,' he said. 'She has been, ummm, fimbling and fumbling with me out of marriage.'

'A grievous sin,' said Pastus. 'I can only imagine what torment awaits her.'

'No torment. She is spared damnation too. She comes with me, if she chooses, or goes her own way. But no devils, no Lake of Fire. Nice things for her.'

'You are a presumptuous and forward fellow.' The devil drew himself up, a smell of sulphur pervading the air.

Osbert steeled himself. Devils were not so very frightening when you realised that, like everything else in creation, they had their desires and wants, could be bargained with, deceived, or even used.

'Well, if I was a shrinking poltroon you wouldn't be after my services, would you? Men like me are rare or you wouldn't be here. A sight rarer since the Plague, I'd guess.'

'A bargain, then. Yes. Salvation for her. I will convey the message through the walls of Hell.'

'Half time,' said Osbert. 'I want something more from you. There is an enchantment on the king. Lift it.'

'I cannot speak of that.'

'Why not?'

'If I told you, I'd be speaking of it, wouldn't I? There are those so great that their works cannot pass low lips such as mine.'

'You've just told me Satan's plans for the earth. There is someone higher?'

'Shhhhhh!' said Pastus, looking left and right. 'Seek the keys.'

'Where?'

'You are a sorcerer, use your art.'

'I'm a piss artist,' said Osbert. 'Though a drink might be useful.'

He went back into the kitchen. Only Pascal, the king's dogsbody, was in there and he lay sleeping against a bench. Of course, the king's bodily functions – his stool and his bed, his dressing and his undressing – were all taken care of by noblemen, who would suffer any indignity to be near to the king. Well, not quite. The king might have given the job of emptying the bedpan to a favoured noble, but the actual emptying was done by Pascal.

Osbert took a scoop from the wine vat and glugged it down.

A hand on his shoulder. A whisper at his ear. A knife, sharp as a razor, shaved the hair from the back of his neck.

'The Lord of Castile is not patient,' said a voice.

Osbert swallowed.

'It is in hand,' he said. 'The matter is in hand. Only today I spoke with a devil.'

'By Christmas,' said the voice. 'If you want to see the New Year.'

The knife fell away and Osbert stood staring into the blood-red liquid of the wine vat.

Footsteps walked away and, when he was sure they were gone, he turned to the empty kitchen.

'Anyone else?' he said. 'Come on, I've only got three impossible tasks, surely someone has another one for me? Sweep the forest clean of leaves? Find the rainbow's end? Lick my own elbow? Come on, Pascal, all it takes is the threat of death or eternal damnation!'

But the room was quiet. Pascal had stopped snoring.

Osbert approached him.

'Pascal!'

He shook the dogsbody by the shoulder. No reply. A ribbon of blood crawled from Pascal's nose. Was he dead? He was.

Osbert glanced around him. Such chaos – so many dead, a king who could do nothing but swive and sleep, a court in disarray. If he said he'd been appointed dogsbody, nobody was going to remember if he had or he hadn't; the master of the king's household had died a month before and no replacement put in. Where to get some smarter clothes? Pascal was himself a stout man.

'Thank you, Pascal,' he said. 'Your dying wish that I should have your clothes and take your place. You cleared it with the higher-ups, you never had chance to tell me who, but I thank you.'

He dragged Pascal's corpse into the pantry and stripped off his doublet, in the king's livery, and his hose too.

He put his own clothes on Pascal and put the dogsbody back where he had lain. He stretched himself up tall. He was now the king's dogsbody, as far as anyone knew or would care to remember. He made his way through the palace, up to the king's rooms to wait outside the door until he was called.

14

The gaggle of nobles who would normally attend the king were not waiting outside his rooms, having decided – Osbert concluded – that the king was unlikely to be in a condition to be influenced by anything but the swing of his wife's tits for quite a while. He wondered where they had gone. Dead? Maybe. Chasing after Charles of Navarre, perhaps, the present big noise at the court, or sucking up to Prince John.

However, sucking up to Prince John was being seen as an increasingly risky activity. You might actually attract his favour and then, if Charles noticed, you were likely to find yourself in the same condition as La Cerda – banished, or worse.

Osbert glanced around. He didn't much fancy bumping into Navarre. The last time he'd seen him he'd treated the king to a faceful of angel's blood – something Charles's devilish nature had found intolerable. It had burned like quicklime. He allowed himself a little smile at the thought.

The rhythmic sound of the amorous couple beating butter came through the door. Osbert did a little dance to it.

'Hey, ho, we're ankle to toe.
Hey he, we're shin to knee
Hey hi, we're hand to thigh
Hey hock, did someone knock?'

He waited a long time. Odd thoughts came and went. That bed in there had withstood a powerful thumping. The king had been ploughing her furrow for weeks and the bed didn't so much as squeak.

'What craftsmanship,' said Osbert. 'I bet that bed is English. No Frenchman could build joints to support such a fearsome knocking.'

He knew this to be untrue but was overtaken by a sudden wave of nostalgia for England. The busy markets, the credulous towns-folk, the poverty that guaranteed a stream of willing prostitutes. He remembered the Southwark stews. When he was a lad' you could get a bath, a tug in a back alley, and still have change for a pie on the way home. Good days. He wondered what England was like now. Full of corpses, he supposed. The available whores could charge what they liked. Mind you, the gentlewomen might be starving so it was as good as it was bad.

'Ah, dogsbody,' said Charles of Navarre. 'I have a job for you.' Three retainers stood at his side.

'Sir,' said Osbert, burying his chin into his chest and making a great study of the floor.

'He's ill, sir,' said a retainer, jabbing a finger at Osbert as if to check him like a baked cake.

'Plague, I suppose. No bother to me, I'm protected by God. Do you think he's got an hour's service left in him? There might be a bit of labour left in him before he dies.'

'I am the king's servant, sir,' said Osbert, feigning a thick Parisian accent.

Charles kicked him hard and he fell forward onto his face. Osbert was used to agonies and this was very much of the lesser, trifling sort. Navarre, Osbert felt sure, had some more serious torments up his sleeve, should he care to use them. He kept staring at the floor, which had the happy outcome of disguising his face and making it appear that he was grovelling.

'How dare you?' said Charles. 'I asked you a question, wretch, how dare you?'

'Don't know,' said the servant into the floor.

'Well, get up. You need to run an errand for me. I need some perfume brought from my chambers. This place stinks and you are making it no better. An amber bottle about so big.' He measured a space with his thumb and forefinger. 'If you die before you return I shall . . .' He ummed and ahhed for a second, clearly trying to think of a punishment that would be worse than the Plague. 'Miss out. And that is an offence before God. You would go to Hell.'

'Where shall I find you, sir?'

'Within, within.'

Osbert scuttled off. He knew better than to ask Charles himself where his rooms were. Instead, he simply tore around the palace until he encountered a devil like a great bat with a bald ape's head hanging upside down from a chandelier above some stairs.

'Do you know where Charles of Navarre's rooms are?' he said.

'You summoned me, did you not?' said the devil.

'Shhhhhh! Let's not go on about that. Can't any of you fiends keep a secret? What's happened to standards of discretion in Hell?'

'There are no secrets in Hell.'

'Well, there are here. Shut it. Now where does Charles of Navarre lodge?'

'Rooms royal, rooms public, rooms private or rooms personal?' said the devil.

'Any of them. Rooms!'

'The one he's in most is up there, third on the left. That's his room personal.'

Osbert shot up the stairs, thanking God for the arrogance of the nobility. Charles almost literally did not see servants of his rank, as so few nobles did. They called them all *Jean* or *Jeanne* to avoid having to learn their names and never looked twice – well, not at the ugly ones, of whom he accounted himself one.

Idiot devil! There were only two doors that way but one did bear the crest of Navarre. He went to the door. There was no guard on it – such men were now scarce in the days of the Plague and many of the nobility complained to their servants that their wage demands were usurious.

He knocked. He tried the door. It was locked. Great.

This was the new way, of course – locks and bars. In a time when no one who woke with the dawn knew if they'd be alive to see the dusk, theft was rife. The penalty for stealing from a nobleman was death but, then, the penalty for breathing seemed to be death nowadays.

So Charles had locked the door. He knew the nobility, however, and doubted Charles would accept that as an excuse for not returning with the perfume. He took out his angel's feather and waved it at the lock. The lock simply disappeared. Years before, this would have caused him consternation but he knew that it would soon return as quickly as it had gone. He went within.

It was an unusually small and dingy chamber that smelled strongly of cat piss. An ordinary table stood at one side and on it, ink and writing vellum. There was a chair and a locked chest but very little else. There was a small glass pot of something. Osbert picked it up. It didn't smell much like perfume and when he held it to the light of the one slit of a window, he saw that it more resembled tadpoles swimming in a jar than ink. Whatever was in it appeared to be alive. A quill lay on the desk, too. Was this some sort of ink? He didn't care. He had to find perfume; this wasn't perfume, there was no obvious perfume, so that was that. He glanced down at the vellum. Three words were upon it, in French. At first, they seemed to swim before his eyes. Then they took shape to form words: 'Our dearest cousin . . .'

No need to worry who that was to. None of his business.

Osbert looked at the locked chest, then up to Heaven.

Surely God would not have put him here if He hadn't meant him to at least look in the chest. If it was gold, there might be a lot of gold. Then no one would notice one coin or small bar gone missing for a while. And might not the perfume be in the chest?

The angel's feather waved again and the lock on the chest disappeared.

He opened the chest. A glow of gold, fierce and bright, illuminated only his imagination, not his face. The chest was full of pieces of vellum and parchment. There was the seal of the House of Plantagenet on one. Another he didn't recognise. Three feathers. Wasn't that John of Bohemia? He glanced up. No one coming. Some of the information might be useful here as a bargaining tool, should Navarre ever decide to move against him.

He read – written by nobles themselves by the look of it; the handwriting was terrible. Anyone who can afford scribes doesn't get the practice. Secret communications, however, could not be trusted to scribes.

The three feathers seal was from someone with whom Charles was clearly making some sort of bargain. It was not addressed, nor did the writer refer to Charles by name:

'We thank you for your gracious offer of safe landing for our men. We are pleased you recognise our father's rightful claim to the throne of Charlemagne.'

The letter was in French but it seemed the writer was someone in the English court – high up in that court.

Then another one. This time with those quartered arms of Capet and England as its seal. Isabella of England? He feared to touch it, such was that lady's reputation.

'You shall have the means to do as you ask. We will send him to you. You shall build a mountain of dead and stand upon it, owner of all you see.'

There was a small vial at the bottom of the chest. He held it up to the window. It shone with a deep ruby sparkle, the colour of foreboding sunsets one instant, of promising dawn the next. He would recognise it anywhere. Angel's blood.

Should he steal it? Yes! He could protect Gilette from the plague with it and be swived in thanks! And, if the worst came to the worst, he could give Charles another faceful and have it on his toes out of the palace before anyone could touch him. He stuffed the vial into his tunic.

There was no perfume, though – none at all. Then he realised. The devil that had directed him had been upside down! Left meant right and right meant left! He sped along the corridor to find the king of Navarre's door open. There, clearly marked on the table, was a bottle of perfume in an amber bottle. He sniffed it. Yes, that was the stuff: rosewater and something deeper, he didn't know what. He turned and ran to find the king of Navarre.

Unsurprisingly, when Osbert returned with the perfume, Navarre was nowhere to be seen. He was accustomed to the whims of powerful men – Charles had, in all likelihood, forgotten about his request to Osbert. That is to say, 'forgotten' about it until he might suddenly remember and expect Osbert to have it immediately to hand. He was still nervous that Charles might recognise him. He was certainly younger-looking than when he had been court magician and now was dressed as a servant, his hair and beard shaggy, rather than a courtier. So perhaps he was safe. And perhaps not.

He couldn't run away – La Cerda would get word of it in a day or two and hunt him down. Beyond this, the situation could be said to be quite enviable. Yes, he was beholden to a great lord, in fear of being recognised by a cruel king, destined for Hell unless he could perform the impossible task of finding a spare key to Hell but, that said, he was warm, fed, clothed. Lots of people were facing impending death without any of those comforts and most were destined for Hell, if he could judge by what he'd seen on his visit there.

So salvation was in his grasp as, presumably, was great reward if he broke the succubus's hold on the king. He gripped the vial of angel's blood inside his tunic. How would this devil, or demon, or whatever it was, like a faceful of that? Not much, he'd guess. Perhaps he could construct a circle using the blood, conjure the names of God, the angels of the four winds, spirits of the north and south, and then trap it within. Its power would not penetrate beyond the circle, for sure. No diabolic creature's could. The king would be free, Navarre would be out on his ear, La Cerda returned, Osbert rewarded or back to summoning devils for a living. That profession, so lately odious to him, now seemed appealing in the extreme.

Yes, what a plan! The king slept from Matins in the middle of the night to Terce in the middle of the morning, judging by the merciful silence that prevailed in the lodge before 'bonk, bonk, bonk,' resumed for the day. A tiny dab of angel's blood on each eye should protect him from the succubus.

He fingered the vial inside his tunic. It was marvellous stuff. Just a touch could restore youth, a mere smear cover a whole magic circle. One of its most amazing uses was as a cure for drunkenness. You could get beyond smashed, take but the tiniest bit, and the body was all a-tingle leaving you sober as a statue and ready to do it all over again.

He secreted himself in Pascal's chamber – next to the king's own. This was a tiny room with a good straw mattress on the floor, with a connecting door, should his majesty require anything during the night.

There was no keyhole but the door had a good knot in it that allowed him a peek of the interior. He sniffed at the door. It smelled like a barn in there. Had no one emptied the stool in days? He looked through, hearing the familiar bonking noise. All he could see was a woman's foot, which appeared to be at an unusual angle. The day grew dim and night fell and Osbert dozed.

Osbert dreamt odd dreams where he was naked, pursuing Aude through a forest, asking for his armour back. He bore her no malice. He wasn't above robbing someone who fell asleep himself. He awoke with a jolt. It was very dark, a thin moon shining through the vellum on the window. There was no noise from the other room.

He looked through the knot again. Nothing. He would empty the pan. That's it. If asked, he was emptying the pan. He took out his little vial and dabbed it to his eyes. The familiar tingle flushed through him. He felt a yard taller, full of energy. Yes, he could do it. Yes.

He pushed back the door and looked inside. My God, what sort of devil was this? She was awake, sitting at the side of the king's bed, her hand in his, gazing into his eyes. Now he could hear the king's breathing, like a stag at bay, heavy, fast with a sawing rasp to it. Even with the protection of the angel's blood, it was easy to see that Blanche was some sort of devil. She softly glowed in the darkness, as if lit with an inner, moony light. All her attention was on the king. Osbert kept a good grip on the vial. If the devil cut up rough, it was going to get it right between the eyes.

The king groaned, like a man in a fever. He came closer.

'Just going to empty the pan, My Lady,' he said. It was as if he wasn't there. She was transfixed by the king.

Emboldened, Osbert stepped further within. God's bouncing balls, the man looked like a corpse. He'd seen healthier looking men on a Plague barrow.

'Wake,' said Blanche.

'I'm sorry?' He smiled a servant's smile.

'Wake, my love, that we may join again in holy bliss. Man and wife, king and queen, blessed by God and releasing the ecstasies of Heaven.'

Osbert moved the pan with his foot. It was full to overflowing and stank.

'May I take this, ma'am?'

No reply again.

He went to the window – in luxurious glass. He removed the panel and then threw the contents of the pot through the open window. Then he replaced the panel. All the time Blanche did not move, but sat enraptured by the king. The king coughed, hard enough to lift him off the bed.

Osbert went and looked down at him. For the first time, Blanche seemed to notice him.

'Is he not beautiful?' she said.

Her attention came over him like the breaking of a wave. He felt weak-kneed, sick, fuzzy-headed and wanted to sit down. This despite the angel blood! This was a powerful devil indeed. Osbert had experienced them in their many forms, but never one so alluring. He had known the fallen angel Sariel and she had seemed as beautiful to him, but he wondered to see such perfection in a devil. Ah well, it was only inhabiting the body of Blanche of Navarre. Perhaps she was already so lovely. He caught himself falling under her spell. No. Time now to get on with his plan.

'Would you mind?' She did not reply.

This was odd. Was she draining the king? He knew this was how succubuses worked – by swiving a man to death. The king had lasted longer than most. But could a devil touch a king without invitation? No time to reason that one out. Just get on with it. He took out his chalk and sketched a circle around her.

'Mind your feet,' he said, like a woman scrubbing the floor, as he crawled past her. She didn't stir. In the devil's own light he sketched the names of God and of the spirits of the winds. He added a few of the archangels too, for extra security. It might be possible to trap lesser devils by using holy water or crushed-up pieces of the communion host. Any devil that could enchant a king needed stronger measures. Carefully, he dabbed the angel's blood around the cardinal points of the circle, then traced the full circumference. The lightest patina would suffice. The devil didn't move. She sat staring at the king. He moved the vial of angel's blood to the king's lips to revive him, but thought better of it. No, it would profit him more to do things differently.

Now for the show that would secure his place in history. Navarre would be undone. His rooms were on the other side of the lodge. Prince John's were much nearer.

'Ready,' said Osbert. 'Ready to ascend the ladder to favour again.'

He crept out of the room and over to Prince John's door. No guard here, either. The Plague had changed everything. He knocked lightly. No reply. He knocked harder.

A great shout from within: 'God's dangling piles, what time is it?' That was not the prince's voice.

'My Lord, come quick. Your father awakes. The enchantment on him is broken.'

Stirring and grumbling, some cursing. The door opened. It was a groom, still half asleep, carrying a rush light.

'What?'

'My Lord, tell the prince. It is I, Osbert the sorcerer, who has been working unseen to restore his father to health and break the enchantment he is under. The enchantment is broken and he is restored to health. Come and see!'

The large figure of Prince John loomed behind the groom.

'Can it be true?'

'It surely is, sir. It is me, Osbert.'

John squinted at Osbert. 'I remember you. Perhaps. There was a fellow . . . What?'

'Your father is free. The reign of Navarre is over. The succubus is defeated and I will restore your father to his full wits and competencies.'

'His *what*-encies?'

'Please, My Great Lord. Follow me.'

John and the grooms traipsed after Osbert to the king's room. The devil still stared at the king.

'My God,' said John, 'he's worse than he was.'

'But the devil is trapped and I shall restore him, sir.'

Osbert strode across the floor to stand beside the king.

'What is going on?' It was Navarre, pushing through the grooms.

'You are undone, sir. It is I, Osbert, who did best you at Crécy, returned to restore the king to health and sanity.'

Navarre tried to get into the room but the grooms held him back. Osbert, suddenly aware of the speed of the cat-like king, thought it best to hurry proceedings along. He reached into his tunic, pulled the stopper from the vial, and put it to the king's lips.

The king clutched his throat. Then he sat up and looked about him.

'Restored!' said Osbert.

Philip put his hand to his throat again and coughed heavily. And again. Osbert smiled at him and bowed. The king coughed once more.

'I cannot . . .'

'Cannot what, sire?' said Osbert.

Later, of course, Osbert would realise the king's attempted final word had been 'breathe'.

Osbert looked at the bottle in his hand and sniffed at it. The bitter perfume scent.

'That was rosewater and belladonna,' said Charles. 'You're not meant to drink it!'

'An error of detail,' said Osbert, addressing the throng of nobles but looking at the king. 'I shall give him angel's blood to restore him.'

He took out the correct vial and applied it to the king's lips.

Wide-eyed, Blanche stared at him.

'Majesty defiled, love cast down. What fiend has done this?'

Osbert now had the correct vial in his hand, unplugged. Oh shit, at least she couldn't get at him. He was utterly certain he'd dabbed that circle with the right vial, it had been the one he'd used on his eyes. He'd give Navarre a faceful of that and then. Play it by ear.

'He isn't dead,' said Osbert.

'Here he is,' said Blanche, 'here he is! I see his soul departing. My love! My love.'

She threw herself forward off the chair, onto the bed and, Osbert was alarmed to note, out of the magic circle.

'Right,' said Osbert. 'Nobles, gentles all, I shall depart.' He gave a deep bow and made towards the door of the dogsbody's room, but Charles froze him to the spot with an outstretched finger.

'Sorcerer! I see you now!'

'My Lord, the devil has escaped!' said Osbert.

'What devil?' said John.

'That devil.'

Blanche looked up at him, her eyes full of hate.

'I am no devil. I am the angel Asbeel, fallen into Hell seeking a way back to God through the love of kings!'

Osbert put his hand on the door to the dogsbody's room but Blanche leapt for him with superhuman speed. He instinctively threw the vial of angel's blood into her face and dived aside. She swiped at him as he moved, knocking him to the ground.

When she rounded on him again, though, she stopped. She was splattered with the blood.

'What's this?' she said. 'What's this?'

She held up her hands.

'Blood of the Archangel Jegudiel, at a guess,' said Osbert.

Blanche screamed, so hard that the men in the chamber covered their ears.

'A sin!' she said. 'An abomination! I am contaminated. I am stained!'

She ran for the main door, skittling the men aside and then was gone.

'You will die!' Charles strode towards Osbert, but Osbert still had the vial and held it up.

'There's enough of this to scald you, Sir Cat!' Charles backed away, hissing.

'Shall I cut him down where he crawls?' said a groom to John.

'Peace!' John held up his hand and the room fell quiet.

He walked over to the bed where his father lay. Osbert, with his pardoner's eye for relics, couldn't help sizing the king up for his worth. If they made him a saint then his hair alone could be sold for a fortune. His teeth, too, were in excellent condition.

'The king is dead,' said John.

Everyone in the room fell to their knees. Osbert, already on the floor, prostrated himself into a full grovel.

'A new king rises.' John stood tall, slightly ridiculous in just his hose and undershirt.

Charles had composed himself. 'Majesty, we must punish his murderer.'

John turned his slow gaze to the king of Navarre.

'Cousin,' he said, 'it is as if an enchantment has been lifted from me. Was your sister a sorceress?'

'She was, Lord, I see it now. She bewitched me and made me forget the deep love I held for you.'

'And my father, whose reign so blighted the kingdom, who brought us defeat at Crécy, who hated all I loved and loved all I hated, is now gone.'

'Poisoned by this sorcerer!' said Charles.

'You said it was perfume!' said Osbert.

'Hold your tongue, you low dog.'

'This man has done us great service,' said John. 'He has freed the court of a witch and, though my father died when the spell was broken, his soul is in Heaven and the earthly realm of France is mine.'

'The king of Navarre helped me in this endeavour!' Osbert thought he might get what favour he could from Charles – a quick death at least.

'Then we are blessed in our friends,' said John. 'Long have I thought we should free this court of devils. Now our sorcerer who brought them here is returned to us. When the cathedrals are renewed, when new churches are built and devils and demons banished from the land, then the angels will return. How can we know if the fiends that surround us work for us or our enemies? They are not beautiful and they are not necessary. Let us be rid of all devils. Sorcerer, can you do it?'

'With a king's command and God's will behind me, I'm sure I can.'

'Let's not be hasty,' said Charles. 'Might not some of these devils be thought to have given good service? Had we more on our side at Crécy, would we not have won?'

'It surprises me you talk of Crécy, cousin,' said John. 'There were those who charged that day's loss to your account.'

Charles audibly gulped.

'I believe,' said John, 'that the dragon that tore the angels was a punishment from God because we associated with devils. I believe the pestilence affrighting the land has the same origin. We shall take steps to banish the devils from this court. A magic circle shall surround all our palaces. No devil shall cross it.'

'The English will use devils,' said Charles. 'You can bet Lord Sloth will be licking his lips when he hears we have cast such help aside. And what of the demons of the poor who fight for Edward? What defence against them?'

'Belief.' John smiled. 'Cousin, you are dear to us and have been so since you were a boy. We know you for a hot-tempered and difficult youth and understand that you are jealous of our love. You were enchanted and are now free. You shall have ample reward in due course.'

'Make me constable!' said Charles.

John held up his hand. 'My father's corpse is still warm. Let us deal with things in the proper way. To each thing its own season.'

Charles smiled and bowed.

'Now to work,' said John. 'My father's funeral arrangements must be made. And we have had enough of hiding in Vincennes. Let us return to the city and our palaces there. Sorcerer, what do you need to work your magic?'

'Money,' said Osbert, gazing up with the continuing expectation of a kick in the face.

'Then you shall have it.'

'And access to relics, of course.'

'Those too. This,' said John, 'is the day France is reborn. Today we rise again, full mighty in the eyes of God. To Notre Dame and to prayer. But first, send word to La Cerda that the enchantment is broken – the court is free and he may return.'

'Amen!' said Osbert, casting a sideways glance at Charles, who looked at him with the expression of a cat who has just caught a canary mocking it behind its back.

John turned from the room and Osbert went scuttling after him, thinking that the closer he stayed to the new king, the safer he would be.

15

The count of Eu wrapped his cloak around him, sheltering from a November squall. His horse was tired, the animal blowing out its complaints as he moved towards the gates of Paris. So long hiding, dodging devils before he'd made it home on a ship whose captain had been made desperate by Plague. Those winter seas! What man who was not near starving ever chose to face them, no matter what the reward. An early snow lay thin on the rooftops and spires, even on the roads themselves. He shivered, though not with the cold. At this time of year the suburban tracks were usually too well used to allow any snow to settle. The city above the walls was beautiful but it was the beauty of a sepulchre, the whited bulk of Notre Dame rising up like a nation's tombstone. He had loved this run in to Paris through the suburbs. This was life at its most vibrant: the tinkers and the labouring men around their fires; the smell of poached game on the wind; the ragged children shouting out to him to buy whatever they thought he might like – women, ale, food. Some would try to touch him for a cure, others would bow as if before God. He felt a sharp duty of care towards these people – they toiled, he fought. That was God's bargain and he was pleased to bring them peace, if not a relief from poverty. He'd often dreamt of making this journey in his long captivity, but now the way through the hovels appeared as if in a dream – empty, cold and silent. A new land; a new king too, if the reports that had reached Guisnes were true. They were saying the old king had swived himself to death.

The horse bowed its head, losing its struggle with the wind. He thought how surprising horses must find life. When they are saddled for the day, they have no idea if they are to be taken for a ride across three fields or three countries. Were men so different? Perhaps only in that they deluded themselves they had some control over their destinies.

'Not long now, old fellow,' he said, patting the horse's mane. 'A nice stable at the court and a bag of oats to chew on.'

'And a nice bed for us.'

Auhert was at his side – one of six good men he had taken from his county of Guisnes on his way through. They'd been delighted to see their lord – though they'd be less delighted when he sent them home with the news that his freedom had been won by promising the county to English control. Still, that was only yet a promise. He hoped to enlist the help of the king in buying the county back. It was of vital strategic importance, but so was the information he was carrying, exposing Navarre's plot. He had thought to send a letter with the man dispatched to alert the king to his approach but had decided that the greatest drama – John was a lover of drama – would be achieved by making the announcement himself.

They waited before the gates of Paris for the king to be informed of their arrival. Not long, he was pleased to note. Trumpets sounded, a great clatter of hooves, and the gates opened to reveal forty Knights of the Star - France's new answer to the Knights of the Garter - in all their bursting colours sent to receive him. At the front was a courtier. He didn't recognise him – some middle-ranking comte in a surcoat of checked blue and gold. It was of good enough material, but not something you'd catch a duke wearing. Not a good sign that no one greater had been sent to meet him. Perhaps they were all dead. He bowed in the saddle.

'My Lord Eu. Comte Dreux at your service. The king expects you.'

'Then lead, sir.'

The great throng engulfed them and led them at a clatter through the streets.

He'd been looking forward to Paris – French voices, French language, French smells of garlic and fine cheese. None of that. The streets were not exactly empty but far from the normal bustle he'd expect. Still, he would begin to feel at home soon. Even the air was different here, not the cold, aching wind of England but a crisp cold with the smell of ash fires in the air.

Much had changed since he had been away – the streets were sparser, the prices greater. The poor were fewer in number, while a mason's house bore a crest in what looked like it might be gold leaf on the first floor. He tapped the purse at his belt. It was a finely made piece in calfskin, worth a year's labour to most of the poor. And yet it was empty, while the toiling wretches – their skills made rare and therefore costly by the Plague – decked their homes in filigree. This was the new world, then – the world upside down, God absent or sleeping.

'You had a good trip from England?' Dreux was at his side.

'Passable, sir, passable.'

It had taken him an age to get back to Paris. The Norman lords were vacillating between England and France – or so it was said. He had no doubt that they had come out for England, following the lead of Charles of Navarre. He had no doubt now that the boy was wildly ambitious. He cherished the constableship and the risk of Eu falling into his hands – or worse, those of his thuggish brother – was too great. He could not risk Dieppe, could not risk Caen. Calais was under Luciferian control under the woman Greatbelly. Anglo-Gascon mercenaries were burning half the south. In the end it had been Sluys and a trip through Flanders in disguise. The count of Flanders would have snared him in an instant if he had known, but he was currently closer to France than England, so less likely to get word of Eu's passage through his lands.

God, the winter sea. It had cost a fortune he didn't possess to get a captain to take him in November. Luckily the man would sail on a promise.

'Not going to the Louvre?' said Eu.

'King John prefers the Tour de Nesle,' said Dreux. 'He finds the air sweeter. He has a mind that the Plague is carried by low vapours, so prefers to spend time as high as he can.'

'As good a theory as any I've heard.'

'My view is that it's a punishment from God.'

'Whatever for? We can't all be guilty – French, English, Florentines, Romans, Castilians and the rest of the world.'

'God is offended everywhere,' said Dreux. 'I blame the devils. We should never have allowed them.'

'John has done well to banish them.'

'Not all of them.'

'Navarre?'

'Still hanging around like a bad smell. It's good to see you, Constable. We've missed your wisdom.'

'And I yours,' said Eu, though he couldn't recall ever seeing the man in his life.

They neared the Tour de Nesle where John had set up his court. A strange place to choose – more of an extended fort on the left bank of the river. All along the bridge to the tower, John's banners stood, gaudy and limp in the cold air, a shivering man-at-arms beneath each – the handsome braziers at their backs doing little to drive away the cold, it seemed. His own flag was missing, he noted, those of La Cerda in the prominent position next to the king's own on the steps. Well, he'd always had to contend with favourites; it would be no different now.

Eu wondered about the cost of all this. The country was crippled, it was well known – bandits, Englishmen, Gascons, Normans, every sort of pillager on the prowl. And now it was facing invasion. Despite his misgivings, Eu had to concede, this was a more kingly display than Philip had ever bothered to put on. And perhaps John was right to offer a little pomp, a little show after the dour Plague years. The count himself thought he might add substance to the appearance of joy with the news he was bringing. A traitor unmasked, an invasion undone. He was pleased to bring the news – to prove his value so quickly again.

A gaggle of pages came forward to meet them and Eu slipped down from his horse. He looked up at the tower. He remembered what had gone on here – the Valois women up to their old devil-summoning tricks again. Was that why John was here? Did he use their summoning chambers? Or did he think protection was possible there – some circle or device to keep away the Plague and assault by demons? God, if the angels could come back . . .

So much to tell John, so much to do to set the realm back on its feet again.

Up the stairs to the tower and the doors were flung open. Two Navarrese footmen on duty. He steeled himself. Now to face Navarre.

'God,' he offered up a prayer, 'let right prevail. Give me the words I need.'

More trumpets sounded and he went within the tower, where the first devils had been said to come to France and where he now hoped to drive the devil Navarre from it.

The interior of the Tour de Nesle was not as Eu remembered it. It had always been opulent – a resting place for royalty and aristocracy – but now its walls glittered with rich tapestries in cloth of gold, candlesticks and rich plates. Carpets adorned the entrance hall, a filthy affectation in Eu's opinion – dirt from the street had already rendered them a dirty brown. *Glitter and shit*, thought Eu, *like a dragon's cave.*

A strange figure greeted him at the top of the stairs – he recognised it as that court sorcerer, the one who had summoned the French devils.

'Ah, My Lord Eu,' said the sorcerer, with a deep bow.

He had a flame-red pointed hat on his head adorned with circles and symbols like a wizard from a story, and wore a pale yellow cape that looked as though it had been made for a man twice his height. To Eu, the man resembled nothing so much as an enormous melting candle. At the sorcerer's back were two extravagantly dressed knights, surcoats of stars picked out in silver. These must be the vaunted Knights of the Star – a body set up by John in response to Edward's ridiculously named Knights of the Garter. How they had suddenly become the flower of European chivalry, Eu did not know. One of them he recognised, Geoffrey Bellerose. The man was no lion of the lists, that was for sure – a very mediocre fighter who was given to passing out after the first decent blow to the helm. His boots, Eu noticed, were adorned with little stars too.

'Does the king send common men to greet the constable on his return?' said Eu.

'These are strange times, sir,' said the sorcerer. 'The Plague, the depredations of the English and their godless horde, nobility possessed and struck down by all manner of infernal spirits. We need to simply ensure no malign force attends you with a small, discreet banishing ritual.'

'I'm the count of Eu!' said Eu, 'Constable of France. By Satan's boiling piss, no infernal force would dare!' He thumped the constable's chain at his neck for emphasis.

'No, sir, no,' said the sorcerer, shaking beneath the huge robe and giving the impression of an oversized chicken blancmange. 'Even the sister of the great king of Navarre was afflicted. The demonic forces know no bounds.'

'I will not submit to it!' said Eu. 'Such an indignity.'

'Suit yourself, squire, but you ain't getting in to see the king without it.'

Eu's hand went to his sword hilt. A tap on the shoulder. Dreux.

'We all have to submit to this nowadays, Lord. The king is afraid of contagion, of devils, of . . .' He drew breath. 'The king is afraid.'

'Very well,' said Eu. 'Get it done and then get out of my sight.'

The sorcerer bowed again and approached down the steps, tripping for an instant on his long cloak before regaining his balance and completing his descent in high steps, like a May dancer.

He waved his hand into Eu's face, muttered a few phrases in Latin, and then fumbled in his cloak to produce a small bottle. He withdrew the cloth stopper and sprinkled it over Eu.

'Safe!' he said.

The two knights bowed and gestured for Eu to come up.

He strode up the stairs and into a throne room. Here the opulence was stunning: rich tapestries showing hunting scenes; a handsome fireplace decked out in carvings of stags, all adorned in gold leaf; a great throne on which sat the imposing figure of John. He was in good shape for a king, tall and broad, and Eu knew him for a brave warrior. A shame his brains were not as formidable as his appearance. To his left was the shit Navarre, to his right La Cerda, shining like the night sky, so many jewels adorned him. Around them the rest of the council. He knew them by name. Blissy and Beaupoil, Armagnac and Laval. Friends, or as close to friends as you can have at court. They eyed him shyly. He didn't like this. Shouldn't they be cheering his reappearance? He glanced at La Cerda, at Navarre. Had one of them been made constable in his absence?

'Cousin,' said John. 'You are home.'

'Yes, Lord.' He sank to his knees.

'Why do you do me such honour?'

'You are my Lord.'

'Not so, not so.'

'Why do you say this, sir?'

'Edward, across the sea in England, is your Lord.'

'I have not been so long in England that I have become an Englishman. All the time I was there, I worked for your interests, sir, I—'

John leapt to his feet. 'Must I be subject to such lies! Dare you say these things to my face?'

Eu's mouth went dry, he felt his head pounding.

'Who has spoken against me, sir, who has slurred my name? Allow me to defend myself!'

John clicked his fingers at Navarre. The youth smiled and stepped forward to hand the king a letter.

He snatched it and threw it at Eu.

'Do you deny this is yours, in your hand, written in a code known by you and the king of Navarre? He has explained your subtle cypher, sir, laid it bare before me. You have intrigued against me and you have attempted to steal away the source of our magical defences against the evil of the English, our perfidious cousins.'

'I have not!' said Eu.

Navarre stepped forward and picked up the letter.

He read:

'Send the court sorcerer who was at Crécy. The work is of a nature I cannot disclose, and he must travel here without notice.'

'You cannot trust Navarre, he himself has been intriguing with the English. I have the evidence!'

Eu produced the letter that had been delivered to him from the Black Prince.

John took it from him and opened it.

'Do you take me for an idiot?'

'Sire?'

'No seal, no writing, nothing.'

'I don't follow.'

'The paper is blank, sir!'

He held it for Eu to see. The count felt his stomach fall into his boots as he realised it was true. There was no writing on the paper at all.

'I have been robbed! The letter has been replaced.'

He took it from the king's outstretched hand. But no. It was the same vellum, the same little drawing of a cat in the corner.

'This is sorcery,' said Eu. 'I am the victim of sorcery.' He pointed to Navarre. 'He has worked magic against me.'

'Impossible,' said John. 'The court is surrounded by powerful wards.'

Eu swallowed.

'Yes, well you might pale, My Lord. We have banished sorcery from Paris. No devil flies here, no magic can be worked.' Navarre coughed his little cat's cough. 'I have a letter of my own, from my spy at the English court. Do you deny that you have signed away the county of Guisnes? Have you not signed away your castle there to our enemies, giving them a foothold?'

'The castle lies behind Navarre's lands in Normandy. Navarre is conspiring with the English and the castle would have been value-less. I only gave them what was already lost!'

'A surprise they wanted it, then,' said Navarre.

'La Cerda,' said Eu. 'Back me here. Is this not a dangerous man, is this not a devious man?' He pointed to Navarre.

'He has strengthened France while you have sold its territories to its enemies.'

Eu should have known. No matter how La Cerda hated Navarre, he had too much to gain by the fall of the Constable of France.

He straightened. 'Well, My Lords, congratulations. You have killed me. Which one of you will have my lands, I wonder? Which one my office? I am a true servant of France. I have honoured my king, I have fought bravely and never wavered in my loyalty. My king!' He turned to John. 'I will not beg for my life nor try to stay your hand. Know only that I will serve you, in Heaven as I hope or in Hell if I must.'

'Get him away,' said John, 'We'll hang him in the morning.'

Eu was seized, his constable's chain stripped from him. Eu saw Navarre's little hand shoot forward to take it but John took it himself.

'La Cerda!' he said.

La Cerda knelt.

'No!' said Navarre. 'Not him! I should be constable. So much was promised!'

John smiled. 'You are still not much more than a boy, Charles. When you are grown, you may come to such high office.'

'He is without connection. He is, he is mere . . .' He searched for the word before spitting it out like a cat in a bate. 'Nobility. We are royal. We are appointed of God!'

'He is connected,' said John. 'For we have some more good news. I am to be married to our dear La Cerda's cousin, Countess Joan of Auvergne, widow of the late Philip who died at our side when we took Aiguillon back from the English.'

'That is a preposterous match!' said Charles. 'She's got a son already. You've got eight children, the place will be overrun.'

'Remember to whom you speak, cousin.' John mellowed, smiling as he had often smiled on Charles in their younger days at courts.

'She brings a great dowry. What do you expect? I should marry your poor sister, so lately my father's bride, and provide my own dowry!'

The court burst out laughing at such great wit.

'She's wandering the streets mad, they say,' said John. 'And may she take her witchcraft with her.'

Navarre gaped like a decked fish.

'We are now surrounded by loyal men. France will retain her greatness now the viper is driven from her garden. You, La Cerda, will be our constable, our right hand, scourge of the English and defender of our right. With this badge, I give you the lands of Champagne, Brie and Angoulême!'

Navarre looked fit to collapse.

'Those counties were my mother's,' he said.

'Oh Charles,' said John. 'The whole of France was your mother's, if we were to listen to you. I wouldn't have you angry at me, cousin. Marry my sister Joan! She's pretty enough.'

'She is pretty indeed. But what lands does she bring with her, Lord?'

'Oh, you've lands enough in Normandy. Have Guisnes.'

'That is pledged to the English, sir, it will bring great troubles to my door.'

'Something to keep you busy. Take Joan back there, knock up a few babies and knock a few English heads.'

Eu spoke, 'Thought you'd be made constable, did you, Navarre? Bad luck. Back to the plots and schemes. Maybe they'll make you constable of England if your treachery rewards you! He'll have the English upon you, sir, do not mistake that.' A man restraining him dug Eu hard in the ribs. Eu headbutted him, sending him crashing to the floor. The second man took a stamp to the knee and collapsed likewise.

'Take him!' shouted John, but Eu drew his sword and neither guards nor courtiers appeared to much relish the idea of putting hands on such a formidable knight.

Eu pointed his sword at the little Dauphin – as Prince Charles was now rather strangely being called, after his father inherited somewhere in the east. The boy, no more than twelve years old, instinctively stepped backwards. 'Your father is beset by false friends,' he said. 'Take care to protect him from them.'

'Father,' said the Dauphin. 'The count has many, many friends in France. Might it not be better to hear more fully the case against him, to allow him to make defence and call witnesses? We may indeed send him to meet divine judgement, but after men have heard his crimes and been able to assess them for themselves. This risks civil war.'

John stood off his throne – *a tall and magnificent idiot*, thought Eu. His son should be king. The Dauphin Charles was mocked by some for his lack of courage and skill in the tilt yard and comparisons made to his father who, docile as a greyhound at table, could be as fierce as a leopard in battle. But if the Dauphin had been king, if he had been king, if . . .

'Am I not loved?' John roared.

'You are loved, sir,' said La Cerda, leading a chorus of approving voices.

'And does he not condemn himself by drawing steel in our most sacred and inviolable court?'

The courtiers brayed their consent.

Some spangled knight stepped towards Eu, his courage – or rather his wish for favour and advancement – pushing him to risk his life. He had no sword, afraid to draw it in the presence of the king. Eu turned his own weapon around and offered it to the man.

'Here,' he said. 'Joyeuse. Charlemagne's blade. Give it to the constable, I feel he'll have need of it in days to come.' The knight took the weapon and the guards advanced but Eu stopped them in their tracks as he turned to face them.

'No need to force me. I only need the command of my king to go to my death. How many of you cowards could say the same?'

John gestured for them to back off.

'Now show me to my cell and send me a priest.'

16

'I know,' said Osbert to Gilette, 'that we've had the Plague, the huge defeat of our armies, Hell has spilt devils and demons upon the land, so many are dead and the king who was our rock for so many years is also dead. But, to the man of cheerful outlook, these things present themselves not as problems but as open doors that may—'

Charles of Navarre appeared from nowhere, causing Gilette to scream and run off, while the little king pinned Osbert to the wall at the point of a dagger.

'Lord, do not kill me, I am a useful man!'

Charles drew back his lips to show his spiky little teeth.

'I am not going to kill you this time, sorcerer,' he said. 'But some time, and it will be soon, I may prick you or cut you a little and eventually I will kill you. Wait for it. Any shadow, any recess or doorway, I may be waiting. You have taken the sceptre of France from my hands and placed it in those of my enemies.'

Charles withdrew and, in his cat-like way, vanished.

Osbert felt sweat running down his legs, or at least he hoped it was sweat. He could banish Charles, complete the circle around the court, refuse him entry. But then one of his men would come for him, abduct him, torture him, cut off his most tender parts and feed them to him. Boiled, perhaps. Osbert, a man given to flights of thought, wondered if it would be a kindness or a cruelty to serve a man his own tadger boiled. Presumably it would be easier to munch on. The thought made him ill. There was no end to the barbarities a man like Navarre could dream up. Perhaps he would boil his bollocks while they were still attached. For a few moments Osbert pondered on this. A coward is an imaginative man.

As he sweated and fretted he became aware of another pair of eyes looking at him. It was Prince Charles, now known as the Dauphin, since his father had bought the right to be named after a fish – and collect some taxes – off some extravagant southern lord. He wore a rich blue velvet tunic embroidered with the vaunting dolphins that gave him his name. Osbert bowed, sweatily.

'Navarre scares you?' the Dauphin said.

'Yes.'

'I took you for a fool but now I see you are a wise man.'

'Will you not plead with him for me? Or is there bad feeling between you?'

'I love him. It is wise to love him and to be loved. Those he hates come to no good ends. Look at Eu. Cynics might say Charles plotted the entire thing.'

'Your Highness's eye is keen and his wit penetrating.'

'Yes. Perhaps I have misjudged you. Perhaps you are a man who sees what needs to be done.'

Osbert could not help but note this opinion had come from precisely nowhere. Flattery. Why?

'What needs to be done?' said Osbert, very much hoping it would not be him who was required to do it, whatever it was.

The Dauphin said nothing, just regarded him with that even blue gaze.

'What does one do when a diseased stray cat haunts your door?'

'Beat it to death,' said Osbert.

The Dauphin gave a little laugh.

'Well, one gets rid of it, at any rate. Perhaps you should speak to the count of Eu.'

'Why don't you, Lord?' For an instant, Osbert thought he had spoken out of turn, but the Dauphin smiled.

'And what would I say? That my father is an idiot who may lose all France between false friends and bluster? That La Cerda means well but imagines he can deal with Navarre when he cannot? That I can save him? Well, sorcerer. None of these things are true. And besides, it is not politic for me to be seen there. Eu's friends would say that I goaded him on his last night on earth – his enemies might think I gave him comfort.'

'And what can I do?'

'I have a feeling the count should be given a chance to express all his lies. I would be interested to hear them, for my instruction, so – like a base foil around a bright gem – they might better show me the light of truth.'

'You are a subtle man, sir.'

'I am a boy. And I am direct in what I say. Never doubt me. Eu is a traitor and a liar because my father says so. My father the king stands in place of God and cannot be wrong.'

'And what will you say if you stand in the same position?'

The Dauphin crossed himself.

'God protect my father. And such speculations are for another day.'

'They won't let me in to see him,' said Osbert.

The Dauphin took off a ring. It was silver, inscribed with a leaping dolphin.

'This is my authority. You are court sorcerer. Eu is a conspirator, a friend of the English, a devil himself in all but reality. You should inspect his cell to ensure the Count had no magical tricks up his sleeve. That is your duty, is it not? What if he were to escape by magical means, as the sorcerer Montagu once did? Think of the problems that might give the ambitious men of the court. Half the nobilfy is on Eu's side.'

'Very good, sir. God's bones, I wish you could give me your wit, along with this ring.'

The Dauphin smiled. 'If my wit was something I could give away, sorcerer, I would serve France better than by giving it to you.'

He turned away, not even waiting for Osbert to bow.

Quickly Osbert made his room and took his most impressive robe, his wand and his chalks and philtres. The wand did no good but reminded others that he was a magician, appointed by the king and so deserving of respect. He ran to the tower of the palace and swept up the stairs towards the count's prison. The guards let him in without question, though he had no doubt they would report his visit.

The room was well-appointed, wood panelled, with a deal of gilt picking out stag designs on the deep bed. Nobles, he had forgotten, lived better in dungeons than ordinary men in their own houses.

Eu had risen to meet him.

'You are in league with Navarre. I ought to kill you,' he said.

Osbert, being somewhat accustomed to this reaction, bowed.

'I am not in league with that catty fellow. It would be a mistake to kill me.'

Eu smiled a cold smile. 'Well, God forbid that I should make one of those.'

Osbert checked the door was shut.

'How did you get in?'

'I have convinced the king that you may be a sorcerer like Montagu who cursed the king of Navarre.'

'Montagu was no sorcerer.'

'Well, which leaves us with another interpretation in order to explain Navarre's feline tendencies.'

'Which is?'

'The king of Navarre is a devil. Or half a devil, as it is said. My lord La Cerda seemed convinced of that.'

'So how can he get into this court? You have sealed it against them, have you not?'

'I have, as best I can. However, the work is simpler than you think. My circle is of little use. It is the word of the king that keeps the devils away. All he had to do was order them to go and all I had to do was pass that order on.'

'And Navarre?'

'Expressly invited to stay. And I suspect his royal blood gives him more independence than your ordinary fiend.'

'Your point?'

'None, My Lord. Though the King of Navarre has taken a rare dislike to me. Only my own vigilance and the protection of King John save me from . . .' He made the gesture of someone being strangled with a noose.

'I cannot see how this concerns me the day before my death.'

'Well, it occurred to me that, in return for your protection and swift removal from this court, I might be able to arrange your own departure. You have friends in France? I could help you reach them. You could chop Navarre to bits as your first priority!'

He produced the angel feather, which glowed faintly in the gloom of the chamber.

'This will open a hole in the wall. It will also allow you to float to the ground.'

Eu was impassive.

'My king has ordered me to die. That is his will. It is the will of God enacted by His appointee on earth. I cannot go against it.'

Osbert breathed out through his teeth.

'Think of your lands, your family.'

'I think of my soul. Navarre may win here but he condemns himself before God.'

'You are a true servant of France.'

'I am that.'

There seemed nothing more to say. Job attempted, he'd report back to the Dauphin and hope to pick up a tip. Wine, Gilette and sleep, in that order, to follow. Lock the door against catty kings.

'Well, I bid you goodnight, Lord.'

Eu looked Osbert up and down.

'You are a sorcerer?'

'I have summoned many devils.'

'Then you can do France a favour.' He went to his bags. Again, Osbert marvelled that he had been allowed to keep them. Still, there was one law for the rich, another for the poor, which was how God had ordained it.

He opened the bag, took out a small scroll and offered it to Osbert. The sorcerer took it and unwrapped it. It bore a magic circle upon it. Around the edge of the circle were Hebrew letters – Osbert recognised them as such. He counted them, lost count, started again. Seventy-two.

'This is the seventy-two-letter name of God,' he said.

Eu shrugged.

'I have heard of it but it is known only to the highest of the high, revealed in insight and dreams,' said Osbert.

'I received it from the highest of the high. The prince of England is a devil. You are to call him here and trap him in that circle. My sword Joyeuse will be swinging at La Cerda's side. He can kill him with that or die trying. There are enough holy weapons to do for him.'

'This will aid France?'

'Of course.'

Osbert sat down on the bed. Eu's eyes widened at the affront but Osbert held up his finger to beg leave to speak.

'I have a better idea. I have the liberty with this feather to come and go in my Lord Navarre's rooms.'

'Then you should kill him.'

'I have thought of that, My Lord, but he is a wonderful climber and chooses to sleep these summer nights atop the highest tower of the Louvre. No ordinary man could get there. However, I have seen certain documents that confirm your view that he is conspiring with the Black Prince.'

'He will have burnt them by now. He is no idiot.'

'Indeed he has, or I should have contrived to have dropped them in the throne room. However, England's last invasion – for all the slaughter of Crécy – was a failure. They have one port, which it is very hard to leave by land, half given over to the rebellious poor. They need allies. What if one of those allies was to disappear? You may be content, My Lord, to go to your death, but what if you could rid France of your enemy and betrayer, as well as dealing the English a terrible blow as you remove their ally?'

Osbert's mind was on something La Cerda had said when he was first introduced.

'How would you achieve that?'

'Navarre is a devil, or so they say. This is powerful magic indeed. There is the matter of the ingredients, we would need something powerful and holy to hold such a devil, to compel it to come.'

Eu went to his bag again. He removed a wooden cylinder, sealed at the top. 'Dust from the tomb of Becket.'

Osbert smiled. 'That will help. It is a holy relic.'

'Can you be certain it will work?'

'Magic is never certain. It's one thing to have the ingredients, another to work the art. Though the men may assemble on a chessboard, it's in the movement of the pieces that the game is won and lost. It might work.'

Eu puckered his lips.

'You are an Englishman?'

'I am.'

'But you work for the French.'

'They have treated me better than ever the English did. In France I am a sorcerer, dressed in fine robes, eating fine foods. In England, I am a beggar. Well, then, shall I be English and a pauper? No, I'll be French and prosper. Hang the English, for that's what they'd do to me.'

'It is hard to be loyal to France in these times. But God does not set this land in such great estate for nothing. Why else are we so blessed with the riches of the earth, the glory of the sun, such a wide and prosperous estate, while England lies dismal under fogs, ravaged by winds and rains that fall like the judgement of Heaven.'

'What?' said Osbert.

'Navarre must not prosper. Whatever happens, he must not. Your hate for him reassures me.'

'It is a necessary hate. When a great man like that hates a low man like me, the low man must hate in return for, if he loves, then he obeys the Lord's wishes and must die. As I love myself I must hate him.'

'Then do God's work,' said Eu.

'Well, let us try.'

'I will need my sword to kill him.'

'I have a feeling you will not,' said Osbert.

17

The Plague ran ahead of Dow. From the towns and the villages of the north, people came fleeing south, meeting those fleeing north like two mighty flows of water. The dispossessed were everywhere and Dow was sorry to see them. The dying children, the bloated corpses of all stations of men by the roadside, knights, rich merchants, yes, but poor men and women too who had never had anything but their lives and now had those snatched from them.

'This is right,' he told himself. This was the price of rooting out corruption, but it had broken his heart to see it. He thought of England. Had the disease, which had a life of its own beyond him, reached England? He hoped so. It would be a blessing on the land, a new start. A year cannot turn from autumn to spring without a winter between.

He had paused a while in Paris – it was too cold to continue, he would have died himself if he had tried. He could not do that with the world only half way to Eden. He took refuge for the winter in an abandoned church – the priest dead of Plague, the churchyard so full of bodies that new ones were piled in stacks rather than buried. He made a fire in the centre of the nave, hacking the wooden rood screen to pieces, tearing down the sculpture of Christ on the Cross. He lit it with the robes he found in the vestiary, watching as the limbs took light. Christ was Lucifer, returned to bargain with the savage God who had usurped him. It felt right to release the light within this image, to watch the fingertips glow the colour of a setting sun, the body illuminate to become the heart of the fire.

The smoke went high into the beams of the church, little sparks flying up like souls to Heaven. No, not that. There were too many. The multitudes went to Hell, one impure thought unconfessed being enough to secure an eternity in torment. Once he had thought he would open the gates of Hell, allow all the sinners back to earth. But wasn't he cleansing the world? Could the murderers, the thieves, be allowed back once Eden was re-established? He shivered, despite the warmth of the fire. He could not yet fathom the answer to that one. Some judgement might be required, some test to allow access to Paradise.

There was a noise at the poor door of the church. Looking into the body of the fire, he wondered why some people survived the Pestilence, though most did not. The mercy of Lucifer? No. Lucifer would forgive everyone. He knew that sometimes, to serve a cause justly and well, that cause must in some ways be betrayed. The stronger metal from the blacksmith's fire contains impurities; the strongest steel endures many hardships, heated and quenched until such pain toughens it to resist all breakage. So he put the world through this fire of Plague, so he quenched it in blood. Lucifer never demanded obedience. He would see, when he returned, that the sacrifices had been worth it.

'It is done.'

A voice behind him. He turned. A poor man, in rags; beside him a woman wrapped in a thick cloak of the sort a merchant's wife might wear. He was surprised by the clothes of the poor man. When he encountered living people nowadays, he saw so few in the clothes of the poor. The houses of the rich were there for looting – why walk around with holes in your clothes when a rich man's wardrobe lay open to anyone who had the guts to go past his body to steal from it? He wondered himself why he was not harmed by the Plague. Protected by Lucifer? Perhaps. He knew his mother had been a fallen angel. Perhaps that was it.

'What is done?'

'Your task. You have accomplished it. Lucifer wants this. I have seen.'

'You have seen what?'

'The reason for all this. The Pestilence, the destruction. You, my friend.'

Dow said nothing.

He heard the man approaching behind him. He felt no fear, no reason to defend himself. Why rob or kill someone like him?

Men with purses stuffed full of gold lay dead on any street – why waylay a poor man with nothing more than a reed pipe to take?

The man came and crouched beside him.

'Two knights, one horse. That is my upbringing. That is my banner and my nature.'

Dow kept watching the fire. He wondered if this man would drop dead in front of him like so many others or if he would go home to die. Or would he survive? Some did.

'I am a Templar. A poor-fellow. A soldier of Christ Lucifer. I am the one they call Good Jacques. Jacques Bonhomme. Everyman.'

'Good for you,' said Dow.

The woman came now and knelt on the other side of him. She opened her cloak. Within was a flash of silver like the sun on a lake. He had seen it before. The mail of the archangel Jegudiel, liquid, enchanting.

'You have killed enough,' said Good Jacques.

'And Lucifer tells you so? How? He does not speak to me.'

'He speaks to you. That thing you have in the shadows. He spoke to you about that.'

'I do his work. I hope to. I do not know. I do not know.'

'I do. And I tell you this thing is over now. Stopped, as much as it can be stopped.'

'And are you the one to stop it?'

'I am that.' He touched his forehead. Dow saw that it was marked with deep cuts, as if inflicted with sharp needles. 'I have worn the crown. I have seen. You must too.'

Dow now noticed that Jacques had a bag with him. He opened it and took out a cheap wooden box, two spans wide and deep, a span tall. The lid was tied down with rough string and Jacques took out a small knife to cut it.

'You have seen this before, I think. At the Sainte-Chapelle where the angel died.'

He opened the lid. Inside was a circle of thorns. The Crown of Thorns.

'I have worn this.'

'And?'

'When the old god Ithekter – you call him the Horror, whatever you will – when he cast Lucifer into Hell, did not Lucifer escape?'

'He returned as Christ to bargain for the freedom of the world.'

'He did. And what did he get for it? Nailed to a tree and sent back whence he came. His glory stolen. The Horror told men it was him on the Cross, so men would call Lucifer's appointed servant – you – Antichrist when he came. You are not an antichrist. You have more of Christ Lucifer in you than all the legions of the dark god. Tell me what will happen when Lucifer returns?'

'No more bargaining. No more concession. God dies. The age of Eden restarts. None are ruled. None are rulers. So Lucifer vowed on the Cross.'

'He did. And this is the crown he wore. The world's crown, the crown of pain. This is how he saw and through this, you can see him still.'

Dow shifted. 'I had not thought—'

'No. It was known by my order but a secret we sought to keep. It is not an easy path to knowledge. I am offering it you now. Would you talk to the Light, he and she that is in us all, he who was tricked at Golgotha into a bargain the mad god would not keep?'

Butcher shifted in the darkness.

'I do not know. I—'

'Then trust me to tell you why you have done what you have done. You have raised an army to storm the fourth gate. So many dead, say the priests, that Hell cannot hold them all. Lucifer sees what Satan wants, even through the walls of brass, even surrounded by the Moat Doleful, even across the Lake of Fire.'

'What?'

'He wants this earth. God lies wounded, unable to impose discipline. Satan stirs, calling in the magic to take over the earth. There will be no middle place. Just Heaven where God lies bleeding and Hell, here, ruled and ordered by devils if men cannot do it.

'Satan cannot be allowed here.'

'Satan must come here. He must. We must help him,' said Jacques. 'No!'

Good Jacques held forward the box.

'Wear the crown of pain,' he said. 'Let the light into your mind!'

Dow took the box.

When he had last seen this crown he had been a boy, overwhelmed in the presence of the great angel, shocked to see it die.

He had not thought what the crown meant, or what it might do. It had touched Lucifer, pierced his skin, the thorns had soaked in his blood.

'I will do it,' he said.

He stood back from the fire and walked towards the altar. Butcher glistened, slick and bloody in the firelight, crawling with flies, hopping with fleas.

Dow put the box on the altar and took out the crown, gently. The thorns were still sharp after so long and he felt them pierce the skin of his fingers. His stomach skipped and he felt dizzy. The church was no longer around him; the fire no longer burned. He was on a hill, looking up towards three crosses. On two writhed the figures of men; the third and central cross was vacant.

The sky was dark, storm clouds blowing over, the sun bright behind them.

He put on the crown. Dow had been cut in his life before – when he was a young child his tongue was sliced by a priest for spreading heresy. He had been branded, too, with the fork of Lucifer, but this was a pain beyond all those. The thorns cut his skin, burrowed into his skull, it seemed, through his skull to his brain, sharp pins sticking through him like pins into a cushion.

Each thorn was a shaft of light cutting through his head, a lattice of pain illuminating inside him. He was no longer a person, just an agony hung on light. Light was in his hands too, and stuck through his feet; he was nailed to a tree of light. He turned his head, or his head was turned. He could not see who was on the cross beside him.

He heard a voice that was like a million voices speaking at the same time, in every tone, in many strange languages, but he knew what it said.

'One to be my herald.'

He turned to his left. On the cross he saw himself, choking and spluttering in agony.

'One to set me free.'

He turned to his right. There was another figure. He could not make him out but he knew him, or rather the pain taught him about him. He was a thief, as Dow had been, a scoundrel. Lucifer would not be lifted up by kings but by the despised of the world

– not those who choose their destinies, who war and struggle because they can, but those who have destiny thrust upon them, who scrabble, strive and struggle because they must, because to do otherwise is to starve and to die.

His mind was carried on the beams of the thorns, his thoughts ranging wide over a burnt and blasted land. Hell. It must be. He saw armies of devils streaming across burning plains, heard the screams of the tormented, driven in columns across searing deserts, saw the multitudes of dead, so many dead. So many. They turned their eyes to him and, in his agony, he was above them and among them at the same time. There were the routiers he had killed, there the many dead of Caffa, the brightly clad merchants, the drab poor who he had slain with the pestilence he had summoned.

They wandered unguided. The devils had no time for them. Vast armies were gathering – slithering eels with men's heads, fly devils and snake devils, devils that seemed put together from a hundred different offcuts.

'The gates will open,' he heard. 'The gates will open!' In voices human, insect, animal.

'Three gates will open,' said a voice. 'And then the army of dead will storm the final gate that controls the way to Dis. With Satan on earth, his devils gone, the way to the gate will be clear.'

Dow's head swam. The scent of burning hair filled his nostrils, he didn't know if he stood or lay. He felt blood streaming down his face. He was on the cross again but not on the central one. He was looking across at the shining body of Lucifer, his side pierced by the lance, his head cut by the thorn.

'God! God!' said Lucifer. 'Why have you forsaken them?'

'Enough!' screamed Dow.

He pulled the crown from his head and it was as if he was uprooting his brain, that it was a mandrake torn screaming from the soil of his skull. His hands bled, his mouth was full of blood, blood in his nose, in his throat. He put the crown on the altar, coughing as if he would hack up his lungs.

'What has happened to me?' said Dow, gasping.

'In sharing his pain,' said Jacques, 'your mind has gone through the gates of Hell to hear him whispering to you from beyond the walls of Dis.'

'I was on a hill when they killed him.'

'I watched that too. I saw you on the cross.'

'You were the third?'

'No. I don't know.'

'Who was that? He was to open the gate. If we can get to the gate, clear the path, he will open it. Who is he?'

'Someone,' said Jacques. 'But for all my art I cannot see who.'

'He will present himself when the time comes,' said the woman in the angel armour. 'For now, we must act on what we know and do what we can.'

Dow swallowed, made the sign of the three-pronged fork on his chest. His body shivered and he was suddenly very cold but his heart was glad.

'What I did was right. There is a mighty army waiting to release Lucifer so it may be free. What can God do to them? He has already locked them in Hell. Lucifer is their hope. Lucifer is hope.'

'And you have done enough,' said Jacques. 'Aude . . .' He spoke to the woman.

She unsheathed a sword. The church filled with light, all the colours of the rainbow dancing off the walls, dancing inside Dow's mind, filling him with dread and elation. He had come to the end of his taste for action, for doing. He just watched as she approached Butcher, the light dancing off the slick meat, a host of flies and hopping fleas falling from it in a swarm before the rainbow flashes.

The thing keened, its calf's tongue clacking against its fleshless palate.

'Yes?' said Aude.

'Yes.'

'You are sure there are enough?'

'There are enough,' said Jacques.

She raised the sword and struck. There was a bright flash, so bright Dow had to turn away, and when he turned back only a pile of meat like a butcher's poor table lay on the cobbles.

Dow felt tears come to his eyes.

'He is coming, isn't he? He's truly coming.'

'He is,' said Good Jacques. 'But it is up to us to open the way.'

18

Osbert pushed aside the bed and chair and drew the circle on the stone floor of Eu's chamber. Even as he inscribed the letters around its edge, he trembled. He had never worked with such powerful magic and, though he knew his Hebrew letters well from his time in the captivity of the priest Edwin, knew how each related to each in their jumble of consonants in order to produce the sounds of the vowels, he would not let himself say them in his head as he drew them. The name of God filled him with fear. He had worked his summonings before, pulled spirits from their wanderings in the air or through the cracks in the lesser walls of Hell, but then he had the names of angels to work with, not the most holy and secret name of God.

'I can bind him while he is in the circle,' said Osbert. 'With this name, I can command his silence, perhaps even return him to Hell, though that will be harder. And yet, I do not think we will even need this.'

'Why not?'

Osbert didn't want to say in case the summoning went wrong, though why he was worried about disappointing a man who seemed determined to be hanged with the dawn, he did not know.

When the circle was drawn, he sprinkled the tomb dust around it. His stomach felt tight and he had the sensation of bitter fruit in his mouth.

'You are taking your time,' said Eu.

'The preparation must be meticulous. We are dealing with a powerful devil, a king too. A slip could be costly. My Prince Navarre is a small man but fast and full of claws. I would not like this to go wrong.'

'It will be dawn soon. I'll be hanged before you're finished.'

'That is your choice. You have the means to leave with the feather.'

'I should fetch my sword.'

'You will be discovered by the guards if you move through the inside of the building. Never mind, the circle is done.'

He stepped back to survey his work. The circle was an exact copy of the one on the manuscript, more detailed and finer than any he had ever drawn. Angels' names intertwined with those of wind spirits, Latin wrapped around Hebrew. Sworls and curlicues graced the edges, spikes and triangles towards the centre but all gave way for that greatest of names at the edge in plain, blocky letters. There was one gap in the circle, to good purpose.

Osbert took the incense from Eu's bag and lit it from the rush light. The sweet smoke drifted up across the room like a spirit stretching itself out in the light, like the angel-bane dragon at Crécy in miniature.

He intoned the names of the angels, called the names of the spirits, made passes with his hand.

'Will this take for ever?' said Eu.

And then he said it again. Directly afterwards, or sometime later, Osbert couldn't tell. That minute shift in attention, the feeling that the world had been knocked slightly off its centre, took him. It was working.

Light streamed through the windows and Eu said something else; Osbert couldn't make it out. Was it dawn? Yes, the pre-dawn. His mouth tasted of ashes, he felt tired, the light was hollow. It was time. He began, intoning the first letter, the second, moving on with a great deep vowel to the third.

'You are too late,' said Eu. 'They are coming across the courtyard.'

The fourth letter, the fifth, and still on, still on.

'Navarre is with them.' Osbert heard that. Part of his mind was still left in the ordinary world and, as an eavesdropper, he heard his own thought. *He would be. He is being summoned.*

The letters tumbled from his mouth. He had the idea that he was spitting up gems, beautiful sparkling gems that cascaded from his lips to the floor.

Footsteps on the stairs, the sound of the guards coming to quick attention. A hard knock on the cell door.

The sixtieth letter, the sixty-first. His breathing was heavy, as if there was a weight on his chest. Was there a light in the circle? It seemed so, an emerald, dancing light.

'We are going to open the door, My Lord. Prepare yourself to meet great men in decent array.'

The seventieth letter, the seventy-first.

The door opened and Navarre pushed his way past the jailer.

'What is this?' he said.

The seventy-second letter. The emerald light burned bright, bright enough to make Osbert turn away.

'What's this? What's this?' Navarre cried out, shrieking and shaking.

The most incredible transformation had come over him. No longer was he cat-like, with catty eyes and sharp little catty finger-nails. Half of him was a cat, a gigantic black cat with ears and fur and whiskers. The other half of him was a man, an ordinary, quite handsome man in that blond Capetian way. The cat aspect of the king had split away, leaving one half of his body feline, the other human.

'What is happening?' the king cried out like a cat. A red line surfaced on his forehead, more than a line – a crack running down the entire length of his face, cutting him in two. The king tore at his clothes, his human hand quite ineffective, his cat's paw shredding them.

'My Lord!' his men cried out.

'Get these off me,' he said. 'Part of me needs to leave!'

He tore still at his clothes, rolling and thrashing on the floor. The crack in his face grew. It was clear the lord was splitting apart.

The emerald light shone fiercely. A crackle, a smell of ozone, and then a thunderclap.

'Sorcerer!' cried one of Navarre's men.

His sword was free and he swung it, but not at Osbert – at Eu.

The count fell, a great wound at his neck, his blood splattering onto the circle.

'I am dying!' screamed Navarre. 'Dying!'

Eu's blood mingled with the tomb dust and the whole perimeter of the circle bubbled like a hot spring.

A final scream like that of a man on a rack and the king of Navarre split in two, the cat half of his body rolling into the magic circle, wrapping entrails around it as it went. The human half lay where it was, its beating heart visible.

The noble with the sword turned to Osbert.

'No, My Lord,' he said. 'I have battled the sorcerer Eu all night. This is bad magic he has wrought.'

The noble brought his sword to Osbert's throat.

'Undo this magic. Undo it, or I swear on the saints' bones that I will halve you as he has been halved.'

A hiss from the human half of Navarre, a wheezing of lungs and his half-tongue struggled to form a sound. His leg tried to stand, while his hand struggled to contain his guts.

'Save me,' he said. 'Save me and I will be in your debt.'

Osbert looked at the body of Eu, the bubbling magic circle, the jumble of organs, blood, bones and fur that was Navarre. A king in his debt. A king reliant on him to survive. A king who had made a vow in front of his nobles. Navarre was split exactly in half, split as by a great axe, down the centre line of his body. An ordinary man would have been dead, but the king was far from ordinary. He recalled when the devil Nergal had lost his head. Navarre's mother had sewn it back on and made it stable with an iron collar. Devil's flesh mended well.

He bowed.

'Fetch me a bodkin and strong thread,' he said. 'And send for a smith. We will need bonds of iron.'

Osbert was acutely aware of Prince John's eyes upon him as he stitched up the king of Navarre. Half the court had turned up to watch. They brought in two ladies of the court who were skilled with needle and thread to help with the work, but neither could face it. When Prince John arrived, and the smirking La Cerda, Princess Joan was summoned – as the betrothed of Navarre she was bound by duty to help with the stitching.

She blanched when she saw him and crossed herself.

Luckily the girl proved of stronger stomach than the other ladies and set to work with her precise, neat stitch. Osbert marvelled that one so grievously wounded could live, though the success of the stitching did not surprise him. He had seen devils stitched before and noted that it proved marvellously effective.

Throughout the pricking and stitching, Navarre howled piteously, though Osbert had heard knights contend that true mortal wounds are not lamented by their bearer.

'Where there's pain, there's life,' one knight had told him. *And where there's life, there's pain*, he'd thought.

Stitching would not suffice on the split sternum, nor on the jaw and skull, so the smith hammered in some firm staples to fix one side of the body to the other.

'Good news, sire,' said Osbert, as they worked upon him. 'Your cock is left whole, so the future of the line of Navarre may yet be a happy one. Hold still while we sew up your, er, derriere. This is tender work is it not, Princess Joan? Not many a bride knows such intimacy in such a pure and helpful way before her wedding night. The, er, rear will require a woman's nimble fingers to make the neatest join.'

It was not easy work, though it was done as best they could. Still, as Osbert had seen in the case of Nergal, the devil who had been decapitated at the Sainte-Chapelle, devil flesh has its own ways. The summoning over, the circle broken and the green orb of light gone, it was as if the cat part of Navarre had been out for long enough and now butted and mewled to be reunited with its former half, the entrails stuffed back inside. The iron staples alone would not have held Navarre together, nor put the internal parts back in their correct order and relationships. Once the stitches were in place, the cat half and the human half melded very well, the flesh not quite fusing, but still making a very good join.

The king of Navarre was quickly measured by the smith and the bands were fashioned well before the last stitch was in place. They were quite impressive – in the style of an eastern breastplate. There were fastened at the back by quickly improvised ties. The smith promised better when he had more time. 'Armour, more fitting to your station, sir,' he said.

Navarre tried to speak – presumably to tell him not to address his superiors unless told to do so – but the cat side of the top lip came away from the human side and had to be restitched. They worked on him until the day faded. By the time they were finished, a very creditable job had been done, at least in the rush light. The king looked quite impressive in his iron bands, his tight leather collar and the riveted band he wore about his head. Osbert suspected it may have been improvised from a barrel but did not share that with Navarre.

'Good as new!' said Osbert.

'That,' said Navarre, in a way that indicated the human and cat halves of his lips were not working quite as they might, 'is demonstrably untrue.'

He was quite a sight – on his left side a gigantic cat's paw and hind leg, half a very good cat's nose, a fine large black cat's ear, a wonderful coral pink at the centre. On his right, a human leg and arm, an ordinary nose and ear. The join between the two was picked out in the best stitching Osbert and Princess Joan had managed – which was very fine for her part, less for his.

A looking-glass was brought for him and Navarre examined himself in the shining steel.

'This band,' he said, his mismatched eyes flicking up to his forehead, 'will need to be replaced by a crown. Joan, you are to be my wife.'

Joan, a lady of breeding, simply bowed her head, registering none of the panic Osbert might have suspected.

Navarre went on, 'See to it that a fine crown is made for me. Let it be softly padded and come with a means of adjustment to stop my head falling apart.'

'What has become of you, Charles?' said John, with genuine tenderness.

'I am the victim of more English sorcery. But let my enemies beware. Other men may have been split in two from shoulder to groin and used that as an excuse to retire from public life, to live in idleness. Not I. Has ever a knight suffered a more grievous wound?'

'None and lived,' said John.

'Exactly,' said Navarre, on the third stuttering attempt. 'So those who would seek to kill me or do me down would do well to look on me and remember how hard that might be.'

'You need some rest,' said Joan.

'How was the king of Navarre so sorely afflicted, sorcerer?' said La Cerda.

'I believe the sorcerer Eu – who knew, eh? – I believe he summoned the half of my Lord Navarre that is a devil. That part was split from the nobility of his human form.'

'I am not a devil, nor part devil.' Navarre spoke like a man with a broken jaw, struggling to control his face. Osbert could not help but notice that the catty left paw had sprouted a vicious set of claws.

'Then you will not mind if I have the sorcerer here perform a devil banishing upon you,' said La Cerda.

'I will not submit to such an in—' Navarre could not get the word out so Osbert did it for him.

'Indignity,' he said.

The claws retracted and came out again. The King was having difficulty mastering his new body, Osbert was pleased to see, because he felt that – were Navarre more able – those claws might be headed in his direction.

'No need for that,' said John. 'But, my Charles, you appear as an abomination, the equal of any that lately affrighted these halls. Though I have no doubt you are no devil, all men might not see it so. You may spark rumour that we are not pure, give solace to our enemies. I must therefore ask you to go to your lands in Normandy.'

'My place is here at c- c- c- c—'

'A furball?' said La Cerda.

The king laughed heartily and, taking his cue from that, so did Osbert. Navarre's human eye, however, cut him short and Osbert put his fist up to his mouth in a gesture that might be taken for stifling a laugh but also might be taken for biting back his disapproval. He hoped.

Navarre stiffened, with something of a creak from the leather collar and the iron bands that helped hold him together.

'Very well. Perhaps you are right. My days at the court, and of courtliness, are over. I shall marry and take to my Norman castles. I ask but one thing, sire. The sorcerer. He has restitched me. I need him in case I split again.'

John shook his head. 'No more devils in France. The sorcerer remains to see to that.'

'Am I to leave with nothing? No mark of esteem? Cast out. My Lords, a less loyal man than myself might wonder if King Edward would be a more indulgent lord.'

'You have my sister's hand in marriage!'

Navarre twitched, in pain or anger Osbert could not tell.

'There might be a suitable gift.' The little Dauphin had spoken; his voice was on the cusp of manhood, rasping like a dog's.

'Yes, Charles?' said John.

'I might go with the king of Navarre. I do love the Norman coast, and who better to teach me matters of policy than my uncle? What greater mark of trust and prestige than that you entrust your heir to him?'

Navarre turned stiffly to the little boy.

'That would be acceptable. Princess Joan is so fond of her little cousin . . . What a bulwark we would make against the English enemy.'

'That isn't wise, sir,' said La Cerda. 'Send him the duke of Orléans instead.'

John stiffened slightly. The duke, John's brother, looked up for a moment with the expression of a puppy discovered by a cook with its head in the pudding bowl. He was a weak-minded boy who was as useless with sword and spear as he was with the arts of diplomacy. He would be a liability rather than an asset and, on top of that, was so far from the throne that Navarre could cut his throat without anyone noticing.

'I have my own affairs, old man,' said the duke.

'Strumming the lyre and making wine,' said John.

'Exactly,' said the duke, as if this was the most important work a man could perform.

'I was all but raised by King John,' said Navarre, curling half his lip, the other staying furrily unmoved. 'I would repay what I owe and raise his son to manhood.'

'I would go with the king of Navarre,' said the Dauphin. 'He could teach me a great deal, I think.'

John waved his hand, clearly bored by the talk and having to mediate between favourites like a father between squabbling children.

'Of course! You are a man of extraordinary wit, Charles. You will educate him far better than I in the ways of kingship. And it saves the boy getting under my feet. I see little enough of him but when I do he is always plaguing me with the most perplexing questions.'

'There is no better king than you,' said La Cerda.

'Yes, but I won't have time to instruct my little Dauphin. I have the affairs of a great state to run. Charles only has a few mouldering castles and that biting Norman wind to occupy him. The Dauphin may travel with Charles and his aunt. It will show the men of Normandy our love for them and secure them in our fight against the English.'

'Or hand them a valuable prisoner,' said La Cerda.

'Don't say so.' John went to hug Navarre but didn't quite seem to know how to approach him. 'Charles is our kin. Charles is family. Charles is blood!'

He finally threw his arms around the bifurcate king. Navarre winced with the pain.

'Yes,' he said. 'Yes. I am blood.'

PART 4

1355-1356

The Battle of Poitiers

I

Finally Clement was dead and Innocent had taken his place – a man more attuned to reason and one who, rather than fritter away his days commissioning paintings and listening to music, was determined to make a mark on the world. He had accepted her request for audience as soon as he had his own cardinals in place, only three years after Clement's death. Innocent was a man of the world, less fussy about allegations of sorcery, and she felt sure she could do business with him.

The papal palace at Avignon was vast – far bigger even than Windsor – and gleaming white in the southern French sun, a huge diamond on a foil of golden, autumnal trees. Liveried servants scurried through the streets; a line of cardinals made its way up the stairs to the palace like a flowing scarlet ribbon; the rich carriages of wealthy pilgrims crowded the palace plaza; hawkers moved among them, selling nuts, sweetmeats, indulgences and relics, broken varieties of every imaginable tongue on their lips: '*Pour la santé de votre ame!* For the good soul! *Por el bien alma! Diese Torten schmecken schön!*'

Isabella gazed up at the great building, footsore from her great journey, her skin baked brown as a field labourer's, her hair bleached to straw. The gritty mistral wind stung her eyes. In some ways Avignon reminded her of the Hunger Garden in Hell. Everything looked fine here but no one sat outside and, even in the heat of the day, shutters were drawn against the salt and the sand of the incessant breeze. And then, of course, there was the river they had passed over. The Plague, which was diminished the last two years, had bitten back in Avignon. The Rhône was a horror in itself: corpses floating past, some stuck on the pillars

302

of the bridge, others bobbing on in a ghastly progress towards the sea. The Pope had consecrated the river, so many dead had fallen, and now it was one long grave throughout the city. How did anyone ever get a drink?

Still, the gaggle of pilgrims with whom she had travelled from Bordeaux were momentarily awestruck by the palace, their gossip and self-congratulation at missing the marauding English ceasing as they gazed up at the building in wonder.

Isabella, more used to grandeur, was still impressed and a flicker of self-consciousness went through her – she was not exactly dressed for the occasion. The clothes she wore were those of a common nun, which she had been for five long years while she waited for Pope Clement to die.

Her pack contained her rings, including her seal. She was sincere in her penitence but had to present herself in a way the Pope would understand, to appear as a queen in the clothes of a poor nun, not as a poor nun.

This Pope was no less indulgent than Clement, surrounding himself with riches, the best musicians and, no doubt, the best whores. But he would expect certain standards. She had her letters in her own hand, only one girl there as a travelling companion, a nun of Navarre – obviously a spy for her nephew but she didn't mind that. She had helped him in the matter of Eu, he must look kindly on her. Entertaining one of his spies would reassure him further. She saw no need at present to betray him in any way, but had lived long enough to know that one day it might be necessary and she did not want him forearmed.

No one had run ahead of her, no one announced her visit, so she climbed the steps of the palace with the other pilgrims, reminding herself to join the queue of common pilgrims at the door. It would have been so natural to walk straight in, but then, it would have been so natural to have been announced and to be greeted with bugles and bows.

The autumn sun was low in the sky by the time she reached the door. Pilgrims were allowed in to the common chapels and those who sought an audience with the Pope were told to go away or fobbed off with a meeting with a lesser churchman. Not so Isabella. She presented her letter, showed her seal.

The priest on the door looked surprised, exchanging glances with the men-at-arms who stood beside him.

'You are a queen?'

Isabella fought her instincts, which were to order him whipped for questioning her. There was no one to order, for a start, but she had put the habits of queens behind her. She bowed her head.

'You don't look like a queen.'

'I am Isabella of France and England, of the House of Capet, mother of the English king and daughter of the last legitimate king of France. I ask audience with His Holiness.'

More glances between the priest and his men-at-arms.

'Why are you dressed like a shitty nun?'

She calmed herself. 'I have done great wrong. I am truly penitent and I would be absolved by the Father of the Church.'

Conversation in Italian. The queen knew enough to pick out what they were saying. She looked well-bred enough to be a queen. She could be a queen. If she wasn't a queen they'd be in trouble for taking her to the Pope. If she was, they could be executed. Best take her.

'This way, Majesty,' said the priest. He led her into the palace and the men-at-arms closed the door to the throng behind her.

Isabella had grown up around indulgence and riches, but the interior of the Palais des Papes was beyond anything even she had seen. Gold and silver decked the walls like something from a miser's dream; rich paintings in the most exquisite style hung there too – not religious scenes, but of hunting and the chase.

Thick carpets lay on the floor, though they were filthy with the dust of the streets; candle holders the worth of a small duchy adorned tables of such fine workmanship that they might have been carved in Christ's own workshop in Galilee. No rude light of nature had been allowed to intrude, the many candles deepening the lustre of the decorations and giving off the wonderful scent of beeswax – no rough tallow nor fish stink here.

For an instant Isabella felt the urge to renounce her life of austerity, to step into fine clothes again, outshine even the most beautiful creations of the craftsmen's hand, but she quelled it. If she was sincere in her purpose, direct and resolute, she would dwell in surroundings like these for eternity, for the Palais des Papes had to be what Heaven was like. There she would sit for ever among gold and silver, fed the most delicious foods from golden plates, drinking nectar and ambrosia from golden cups. She would endure and she would wait.

Isabella was led through many corridors, through a palace more populous than any she had ever been in. Sometimes it was hard to get by for the press of officials and messengers, of servants bringing food and wine. You'd think the Pestilence had never happened. Eventually she came to a huge gilded door. Outside it, on cushioned chairs, sat twenty or so nobles in their best clothes, long beaked plague masks on their faces so they resembled birds of gaudy plumage, their servants around them. The atmosphere was stuffy and close, and some of the servants fanned their masters with cloths or wiped their brows with perfumed worsted.

'Madame,' said the priest, 'I beg you that if you are not who you say you are, you admit it now. Perhaps you are some gentlewoman who has fallen on hard times and who hopes an audience with the Holy Father will restore your fortunes. Perhaps you are the spurned wife of a nobleman. If this is the case, say so and I will arrange for you to meet a court official more suited to your station.'

Isabella raised her eyebrow.

The man bowed his head. 'You are a queen. If you wait here, Your Majesty, I will see if His Holiness's secretary might give me a date on which he might see you.'

She inclined her head in the attitude of a humble supplicant, though the words 'He will see me now' went through her head.

The man slid through the door.

'Who let that pauper in here?' an upper-class French voice enquired.

'The poor door's at the back,' said another.

Isabella said nothing, kept her eyes fixed on the door.

'Remove her!' Another voice spoke.

'Yes, throw her out, this is the palace of the Holy Father, for the sake of gentle Jesus, not a goose fair. I don't care if she is a nun, we want a better class than that in here.'

Still Isabella fixed her eyes on the door. She was aware of a kerfuffle behind her. A hand took her arm but she turned to face its owner. It was a young knight of around sixteen.

'What is your name?' she said, in her immaculate court French. The boy paused.

'Gaston.'

'Of where?'

'Of House Arenberg.'

'The Holy Roman Empire,' she said.

This gave the boy pause.

'She knows my house, sir,' he said to someone unseen.

'How the devil does she know that? She's a low woman, it is plain to see.'

'She doesn't sound like a low woman.'

'My God, you idiot boy, if you won't do it, I will.'

A man dressed in a fine deep blue cloth strode towards her. He grabbed her arm.

'What's this fine ring on your finger? Who—My God, that's . . . That's House Capet!'

Her eyes settled on his hand. He instinctively took it away from her arm and stood with a foolish look on his face – rather like an old lady seeing her daughter-in-law cooking something of which she disapproved for her son.

The doors swung open, revealing a vault of scarlet and gold. Bugles sounded, drums beat.

'His Holiness the Pope welcomes Isabella, queen of England and France! All others are dismissed until tomorrow. The Holy Father will see this lady alone.'

The man sank to his knees, squeezing his hand as if to chastise it for its cheek.

'Spare my lands from your son. I meant no harm!' he said.

Isabella bowed her head, walking in all meekness to beg her absolution from the Pope, prepared to embark on whatever course of slaughter it might require.

2

The boy, of all people, the ridiculously named Dauphin, had suggested it one freezing night at the castle of Mont-Saint-Michel, which towered above the mud flats of its broad estuary.

'Kings,' said the Dauphin, a pale youth who, to Charles's eyes, had the looks of a stable hand, 'cannot see men as others do. We cannot harbour grudges and hatreds but view all men as pieces on a chessboard, to be moved this way and that.'

Charles smiled half a smile, the cat side of his face refusing to lift.

'Do I not know it, cousin? Am I not a king?'

It was not just Normans who lined the tables. There were Clermont and Audrehem, men who might one day be marshals of France. There was the Scot William Douglas, who rode with a retinue of two hundred. All around the rest of the hall sat great men of France, united by one thing. They had all been friends, or admirers, of the count of Eu. Now they were flocking to the king of Navarre, whose outrage at Eu's murder was said to have shaken the foundations of the castle of Vincennes to its foundations. He had tried to save Eu but the sorcerer La Cerda had laid a foul curse on him, redoubling the one Montagu had enacted, splitting the king in two. Such was his holy indignation that he had stood again. God had granted him a reprieve from death in order to do his work. Or so Charles's friends said. He did not care to hear what his enemies said – though he heard it. A king always seeks to hear bad things about himself, then he may come as a surprise to plotters, rather than they to he.

A treaty with the English was in the offing. The Black Prince's wasp devil buzzed around the candles, the size of a rook but ten times as noisy. He would have had it killed were it not so useful.

'You are a king,' said the Dauphin, 'and a great one. You could be greater still. I tell you this, cousin, were I the king of France, you would be constable, no mistake. Why, with a man like you at my side, I'm sure I would confine myself to hunting and pleasure all my days and let you do all that tiresome finance work. How can anyone bear to hear of the re-minting of coins, and yet it's the only thing the letters from the court speak of!'

Charles inclined his cat ear. This boy was an oaf, for sure, a galumphing, tactless oath who sought to buy him with bribes of preferment. Good. When you have been torn in half, stitched back together by a trembling drunk coward, and then corseted in iron like the hull of a ship, your patience wears thin. The Dauphin was a great asset to him and might prove more so.

'You are more inclined to the chapel than the hunt,' said Charles.

'My Lord, My Lord,' said the Dauphin,. 'only so I might understand the will of God, to see what He requires of us to rid ourselves of the English, of weak men at court, and return France to its former glory.'

'Does God answer?'

'Of course.' The Dauphin picked up a capon, split off its tiny wings, and returned it to the plate in front of him. The boy hardly ate. Again, Charles wanted to find that irritating but he had to confess, it made him marvellous cheap to keep. His retainers could hardly go to it like pigs in the byre while their lord nibbled half a nut a day.

'And what does he say?'

'Kings cannot see men as others do. A king has no friends. A king has no allies. He has only resources. A king, a true king, cannot be a sentimental man. Your Edward of England knows this well. See how he keeps with him the sons of those he hates. Montagu, who betrayed him in what way we cannot guess, but who those of us who like a wager would say "He did travel where Edward emerged, the route of his mother's skirts.". Mortimer, grievous killer of his father, tyrant who stole Edward's royal power. And yet there is his grandson as part of Edward's garter knights. There, I think to myself, is a wise king.'

Charles licked at a kipper. If he tasted it on one side of his mouth – the feline – it was delicious. When the taste moved to the other, however, he found he did not care for kippers.

'A wise king to reward treachery?'

'No. Do you know the game of Tarot?'

'I have seen it played. It is new, is it not?'

'Quite. And yet fascinating. When one has in one's hand the trump of the Moon, one does not say: "How now, Moon? The last game you were in my enemy's hand and quite undid me, when you shone your light on my poor Hermit and sent him from the game. I do not forgive so quick. I shall not use you. Get away!"'

'I am at a loss to your point, My Prince.'

'How many able men does my father have around him?'

'Few. He prefers fools.'

'Not quite. Does he not know the worth of La Cerda?'

'He knows it.'

'And does he know your worth?'

'I believe he does.'

'Who else, then, might be constable?'

'There is no lord he trusts so well as we two. Him, me or no one.'

Now the Dauphin did lift the capon to his lips. He tore off a morsel of flesh and swallowed it.

'Well,' he said, 'I don't suppose he'd opt for no one.'

Charles looked out of the little window at the cold Norman moon – a sickle, God's fingernail pointing down at him. He glanced at the wasp devil and did a quick calculation. La Cerda dead. The English betrayed. France saved. Him as constable. It was attractive. But surely him as king looked better.

'Would that you were king, Dauphin. God saving your father's life and all, of course.'

'I will be one day. I shall tell you a secret about this land of France, if you like. It is this: The English will never be our masters. They will ruin the land, they will despoil, and they may hold large parts of our kingdom for a while but the game of it – the pushing of men as counters, of angels and devils as trumps or pyramids – that cannot be won. All the English will alter is whoever is their eventual vanquisher.'

'Edward is a powerful king.'

'From over the sea with an army he only half controls, hated by half the nobility of France, distrusted by a third, and relying on bowmen who one day aspire to cut his throat. Why has England declared for Satan, My Lord Navarre?'

'For the devils, for the power—'

'From desperation. They have declared for Satan like a ship-wrecked man declares for a piece of wood that floats by. Because they can do no better. My Lord, God will rule again in this land.'

'The sooner you are enthroned the better,' said Charles.

'No, that would be treason. I dread the thought of my father's death. And yet, if the English have another Crécy, I fear his valour and his fearlessness may cost us. Only your stalwartness stands between him and defeat, cousin. I swear to the saints that, if the English could land easily here, France would be won by you in a week. My father does nothing, or nothing effective, against the roaming bands of brigands that have plagued the country since the last incursion and, were the people of Paris so provoked, they might rise up against him in hope the English king would take over and bring it to a stop.'

Charles had to admit, there was more to this boy than perhaps met the eye. He would send the wasp devil back to England with a 'yes'. Normandy and Navarre would stand with England. La Cerda dead, King John slain or captured, the Dauphin here in Normandy under Charles's power. The future looked fine. He would have a mouse to celebrate. He would enjoy that, if only he could stop it crawling to the human side of his mouth.

'We would not like to see Edward on the throne.'

'Of course not, but I fear that with La Cerda's counsel and my father's inaction, that is what would happen. Unless a more able man stood in the way of the English once my father was gone. They couldn't hold the country after Crécy. So even if they, God forbid, killed my father then they would simply create a void into which someone else would step.'

Charles stroked his whiskers. He saw what the boy was saying. Chaos in the country; the English take Paris with the mob at their backs. Of course, no Frenchman would really stand a single summer of English domination so, with John out of the way, someone ideally placed to strike, such as Charles with his Norman armies; someone loved by the Parisians, again Charles who had brought in his sister, the white angel, and ended the Plague – that was truly what the idiots said – might throw out the English and put the Dauphin on the throne. It was good reasoning and only faulty in its last part. It wouldn't be Charles Valois that was put on the throne but Charles of Navarre.

'La Cerda is safe in Paris,' said Charles.

'Is anyone safe anywhere?' said the Dauphin. 'Often I wonder why someone with so many enemies isn't simply killed.'

'I would but for the repercussions.'

'Really, sir, with La Cerda gone and the English at the gate, do you think my father could afford to do without you?'

Charles smiled, wincing with pain. Yes. Yes. Why not just act directly? The pain of his splitting had made him irritable, permanently. He often felt the need to kick someone and often did. But why not kick La Cerda, and hard? Very hard.

A young page made his way across the smoky room, bowed before the lords.

Charles nodded to indicate he might speak.

'There is someone at the gate, sir,' he said.

'There is always someone at the gate,' said Charles. 'That is why we have a gate. If there was no one at the gate all the time we wouldn't need a gate and so there could never be any one at it. As it is, there is always someone there, so we put a gate there meaning there is someone always at the gate. Gates are placed, in my experience, where people tend to be "at".'

The boy coloured, dipped his knees.

'It is a devil, sir. At least I think so.'

'What makes you say so?'

'He has the face of a man but maggots writhe at the back of his head.'

'Not a suitable supper companion,' said Charles. 'If he wants work, let him see our Master of Devils.'

That was a poor name for what they had – an eel devil from the first level – well, eel-bodied but with the head of a man and an unaccountably large genital area. Devils had been coming to the castle seeking direction since the ban of devils in France proper, and he had done his best to accommodate them. They had been a poor lot. It was said the best of the French devils were going over to England, thinking Edward the best chance of them finding employment doing God's work. France wouldn't have then anymore – John had dismissed all his under La Cerda's influence.

'He says he has news. News you will like to hear.'

The Dauphin stirred the pile of sucked capon bones with his

middle finger. 'It would be good to get news. Isn't the maggoty man Simon Pastus, late of the court? A man of good manners.'

'I recall him very well,' said Charles, 'but keep him facing forwards. I can't bear maggots. Well, half of me can't. The other half finds them fascinating and I cannot deal with the headache tonight.'

'You can come in,' said the boy and, in a blink, the devil Simon Pastus stood before them – fine brocade robes, a sable muff covering his hands, bowing just low enough for a writhing maggot to appear on the top of his head.

'My Lords,' said Pastus, 'I am here, a friend to your friends, a bane to your enemies.'

'Swear before God that we can trust you,' said Charles.

'I so swear, on my allegiance to the Father of Creation.'

'And which of my enemies would you be a bane to?'

'Name them, Lord.'

The king of Navarre leant forward stiffly, his movement inhibited by his corset and steel collar.

'La Cerda.'

The devil smiled, his mouth a chasm of jagged teeth.

'Give me a moment to consider. Yes, I have considered. That should be eminently possible.' Clearly this devil had lost his place at the French court and was looking to do his ambassadoring somewhere else to avoid going back to Hell. Even devils hate Hell.

'He never leaves Paris,' said the Dauphin. 'How can you harm him, surrounded by his men, by charms and wards, protected by the great sorcerer Osbert?'

'The sorcerer too. Bring him. He can undo what he did to me!' Or die trying. Charles had long ago concluded that, had Eu wanted him split in two, he could have done it with his sword when he had the chance. The sorceror was the most likely user of sorcery. His request to have Osbert delivered to him had met with no answer.

'Put it in my hands,' said Pastus. 'Everything can be done. The sorceror is the key? La Cerda fears that France might fall without him and worries what might happen should such a powerful servant fall into the hands of his enemies?' He gestured to Charles.

The Dauphin studied the devil carefully.

'Do devils have agendas beyond those of their masters?' he said.

'I have no instruction from Satan,' he said. 'No pact has been brokered with England yet. It hardly could with Satan still locked in his own prison, unable to sign it.'

'Is Satan your master? Do not devils ultimately take orders from God?'

'When God issues orders,' said Pastus, 'I shall be delighted to obey them. Until that time, I am left to follow his appointed lords of Hell and earth.'

'Give me La Cerda,' said Charles, 'and I will make you my head devil. All you do approved and blessed by an anointed king. But you cannot get a French devil to him. They are all banished by France.'

'He cannot banish human weakness,' said Pastus. 'And it is that which will deliver you La Cerda.'

3

The rush of nobles, secretaries, attendants, ladies-in-waiting, and even two hawk handlers leaving the hall, birds asquawk had subsided, and Isabella stood in the great hall. In front of her was a tall reliquary of gold and ruby. Alongside that, in the brown habit of a monk, sat a scribe. The hall was lit entirely by candles and was warm and stuffy enough that she felt hot even in her pauper's gown.

Isabella walked forward down a long, deep blue carpet to approach the scribe. As she did, she saw that what she had taken for a reliquary – a structure of gold and precious jewels – was in fact a man. He wore the white habit of the Pope but about his shoulders was a rich cloak of red velvet, trimmed with brocade; his shoes were encrusted with jewels, and he wore a golden crown on his head. As she drew nearer, she saw that he was sweating, though he drew his cloak about his shoulders. He was a brown little man, tanned by the sun, his eyes a watery blue, calm in his puffy face. Pope Innocent, that complex, practical man, Father of the Church.

She knelt before him and he extended his hand for her to kiss the Fisherman's Ring. As she did so, a cold tingle spread throughout her as if each hair on her body had a life of its own and was suddenly awakening, as the shoots of a flower beneath the spring sun. She had known that feeling before – as a girl before angels in her father's court. Jegudial had made her feel like that in the Sainte-Chapelle, St Denis at the Basilica, others too.

'Your Holiness.' She said it, and she meant it. She had heard the Pope was a man of great luxury, someone who – as kings said – 'knew how to be Pope', with great feasts, entertainments and indulgence. Here was another son of the nobility who had stabbed and bribed his way to St Peter's throne just to spend the

Church money on living like a god on earth. And yet . . . And yet, the feeling she had, before him on her knees, was one she had only ever experienced in the presence of God's own messengers.

'My Lady,' he said, 'I wondered when we would be seeing you. I apologise for the heat. My doctors advise it to keep away the Pestilence. It protected Clement.'

'No thing of Hell could touch you, Holy Father.'

'It may be so. I have worked among the victims of this monstrosity and come to no harm. But even if I am blessed by God, my people may not be and it is wise to take precautions.' The scribe scratched away, recording every word.

She bowed her head further.

'You have had some strange bedfellows, Queen. You have called friend those who call God their enemy.'

She looked nervously at the scribe.

The Pope seemed to read her thoughts.

'We record everything,' he said, 'though it will go to the archives, not for the eyes of men. At least of these times. You have dealt with Hell?'

He saw her astonishment.

'I . . .'

'Lady, there are three angels in the chapels of this palace, unmoved by the events of Crécy field, still sparkling in our light. And there is greater than they here for those who are deemed worthy.'

'Do angels reveal such things?' In her experience she had found they talked largely gibberish.

'To those who have spent generations working to understand them.'

She prostrated herself. She had never done such a thing in her life.

'I have only traded with devils, Holiness. God's servants. I have never had commerce with the demons nor other prisoners of Hell.'

'You have traded with God's enemies. Though you do not know it. And perhaps neither do they.'

She turned her face up to him, completely at a loss.

'Satan,' he said.

'I understood he was God's servant, His jailer who keeps the rebel Lucifer under lock and key.'

'So he was. But now he seeks to open the gates of Hell for himself. He would make this world his own.'

'Why does God not order him to stop?'

The Pope's face remained impassive.

'What is the Church for?' he said.

'For . . .' she struggled to say. The Church had been such a natural part of life that its function had not really occurred to her.

'To stand between man and God,' she said. 'Connecting them.'

'It is that,' he said. 'But also is it not to defend the faith?'

'Yes. Of course.'

'Why should it need defending? It is of God. Can God not look after His own faith?'

Isabella said nothing. She had never thought about these things before. The Pope went on.

'Why do evil men prosper? Why does this world, made by God under the will of God, contain so many who defy His will?'

She kept silent still. She sensed the Pope wasn't looking for her to answer.

'I will tell you, Queen. It is because God is wounded. In the struggle with the bright angel Lucifer, all those years ago, the evil one put a sword into the Lord of all creation.' The scribe had stopped writing. The Pope smiled. 'God is not what He was.'

'How could God, who is all-powerful, be wounded by something He made?'

'Perhaps it was His will,' said the Pope. 'Perhaps, He who knew everything did not know one thing. What it is to suffer. He who controls everything did not know what it was to lack control. And so He allowed it. And He allowed it again on the Cross, where He died for our sins. Why are you here, Lady?'

'You do not know?'

'Yes. I do. But I fear you do not.'

Isabella's knees were painful from kneeling for so long; she felt sick with the heat of the great room.

'I want you to hear my confession. And sanction and enable a way forward.'

The Pope waved away the scribe and she told him: the murders, the killings; the deals with devils; the corruption of an already corrupt line; how she had caused the good Montagu to be damned, but how it had all been – had she but known it – the will of God.

The Pope thought for a time, his flabby face as still as a tomb effigy's.

'I have heard troubling things about England. The future . . .' He waved his hand.

Isabella bowed her head, waiting for him to finish. He sat for a long time in silence.

Then he said, 'The angels have long said England might prove the Church's most troublesome child. Its kings are too much their own men. It cannot be God's will that they thrive. And, if they are devils . . . England must be brought to the field again. The whole line smashed.'

Innocent stood evaluating her for a long moment, deep in thought.

'I want to see God,' she said. The scribe scribbled that down.

The Pope nodded. 'Yes,' he said. 'I know.'

He clapped his hands together. 'Follow me.'

4

Osbert had stuck rather close to La Cerda in the years following the great 'splitting of the cat', as the unfortunate division of the king of Navarre had come to be called. And, bizarrely, La Cerda had stuck close to him. He had appointed a couple of men to watch him – which was fine by Osbert, as they were agreeable fellows who liked a drink as much as any man and were tasty types if it came to defending him in a scrap. Beyond this, the lord had been at his side for much of his work, watching him intently. Osbert had the feeling La Cerda had been quietly impressed by his trick of tearing the king of Navarre in half. The court knew the official explanation – that Eu was a sorceror – was rubbish. Osbert had impressed himself by stitching him back together again. La Cerda had been less pleased with that, but had conceded Osbert had little choice, being under the instruction of King John.

Now he sat looking at Osbert as if at a great treasure. The banishing of Blanche and the death of King Philip had been excellent events as far as La Cerda was concerned. Add to that the bifurcation of Navarre, and it was safe to say that La Cerda regarded Osbert as a splendid fellow indeed, the key to all possibilities. The Plague had abated in the last couple of years – not gone, far from gone, but now it took one in ten instead of two in five or more, like it had before every summer.

'Do you hope to learn my art?' said Osbert, as La Cerda peered into one of the wax seals he was placing around the door frame.

'I struggle to read,' said La Cerda. 'But a lord must know his defences. As I would supervise the construction of a wall or a bailey, I supervise the building of these magical walls.'

That day, Osbert was on the roof of the tower of the Louvre, inscribing a magic circle and placing on certain seals in order to forestall attack from the air. La Cerda poked about as he did so, examining the seals, asking the odd question.

'This is the name of Our Lord?'

'One of the secret names.'

La Cerda squinted nearer. 'And yet you've written it in a public place.'

'For those who can read it, who are few. Is it not right that great lords like you should know the names of the Almighty who rose them to great estate?'

'Abba . . . Ab . . . A . . .' said La Cerda, before giving up. He showed no embarrassment, as no noble would. You could pay someone to read; you can't pay someone to win you personal honour in battle or to spear a flying boar for you, the things the nobles cared about. Well, you kind of could, but it was much better if you did those things yourself.

Paris was a wonderful city now the Plague had largely passed. The corpse fires still smouldered, the working man charged a fortune for his services, the working girl even more. Osbert, who accounted himself as somewhere between a craftsman and whore, took their example and billed Prince John handsomely. Osbert was briefly rich, though he couldn't really work out what he wanted to spend the money on. Not having to work would have been his number one choice, but you didn't have to be rich to do that. Nor was it an option. The king commanded France be free of devils. Free of devils, though not for free. That might have been another motto.

Osbert, in his fine court clothes, his long tapering shoes, his beaverskin hat and carrying his gold-topped staff, had been giving a lot of thought to mottos, largely on the grounds that he'd got everything else in life, so he might as well have one. 'I have everything else in life so might as well have a motto too.' He tried translating it into Latin, but gave up and carried on stamping seals in wax around the door that accessed the roof. Behind him moved one of the serving girls, a handsome little thing with tits that were monuments to the glory of God, he thought. She was new. Most of the staff were new. Most of them could hardly speak French, or rather had country accents so thick they were unintelligible.

Gilette was still there and Osbert was flat in love with her. He thought he'd ask her to marry him. Something held him back, though. He couldn't quite say what it was. Did he feel worthy of her?

'Will this keep Navarre's sister away if she decides to come back? The succubus?'

'Hard to say,' said Osbert. 'What was she? An angel trapped in human form, they said.'

'What do you think she was?'

'I have seen such before. It would not surprise me if she was one of the fallen.'

'I should track her down. She should die like a dog for what she did.'

'In my experience,' said Osbert, 'fallen angels are not easy to kill.'

'I can kill anything.'

'I believe it, My Lord, on my faith in Christ.'

He whistled as he painted some holy water around the doorway. This was pleasant work on a sunny day. Where once his work had been in calling devils, now he was employed in banishing them. It was good to see the great spider devil go scurrying from the lodge at Vincennes, to see Pastus pack his bags and slink from the Palace of the Louvre.

'I thought they would disappear in a puff of smoke,' said La Cerda to Osbert. The two men stood on the ramparts of the tower of the Louvre, breathing in the fine cold air of a May morning.

'I think that is possible under certain circumstances, but here we have merely forbidden them to enter a prescribed boundary,' said Osbert. 'They leave as quickly as they can but it is not as if they are washed away by a flood.'

'Your magic is impressive,' said La Cerda.

'I am too modest to accept that. Though the truth of it is plain enough.'

He didn't bother to tell La Cerda that the work of banishing all devils from Paris, or even from the royal palaces, would take years if they required the puff of smoke and crack of lightning option. The easiest way to get rid of them was simply to tell the devils that King John wanted them to go, show them the seal with which the king had entrusted him, and tell them to close the doors on their way out.

They were creatures of impeccable respect for hierarchy and it was in their very nature simply to obey. John was an idiot not to have thought of just banning them directly from his whole realm. Would they obey? Probably, unless Edward persuaded them he could be king.

The rest of the time he had spent sweeping dust from saints' tombs, extracting bits of blessed oil, crushing up holy teeth and bones and making a sanctuary – firstly in his own lodgings and then around the palace itself. He had commissioned priests and monks to start inscribing a great magic circle all around the walls of Paris but that would have taken years, even assuming the holy idiots knew what they were doing. 'Look busy, don't be busy,' might have been his motto. So many dead. Why not me? La Cerda joined him on the balcony.

'I have word from England,' he said.

'Yes? From who?'

'Our spy at the court. We have a woman there close to the old queen. Close to Edward. Very close.'

'And?'

'They are summoning devils. Declared for Satan and determined to bring him to this world.'

'Good luck with that,' said Osbert. 'They would need the keys of Hell. We have one, one of them is with the Antichrist and the other two are God knows where.'

'Find out. These are mighty weapons. We need to get them before England does. If only to lock them away.'

'They will never be found. Never. We are safe there. If they were around then men would have used them all long ago.'

'First time for everything in my experience.' *So holy*, thought Osbert. The man even smelled of incense.

'Are our defences safe?'

'For the tower of the Louvre, yes,' said Osbert.

'King John is a brave man and a righteous one. There will come a time when all devils are gone, all demons too. Then we shall have no need of sorcerers.'

Osbert touched his breast. 'I would love to retire to tend grapes. And free myself from this foul work with fiend and hellhound.'

'The day there are no more devils is the day you die,' said La Cerda. 'I blame you for much of this mess in the first place. If you weren't so useful to us then I'd have you executed on the spot.'

'I endeavour to be of service,' said Osbert. 'But there must be other men like me. Killing me would not stop them. There are priests who have communed with the Pit.'

'None of them seem to have your talent for it. And all of them are beholden to Rome. You're my sorcerer. I understand you completely. You are not a seeker after knowledge, nor even after power. You are a man who wants a comfortable life. You'll never have one. It's not what you deserve.'

He said it as if it was some sort of defect. If more people looked for a comfortable life, and fewer went seeking after knowledge and power, it struck Osbert that the world might be a very much better place. La Cerda left the roof and Osbert took the opportunity to begin loafing, gazing out over the town.

In the sky, he saw a mote, what he took for one of those strange spirits that seem to float within the eye when you look up into a clear day. But against the blue, he saw something taking shape – a dark form, like a little man with long plumes rising up from his shoulders. A devil! He reached for a case at his side, the one that bore the king's order that no devil should be in the land. It fluttered towards him, or rather spun, or did something. As it neared, he could see its body was made of two snakes that danced around each other in a dizzying helix. Were they attached? Were they separate? It didn't matter. Clinging to their tails was none other than the maggoty Simon Pastus.

'Hi, ho, and hold your horses!' Osbert said. 'Hold it right there. Out, the pair of you. Not allowed in France, by declaration of the French king.' He waved the piece of vellum at them. 'Go on, scarper! What will you be doing for my reputation?'

'I have a message for you,' said Pastus.

'Not another one,' said Osbert.

'One knows something,' said one of the snakes.

'Then one must say,' said the other.

'Not listening,' said Osbert, putting his fingers into his ears.

'I bear a message, sent from a prince,' said one snake.

'He bears a message that must be heard,' said the other snake.

'It must not be heard,' said Osbert. 'I have heard enough of devils. Now go – a king commands.'

'I am technically ambassador to the court and so exempt,' said Pastus.

'Yes, but they aren't and they have conveyed you here. They can go and you with them.'

'Montagu is near,' said Pastus. 'Possessor of the second key.'

'Well, you get it off him.'

'A devil cannot face such a hero. It must be won by tricks,' said Pastus.

'So you're from Navarre,' said Osbert. Years of street skulduggery had taught him to very quickly work out whose hand was thrust up any particular puppet. Osbert had worked out that Montagu had the second key. Only one other person was in a position to do that and that was Navarre, who had been in the tower when it was taken from him.

'Montagu would meet with you forthwith. He is the sword of God.'

'I'm not leaving this palace, mate. Nice try. Navarre would have me in bits in minutes. Or summoning devils or something that is out of the line of work I currently enjoy. So hop it.' He gestured with his thumb for the creature to disappear.

'Remember, you escape damnation according to our deal, if you find the keys,' said Pastus, dangling from below the creatures.

Osbert clung to the balustrade before him, as if he feared the snake would tear him away.

'No, no, no, no no,' he said.

'You are in peril. France is in peril.'

'Well, I expect there'll be a crumb in it for me – there normally is,' said Osbert. 'And . . .' He had been looking at the two gyrating snakes for rather a long time. His head felt dizzy. Very dizzy. He touched the bone of St Aaron he kept in his pocket, offering a prayer to the saint. His head cleared.

'Piss off,' he said. 'The three of you.'

'You will come,' said the snakes. 'By bait or by hook, you will come. By the baited hook.'

The two snakes shimmered and twisted, then vanished upwards, Pastus beneath them.

Cheeky bastards, sneaking in on the orders of Navarre. Yes, by the book they were obeying a king, but they must have known full well they were countermanding the orders of a much greater king. Pastus might have had a point with the ambassador thing, he supposed. He shivered.

'One banishing for the day, lots of protection work, one quest avoided,' said Osbert to himself. 'Time for a glass of wine and a walk with Gilette.'

He began to wonder what was happening to him. His normal state of raging lust had faded. He thought not so much about other women now, though he naturally did think of them. He thought of her, standing by his side. Sometimes he thought the whole world would die and he would be left with her – a new Adam, a new Eve, to start all over again. So Pastus had ended up in Normandy, had he? Clearly now advising Navarre. Osbert was no fool and saw exactly what he was – a weapon. Navarre might hate him but he would covet him too. He probably wanted him to find a way to stitch him back together.

He made his way down to the kitchens to find Gilette, but she wasn't there, just cooks busying themselves about the place. He tasted a pie here, licked gravy there for a while but Gilette did not appear. He did not feel like wine. Why did he not feel like wine? He always felt like wine. When dinner was served and she still did not return and the cook cursed her for not being there to help with the cleaning and stacking of the plates, he knew.

He walked out into the kitchen garden, looked up at the night sky. She had gone – been taken in order to draw him out of the protection of Paris and into the clutches of Navarre, at last. No devils to help him, no cloak of angel's feathers. All magic banished.

He should, of course, have let her go. She was as good as dead in the hands of Navarre, more than likely raped and murdered already. He knew what was coming on the other side of the garden gate, knew where he would be going – on a pretence to bargain for the life of Gilette.

He went up into the body of the Louvre to find his rooms, collected a few things. He would need to escape from the palace – La Cerda would never give him permission to leave. That would not be difficult, in truth. There were guards on the main entrance but the kitchen and the attendant gardens were not policed, though they were locked from the inside. And, if he was stopped, he would make some excuse.

The kitchen was quiet and a mist hung over the garden as he left the Louvre. He walked through dingy streets that led from the palace, close-lying alleys that radiated from the king's dwellings, places of vice and danger – in normal times. Now they were eerily silent, so many had died in the Plague years.

Osbert knew what to expect – the footsteps following him, the sense of being a target. It was dark and only a weak moon lit the streets. He could scarcely see his hand before his face and he stumbled as he stepped on. Then there was the flash of torches behind him. He kept walking, secure in his judgement that whoever had taken Gilette – and it had to be Pastus acting on Navarre's say-so – would be coming for him then.

Torches before him now. Nowhere to walk so he stopped. A hissed voice.

'Stop in the name of Navarre.'

'I thought I smelled cat's piss,' said Osbert.

A man strode forward, his face obscured by the light of a torch, and struck Osbert very hard across the face with his open hand.

Osbert saw a white light at the side of his eye but he did not cry out or sink to his knees.

'You boys are going to have to keep me sweet if I'm going to do as your lord and master wants,' he said.

Another heavy blow, this time to the belly. He sank to his knees and looked up in anticipation of further punishment. A tough-looking man, a fighter by his build, was standing above him.

'I'll explain to the king of Navarre why I can't heal him owing to the ringing in my ears after the blow you've given me. The same goes if you hurt Gilette. I cannot mend kings in a state of grief.'

The fighting man said nothing, just pulled him to his feet.

'The marshes,' he said.

Hands grabbed him, and pushed him on through the tiny streets. *Why the torches?* he thought. *Why the torches? It's like they want to be seen. Of course! He was bait! Get La Cerda to chase him and leave the door to an unimpeded meeting with King John open!*

'Hurry up,' said a voice.

Osbert didn't resist but let himself be bumped along. A torch was beside him, blinding his eyes. Then it was on the floor. Two torches on the floor. Three. They were throwing their torches down. No they weren't – they were falling. The man who had hold of Osbert threw his own torch away, drew his sword.

A flash of something brighter than fire – so bright it lit the whole street. A cry as another man hit the ground. Only two left. He felt a sword at his throat.

'Move and I cut his throat.'

'Cut it, then. You'll save us the trouble.'

It was a voice he recognised. Dowzabel – the boy who had sent him to Hell in the first place, his only real companion of the years of magical apprenticeship trapped in a magic circle in a cellar in Bow. He was under no illusions, though. The boy was not his friend. He was a fanatic.

Osbert spoke to the man holding him.

'We're both dead,' he said.

But he was wrong. Only one of them was.

5

'I wish I knew where that sorcerer was – I would feel more comfortable about this.' In truth, Charles of Navarre hadn't felt comfortable since he had been split in two. His iron corset chafed him, his neck collar gave him an ache, and now he wore a great padded coat on top of them, a coat of mail on top of that. He'd be out of the armour as soon as the business was done but he bore no hope it would bring him any relief.

Navarre looked down on the little wayside inn from the hillside. It was dusk and the smell of a fire was on the air, roasting meat for the presence of the nobility. Ten good horses were tied to the trees and the standard of Castile dropped limply from a lance sunk into the turf, beside it the fleur-de-lys of the Constable of France. The spleen of the man! A fancy wagon, painted in the colours of the Constable of France, blue and gold, sat there too. They had demanded a good ransom for the sorcerer they didn't have. A couple of pages had made a fire outside to cook on while they guarded the horses. A rabbit or a hare turned on a spit above the flames.

'La Cerda cannot know we don't have him,' said Pastus, 'or he would not have ventured here.'

'Where is he, though?' said Navarre. 'He must restore me to what I was.'

Pastus raised an eyebrow.

'He has a greater purpose than that. He is a living man who has been to Hell. I did not think that possible. He could use the third key. He could release Satan for you – strike a mighty pact to do so.'

'What happened to my men in Paris? You were sure the girl was the key to luring the sorcerer out?'

'Sure. And I was right, was I not? La Cerda would not be here if he was not.'

'No. And we have no word back from the Dauphin who conveyed our message to this imposter.'

'Don't worry about it, brother,' said his brother Philip, mounted beside him. Nearly twenty years old now, a prodigy at arms, his chest as broad and deep as a bull's.

'Let's get going, then,' said Navarre.

He walked stiffly back up to the brow of the hill.

A hundred Norman men-at-arms waited on the hidden slope.

'Follow,' he said.

The horsemen made their way over the hillside. It was impossible to hide so many, but Navarre did not think that La Cerda would run. Why should he? He was on the king's business.

The pages, of course, saw them coming and ran inside. Before the stream of men was a tenth of the way down the hill, men had emerged from the inn to watch them – knights by their swords, but unarmoured and unconcerned, too. No panic, no running for weapons, no mounting of horses. Good. That was what Navarre had expected.

By the time they got to the road and made their way up to the front of the inn, the innkeeper was on his knees before them making the proper signs of respect, but La Cerda was nowhere to be seen.

Charles rode at the head of his column, his horse lumpen beneath him. It was a torment to him that he could not ride a mount more fitting to his station but had to make do with this old plodder. It was the only one that had the nerve, or the senile stupidity, to carry him now.

He was greeted by Osorio, a knight of Castile – a lean man with one of those sharp Spanish beards. He was backed by ten men.

Osorio bowed, not deeply enough for Charles's liking. He didn't bother to acknowledge the formality.

Osorio stiffened.

'Where is our man?'

'What?'

'The sorcerer?'

'Where is La Cerda? I don't talk to the likes of you.'

'He is within. The Constable of France does not come out to greet the likes of you. A thief and an extortionist.'

'Kill him,' said Charles to his beefy brother Philip at his back. The knight drew and spurred his horse forward. He raised his sword uncertainly.

Osorio rolled his eyes.

'Even you are not stupid enough to kill the retinue of the Constable of France,' he said.

'I said kill him,' said Navarre.

'Really,' said Osorio. 'This charade—' He never finished his sentence as Philip spurred forward his horse and caved in his skull.

The other nobles drew but Charles's press of men were upon them, hacking them to pieces where they stood. Philip took three himself.

A couple of the pages ran for it and horsemen went after them, but Charles called after them.

'Catch them, don't kill them!'

He got down from his horse and strode towards the inn.

The innkeeper was still prostrate in front of him.

'Well, get me a drink,' said Charles. The man stood and walked shakily into the inn.

'Only you or staff?' said Charles. Pastus was behind him, five men-at-arms at his back, along with Philip.

'My wife and daughters are away,' he said. Customary when large bands of nobles visited – wise too. Probably up in the hills for a few days, thought Charles.

'You know who I'm after, lead me to him.'

The interior of the inn was dark, windowless. A tallow candle burned in a nook and the innkeeper picked it up. They went in to an inner room, comfortable, draped with heavy cloths that you'd struggle to call carpets but would do a job of reducing draughts. In the light of a candle sat La Cerda, two lieutenants beside him.

He did not stand, hardly raised his eyes.

'Are you mad?' he said.

'Well, to be perfectly truthful,' said Charles, 'the idea has occurred to me that I might be. I prefer to say "a little odd". Off-centre, you know?' More of his men-at-arms came in behind him; he heard them as they came in.

'You'll die for what you've done today,' said La Cerda.

'Well, may as well get hung for a sheep as a lamb, then.' Charles drew his sword with his human hand.

'You're going to kill a Constable of France? This makes no sense. Look, we've a cartload of gold here. My ransom alone will buy you half of France. You're acting like a barbarian, man.'

'France needs me,' said Navarre. 'It needs you too. It can do without one of us but not both.' He strode towards La Cerda, but La Cerda jumped up from the table, picking up his own sword from where it lay behind him and drawing it in the same movement.

'You'll not best me in single combat. I challenge you,' said the constable.

'A little old-fashioned for my tastes. Not quite in fitting with the times,' said Charles. 'With me!'

He pushed the table aside and swung his sword towards La Cerda's head. Unfortunately, the ceiling was low and his sword caught a beam. La Cerda drove his blade into Charles's ribs but the mail, the coat and the iron corset were impenetrable to it. There was no second attack. Charles's men were in the room now, a dozen or more of them, and they swept La Cerda and his men to the floor, less like knights in combat than toughs in a game a of village football. The three went down under the weight of numbers and were quickly dispatched with misericord and knife.

Charles knelt over La Cerda.

'I played the game subtly,' he said. 'I connived and used sorcery to get my way. For what? This is so much better, so much more direct. One blow of the sword yields me all the progress that years of intrigue failed to do.'

He stood. Two whey-faced pages were dragged in.

'You said you wanted them alive,' said a man-at-arms.

'Of course,' said Charles. 'Welcome, fellows. Innkeeper, fetch them a meal. Tell my pages to ready them good horses. Boys, boys, you ride for Paris with the news that Navarre has butchered the Constable of France. The killer will be coming to the court at the Louvre forthwith. Make them prepare the way! Prepare the way!'

6

'Gilette! You're safe!'

'No time for that now, Osbert, no time. With me.'

She grabbed him by the hand and ran him on through the darkness of the narrow rat runs, Dowzabel behind her and two others Osbert hadn't time to see.

'We need to go back to the kitchens, my love. There is a warm pie there, or a piece of one, I'm sure.'

She said nothing, just kept dragging him on.

Eventually the low door of a low house. Osbert was bundled inside. The others followed.

Osbert saw that he was in a very poor person's dwelling. There was no furniture, not a scrap of anything. The surest sign of poverty was when even the rags had been burned. The ceiling was low and sagged and a thick air of damp pervaded the one tiny room.

'Light a candle, for God's sake. I cannot see what's what.'

Instead a sword was drawn from a scabbard – a sword that glowed with the light of the dawn. Osbert's jaw dropped. It was Aude from the village where he had killed Richard, where he'd fought for the poor. She wore his coat of angel's mail, carried his angel's sword – the very thing that was now illuminating the mean little room.

Beside her was someone Osbert had never seen – a squat little man, old, but with the body of a warrior. He was a pauper and in rags.

'Who's he?' said Osbert. Everyone ignored him.

'You've got something we want,' said Dow.

'And pleased to see you after so long too,' said Osbert as Dow searched him. The boy was thorough. 'Gilette, what has happened? Why are you with these people?'

Gilette kept her eyes fixed ahead. She was changed subtly, he thought. She stood taller, more proudly, and, though she still wore the plain kirtle of a scullery maid, she carried in her hand a bodkin of the sort the English archers used, largely for punching through the armour of stricken knights.

'Search him,' said Dow.

Gilette searched him, running her hands under his clothes, feeling down his legs – everywhere. Osbert felt he might cry. It was a parody of the loving intimacy he had imagined existed between them. She found the key to Hell in his codpiece. The angel's feather was tucked down his boot.

She offered the key to Hell to the pauper. 'No,' he said. 'Give it to the Praenuntius.'

Osbert recognised the Latin for 'Herald' or 'One who comes before'.

'He used to have an angel's toe around his neck,' said the pauper.

'How did you know that?' said Osbert. 'I've never seen you before in my life.'

'I've seen you.'

Osbert was having difficulty taking all this in. He'd dropped the angel's toe on the field of Crécy. It had belonged to the body the Archangel Jegudiel had taken when he came down from the light, the body that had been killed by Orsino, the mercenary. And then possessed by Hugh Despenser. Something about the toe had made him fear Despenser might find a way to come back again, to reinhabit it and find a way to get back at Osbert for killing him. Accidentally! Accidentally! That wasn't the sort of excuse Despenser accepted.

'Have you now?'

'I saw you at the Temple, I saw you at Crécy. I know where you went, what you did. There's only one thing I don't know. Where is the Evertere? Where is the dragon banner? Our ympes lost you in the dark of the angel's death and did not pick you up again until you had rid yourself of it.'

'I got a long way south,' said Osbert.

'Where?'

'At Poitiers. I had met a fellow who assured me he could get a good price for relics and stood in good esteem with the monks of the town. I sold it to them.'

'Did they know what it was?'

'I think so. Their abbot had a number of such relics. A piece of the True Cross. I think he sought to put it where it could never be recovered.'

'How much did you get for this act?' said Dow.

'I don't know,' said Osbert. 'I was low on money and they have some very strong ale. A bit, I think. I was drunk for a month after.'

Gilette put her head into her hands.

'Well, it was beginning to spook me. It made a lot of noise. I mean, it could have been digesting the angels. It's a sort of snake, isn't it? They say the snakes of the Indies only eat once in their lives. They must have awful gut rot after that big meal.'

'We will need it in Hell,' said Dow.

'What do you stand for, sorcerer? When the final trumpet blows, whose side will you be on?' said the pauper.

'My own. And I would have been on Gilette's too, had I not been cruelly deceived.'

'But you are a strange man, Osbert the Sorcerer. A very strange man. Things happen around you. You are a man of destiny.'

'God forbid I should be marked by destiny,' said Osbert, and crossed himself.

'God's good at forbidding,' said the pauper. 'But I find myself wondering about you, sorcerer. Someone or something has marked you out. It makes me wonder if I should kill you here.'

Osbert laughed. 'Murder. How quaint. The world paved with bodies from the frozen castles of Scotland to the boiling lands of the Middle Sea. Well, be quick, sir. These are no times for lazy or sluggish killers. You are apt to find your victim dead in the street before you reach him. The Plague must return soon, it always does.'

'You are no instrument of God,' said the pauper. 'So who do you serve?'

'Whoever shouts at me. Whoever shoves and bullies. Would you have me serve you, sir? All you need to do is whip me or kick me and you will find me most compliant. I'm surprised you didn't just have me worked about the ears with sticks and bricks. No need to fuck what you wanted out of me.'

'You weren't always so easy to beat about the ears,' said Aude. 'I've seen you fell a charging knight without getting off your arse.'

'But why her?' said Osbert. 'Why Gilette? To offer me sweet kisses, to exchange gifts and have her call me "Darling". It seems so unfair.'

Now the pauper laughed. 'Unfair? Look at the world around you and cry "unfair" that we sent you to bed with a girl so soft and lovely.'

'You are a spy,' said Osbert to Gilette. 'How did you even know I had the key? I never mentioned it!'

'You sent a creature to ask for the other two,' said the pauper.

'You could just have asked for it, Gilette.'

'It was safest in the King's court until we needed it,' said the pauper.

'Why drag me out here to get it?'

'We were saving you, if only you knew it.'

'From what?'

'Navarre had ordered you kidnapped. Those were his men.'

'What are you going to do with the key? It's mine, I should know.'

Dow approached him. Looked into his face.

'That,' he said, 'is the business of Lucifer.'

'I wondered how long it would take before he got a mention,' said Osbert.

In his experience, Dow never went more than a couple of breaths without saying the name of the bright angel/fiend of the Pit/depends on your point of view. He turned to Gilette.

'So it all was . . .'

She lowered her eyes.

'We work to greater purpose. What does it matter what I felt for you? What does it matter what those who loved the dead and the gone felt? This world is fleeting. We seek a better one.'

'The thing I have noticed about those who seek to improve the world,' said Osbert, 'is that invariably they make it worse. Kings, rebels. You're all the same, shitting on the little man. Shitting on me from a height. Who are you?' He pointed at the pauper.

'A sorcerer,' he said. 'But not one of your worth. I am Good Jacques of the Knights Templars that were. The servants of Lucifer, bright angel and maker of the world.'

'And what do you want the key for?'

'Lucifer is coming to earth. Eden will be here again. We will let him from Hell.'

'Aren't there four gates of Hell?' said Osbert. 'You only have three keys.'

'We may not need the fourth,' said Dow.

'Why not?'

'Because Lucifer works through me,' said Dow. 'And has done things I could not imagine. How many dead surround us?'

'A multitude,' said Osbert.

'An army,' said Dow. 'Now go, back to your drink and your women and, if you like, your devils. Lucifer is coming and, when he does, you will, I hope, turn to him.'

'And if I don't?'

'Who would not?' said Jacques. 'Who would refuse a place in Eden?'

'Depends on the rent,' said Osbert, glumly. 'Gilette, my love, say it was not all lies.'

'It was not all lies,' she said. 'Only some of it.'

Osbert smiled. 'Then it was as good a tryst as ever man and woman had between them. For some of it is always lies. Will you kiss me?'

She put her arms around him and kissed him.

'Cannot I come with you?' he said.

Jacques shook his head.

'You are a hare now. And soon the hounds will be released. We must be as far from you as possible when that happens.'

'But what shall I do?'

'What you always do,' said Jacques. 'Prosper. You seem to find that easy. Follow and I will kill you.'

Osbert put his hands in the air. 'Shan't follow, then.'

Gilette kissed him.

'Goodbye, Osbert.'

'Where will you go?'

'South or north,' she said.

'Well, glad you've narrowed it down.' He held her hands. 'I shall find a way to make you have me back.'

'I loved you, Osbert, but in these days, love is not enough. You are a liar. And, because you could not be swayed by duty or by the love of the light, you made me a liar too. When you stand in the light of truth, when you are within what you appear without, then perhaps. I loved you, Osbert, but in these days, love is not enough.'

'I shan't hold my breath, then.' He kissed her.

'Come on,' said Dow. 'We must get away before he is missed at the palace.'

Good Jacques made the sign of the three-pronged fork. 'I am sorry to have to take all the available Ympes.'

'Your mission is clear,' said Dow. 'You need them more than we. Let them fly you swiftly and safely in your great business.'

They went through the door and into the street.

Osbert followed them out, but by the time he entered the alley, they were gone.

He stood in the gloom, in the pissy, shitty smell of the alley. Rats scuttled at his feet. He could not go back to La Cerda now – the loss of the Key of Blood would be enough for that great lord to hang him. Where could he go? Somewhere quiet, somewhere free of devilry and horror, free of people.

What a world. Nothing as it seemed, nothing pure or decent, deception at every turn.

'So I have lived,' he said to himself. 'I have gulled men with false nostrums, I have sold the bones of pigs as those of saints, the teeth of debtors dead in jail as those of holy saints. I have been a bad man who has lived by lies. But now I forswear lies. From now on, I am a man of the truth. I shall deceive and trick no more. I shall live the life of an honest man and no saint shall ever have been as innocent as I. Women, I have lied to but I shall lie no more. Nor shall I pay them for a mocking echo of love, a false silk that frays and discolours from the moment it is worn. I shall be worthy of love, if not from Gilette then from . . .' He stumbled for words. 'Just worthy of love.'

He looked into his purse. A good amount. He was off to find an alehouse.

Isabella was led through the winding corridors of the palace, through backstairs and dusty archways she would have thought never to have seen in her adult life. A queen may play with the servants in such places when she is a child. Grown, come to power, she never sees the grimy bowels of her palaces, the cobwebs and dirt that serve as channels between the gilded rooms where the nobility dwell.

They passed through a series of locked doors and Isabella noted how each one was marked with odd writing. She recognised it as a jumble of scripts – Latin, Hebrew, Greek – and she knew enough of the first to know what the words said: the names of God.

'Each one of these names,' said the Pope, 'is most secret, and each more secret than the last.'

'To keep devils out?' said Isabella.

'No devil would want to come in here.'

They continued on, the passage ever tighter. Now it rubbed both her shoulders and she – a slender woman – was obliged to turn sideways to pass through.

Finally they came to a door of steel, engraved with many circles and names.

'What is this? A prison for me?'

'No such thing, Lady,' said the Pope. 'This is La Tour des Anges.' And then, in clicking English, as if she could not understand the French, 'The tower of angels.'

He opened the door and she now saw they were in a magnificent chapel, high above the city. There were seven stained glass windows – glorious works of red, green, gold and blue – showing the making of the world from the inception of light to God's rest, depicted as a shining cloud looking out on the mountains and lakes of creation. Some of the high panes were missing, their arches open, and she could see far over Avignon, which seemed baked umber in the falling sun.

A magnificent altar was the centrepiece and upon it, housed in foils of gold and silver, some in cups, some in maces, some in dishes and some in crowns, were the most precious jewels she had ever seen. They all shone with a light deeper than any natural gem. She heard high voices all around her, calling out praises to God, songs of devotion and delight.

'Angels,' she said.

'Yes,' said the Pope.

'How many?'

'I don't know. This is a safe haven for them.'

'They need a haven?'

'We knew from the Bible that one day the dragon would come. Years ago we built this place to protect against it. When it became clear its arrival was imminent, we moved all the angels of Rome here to be protected until God showed himself.'

Isabella's head was spinning, as if after the first sips of summer wine. A great elation filled her. And then a dread. She had drunk the blood of these creatures. Too late to worry about that now. She was where she was and could not turn back.

She bent to see a crown, stared into its jewels. Voices. 'Servant,' said one. 'Savage servant.' The jewel seemed to her like a house of many rooms, shining floors shifting within it.

'Do they speak to you?' said Isabella.

'They do,' said the Pope.

'And what do they tell you?'

'That you have served the light. You have served God.'

'In dark ways.'

'You have rid the world of angels who have taken flesh. You have put their bones and their blood to good service.'

'I have.'

'You are a daughter of God. Ask what you want.'

'I want Mortimer from Heaven.'

The Pope smiled.

'Only God can grant that.'

'And how do I speak to God?'

'God has abandoned the world. The angels cannot find Him. He has sickened Himself on our sins, sent a plague to torment us. God has gone. There are no rulers.'

Isabella bowed her head.

'I have often wondered in these strange days of heresy. It seems the Bible is not as it is written. Lucifer and Satan are not as one.'

The Pope looked surprised. 'And where in the Bible does it mention Lucifer?'

'Is he not the Devil?'

'Not according to The Bible. Lucifer is mentioned four times. Three of those times "Lucifer" is a name given to Christ.'

'I don't understand. Are you saying the Luciferians are telling the truth?'

'No, they are liars who have twisted the word of God.'

Isabella kept quiet, not understanding at all.

'The Bible says Lucifer fell, in one reading of it. It also says Satan fell – Jesus says, does He not, that He saw Satan falling from Heaven like lightning?'

'He does.'

'So the Bible clearly has Lucifer and Satan as separate beings. But the Bible does not talk much on the subject of Hell. Our God is a god of love, after all. He made the world. That we know because it is written and because the angels say so. But God was too good a maker when He made Lucifer, and only after a terrible fight did He lock him in Hell and there contain him. A man, a low man, can make a son who kills him. So why can't God? Nothing is impossible for God, even to make a being greater than He.'

'So what do I do?'

The Pope smiled.

'Our angels have identified you as chosen of God. They would work with you.'

'For what?'

'For the establishment of the kingdom of God. Lady. Queen. Look around you at these days. The Plague, whose victims I minister with my own hands. The devils and demons in the sky. Is it not obvious?'

'What?'

'These are the last days.'

'God is coming back to judge us? The dead will rise?'

'Most certainly.'

'My Mortimer! When will this occur?'

'When,' said the Pope, 'we make it happen.'

Isabella crossed herself.

'Do not the last days proceed according to prophecy?'

'Prophecy is only a foretelling of the decisions men make. We cannot sit back like hermits and wait. There is dispute as to where we are, dispute even among the angels. But I think it is safe to say that we are somewhere near the end as prophesied in the Revelation of John of Patmos. Where depends on how you read the text – literally, as a symbol, or as a mixture. One thing is certain – nothing but God's grave displeasure could have caused the Plague, these wars. We must make Him return.'

'Can you make God do anything?'

'You do His will. He sets the course. It is up to us if we follow it.'

'And how do we do that?'

'We release Lucifer from Hell. God must return to the world then. It says so in the Bible.'

Isabella crossed herself. 'And how do we do that?'

'You need to meet someone. He will be here in a moment.'

'Who?'

'An enemy.'

Isabella stood marvelling at the work of the chapel; every pillar was coiled with gold, the roof decorated in rich paints and gilt.

On the altar stood a crown and beside it a sceptre.

Presently there was a noise at the door. It opened. A man, worse dressed than her, stepped in. His clothes were in rags but he was well fed, well muscled – too well muscled to have been a labourer fed on barley and millet. Only warriors were so thickset.

'You do not bow?' she said.

'This is our enemy, Queen. Do not expect him to bend the knee. This is Jacques Bonhomme. Good Jacques. One of the poor knights, the Templars, accursed of God. A friend of Lucifer. They do not call Lucifer Lord, did you know that?'

The man looked around him at the beauty of the chapel. He seemed to find it rather distasteful, by the tight-lipped expression on his face.

'There are angels here?'

'There are angels everywhere,' said the Pope.

'Not in France – they cower from the Evertere.'

'No longer. The Evertere has not been seen in a long time. Though I suspect you will know where it is.'

The Templar grunted. 'We're here for business, aren't we?'

'Yes. Tell the queen what it is.'

'We bring Satan to earth.'

Isabella almost ducked. The Pope smiled.

'Do you think his devils can come here to Avignon? Do you think his spies can slink beneath the gaze of angels?'

'Do the angels not hear us?'

The Pope shrugged. 'They are in rapture in the gems. They will not make themselves present unless called.'

'Why would you bring Satan?' said Isabella to the Templar.

'To kill him. Or to distract him long enough for us to break through the last wall of Hell and release the light.'

'You can break through the wall?'

'We can try. If we can summon Satan. If you can call his devils.'

'I have forsworn the calling of devils. God placed devils in Hell. It is unholy to call them.'

'Would they not just step from Hell once the gates are open?' said the Templar. 'I can't think any of them can like it very much there.'

'I think not,' said the Pope. 'He would need to be called, devils would need to be called. It might be possible minor devils would come to the call of a sorcerer or someone God has allowed to discover His secret names. But Satan – he would not come from Hell other than from the summons of someone elevated by God to the highest level. The Devil could not come forth on his own volition, no matter how he wanted to.'

'You could call him!' The Templar jabbed a meaty finger towards the Pope.

'And risk damnation? God set Satan in Hell. To call him forth, even in the best interests . . .'

Isabella thought hard.

'My son, though he has devil blood, is an appointed king. Could he call Satan forth?'

The Pope pursed his lips.

'I don't know. He has been crowned and anointed, angels have spoken to him. And yet God worked through you to oppose his line, to control them if not to end them. This is a question of deep theology. God may not respect the man but He respects his position. Somehow this contaminated line thwarted his will to come to power – but now . . . But now! As kings they must be granted the rights of kings or kingship means nothing. I have thought long and hard on it and I have concluded this is why we have wars.'

'For what? The ambition of men?'

'Yes. But it is God's way of making adjustments to the world, or removing sinning or corrupt kings, corrupt of the mind or corrupt of the flesh. If a king removes a king then the order remains. I think it very likely your son could invite Satan over the threshold of Hell and into the world. Though God may despise what he represents, He loves the office of king and His will should respect that.'

Isabella felt her heart skip. To kill her son was one thing but to damn him for ever, before God? But then she thought of her own line: *Dieu Donné*, as House Capet's motto said – God Given. Was she not descended from Saint Louis himself? And yet she had been married to the devil-blooded Edward, borne him children, corrupted her line. She felt soiled just thinking about it.

'Satan cannot be allowed to roam free, or to ally with the English,' said the Pope. 'He must be bound.'

'If we do not release Lucifer then Satan would put a grievous yoke on the people,' said Jacques.

'Can you not bind him?' said the Pope.

'How?' said the Templar.

The Pope put his hand to his chest, affronted.

'I am not a sorcerer. That is a gift of men like you and the Capetian queens. How might it be done?'

Isabella thought.

'The blood royal dominates these creatures. I gained an audience with Satan by presenting him with the heart of my husband.'

Even the Pope, a sophisticated and worldly man, blanched slightly at that.

'There may be a way that suits all our needs. We need a grand summoning. A field red with the blood of kings. Angels at the cardinal points of the circle. Relics beyond compare to compose the dust of its drawing. We call Satan and then, as the Bible says, we kill him.'

'And then? How do we kill Satan?'

'The Archangel Michael,' said Isabella. 'He is the bane of devils and demons alike. If he knows Satan's plan to inhabit the earth, he will not allow it. He will not see God's great creation turned into another Hell. If Satan comes to earth, he will kill him.'

'I can show you Michael,' said the Pope. 'Or at least somewhere he inhabits. You will not have much luck, I think.'

He went to the altar. A great sceptre lay upon it, topped with a pink diamond, the size of a pigeon's egg. Isabella, who had seen many jewels in her life, had never seen anything like this one. It shone and glittered in the chapel light, revealing shining flaws, split angles of colours. She gazed within. The light moved in an enchanting play, offering sharp angles of colour that touched, vanished and reformed to reach out to each other again.

'Michael,' she said.

'Queen.' A delicious chill went through her. The voice came from all around her, as sweet as a child's song but as terrible as the sea.

The Pope crossed himself. 'He hasn't spoken in ten years.'

'Will you appear for me, Michael?'

No reply.

'Michael, come from the gem, step out of the light!'

'I am enraptured.'

'The world is in peril. Satan is coming to earth.'

Now the gem radiated light, sending patterns of green and gold shimmering out against the floor and roof of the chapel.

'A queen says so?'

'A queen says so.'

The light intensified, the gem shining so brightly that Isabella had to look away. Patterns danced on the roof of the chapel in colours more lovely than she had ever seen.

'Satan is a servant.' The voice was like many voices all talking at once. 'Let every person be subject to the governing authorities. For there is no authority except from God, and those that exist have been instituted by God. Therefore whoever resists the authorities resists what God has appointed, and those who resist will incur judgment. For rulers are not a terror to good conduct, but to bad. Would you have no fear of the one who is in authority? Then do what is good, and you will receive his approval, for he is God's servant for your good. But if you do wrong, be afraid, for he does not bear the sword in vain.'

The Pope now spoke.

'Michael. Does it not say, in the Holy Book, "Now war arose in Heaven, Michael and his angels fighting against the dragon. And the dragon and his angels fought back, but he was defeated, and there was no longer any place for them in Heaven. And the great dragon was thrown down, that ancient serpent. He who is called the devil and Satan, the deceiver of the whole world – he was thrown down to the earth and his servants with him. And I heard a loud voice in Heaven, saying, 'Now the salvation and the power and the kingdom of our God and the authority of His Christ have come, for the accuser of our brothers has been thrown down, who accuses them day and night before our God. And they have conquered him by the blood of the Lamb and by the word of their testimony, for they loved not their lives even unto death.'"?'

'Are these the last days?' said the angel.

'Yes,' said the Pope. 'Yes!'

'When Satan rises up, call me from the light of this gem. Until then, I will dwell in rapture.'

The light went out and the chapel seemed dull without it.

'Take the gem,' said the Pope. 'And take the Crown of Five Angels.'

'How will Hell's gate be opened?'

'I will see to that,' said the Templar, 'it's why I came here. These days make strange alliances.'

'Where?'

'At Poitiers,' said the Templar. 'When you receive the message, see to it that Edward's army meets that of John there – they cannot go to the north. We will bind Satan in a circle made from the blood of kings. Be certain they are there to spill it.'

'The angels will do for Satan?'

'Possibly. Remember, he threw down the most powerful. He must be bound if he is to be killed. Like any devil he can be compelled and constrained, but the magic must be a great one.'

'I can persuade John to the field, if I have angels at my back. My son, he is already pledged to Satan,' said Isabella.

'I will get him there,' said the Templar. 'We have prepared for this day for a long time. He is a great spiller of blood. He will mark the circle well.'

'Holy Father, I give you my pledge. We shall restore God to the world and stand in his wonderful light.' She knelt and kissed the Pope's ring.

'The light you stand in will be the light of the dawn. Lucifer's kingdom is coming. Beyond death, beyond suffering, beyond kings and queens,' said the Templar.

'We will see,' said Isabella. 'Two travellers walk by the same road but only one will arrive at the destination.'

'There will be room for all,' said the Templar.

'None for the rebellious poor,' said Isabella.

The Templar shook his head, walked to one of the open arches and stepped out into thin air. A huge cloud of ympes descended and bore him up.

She turned back into the room and took up the crown.

'How shall I transport this?' she said.

'It is full of angels,' said the Pope. 'It will transport you.'

8

The girl Alice had been busy. Her art was faltering and she proceeded with some error at first, but soon very promising devils were being pulled through the cracks in the walls of Hell. Above the English fleet floated twenty huge jellyfish, their tentacles swaying in the light breeze. On the quay, three legions of the Boar Men of Gehenna stood with gleaming spears, and beside Lord Sloth and his leopard warriors, eight flaming men stood on the deck where sheets of iron had been laid down to prevent them burning a hole in their own ships. On each ship stood one strange creature – an impossibly thin man-like thing, but with folds of flesh falling down from its face and neck to cover its feet and spread out on the deck like a huge and grotesque cloak.

Next to the cross of St George flew the barbed whip symbol of Satan, its design and manufacture personally overseen by the Iron Lion himself. He stood gazing up at it from the deck of the *Christopher*, the latest ship to bear that name, clearly proud to see such a day come to earth.

Philippa was beside them, ready to travel with her husband, to fight with him if need be. She was going for a purpose. If a dialogue could be achieved with King John – if Edward could be made to bow the knee, to accept his role as a vassal king – then perhaps his position on the throne would not be such an affront to God. Perhaps John could banish the hideous thing she had taken for her son. She was desperate, she knew, her whole world shaken to its core.

'Not as many devils as when my mother was with us,' said Edward to Philippa. 'But a fair show.'

Philippa shivered. She hated to see these things.

'Your army of men is a mighty one.'

'Since we won Crécy and Calais it is easier to get men to answer my call,' said Edward. Indeed, there was a formidable fleet of ships. The ports from Hull to the Solent had been stripped to provide the navy.

'Where will you land?'

He smiled at her. 'Am I to have you burnt as a spy?'

'I'm sorry. I never get used to this need for secrecy. There have never been secrets between us.'

'Some must be kept. For habit. If I tell you, I might tell a baron and he a knight, and he might reveal our secret to whatever French spy is sitting next to him across a cup of ale.'

'I understand.'

Am I now your enemy? she thought. *Are we to believe that Satan is God's servant? Does the blood of devils truly run in your veins? Have I carried devils in me? All my pretty children, reeking with the stench of Hell.*

And yet, if devils were God's servants could they truly be said to be evil? Perhaps it was worse than being evil. They were things meant to serve and to obey, not to rule. It would be a violation of the holy order of God to set them on the throne. And yet here was one, her husband, her beloved husband, in the crown of a king, ready to throw down a true king, a man who was surely appointed by God. She loved him beyond question, but could she follow where he was leading? To Hell!

She thought of the glass the man Tancré had brought her. She had feared to look in that again for what it might show, and had thought to bury it. But no, it was with her, in the bottom of her sewing bag where no one but she would ever look, or have reason to look.

'Those things make me shiver,' said Philippa, nodding towards the thin man that stood on the deck.

'They are windbags,' said Edward. 'In Hell they blow their rancid breath for ever into the faces of the over-talkative, the chatterbox and the gossip.'

'Such small sins,' said Philippa.

'When this war is won, perhaps we will pray that such are not punished. God may answer.'

'Will he?'

'I don't know. But I do know we have no choice in this. We take France, we impose order or the world will fall to chaos. Already God has chastised us with a plague. What will come next if we allow weakness and uproar to own the land?'

'What will come next when the devils are king?'

'We have declared for Satan,' said Edward. 'But Satan's appointed realm is Hell. Once God's order is restored under me, he will have no choice but to go back.'

'You know devils so?'

Edward pursed his lips, set his jaw. 'Let me tell you, my queen. All men are devils. Is this not so? How long have the kings and princes, the queens and princesses of our lands mixed their blood with creatures of the Pit, in hope of preferment, in hope of power? The boy Navarre who waits for us in Normandy, he . . .'

Edward had said too much.

'You put your faith in him?'

'He has a similar interest to me. What angels will come for him? Will stone saints sing for him? Perhaps, but grudgingly. He is not born in God's favour so, like me, he must work his way there.'

'Angels came for you once.'

'And they will again. When order is on the earth, when low men kneel and high men rule justly, when the rightful king, which is me, rules France. Then God will come and the angels will burst with song.'

Philippa looked into his eyes. Did he believe it? She thought he was taking a big risk. Last time, holding France had proved beyond them. Calais had been militarily useless, bottled in to the marshes and there was no base within the country to fall back to, on which to build supply lines. With the Norman castles open to the English army, conquest might be possible. But then what?

Her son came on deck next to her. He looked magnificent, a head taller than other men, clad in his black robes embroidered with silver garters. The badge that held his cloak was a red cross circled in blue – the sign of the Order of the Garter.

'Any word from Hell's walls?' said Edward.

'We have messengers crawling as far as the Falls of Blood. The captains of Hell are sympathetic to our cause.'

'But no word from Satan himself.'

We have no resistance so far. And these devils are sent. Take that as a good sign, Father.'

'I do, son.' Edward hugged the boy. Once Philippa would have simply felt aggrieved that her son would allow his father an intimacy he forbade her. But now she knew. The prince could touch his father easily because his father carried devil's blood too.

'Set sail?'

'Set sail.'

The prince raised his hand and the sails were raised. There was a light offshore breeze that might have carried them well enough, but the windbags sucked in, inflating hugely, gigantic bladders of air. As one they blew, filling the sails, driving the ships forward across the sea, the boar men of Gehenna pouring into the water behind them, the floating jellyfish serenely following.

It was a good crossing, the sea as flat and unruffled as a sheep-bitten field. Once at sea, Edward summoned the girl Alice to him.

'You are sure of the loyalty of these fiends?' he said, jabbing a finger at the gigantic jellyfish that floated above them.

'I am.'

'Then I announce our landing spot. Queen, Princes, Lords, knights, freemen, and devils. Know that we shall be landing by Mont-Saint-Michel. The monastery has been turned over to our good offices by the King of Navarre, who commands the Norman lands. This shall be our base and our impregnable fallback position. From it we shall move to conquer France, and claim our right.'

A great cheer went up from the ship, and the cheer caught as the news was relayed from ship to ship in the mighty fleet.

'Will we meet resistance?' said Sloth, licking his lips, his great jumble of teeth spreading wide, as dull as boat nails and just as big.

'No. Navarre has given me his word.'

'You can trust him?' said Philippa. 'He has led us a dance in the past.'

'This time he has more to lose. He has played for the highest stakes. My man was there when he murdered the Constable of France.'

'Bold but ungodly,' said Sloth.

'Sometimes,' said Edward, 'God is served through sin, just as masters are sometimes best served by disobedience.'

The lion looked shocked and rattled its mane.

'You are a king,' it said. 'And so I must defer.'

The windbags blew their stinking breath and before long the Norman coast appeared. Every time she made the journey in good weather, Philippa was struck by how near France was to England, how slender and slight a barrier seemed the sea. Every time she made it in bad weather, though, she thought it an impenetrable moat, a protection to rival the walls of heaven.

They had set off at dawn and, by the time the fleet assembled for landing and the tides made it possible, it was mid-afternoon. Mont-Saint-Michel rose from the water like a little England, like an image of God's design for the world – a broad base tapering up to a narrow spire that pointed like a needle to Heaven, a cross on top for anyone who had missed the message.

'It's like a castle from a romance,' said Philippa.

'It's a stronghold,' said Edward, 'and we shall have it. Sloth?'

'My King. Give the order to— In the name of Christ's blood, what is that?'

Something was happening on the spire of the monastery. The flag of Navarre which flew above it was coming down, its distinctive red lowering and disappearing.

'I don't like this,' said Edward.

Above the island monastery the air itself sparkled and shone, silver, gold. For an instant Philippa thought it might just be some trick of the sun catching a rain-cloud. But no, the light took shape – great shining beings that spilt rainbows from their forms. They towered over the monastery, as tall again above its spire as it was from the water.

'Angels!' someone said.

She counted five. Five! Had ever so many been in a battle before? *France has angels?* No, it did not! The angels had fled at Crécy, yet here they were. A wind blew from the shore, cold and full of grit.

'Pray, Edward,' said Philippa. 'Pray for forgiveness. Pray to know God's mind.'

She sank to her knees herself. The wind blew harder. The ship lurched violently. The windbag on their deck struggled to hold on to the rail of the ship, his great flesh folds flapping. The wind blew harder and he was gone, whipped over the side of the ship and cast in to the sea.

'I am a queen,' prayed Philippa. 'Appointed by God. Hear me, angels, hear my plea and my petition.'

The wind did not abate. Devils and men clung at ropes. A boar man, who had been swimming in the water alongside the ship, was tossed on to the deck and landed with a crash, splintering the boards. She was thrown violently sideways, knocking Edward clean from his feet. She grabbed at him, imploring.

'Pray, Edward, pray! Whatever you are, you are a king, crowned and anointed. Pray!'

Edward put his hands together.

'Great angels, great angels!' he screamed. She did not hear the rest but mouthed her own prayer, reminding the angels of all the good works she had done, all the contributions she had made, the churches she had invested, the priests she had sponsored.

The storm grew quieter, though the swell was still heavy, the wind full of grit.

She wiped her eyes, looked out above the monastery.

The great figure of a woman floated in the sky, her dress shining with jewels of every colour. In her hand she bore a spear. She raised her other hand and pointed, back across the sea to Dover.

'Bargain with it!' said Edward to Philippa. 'We can go to our own lands in Calais and in Aquitaine. I am rightful king there, I should be allowed there!'

'Dear angel, whose name I do not know, but whose divinity I recognise and adore. I am Philippa, Queen under God of England, of Calais and Aquitaine. Acknowledge our right to pass to these lands.'

The woman's colours deepened, the jewels of her dress sparkling red and green. Then she flickered and faded to nothing.

On the spire of the monastery now flew the blue and gold of France.

Edward got to his feet and embraced Philippa.

'You have saved us. You have saved us.'

'But Navarre has betrayed us,' said Philippa. 'And now France has its angels back.'

'Then now what?' said the Black Prince.

'We do what we always did,' said Edward. 'Though we cannot overthrow France, we can destroy it, show God that its king cannot care for it. My son – go south to Aquitaine and await our instructions. We will go to Calais.'

'What for?'

Edward said nothing.

'You cannot trade with the men of Lucifer again,' she said. 'We should be seeking a way back to God!'

'God is gone. Or sleeping.' He turned to his son. 'Rip the guts out of France. We'll force John to meet us in battle and we'll have another Crécy!'

Philippa's heart leaped in her chest.

'Crécy was nearly lost if it hadn't been for the dragon that ate the angels.'

'It came once,' said Edward. 'It will come again. Faith. Sacrifice. Courage. The piety of kings.'

Philippa crossed herself.

'It is a thing of Hell!'

Edward looked up into the sky, where the angels had been.

'So am I,' he said. 'So am I. *Honi soit qui mal y pense!* It is as it is!'

9

Charles rode into the city with his banners streaming – the golden chains of Navarre bright in the summer sun. As he had expected, he met no resistance and the gates were thrown open to him. His brother, big Philip, rode beside him. My God, he'd seen those bull devils riding their great beetles before but Philip had a neck as thick as any of them.

If there was meant to be some sort of magical edict on devils entering France now, it hadn't worked against Charles. He had a creeping sense of unease, true, but his human and kingly half rightly commanded his catty and devilish side, which enabled him to progress.

'You're sure about this, brother?' said Philip.

'As ever I was about anything. Our Dauphin will prevail upon the king to see wisdom. We may have to throw him a couple of freezing castles here and there, or some shit pit of a county, but he has to see sense. He has no one but me to advise him and no one who has ever shown their love so well.'

'If you are wrong?'

'I've sent word to the English. Our invasion is back on.'

'You might be dead by then.'

'I command the loyalty of Normandy. If the king wants me to betray the English, he has to do business.'

'There are a lot of men-at-arms in the city,' said Philip.

And indeed there were. Throngs of them. For the first time, Charles felt a little nervous. He put his finger inside his stiff collar – between the metal and the fur of his left-hand side. Philip, he suspected, was inwardly smiling to see his scratching but said nothing. Anyone, even his brother, who said 'fleas' would be in for an inventive punishment.

On they went through the streets. He was popular still, he was pleased to see. People thrust babies at him, withered old men tried to touch him. It did not seem to matter that he was half cat but he understood why. To these people, the nobility were like creatures of another race anyway. They looked so different, with their pale skin, their bodies tall and well fed, their rich clothes. The worth of the cloth of his nosegay would keep a poor man for a decade, the incense inside it his entire life. As was right in any ordered world. But Charles did not want an ordered world quite yet, if at all. If he could be king of France, then fine. If not, chaos. These merchants, always grumbling, these low men – whispering of Lucifer in the shadows – needed encouragement. Perhaps one day they might even revolt.

Trade was not doing so well, he noticed. The big market at Les Halles was threadbare. The remnants of the Pestilence, war, harvests left to rot in the fields – what could you do? Well, something.

A voice cried out, 'Lord Navarre, tell the king to save us from the English.'

'My first task!' shouted Charles. 'Paris is dear to me and we will drive the scum from our lands!' He recalled his letter to the Black Prince:

'You will land in Normandy and muster men there. I will secure the people of Paris and the invasion will be over quickly.'

He stopped at a market stall and had his men buy some leatherwork. He didn't need it, but it stood him in good stead to be in the good books of these people. A monarch has two ways of sitting secure among his people – generosity and tyranny. King John was incapable of either. Charles, who had studied the Romans as part of his upbringing, knew well the power of the mob.

'How much?' His man Sangiz had been buying a belt. He now looked as though it had been tied around his neck, so red was he in the face.

'That is the price now, sir.' The leatherworker looked the knight straight in the eye. My word, here was a saucy fellow. Charles was sure Sangiz would strike the greedy merchant down, which would have defeated Charles's attempts to build goodwill.

'I will pay, I will pay,' he said.

The leatherworker smiled.

'Your man is welcome to try any other leatherworker in the market, if he thinks he can get a better price.'

Charles looked around. The market was sparse enough for him to see nearly every stall.

'I see no other.'

'My point exactly. You are a good king, sir, and we respect you. But I see what is in your knight's eyes. He would strike my head from my shoulders. Well good. Let him. But I say then that the court will want of repair for its saddles, no fine leather will be prepared to make the gloves you wear, no belts cut, no buckles fitted. He would be an unpopular man with his fellows.'

'There must be some other leatherworkers left alive.'

'There are twenty in the city, and we are guildsmen whose bond has been strengthened by Plague. Strike my head from my shoulders and you may as well strike all for all the work you will get.'

Charles doubled the amount he was about to pay for the belt.

'You are right to think so,' he said. 'For too long lords have ignored the worth of the toiling man. Increase your prices further, is my advice.'

'We cannot,' said the leatherworker. 'We are under sharp edict from the king, who has banned further price rises. He says they are ungodly.'

'The king is poorly advised. Let it be known that, to free the people from his yoke, I have struck the head from the shoulders of the tyrant La Cerda. I will be constable within the hour. Put up your prices as you so wish. These are new times and we must find new ways.'

'God bless you, sir.'

'And you. Recommend me to the masters of your Third Estate and tell them they always have a friend in Navarre!'

He took the belt and passed it to Sangiz.

'Ride beside me, Sangiz,' he said.

The knight, almost boiling with rage, did as he was bid and the procession turned towards the Louvre.

'Pay it no mind,' said Navarre. 'In five years we'll have recovered from the Plague. There will be leatherworkers aplenty and I promise you, I'll have you a belt made from his hide.'

'It's not right to yield to such low men.'

'Did you have poachers on any of your estates?'

'We did.'

'And how did they trap a boar? Did they fly through the woods as we do, shouting and hooraying, chasing their hounds?'

'They would have been hanged if they had.'

'Then how?'

'They dug a pit near its common places of forage and covered it with thin branches and soil. Then they baited it with acorns and waited.'

'And did not those branches yield to the boar's foot? Yet it was not much good for the boar. We yield a little, sir, only to increase the force of the fall. We take what allies we can while we must. When the wind changes, so does the setting of the sail.'

At the Louvre, his banners were not flying. Well, he would hardly expect that.

He strode as best he could up the steps to the Louvre. God's balls, he hoped that sorcerer was going to be in the palace. He'd have him working day and night to put right the harm he had done.

Trumpets sounded, drums were beaten. The king's guard were out in force.

'If it looks like trouble . . .' said Charles.

'Oh, it looks like trouble,' said Philip.

'If it—'

'If it looks like trouble, brother, we are sarded. Up the rear with a red-hot poker the way old English Edward went.'

'Come in and get me,' he said.

'Well, I'll try. Shouldn't I come with you?'

'He won't murder me in the palace,' said Charles. 'His wife doesn't like the sight of blood. Well, the last one didn't, and I don't suppose the latest is much different.'

Such a familiar place – the mosaics of unicorns, the gold and the blue of the halls. Already he saw that he was accompanied by armed men, though only in the style of an honour guard. He hoped to God that the Dauphin had done his job for him.

He paused at the door of the throne room. The air was thick with incense. He was announced: 'Devil, traitor and servant of evil, Charles the Bad of Navarre.' Not promising.

He stepped forward to go inside but found he could not cross the threshold. Through the smoky air, he could make out King John and the Dauphin at the other end of the throne room. John made an impatient gesture with his hand and a servant came to the door. He took down a plaque that was hanging there. Relief swept over Charles. A magic symbol. A name of God? That sorcerer, he was sure.

Charles walked in and bowed to the king. John stood, furious.

'I commend you on your bravery on coming here, cousin, and on nothing else. Is it true what they say you have done?'

'True as you like,' said Charles. 'Yes, I butchered him with my own fair paw. Swack, snick, tick, scritch, scratch!' He illustrated by waving his paw about, its long claws exposed.

John shook his head.

'For what?'

'For leading you astray, cousin. Listen to me carefully. Your realm is in peril. Bandits roam the land, killing what the Plague left. The English gather on their shores waiting to invade, their armies bolstered by devils who accept Edward as king of France, who will fight against your men. The only thing that has stopped the Luciferian heresy spreading through every town and farm is the number of dead in the Plague. You need to impose yourself on the land. You need to wipe away the English bandits, summon men to defeat the English when they come.'

John snorted.

'What do you know?'

'I know more than La Cerda and that is why he had to die. Why do you not come forward like a lion to save your realm? Why hide here like a sheep?'

Charles enjoyed the force of his words. This idiot would not dare harm him and would bend to his will.

John stiffened.

'He said that if we endured God's wrath, that if we took our punishment in all humility and contrition, then the angels would return.'

'So where are they?'

'I will lock you away for this. You were my special delight as a child but I saw in you things you didn't even see in yourself. You turned bitter and ambitious. Men, take him to Le Châtelet.'

Charles shrugged.

'As you wish, cousin. But how am I to help you, then? You are to need my help, I take it. The English are currently sailing for the Norman coast. My men will naturally oppose them vigorously. However, when it is learned – as it is always learned, as it must be learned if I am to be made an example of – that you have imprisoned me or killed me, then they may well be inclined to side with the English. What say you, cousin?'

He extended his hand to the Dauphin.

Now the boy stood.

'I would do what I can for you, cousin, for all the help you have rendered me,' he said. 'I have cried salt tears over your fate but I can see no way round it. You have killed a constable of France.'

Charles bristled.

'Explain to your father clearly what happens if harm befalls me.'

The Dauphin addressed the king.

'Sire, if Navarre is allowed to advise you then we are secure from the west and the English cannot dare face us without his support. They cannot rely on their devils once they see your banners in the field. They may well bow down and accept your God appointed-right, even turn to side with you. They need Navarre.'

Navarre bowed deeply.

'Furthermore,' said the Dauphin, You require good advice. Navarre is full of it.'

'I brim!' said Navarre.

The Dauphin bowed to him. Navarre did not like this. There was something in the boy's manner. A regret? No. Something. Navarre sensed a 'but' coming, and one he thought he might not much like.

'But,' said the Dauphin, 'all this is by the by.'

'By the what?' said Navarre.

The Dauphin gestured to the throne. Charles had taken very little notice of the veiled figure sitting beside John. He had thought it was a handmaiden or a maid, some low woman brought in because the Plague had killed anyone of better breeding. But now he saw by her bearing that this was a very different kind of woman indeed. She stood tall, possessing the room.

She drew back her veil. My God, it was his aunt Isabella! 'France is the domain of God, not devils. I have defeated one English army and can defeat another.' She removed the veil to reveal a five pointed crown, each point tipped with a brilliant diamond. The light in the room grew fine and bright, like a snow field in the sun.

'The angels are back in France. England will fall and a true line take its place. I'm sorry, little Charles, but there is no place for fiends like you in this bright future,' she said.

'I am a king!'

'Half of you is,' she said. 'The other half is a cat. And, like a cat, it shall be put out!'

'I have shown you what he is, father,' said the Dauphin. 'Now act upon it putting all sentiment aside.'

'Remove him,' said King John.

'You have betrayed me,' said Charles.

'Those who deal in betrayal are paid in the same coin,' said the Dauphin. 'Eu wa a noble man. In one strike I avenge him on you and the English.'

Charles tried to run, tried to draw his sword, then tried to struggle as strong hands gripped him but it was no good. He heard the angel's name 'Jophiel' and his limbs would not do as they were bid.

'This is God's day,' said King John. 'Through Isabella, we will restore his order on earth and vanquish the line of devils that have stolen the English throne!'

IO

Philippa looked out over the Pale of Calais from the high watch-tower, out over the road through the marshes. A camp had sprung up there, refugees from the Plague and from the routiers – the gangs of unemployed English soldiers who had been ravaging the French countryside since the truce imposed on England and France by the pestilence. A swarm of ympes – the tiny demons of the Luciferians – turned and wheeled above the throng; for what? For joy? Or were they, like she, just trying to work out how best to help these poor people?

Edward was beside her. Since Normandy, he would not let her from his side.

'You persuaded the angels away,' he said. 'By your holiness, outweighing my corruption, you saved England.'

Philippa felt sick. She did not know what she had done. In truth, she had panicked and simply prayed by instinct. 'This was always known,' said Edward. 'Now I see the wisdom of the old King Philip who took lame Joan for queen of France. Her piety was his protection and so yours is mine and, through me, England's.'

Edward scared Joan now. She had borne him so many children, and yet he was becoming someone she didn't know – feverish, angry. His moods were dark and he sometimes was full of regret. 'If we had not declared for Satan, the angels would still be with us.'

'It is not too late to renounce,' she said. He squeezed her hand.

'Satan is of God. When Lucifer rose up against Him, God threw Lucifer down and put Satan as jailer of the Pit. He is His most trusted servant and, through Satan, we serve God.'

'As you are my king, and my husband, appointed by God as my master, I believe you.' She had to. The alternative? Madness.

Whatever Edward's mood, he needed her. She would use that to her advantage if she could.

'Can we not let these poor people in, my love?'

Edward laughed, too hard for her liking. 'Well, we wouldn't have gone to all the bother of driving them out if we were going to do that.'

'These are not the people of Calais. They've come from further afield.'

'They should stay where they are. Half of them are serfs and you can bet what you like that they have no permission from their masters to move. It's unnatural that they should be here.'

'Yet they are here. And in part because of us.'

'Nothing to do with me!'

'It is our men who ravage the country.'

'Not on my orders,' said Edward. 'I brought them here to take France and to hold it. If God does not provide enough work for them at home and the Plague means there is no war for them here, what are they to do? You cannot control it and I will not share what I have won. These are the poor, are they not? Let the Luciferians look after them.'

'They are starving themselves from what I hear. Could you not at least send them some bread?'

'I can do that. Though you are too soft.'

A page came up on to the roof of the tower, bowing deeply and going down on bended knee. He bore in his hand a note.

'You read it, Philippa,' said Edward. 'You know how I struggle.'

She took it.

'The Luciferians want a conference with you.'

'Do they? Tell them to whistle for it.'

She looked at him oddly. 'I thought we were here to gain Luciferian support?'

He waved the page away.

'My love, we are here to strike when Philip marches south to meet the Black Prince. Our army will attack his undefended rear at Paris.'

'You will never hold it.'

'The people of that city bear him no love. With encouragement and a little chastisement, they will recognise me.'

Philippa studied the note.

'The note bears a mark. What do you make of that? I haven't seen that in years.'

There was a seal on the note showing two knights on a single horse. The Templars. They'd been put down years ago by the last of the Capetians, their castles given away, their lands sold. She passed the note to him.

Edward studied the seal. He passed it back. 'Read it.'

'They want to meet you.'

'Where?'

'At Fort Nieully.'

The Luciferian headquarters. She shivered. It was a den of thieves and murderers, she was sure.

'Does he think I come crawling like a dog?' said Edward. 'If the Templar wants to meet me, he can come here.'

'What Templar?'

'He is a man, a useful man, I once knew. Page, send back and tell him the king of England does not come running on the command of a beggar. I have fulfilled my bargain and given them their stinking Eden, for what it's worth. I have no more need to deal with him.'

The page scampered away.

They spent the day walking the city, taking Mass at Notre Dame, visiting the fort that Edward had built to stop supplies getting in to Calais by sea during the siege, dining in the warm open air by the riverbank, the courtiers sprawled out beside them. This was a rich court now, dressed in all the glory of the plunder of France, their raids into the surrounding lands, and not least that they had from Calais itself. In their russets, greens, reds and golds the courtiers reminded Philippa of leaves spread out on the riverbank, the fall of an exquisite autumn.

It was here that the page returned, quaking. Another note, clearly intended for a king because it bore no words to tax his reading. On it were simply scrawled images of three keys and the words "Hell is ours".'

Edward's eyes widened.

'With me!' he shouted. 'With me.'

Every man of the court, and some women too, fell in behind him as he raced from the riverbank. Philippa's heart leapt. She had no good presentiment about this at all. She chased the throng through the streets of the town, shoving through the barricades that separated the Luciferian quarter from Edward's part.

The guards had been told to let them pass, evidently, because they had no problem getting through – a relief, for Philippa well knew that anyone trying to deny her husband in that mood was likely to end up dead on the cobbles.

Over the filth and the muck, lifting her skirts to keep them above the shit. Already this once prosperous side of town was turning into a slum – the commoners completely unable to keep any standards of decency.

The fort lay by the side of the Strait of Dover, a low affair that seemed to peer across the water like the brow of an angry giant.

Edward ignored the guards and strode straight in, ducking as he descended the stairs. His men tried to follow him but he barked at them to stay at the entrance and watch for trouble.

'Philippa – with me. Only Philippa.'

She followed him down. It was a dark and dingy place, a true military emplacement designed to hide crossbowmen and archers, to resist the hardest of gunstones or trebuchet attack. Inside its narrow corridors, picked out by torchlight, she saw the three-pronged fork of Lucifer daubed on the walls. It made her shiver.

'Jacques Bonhomme! Jacques the Good. Where are you?' Edward was calling out.

'This way.' A man with a torch met them.

Finally, Edward entered a mean and small inner room lit by a weak, fishy candle. At a table made of two upturned baskets and a plank sat a figure in a torn tunic, hose that were darned beyond guessing what the original colour had been. Two flags were behind him. One bore the image of a sun – the sign of the Free Legion of the Dawn Light, an irregular force of freed souls. The other bore the sign of an open hand. Some other hastily cobbled together band of refugees from the torments of Hell, no doubt.

'Jacques,' said Edward, almost with familiarity.

'Edward,' said the man. He did not bow but met Edward's eyes squarely. 'It would be best if this were a private meeting.'

'You may speak to my wife as if you were speaking to me.'

Jacques pursed his lips, a southerner's 'as you like it' expression. 'André,' he said to the man with the torch, 'please close the door.' The man did as he was bid.

'We have a mutual problem,' said Jacques.

'Which is?'

'We both need access to Hell.'

'It seems you do well enough,' said Philippa, nodding to the banner.

'Indeed. But you know such demons as we have at our disposal are won hard, by bargaining and by deceit. We pull them through the cracks in the walls of Hell, bribe the devils at a postern gate.'

'I hear you have a key to the first level.'

'We now have the keys to the first three levels, though we fear to use them. Open the big gates for too long and, though our friends emerge, so do our enemies. On balance we have restrained ourselves.'

'Wise,' said Edward.

'Yes. But the time for wisdom is over. I am willing to do you a deal. Not even a deal. I am willing to make you a gift.'

'What sort of gift?'

'You have declared for Satan. The English race faces extermination if Isabella can persuade her angels to fight.'

'She will persuade them,' said Edward. 'Persuasion is her art.'

'Exactly.'

'So?'

'I offer you the greatest aid any king has ever had. I will help you call and bind Satan to your will.'

'He cannot defeat angels!'

'Can't he? He keeps the brightest angel of all locked in a prison. He keeps Lucifer in Hell. I would suggest the angels your mother can employ are of lesser strength entirely.'

'You cannot be bound to Satan!' said Philippa. 'It is one thing to invoke him, to use his devils, but to be bound entirely!'

'You will not be bound. You will do the binding. I have in my possession certain items. The Crown of Thorns. The lance that pierced Christ Lucifer's side. At a certain monastery I know there is a piece of the True Cross. All these things were made by

364

God and pierced the greatest angel's flesh. They are holy to God, invested with His power. We will use them to bind Satan. Or you will. The whole armies of Hell will be at your disposal, not the mere stragglers you have now.'

Edward snorted. 'And what do you get out of it?'

'Eternal torment, more than likely,' said Jacques.

'What?'

Jacques picked up the little candle, turned it around in his finger. Then he replaced it.

'I will not play you false, King. Remember that at Nottingham I set you on your throne when I opened the way to Mortimer's chamber. I am offering to secure that throne now.'

'For what reason? What do you get?'

'I get to take part in a race.' His voice was flat.

'Who against?'

'You. I will tell you plainly what I am planning. My men will lead an army against the walls of the Night City on Gehenna plain, where lies the last gate of Hell. I try to release Lucifer while Satan skips to your command here in the realm of men.'

Philippa crossed herself.

'You have three keys?' said Edward.

'Yes. The fourth remains lost.'

Edward glanced at Philippa. She knew that look. He was not looking for encouragement, not at all. But he feared she might hold him back.

'Cannot peace be made?' she said.

'You know what our spies tell us. She means to clear out England, root and branch. What if she persuades the angels to do that?'

'They would never agree. God has already taken the unholy in the Plague. That is what it was sent for.'

'It took the good and the bad alike,' said Edward. Philippa saw Jacques shift in his seat. She sensed deep discomfort.

'Our souls will be in peril.'

'My soul is damned,' he said. 'I was born damned. I see that now.'

'And so England will be damned with you?'

'God will receive the good into His heaven. And this is a good we do. Order will come back here. England will be protected. These

. . .' He gestured to Jacques, 'will be in Hell. If Lucifer cannot break out, how can these break in?'

'And if it goes wrong you have made the world a hell.'

'I have cast myself into the hazard all my life. This is no different.'

Philippa despaired. But what could be done? Her husband saw no difference between his own interests and those of the state – those of the world.

'I will pray for you,' she said. 'Have faith now in my piety. I am your protection against angels. I am your bulwark. Through me find a way back to God. Renounce the banner of Satan.'

Edward shook, such a physical man, his body trembling with his inner turmoil.

'You kept the angels away once,' he said. 'You must be able to do it again.'

'Or persuade them to your cause,' said Philippa. 'Your mother is a vile woman who has done vile things. I have kept myself in virtue because it is my nature to do so, but I see now that I served God's purpose. You cannot give the world over to Hell – you cannot!'

Edward sank to his knees, took both her hands in his.

'I have faith in you,' he said.

'And I in you.'

Edward kissed her hands. Then he stood.

'Keep your deal, Templar. My wife's holy nature will preserve us. England will use devils but it will not turn earth to Hell.'

'André!' Jacques called out. The door opened.

Philippa breathed out deeply. At last he had seen sense. At last come directly to God rather than fall down before some sulphurous imposter.

Jacques moved his hand. For an instant alarm gripped her. No, they were not going to attack Edward. In such a small space, it would be suicide. The king was worth thirty Luciferians in a fight.

'Stay a moment,' said Jacques. 'I promised that I would return something to you. You fulfilled a bargain, Edward. For the help I gave you to take the throne, you promised Lucifer a place in France to establish New Eden.'

'I did.'

'But you also agreed something else – a clause I included to speed you on your way.'

'What clause?' said Philippa.

'If the deal was not done in seven years, a child. Then another three and a half, another child. And so on. King, Queen, let me introduce you to your children – William of Hatfield, Blanche of London.'

Into the room came a young man of about eighteen, dressed in the poor garb of a Luciferian. Behind him was a girl a few years younger, also in plain attire. Unmistakably, they were Edward's children. The boy could have been him.

'What have you done?' said Philippa.

'What I needed to! It is as it is!'

Philippa thought she would collapse. Her children. She had seen the bodies!

'What cruelty is this?' She went towards the boy, to the girl, to touch them, but the boy drew back.

'I do not know you, madam,' he said.

'William, Blanche,' said Jacques, 'meet your mother and father.'

'I saw them dead!' said Philippa. 'I wept tears over their little bodies. I saw them buried.'

'Your husband is a marvellous deceiver,' said Jacques.

Now Philippa did embrace the pair and they accepted her, however stiffly.

'No wonder you ally with monsters,' said Philippa. 'You are one! You bargained away our children.'

'I had no choice. It is how it is.'

'How I despise that saying. It is how you make it. It is how you choose it to be! You stole my babies! You told me they had died!'

'I stole nothing. These . . .' He gestured to Jacques. 'These took them by demonic means. Do you not think I wept too?'

'I care not what you did,' she said. 'Go to Satan. You are a good match. And when the angels rip you down, do not expect me to raise a hand in protest.'

'Other people's sons will die. Others' daughters.'

'As if you care. As if you would ever care. You have a devil's blood, they say, and marvel at it as you are so fair. Well I know the rot inside you, Edward Plantagenet, and may it destroy you. I curse you. I curse you for what you have done.'

'You will obey me, madam. As God commands.' He stood tall.

'I will disobey,' she said. 'And if that means I go to Hell, so be it, for no torment below can match the one I endure here. Come, children. My daughter. My son.'

Edward flew at Jacques, catching him squarely on the jaw with a jolting punch, knocking over the table plank, scattering the baskets.

The old Templar fell backwards flat on the floor.

She took her children by the arm.

'Come, let us go away from this man,' she said.

'What do I need to do?' said Edward to Jacques.

The Templar wiped his mouth, coughed. 'Go to Poitiers. There we will open the pit of Hell. Get there quickly, with all your might.'

'This is foul work,' said Philippa. 'Come, my children. I have mourned you for too long.'

'Keep the lady out of churches,' said Jacques.

'For what?' said Edward. 'This is my wife and a queen of England. She does as she pleases.'

'The angels have noticed her once. They may notice her again and our plan may be revealed.'

'Angels can't read minds,' said Edward. 'Are you suggesting my wife would betray me?'

'Just keep her out of churches,' said Jacques.

I I

An ympe, settled on Dow's arm in the Bois De Boulogne. A message from Calais. He stood, pissed, and looked up into the air. Already the ympes were swarming, called by Murmur beneath the stormy sky, the sun igniting the edges of the black clouds like cinders.

'It is time,' he said.

'Then let's away,' said Aude.

The tiny people seized them, two hundred each, bearing them up into the hollow light of the building storm. They flew before it, outrunning it south. Both wore encompassing dark cloaks and thick mantles – to disguise Aude's angelic armour, but also to protect Dow, who had no such divine protection against the elements or from the cold. This land was untouched by routiers, unburnt, but they flew over many farmsteads that were overgrown, with no signs of life. Three years since the worst of it, but the pestilence had altered this land so much, so very much. Dow shivered. What was to come? Worse? Maybe but, when Hell was split open, and Lucifer free, this would be a paradise.

Ympes were sent to the English army. It was turning north from where it had landed in Aquitaine, burning the land as it went, heading for Poitiers under Edward's instruction. From high in the Ympe cloud, Dow saw the pall of smoke over the land, until rain came down in torrents and he was forced to land for a while.

When the sun came, the ympes fluttered and scurried into the sky.

'Ask the English why they do not come,' said Dow.

'We are stuck at Tours,' came the reply. 'We cannot take the town without devils and Tours is still in France, bounded by great wards.'

So John had finally worked out he could ban devils from France. But the English were clever. They were expanding Aquitaine, their sovereign land, by use of ordinary men. The devils could then come in behind them, once the claim was made, or even fight in disputed territory. However, they could not set foot in France proper except under orders of the French king. Or, at least, their morale would suffer very badly if they did.

He sent a message back.

'Ignore Tours, make the land around it your own and then you can defend your back with devils. Come here in force and I will give you all the devils you want. They will stream from the mouth of Hell.'

A day, two days, watching and the ympes reported movement – not in the town but in a graveyard outside the walls. Monks were seen entering the graveyard by night and descending into what appeared to be a tomb.

'Do you think this is it?' said Aude.

'We must look,' said Dow. Up they flew, under the silver clouds of a half-moon night, skirting Poitiers. Dow could almost feel the apprehension of the people within its walls: mothers putting their children to bed not knowing if it would be for the last time with the English so near; the people drunk in the streets out of fear; the churches and the inns equally full. If they knew what was coming, he thought, many of them would die on the spot out of fright. He made the sign of the Fork with his fingers. Faith, now, was his only hope. Lucifer would redeem everything. Redeem Dow too? He couldn't allow himself even to question it. Of course, of course.

The ympes set them down at the edge of the churchyard. A vast party of monks had now arrived – fifty or sixty of them. They were Black-clad Benedictines, a severe order, Dow knew from his time in London. They stood in utter silence, a single torch illuminating them enough for him to see that many of the brothers bore clubs or maybe even maces – at such a distance and in such a light he couldn't tell. It was certain, though, that a couple had mail beneath their habits – he could see its glint.

'Do we wait for them to drag it out?' said Aude.

'No. They will have sealed the tomb with wards and sigils. They might be useful to us and we wouldn't want to see them broken.

370

If they have enough magic to keep the Evertere in, perhaps there is enough to keep angels out.'

'I doubt it.'

'I too. We can best defend the tomb from inside, where the way is narrow.'

'I can defend against men anywhere,' she said.

'But not perhaps against angels and holy swords. We need every advantage.'

She nodded.

'Now?'

'Now!' said Dow.

Aude cast aside her mantle and cloak, unwrapped the shield and sword. The angelic armour lit up the copse around them as bright as any fire, the sword shone with a wavering light, and the shield shone like sun on water. Dow touched the hilt of his falchion but didn't draw it yet. He was nervous. Aude said the angelic armour could defeat any number of men. Time to find out.

Immediately the monks turned to face her.

She walked out of the copse and the brothers gasped as one. A couple sank to their knees, and then one more, and one more. Dow smiled to himself. They had mistaken her for an angel. He stood beside her, the monks' gabbled prayers washing over them.

'What now?' she asked.

'I don't know. What do you think?'

'Just walk in.'

They walked across the clearing towards the tomb. In the angel light Dow could see it was very large, wide steps going down into blackness.

A voice mumbled something.

'Forgive us!' It was a contagion, all the monks prostrating themselves, crawling towards Aude's feet, begging forgiveness.

'Forgive us! Forgive us!'

They were blocking the way to the tomb, coming forward in a mass. Dow broke from Aude to skirt round behind them and make the entrance. Such was the distraction provided by Aude, he had remained unseen.

'Forgive us! Forgive us!'

They were at Aude's feet. She stood rooted, not knowing what to do.

'You are forgiven,' she said.

Dow got to the entrance. It was very dark within. He needed a light, or at least Aude with him.

'Does an angel talk like a tavern whore?' One of the monks stood – a senior fellow by his age and girth.

'What is your name, angel?' said the monk.

'Aude,' she said.

Dow hesitated at the mouth of the tomb. He saw it bore heavy iron doors at the bottom of the stairs.

'Aude!' said the fat monk, mockingly.

Aude's voice. He had given it no thought, but she was an ordinary girl who spoke in a thick, crunching peasant accent. The only angel he had ever heard speak spoke like a king.

'So an angel has a name like a tavern whore, too.' He hefted a mace in his hand. 'If you are an angel, show us. Shoot forth holy fire. Swear to protect us against the English. Praise God on high and curse the Devil and all his works.'

More monks stood. One said, 'Father, do not doubt the divine,' but another said. 'What does an angel want with the dragon banner?'

'I come to guard it,' said Aude. More of the monks stood.

'An angel would not talk like that!' said another.

'Who's that?' Dow had been seen.

The monks were still undecided but the fat one with the mace jumped at her, treading on the back of one of his brothers to do so. The mace came down in a swift arc but the shield flew up to meet it, shattering it. A monk grabbed Dow's arm. Dow had trained under the mercenary Orsino for most of his childhood and didn't even have to think. He put his hand on top of his attacker's to stop him taking it away and turned the man's wrist sharply, breaking it. Then he had his falchion free.

'Isabella!' he shouted. 'Queen of England! Attend us now.'

The monks swept in on Aude, hammering with their maces and clubs. Even the shield could not be everywhere, though it was most places, but those blows that did make it through sparked off her armour. She swung her sword and it was as if a rainbow flashed among the flailing monks, so little resistance did it meet, but what fell from it was not rain, nor gold as in the tales, but blood. But the blood did not fall. It hung in the air like a mist, sparkling with its own light.

Three monks ran at Dow, but took only a few steps before they clutched at their eyes, stumbled and fell in a rain of tiny spears and arrows. A flock of ympes wheeled away, and turned, ready for another pass.

'Isabella!' shouted Dow. 'You who call yourself a queen. Hear us, fulfil your bargain.'

Soon Aude stood among a pile of bodies, ten men dead at her feet. The other monks backed away, hurling insults, crying out to God, some throwing clubs or loose stones they had found on the ground. The Sacred Heart shield deflected them all.

'I am no whore,' shouted Aude. 'Though I should not count it a shame if I was. I am a tavern girl who saw the light of Lucifer, to whom ympes whispered in the dark. I am nothing, not considered by great men, not written of in chronicles or verse. No statue has ever been raised to me, nor will there ever be. And yet here I stand before you. The future. Your time is over.'

The monks had now noticed the sparkling mist of blood that hung in the air. Dow felt his hearing go muffled, a pressure in his head as if he dived to the bottom of a lake.

A voice in the air, deep like thunder.

'I am Shamsiel. The constrainer.'

Another voice, with the sound of chanting, the names of God.

'And I am Jeduthun, Master of Howling.'

'And I Jophiel, God's Spy.' This voice came with the sound of many whispers.

'And I Qaspiel, angel of the moon.' Bells sounded, deep and sweet, and a flute rose high above them. Next, the sound of a great burning, as if from an enormous bonfire.

'And I Soterasiel, who stokes the fires of God.'

'Make way for God's queen! Make way for God's queen!'

From the mist of blood a shape formed, the sparkling droplets condensing to lend it substance. At first it appeared only as a floating crown of gold, topped by five points of white fire. Then a sceptre appeared, with a shining jewel on top of it. Next a woman, in the plain garb of a nun but with her golden hair uncovered.

The queen stepped out of the mist of blood. The points of light split from the crown and flew off into the night, to emerge as great pillars of light in a circle a league about. A fifth hung like a great star above, lighting the land for miles about.

'Our God is a god of love but a god of blood too,' she said, jewel in the sceptre in her hand burning crimson. 'Christ's blood he gave for our sins, the blood of the martyrs flowed in times gone by and flows today in memory of that sacrifice, as your blood has flowed here, to rid the world of sin. The first consecration has commenced. Brothers of Benedict, do not mourn your dead, for they have fallen for a great purpose. We have work to do here and it is God's work, as you see by these, his servants. Here you will see a great magic, performed with blood of the English king!'

Dow's instinct was to stay and watch the beautiful angels burning white over the countryside, but he had work to do.

'Come on, Aude,' he said.

'To Hell,' she said.

'To Hell,' said Dow. They dived into the darkness with the prayers of the monks to the angels at their backs. Aude split the doors to the tomb with a single blow.

12

Philippa lay in her bed, but no sleep would visit her. She was alone, for a queen, with only three ladies-in-waiting sleeping on beds around her, though she knew there was a guard just the other side of the door in her room in the Château de Calais. Her two children were with her too – full-grown, their long limbs and golden heads lying on couches. She had kept them with her, though they had found her company strange. They had been raised as Luciferians, unused to the riches befitting their station, unused to servants and to prayer. But they stayed; there was that. She would win them eventually, and though she could never reclaim their infancy – games in the gardens at Windsor, boats on the river, seeing her son fitted for his first armour – she could love them in their youth.

A single wax candle burned, though she had nothing to read. Her husband had seen to it that no book came anywhere near her – for fear that a Bible might be slipped to her and of the damage she might wreak with it. They said she could summon angels. She wished that were true.

She went to her window, past the softly snoring ladies, and looked out through its arch to the sea. Her husband's ships had arrived with provisions and troops from England, flying the banners of St George, and of Satan. Once unloaded, the army would march south for Poitiers. This town was England, or at least half of it was, so devils massed about the quay and flew thick in the air. She saw a multitude of winding, flying snakes writhing in the air above the mast of her husband's ship, great flies above them. On the dock, men who seemed made all of water themselves, living fountains in the image of men, slid into the water while the devils of the imagination, horned, fanged and winged, collected spears from human soldiers.

News had come that the king of Navarre had been imprisoned by King John and – even better – that John was marching south to meet the Black Prince. Navarre was held under close guard and his captains in Normandy had received no new instructions. Being disinclined to fight, they were holding to their castles. They would not help Edward but they would not oppose him. He could land on the Norman coast and was fairly confident that Le Havre would allow him passage. No fighting his way out of the Calais marshes.

There were no bowmen here. They had disembarked in Aquitaine with her son, the one they called the Black Prince. Was he still alive, the boy they had swapped for that monster? There was something cold in Philippa's heart; her stomach seemed turned to stone.

How could a man like her husband be allowed to prosper? He had taken her children, used them to further his ambitions. She had no holy objects, no focus for her prayer. For want of something to do, and out of habit, she took out her embroidery. She was completing a little design for Edward – a cross of St George with the motto of the Knights of the Garter below. In truth she had not much enthusiasm for the design, but a lady must always be sewing – so had said her mother – and it calmed her to do so.

She could not allow Satan to be summoned to earth. God had places for everyone and His place for Satan was in Hell. What calamity if he escaped! What calamity if he neglected his duty! A pact with the Sons of Lucifer, a pact with demons and the damned! No! No!

She went to calm herself by sewing but she quickly saw that God had guided her hand. At the bottom of her bag of bits, where she kept the buttons, thimbles and odd bits of thread, she saw a glint. The fragment of glass the pauper Tancré had given her. She crossed herself and looked hard at it. The light shifted inside, reaching out to her like a sunbeam. She had not mentioned its existence to her husband, nor to anyone, and had put it away for fear of what it had shown. Tancré had said it was part of a window from the church of Gâtinais. Was that not, in its way, a holy relic, and did it not shine with holy light?

She held it inside her hands, stroked it. Then she pressed it between her palms and knelt in prayer.

'Holy Father, by this relic, grant me to know your wishes.'

She cupped her hands. The fragment glowed blue like a little star. Philippa renewed her prayer. 'Angels, who spoke to me at Mont-Saint-Michel, come and attend me now.'

What would she do? Who could replace her husband and the monster that stood in for her son on the throne? Even the children she carried had been infected with devil blood. These beautiful young people who slept beside her had devils' blood coursing through them. Could she see them rule? She didn't know. All she could do was love them and trust to God.

The star's light dimmed and she held it close to her eye. She heard a voice, from within like the shift of sand in a box: 'Mortimer.'

Philippa crossed herself.

Not him, not the man who had usurped her husband's power.

'Mortimer.' The voice again, as if far off.

'Lord, be clear with me, let me know your mind.'

'Mortimer!'

And then a vision, in a blink. He was there, in front of her, reaching towards her, 'The Mortimer' as Edward II had called him, splendid in a raiment of light. He bore in his hand a sword of light and on his head was a crown wrought in the shape of three brawling lions.

'Mortimer!'

She closed her hands over the fragment, her heart thumping. She knew what to do. There was no doubt. It was a choice between her husband and God. There could only be one winner. She woke one of her ladies.

'Get up. Tell my husband I would wish him goodbye. Let me see him on the dock.'

Who for the throne of England? Anyone but Edward. Anyone but the devil posing as her son.

Morning came.

She waited as the other ladies woke, emptied the chamberpots, took out the queen's clothes for the day. After she was dressed and anointed in oils, the lady returned, begging pardon for the length of her delay.

'He will see you, escorted, at the water's side,' she said.

Philippa rose, gripping tight on the glass fragment as if she feared it would float away.

Her ladies and the guards took her down to the waterfront. The boats were in mighty array, forty of them, unloading provisions from England, the army ready to march on Paris once the Black Prince had drawn John to Poitiers.

Edward emerged on the deck of the hulk, that damned lion at his side as always. She offered a prayer again, to save herself from its teeth. That was unworthy. If God wanted her as a martyr, she should accept it. It was also cowardly. Such a devil wouldn't try its claws on a queen.

In the morning sun the king looked magnificent, his breastplate shining silver, his caparison red, a page behind him carrying his helm and weapons. There was no need to be wearing such gear so far from a battle. But to all his men the king was saying, 'Look at me. Was I not built for war? Who could stand against such a king?' She could.

He saw her and bowed his head, came down the gangplank towards her. In his armour he moved as easily as a boy, as he had been when she first knew him. Now his limbs were thicker, his body solid and wider, but his grace was undiminished.

'Philippa,' he said, 'are you ready?' They had not spoken since her children were restored to her.

'I am ready.'

He knew her too well; he could see her disapproval in the force with which she clasped her hands, the tightness with which she held her shoulders.

'You will board the ship,' he said. 'Lady, you are a queen and your responsibility is to England. You will protect us from the angels.'

'What is England? When we were young we never spoke of England, just family and our right.'

'I am England,' he said. 'And everywhere that I rule is England too.'

'Then England has betrayed me.'

The king looked pale.

'I did what I did for the greater good.'

'You speak in French now, like a ruler. Not English, affecting to have something in common with the low born. As if their cause was your cause.'

'Their homes and livelihoods are at stake if we lose to France.'

'Really? Or would it be just another set of masters? Your home, your livelihood, mine too, are at stake, not theirs.'

'They fight for me because they love me and their homeland!'

'They fight because God says that is what they must do.'

'Good enough reason, I should have thought.'

'I wonder. I wonder if that is what God wants.'

She held forward the fragment of glass.

'What is this?'

The glass glowed blue in her hand.

'If you think to bewitch me, I . . .'

A kaleidoscope of colour burst over his face from the glass, dancing patterns of red, blue and green.

'This is a thing of God,' she said.

'It is . . .'

He swayed, unsteady on his feet.

'You stole my children,' she said. 'And you frustrated God's purpose, wedding me to your unholy cause. Look into this glass and behold what you should have done. You are God's enemy, yet you would raise His servant Satan up as a lord.'

'What's going on?' Sloth roared from the deck, his voice like a fist in the face.

'Mortimer,' said Edward. 'Mortimer is in that glass.'

'He speaks from Heaven,' said Philippa.

The king rocked back and forth. Philippa herself felt giddy – the blue of the day, the play of the colours on Edward's face. Sloth sprang over the gangplank, his teeth bared.

'I am a sinner.' Edward collapsed to the boards.

'What magic is this?' said Sloth.

'The king is inconvenienced,' said Philippa. 'Prince Edward is away. I am in power here. Bow before me.'

Sloth looked around him, his great mane rattling, as if asking for advice. Then he knelt and bowed his head.

'Take King Edward to his chamber,' she said. 'Stand down the sails. We ride for Gâtinais.'

'The Black Prince will be slaughtered,' said Sloth. 'We must get word to him! I'll send a devil!'

'What was it my husband said at Crécy? "Let the boy win his spurs." No word will be sent, by my command, appointed by God. My son's fortune is in the hands of God. I leave on God's business. Now get me a horse saddled, we'll be gone within the hour.'

13

Five monks cowered in the darkness. These were not warlike men and were unarmed. Aude kicked them on down the passage.

'Where is it? Where is the banner?'

'We cannot tell you that.'

'I will kill you.'

'Keep them moving,' said Dow. If they were holy men, their blood would be useful to his ritual.

Aude drove the men on into the depths of the tomb.

As Dow had suspected, the tomb was well marked with sigils and magical devices. They were carved into the wall in a style he had not seen before – figures of angels and the stories from the Bible. Each was beautifully rendered and, in the glow of the angelic armour and weapons, he could see they had been exquisitely painted and inlaid with gold.

Would such things work against the Evertere? Would they work against what he was planning to release upon the earth – all the devils of Hell? He doubted it.

The tomb went down two levels into a short corridor. In one small dusty room were three sarcophaguses. In another, through a doorway engraved with magic circles and the names of angels, just one sarcophagus.

'No! No!' said a monk.

'If you can't keep quiet I will kill you here,' said Aude.

The monks all crossed themselves.

Dow approached the sarcophagus. He touched the lid and withdrew his hand on instinct. Something was stirring inside.

'How did you get it out of its box?' said Dow. He recalled the banner had been in a specially sealed container, when he had put it away at Crécy.

'It's still in the box,' said a monk. 'We put it in without opening it.'

Dow slid back the lid. It was not the box as he remembered it. Someone had constructed an outer steel skin around it – another metal box held together with rivets. There was no lock, no hinge. It was sealed shut.

'Get it out,' said Dow.

'You will use it for evil.'

'Kill one of them, Aude.'

Aude raised her sword.

'All right! All right!'

He took out the first key to Hell from his bag, opening the little case that carried it very carefully.

There it was, gossamer thin. A breath might blow it away.

'It will want blood.' Dow passed the key to Aude. The monks quailed.

Dow cut a little nick on the side of his forearm. A bead of blood appeared. He sheathed the misericord and gestured for Aude to give him back the key. She did so and he held it so that the blood dropped on to it. The little bead sat for an instant on top of the key and then was sucked within as if it had never been there.

The monks fell to their knees, praying and crossing themselves.

He laid the key on the ground. The smell of smoke. Were the monks above trying to burn them out already? Would Isabella allow that?

He had used the key before, with invocations and with circles made from the dust of the tombs of saints, but never like this. No circle. No protection against whatever might come through. What did he expect? An increase in the closeness of the room, a ringing of bells, the feeling of teetering on the edge of a great precipice. The key had drunk blood. It should work. But it did not. He squeezed more blood on to it, but nothing.

The smell of smoke came drifting through the door.

'I thought you could do this,' said Aude.

'So did I. Kill one of the brothers, we'll drain his blood onto the thing.'

'No!' screamed a monk.

Aude grabbed one by the habit but the others ran to the door, wrenching it aside, jumping through and falling into the red light of the first layer of Hell. A heat blast like a smith's furnace hit Dow. He went to the doorway and saw that it led to a precarious, crumbling terrace on the edge of a huge wall of red bricks that ran with ichor and slime. Aude cried out.

'How can they get out, how can the devils get out? If they come here?'

'They'll find a way!' said Dow. 'Let's open the banner as soon as we are in Hell.' He pushed the box containing the Evertere in front of him, steeled himself and stepped out onto the terrace. Clouds of stinging black smoke bit his eyes and he blinked for vision. He was impossibly high up. He had seen the cliffs at Dover and this wall towered way beyond their height.

He took a step on the terrace, the heat rising up through his boots. Aude stepped out beside him.

'Does the armour protect you?' he said. 'Can you see?'

'Yes!'

'Strike the box! Free the banner.'

He leant back against the wall of the terrace but the ground crumbled beneath his feet.

'No!' he heard Aude say and, blinking through the smoke, he saw the Evertere falling away far below.

No time for panic. He could retrieve it. 'Be my eyes until we get down!' he said.

Aude crossed herself out of habit but then made the three fingers of Lucifer on her chest. It was the last he saw, his eyes shutting tight against the smoke.

She took his hand and led him down. As they descended, the smoke cleared and he could see better. Coming up towards them was a man who appeared to be carrying an armful of rope. Dow saw when he got closer that it was his entrails, which spilled from a ragged hole in his side.

'Are you one of the damned, brother?' said Dow. 'For the way is open to you!'

The man hissed and threw his entrails like a great ensnaring rope. Aude was in the lead and, though the shield raised itself to protect her, the entrails wrapped over it, engulfing her armour. Three snicks from the rainbow blade and they were severed, the devil – for he must have been a devil – staggering backwards and falling from the wall. Dow wondered what happened to these Devils when they died in Hell. Did they cease to exist or did they simply live on, terribly maimed, for ever?

'Don't kill everyone who comes this way or they'll never find the gate is open,' said Dow. He was crying with the smoke and with the emotion. So close to his goal. When Hell had opened before, God had bargained with Dow for the release from Hell of his beloved Nan. Now he would take her and restore her to life, with all the unjustly damned.

They stumbled on down the stinking walls, their feet slipping on the slime that thrived in the heat.

The fall of the first devil was attracting the attention of others now. Dow saw them massing at the distant foot of the stairs – hundreds, maybe a thousand devils, great grey bodied things that, even at such a distance, looked enormous.

'Can we fight them?'

'Yes, but can I protect you?' said Aude. 'I don't know. Perhaps if I go down there alone.'

'No. We can't fight all of Hell, or at least I can't. And they kept angels here too, I know it, ones who fell with Lucifer. There might be things to harm you. Let us see if we can talk to them.'

'About what?'

'Their freedom. Their master's wish to leave Hell.'

They went down. As they got closer they saw that the creatures resembled the hippopotamus of legend – giant things as big as houses each. As Dow and Aude approached they all roared as one, and Dow could see that in their peg-toothed mouths were living people, striving to get out but quickly chomped back down again by the devils. There, embedded in the floor, was the box with the Evertere in it.

'Who here?' said three of the devils simultaneously.

'What purpose?' said another three.

'That is angel light,' said another three. 'And it hurts our eyes.'

'We are men of the upper world,' said Dow, 'come to offer the jailer of Hell his own freedom.'

'How can men offer Satan freedom? You are damned souls for sure.'

'We have the keys to Hell. No damned soul could touch them.'

He produced the first key.

The great hulks chattered and clacked their jaws, the people within groaning and screaming in pain.

'Do you know where the second gate is?' said Dow.

'We know but we will not show you. We are creatures of God and know our Lord Satan attends his duty here.'

'Would it not be better to allow Satan to decide that for himself?'

The creatures said nothing, just came lumbering towards them across the burning ground.

Aude drew the angel sword while Dow hid behind her. Each creature was enormous, the size of a cathedral, and they came rumbling in, shaking the ground as they came. One stamped down its foot but Aude threw up the Sacred Heart shield. The creature screamed as loud as any storm and hopped backwards cursing, crashing into some of its fellows who went tumbling to the ground, spilling the people from their mouths as they did so.

'Get to the Evertere!' shouted Dow.

They ran, lungs bursting in the heat, dodging the ponderous behemoths as their feet came crashing down, Dow clinging on to Aude as she deflected their feet with shield and sword, toppling the creatures as she went, sending the damned souls in their mouths scrambling for freedom. They tumbled into a crater made by one of the great stomps.

'They can't hurt us!' said Aude. 'The shield will save us!'

It was as if she had called a curse down on herself. A plague of tiny winged devils came sweeping in, each one no bigger than a thumb, but so many that they blackened the sky. Dow fought for vision, flapping at his face to beat them away. Each one was a little warrior clad in shining black armour and bearing a surcoat marked with a clenched fist – some flew banners showing the same.

'Amaymon!' they cried. 'Lord of the first circle!'

Dow was driven wild by the presence of the devils and thrashed with his falchion but, he realised, they were not going for him. The tiny creatures were encircling Aude in a black crowd. A noise like frying bacon, and the little bodies dropped to the burning earth, but more and more poured in, mounds of them piling at Aude's feet in a great sizzle of burning flesh.

He tried to drive them away from her but it was no good. Her shield had been undone from her arm, each creature giving its life

to pull the strap a little more. Her helm floated away, dropping
bodies as it did so, but others were always coming in to lift it a
little more and die. The shield, too, floated up, a fall of bodies
pouring down as it did so. Her mail was unbuckled and pulled
over her head, another silver cloud floating up into the red sky,
dark bodies falling as rain from it as it went. Aude fought to grip
her sword but the creatures were stabbing at her exposed fingers
and it dropped to the ground.

'Release the Evertere! Free the dragon!' she shouted but Dow
could not even see the box.

Dow cut and smashed with his falchion, but he too was now
beset, needle swords and arrows raining into him. As suddenly as
they had come, the creatures dispersed. He ran for the box with
the Evertere in it, Aude at his side, and scrambled it into his arms.

A great foot loomed above them, wide as a house. He and Aude
scrambled to get out of the crater but they could not. An arm came
down, extending to him, another to Aude. He grasped it and was
pulled from the crater as the foot smashed down. It was one of
the damned souls who had tumbled from the mouths of the giants.

'Satan!' shouted Dow. 'Hear me! I have the keys you need!'
He had his hand on the box with Evertere in it but he could not
open it.

The sky blackened, a great foot loomed down.

'Yes,' said a voice, and Dow was flying up into the heavens,
borne on tattered, burnt angel's wings. He screamed for Aude but
it was no good. The burning plain was below him, the giants as
small as mice, the Evertere left where it lay.

14

The parley before the battle, the grand talks with the aim of limiting bloodshed, was held on the field by Des Dunes, with the five angels towering in their columns of pearly light into the night sky. Torches burned around the tents of the camp, lit from habit more than necessity. Isabella had called the talks herself – for tender love of all concerned. The real reason was more pressing. Edward had not appeared. Without him, no blood of an anointed king would spill on the battlefield. Without that, would Satan be contained? She looked up at her angels. They might kill him and they might not. She certainly didn't want to be the vassal of that hideous brute here on earth.

The plan would need to be changed. The battle would require another victor. French blood must be spilled.

The banners of France were outside the tent – the blue and yellow of the royal fleur-de-lys, one hundred and twenty banners of twenty-six earls and counts. So much blue and yellow – so many of the royal houses of France directly related to the royal line. At least thirty of the banners bore the royal flower in some way, whether blazoned with silver lions in the case of La Marche, or with windmills and castles in the case of Étampes. What a watering this would be if France could lose – or not lose, simply suffer great loss! My God, they would sell this soil to pilgrims and the sick for years to come once it was enriched with so much royal blood.

There was the leaping blue dolphin of the Dauphin, its red fins bright beneath the angel light, and there the heart and stars of the Scots – the Earl of Douglas. Isabella was pleased to see that lord in good health. He was short, as Scotsmen tended to be, but well-knit and muscular. Half his countrymen had died of the Plague.

And here were the banners of the poor English – their red crosses and their Satan's whips. Her jaw tightened as she saw the three red diamonds of Montagu – belonging to the son of her hated enemy, now Earl of Salisbury himself since his father had died, or been gone so long he might as well have been dead. Her son King Edward had great powers of forgiveness. There was the white and red quarters of Edward le Despencer, grandson of the hated Hugh Despenser who had charmed her husband from her. It was as if God had set up the whole battle solely for the purposes of her revenge.

Yet that would have to wait. The Black Prince was a devil true and no one who stood beside him had any real claim to the throne – except perhaps Montagu, now calling himself Montacute to distance himself from his shameful father – but alone she could not guarantee that would be enough. To open heaven, Satan would need to give up the secrets of the fourth key and for that, she needed to bind him and bargain with him.

At her side was Good Jacques, the Templar, in his monk's robe, a hood upon his head.

'Where is your son?'

'I don't know.'

'He is a great killer.'

'He is. But my grandson does well enough in that way, too.'

'The English are outnumbered. His blood alone will not be enough to mark the circle.'

'There is royal blood aplenty here.'

'Are there the men to spill it?'

Isabella thought. Her grandson was a match for anyone in single combat and there would be no shortage of royal knights ready to face him. If a deal could be made . . .

She entered the parley pavilion, a guard opening the flap of the great tent for her as she went in.

All the men save John and the Dauphin stood at her entry. She kissed the hands of the French king and took a seat offered by an attendant knight.

'Grandmother,' said the Prince of Wales. He was a magnificent sight – taller than all the others just sitting down. His armour was lacquered black and on his surcoat he bore the whip of Satan quartered with the English lions. Behind him stood

Despencer, just as tall and strong as his Marcher lord grandfather, her husband's lover. Next to him was Montacute – not quite the basilisk his grandfather had been, England's avenging hand, but she fancied him rough enough in any fight. Both wore the cross of the Garter.

Despencer spat as she gathered herself. She had hanged his grandfather on a scaffold fifty feet high. Her only regret was that she couldn't build a bigger one.

'Edward,' said Isabella.

'Are not devils banned from France?' said Étampes, a gruff, dark-haired man with the build of a giant.

'You refer to me or to my grandson?'

Étampes pointed to the prince.

The prince smiled. 'I have devils with me, true. But I am commanded by the king of England and where his men stand is his land, won by his men with the blessing of God. The king of France has no jurisdiction there.'

'I'll show you jurisdiction, you English dog!'

'I am a Norman true,' said the prince. '*Lord* of the English, not of the English.' His French, though, announced him as an Englishman. It had been a long time since anyone in France spoke with such flat vowels. Without warning, he thumped the table. The Duke of Orléans, who had been idly plucking a lyre, flinched.

'Where is your father?' said King John. His voice was relaxed, though he clenched and unclenched his fist, clicking the rings on his fingers.

'He will be here presently,' said the prince.

'Really? Our spies tell us he has not left Calais.'

'He had not left when your spy left, but he left an hour behind. Our devils tell us so.' Isabella thought the boy a poor liar.

'Then you would have thought he'd be here by now,' said the Dauphin. 'Or at least the flying devils that attend him. They move quick enough, don't they?'

The Black Prince smiled a smile that was no smile at all. 'Since devils were banned from France, they have to fly over the sea. I expect them before the night is out.'

The Dauphin said nothing, just let the lie hang in the air, his gaze unwavering on the Black Prince. The Black Prince returned the gaze.

'Perhaps,' said the Black Prince, 'we should settle things here and now. Single combat is old-fashioned but it has its appeal.'

Isabella raised her hand. One body full of prince's blood wasn't going to be up to the task in hand.

'Your martial spirit does you both great credit, My Lords. But I have asked for this parley so that it may be contained and channelled in a way most pleasing to God. You see that I bring five angels with me.'

'Difficult to miss,' said the Black Prince. 'And you know we have our angel-eating banner.'

Isabella raised her eyebrows. She knew from Good Jacques that was not true, though it might profit her to make out that she did not.

'I do. So this is why I ask, in the name of God, that we conduct our business here most gently. It cannot be pleasing to God to see His angels torn from the sky, nor is it safe for that dragon to enter the world again.'

John waved a heavily ringed finger. 'Your plan, lady?'

'That we do what is most pleasing to God. Each of us has a station, set by the Lord. The low men toil and, by our grace, we allow them a portion of the bounty of our lands for their efforts. The Church administers to the spiritual health of men and by constant prayer saves us from damnation. We, the nobles, the royalty, fight. That is our calling and our God-given purpose. You, my King John, bring with you ten thousand or more low men. You, Prince of England, bring many archers and men of little worth. Let them return to their lands to provide us with bread. Take a hundred of your most royal knights, King and you, Prince, bring one hundred of your noble warriors and face each other in the field. Let God decide who lives and who dies.'

The Black Prince put his hand to the hilt of his sword.

'It is a path that meets with tradition and spares us all the risk of freeing the dragon,' said the Black Prince.

John drummed his fingers on the table. He was an oafish man, huge and beefy, sentimental, but an excellent and brave warrior. He would not shirk the challenge.

'Do you have the banner of Lucifer, though? Do you have the Evertere?'

'Do not doubt it, cousin,' said the Black Prince.

'I do doubt it.'

Isabella stood.

'Is this the question? Surely the true question is, "Are the knights of France men enough to take on the English in equal combat?"'

Étampes banged his fist on the table.

'I am more than man enough!'

The Dauphin stood – his surcoat yellow and marked with those jumping blue dolphins.

'Are you willing to indulge in this combat, Edward of Wales?'

'Very willing,' said Edward.

The Dauphin nodded. 'Then let us refuse it. I think your King Edward is not coming. We shall have a battle. You are already sunk to the level of a devil, Edward. Some say you even are a devil. If you have the banner, use it. Tear God's angels from the sky and let God pass His judgement on you for that.'

'God is gone from the world,' said the Black Prince.

'I have more faith,' said the Dauphin. 'Father, let us have a battle.'

John mulled for a while.

'I think we should accept the combat,' he said.

'Yes!' said Isabella.

The Dauphin bowed to his father. 'Your wisdom is great. But what would happen if we defeated the English, or managed a truce? They would release their soldiers and devils to devastate our lands. Let us instead annihilate them. Let not one English devil or low born bowman or murderous gunman live to stain our soil with French blood. Instead of minimising bloodshed, we should rather increase it until we make a river from here to the sea. God is on our side! See the angels above us. Let the English feel His justice.'

Isabella went to speak but John held up his hand. He spoke to Edward.

'How many towns have you burned since you landed?'

'Many goodly ones. I have lost the count.'

John nodded. 'You'll burn no more. My son is right. Death to the English. All of them.'

Isabella crossed herself. She had but one hope – as many of the nobility as possible would die.

'At Crécy no quarter was given, no ransoms taken,' she said. 'The flower of French chivalry was butchered by common men, slaughtered with knives like pigs in a shambles.'

'Yes,' said John, 'there will be no quarter. Today, Prince, you meet your maker – whoever that may be.'

He clapped his hands, stood and strode from the tent, Isabella tailing after him.

Good Jacques met her at the entrance to her pavilion.

'I heard,' he said. 'We have but one hope. Can you get me a horse and harness?'

Isabella looked at him. 'You hardly seem able to ride,'

'We must do as was done at Crécy, as Navarre did. The charge must be premature.'

'That won't work,' she said. 'Let me do what I can. Do you have the Crown of Thorns?'

'Yes.'

'Prepare the ground, powder it and break off its thorns. We shall have a magic circle. Then we shall have our summoning. Where is the English king? Where is he? His blood alone would be enough, I am sure. Or he would have killed so many men of royal stock on the French side that the spell would be sure. Now . . .' She threw her hands into the air.

'I have a feeling you will overcome this,' said Jacques. She didn't like the way he looked at her – not enough deference, too much judgement.

'The French must lose,' she said. 'I'll start by calling off my angels.'

15

The Burnt Angel flew him on over the searing plain of brass for a very long way. The red of the soil changed and became darker. Was it a sea?

The dark below was vast, stretching out from wide horizon to wide horizon, undulating and shimmering in the heat. Above it, long devils flew on wide black wings, dropping sand and rocks, shitting and pissing. The sea called out as they passed – human screams and curses.

'What is that?' said Dow.

'The newly dead,' said the Angel.

'Why do they stand in such numbers?'

'Hell is a bureaucracy,' said the Angel. 'And they have not yet been processed. Perhaps they will never be processed. Perhaps that is punishment enough.' Its voice was dry, like the shifting of dead sticks.

'Are they all newly dead?'

The Angel swooped down over the plain. It was a vast crowd, packed together tight: women, men, children, dancing on the hot metal ground for what relief they could gain from the heat. He saw they all bore weeping sores and great boils, their skin pale, their eyes hollow. He could not deny it, they were all dead of the Pestilence. As they passed they all threw up their arms to grab at the Angel, as if it might carry them away.

He wanted to reach out to them, to tell them help was coming, but he could not. The Evertere needed to rally them was back among the peg-toothed giants, lying next to the corpse of Aude. How could he storm Hell without it? Never mind. With Satan gone, with all the devils gone to earth, he would find it.

'Hold fast,' he murmured. 'Lucifer is coming and will cure all your wounds.'

They flew to the great encircling Lake of Fire. The second wall of hell – patches of cooler earth within the red – stepping stones that the brave, the mad or the desperate might emerge through, though no barrier to flying devils. Dow's arms were numb from where the Angel's claws gripped him and he felt dizzy from the heat.

They flew on to a great wall of living flesh, flying devils shovelling ever more people into it to build up its height, which seemed limitless, stretching up. A great slope led up to the tumbling Falls of Blood.

'I cannot go on,' said the Burnt Angel. 'You must enter yourself.'

It dropped Dow before the Falls of Blood. They roared down from a great height, terrifying.

'In there?' shouted Dow above the roar.

'Step in,' said the Angel.

He could not think the Angel had saved him just to trick him into entering the falls. So he stepped into them. He was engulfed, cast down by the great weight of blood, smashed to his knees, fighting for air. His hand went to his tunic and he reached within to take out the Key of Blood, but the pressure of the torrent prevented him from reaching it. He wanted to die, to give in to the pull of the falls and sink under, but he could not stop now after all he had done. He thought of his Nan, killed by the priest on the moor; of Orsino, his teacher, dead in the House of God; of the nations of dead waiting on the burning plain. He could not be weak for them. His hand made his tunic and he took out the key.

The falls stopped. Hell was silent and then the sky collapsed.

Blood and bodies all around him, the walls of flesh tumbling. This was no key he had in his hand but an explosive charge, a thing to cast down the wall of living flesh. A noise like a great burning, wings about his head. Bodies crashed around him and he feared he would be buried in the fall. From above came Aude, riding the dragon banner, her shield and sword reclaimed. The dragon plucked him from the tumbling bodies, shooting him high into the sweltering air. The great devil had driven its foot down on him. It must have smashed the casket as its foot came down. The dragon must have done for the giants!

The walls fell for what must have been a day and a night, the damned souls free of their torment but entering another, scrambling and climbing to be free. When the last body had fallen, the whole vast plain of the second layer of Hell was crammed as tight as a May Day market, stretching out to the horizon.

At the centre of it all stood a garden, still untouched by the hands of the damned. On a long table squatted an ape with a crown on its head. The dragon swooped down towards it but the ape did not flinch or cower. In its hand it bore a wicked long lance of burnt wood, a shield of bones on its arm, and a helm of a thousand horns on its head.

Dow and Aude stepped down from the dragon. Its long tail stretched up from Dow's hand and the dragon expanded to fill the sky.

'Oppressed and damned, tortured of God. Know I am here to lay siege to the walls of the fourth layer of Hell, to free the bright angel Lucifer from his prison in the city of Dis and restore Eden to earth!'

A great cheer went up from all those around him and the message was conveyed throughout the great throng, the cheer echoing to the hills as it spread. It was a summer hour before it died.

The ape scratched itself.

'You have the third key,' it said.

'Yes.'

'And the second and the first?'

'Yes.'

'But not the fourth.'

'We will not need the fourth, jailer. We will storm the fourth wall. See how mighty our army is! All those God has cast down, rising up to free themselves.'

The ape looked up at the dragon. It stood up and was suddenly massive, itself stretching up to the sky. The dragon snapped and writhed but it did not strike. The ape stooped and was small again, standing on its table.

'You will go nowhere and do nothing,' it said.

Aude drew her sword but the ape turned a lazy eye to her.

'Do you think that I, who cast down the brightest angel, fear a tavern girl?'

394

Aude screamed as the grass of the garden snared around her feet.

'I can't move, Dow, I can't move!'

'I know what you are seeking,' said Dow. 'Call your lords. Call Belphegor and Asmodeus, call Leviathan and all the infernal captains. God has abandoned the upper world. He is nowhere. Anarchy reigns. Step up into the light and order creation to your liking.'

The ape smiled. 'You would tempt the Devil!'

'You need no tempting.'

It showed its teeth again.

'I will kill you,' he said. 'And you will be the foundation stone of my new wall. And then I will go to the upper world and set my order.'

'Dow!' shouted Aude, reaching for the table. She tossed him the holy lance that had pierced Christ Lucifer's side.

'Then come,' said Dow. 'For I am half angel myself and in my veins flows the blood of a king. Strike at me and hazard it all. Perhaps I will make you my foundation stone.'

The ape scratched and gibbered.

'Why should I let you pass?'

'I have the second key, and the first. I will give them to you. You can go.'

'And leave the fourth wall undefended?'

'Yes. And I know this for true. You cannot pass the first gate unless you are called and in a way pleasing to God – His old way, the way of blood and sacrifice. So the Templar told me and so I believe.'

'And who will call me?'

'Once you are at the first gate, Edward of England will call you. He will spread the blood of the French kings on the earth to carpet the way for you.'

'You swear this, by your faith in Lucifer?'

'I swear it. Then you must swear to leave.'

The ape smiled. 'I swear it, on God's bones.'

'You must show me the way to the fourth wall.'

'I swear it. On God's teeth!'

Dow threw the key pouches towards Satan and he caught them neatly.

'You will be here for ever,' he said.

'We will release our friend Lucifer!'

The ape let out a pealing shriek. Wings sprouted from his back. He called to the skies for the legions of Astaroth and Beelzebub, of Azazel and Belphegor, and they came on beating wings, on flying chariots of fire, on beetles' backs and in wasps' claws; they came stomping as giants, crushing the damned of the living plain, as water spirits evaporating and reforming in the heat of Hell, as burning men and maggot men, fly men and bird men, half-snake, half-cockerel, the boar men of Gehenna, the skull-faced legions of Drax, the copper rooster of Karth, the screaming women of Lady Sirlo's banner, the dog men of Duke Morax, who brought with him thirty legions of other spirits, and the Croaking Devils of Pandemonium who rode under the Black Moon banner on blind horses with saddles of human pelts.

For two days the horde of the damned parted as the lords of Hell flocked devils to their banners.

'Sinners go unpunished!' cried Asmodeus, his great fly eyes black in the shade of the dragon's wings.

'We go to do God's work!' said Satan. 'Order will be brought to the realm of men. When Satan sits on the throne of the world, no sin shall go unchastised, in life or in death! To the light! I have the key!'

'Show us the fourth gate!' shouted Dow. 'We will besiege it!'

'You will be there for eternity,' said Satan.

'Our forces are legion. I have seen to that.'

Satan spat and clutched his balls.

'In the garden,' said Satan, 'look to the statue's eye! Now my duty is discharged and I fly to bring God's order to the realms of men!'

16

The great crowd overwhelmed the garden at the heart of Hell. It was hard to say where the table and the fountains and the statue had been beneath the smothering weight of the damned.

Dow tugged on the dragon's tail. It encircled him, lifting him up into the air.

'Friends,' he said. 'We are so many. In front of the final gate we must prepare ourselves.'

'God!' shouted a voice. 'We must have faith in Him!'

Others in the multitude picked up the call.

'God put you here!' said Dow. 'God punishes you. But any who wants to side with Him, leave with the devils! The second key will open the Lake of Fire, the first will open wide the first wall of Hell. Go out and leave if you want to seek forgiveness from a God who cannot forgive!'

In the far distance, Dow saw the Lake of Fire, the vast army of devils streaming towards it. A darkness spread across its centre – a bridge building out from Satan's key.

'There,' said Dow. 'There is your half-freedom if you want it! Lucifer will come and heal you in the end.'

His words were relayed through the throng again and, as they spread, many turned away and ran towards the spreading bridge, following their tormentors. But many stayed, ready to fight. The throng was still mightier than Dow had ever seen, more densely packed than a London market, wider by far than Crécy or the siege of Caffa.

'Can we die again?' said a voice.

'I do not know,' said Dow. 'I tell you truthfully that I doubt it. But chewed up, mutilated, guts split or head cracked, reduced to nothing but bone and flesh, I think you will live. It will be unendurable, yet you must endure it. Know this before the siege begins!'

'This man here is a murderer and should not be released,' said a voice.

'This one killed a child and said it was the mother,' said another.

Dow shivered. 'I am not judge. When Lucifer comes we will all return to the light.'

'This one deserves the darkness.'

'He will be a bane to the world!'

'Get away!' shouted Dow. 'I will not stand as God stands. Go!'

More peeled away, the thick air of Hell deadening their steps. They marched away for a day but still a vast number remained. Dow felt glad so many had gone. A horrible thought had arisen when he had seen the living wall collapse, seen so many ready to fight.

It's all been for nothing. The Plague, the terrible deaths of fever and blood. Nothing.

Yet now, the newly damned, the vast dead of the Plague, would be needed for the great reckoning. Some bore arms, some were nearly naked, but they were all beyond suffering, ready to stake it all on releasing Lucifer, friend of peace.

Dow pulled on the dragon's tail to hover above where the garden had been, calling out and gesturing for the damned to step back.

They did so, retreating to make a vast circle of the dead looking in at the trampled grass, the broken table. Still, though, the statue stood at the centre, Aude beside it.

Dow had not seen it before, or at least not registered it. Now he did and he felt his heart come to his mouth.

It was the statue of a youth, tall and handsome, his arms outstretched to hold the globe of the earth. Dow stepped down from the tail and approached it. Yes, it was the earth. As he looked at it, it seemed to sparkle and shift. He saw the blue of the seas, the green and brown of the land, little flags of noble houses or the crescent of the Saracen, the lands of the headless men or those where the phoenix clatters its wings of gold.

He recognised the youth's face, its impossibly handsome features, the feeling of vast spaces that sprang up in him when he looked into its eyes. This was an image of God, bearing some of His power.

He recalled the chapel of thorns, how God had begged him to remove the sword Lucifer had put inside Him, how God had offered to make him a king over men if he would only take out the sword and bow to Him. He had offered to free his Nan from Hell. Where was she now? Still pursued by the personal devil that God had set on her?

At the centre of the great crowd, in the trampled and ruined hunger garden, the statue seemed vast, as big as the sky, and then it was small again, only the size of a man. He touched it and trembled. This was a thing of God, a being so powerful He had cast the creator Lucifer down into Hell. The wide spaces of the stars were in his mind, the planets moving in their circles, comets streaking across the heavens. He felt the depths of the oceans as a pressure in his mind, the heights of the mountains too. Cold winds streamed through him, giving way to the hot, gritty winds of the south. He was simultaneously at Caffa, in London, on the moor in Cornwall where he had lived when he was small. The sensations were exquisite, ecstatic. He tore himself away from them. One of the statue's eyes was a glass marble and it swam with colours of blood and fire.

Aude was beside him.

'Is this the key?'

'It must be. Satan said what we sought was here and he was under solemn oath to God!'

He climbed up on to the statue and took out his knife to prise out the glass. It came out easily, but when it fell into his hand it was so impossibly heavy that he dropped it to the ground. It settled on the plinth of the statue. Dow tried to lift it again but he could not. His fingers clasped around it, but he could not shift it at all.

A man approached him, his body swollen with Plague.

'Our army stands ready for the siege, Lord.'

'I am not your lord. Where is the fourth gate?'

'I do not know.'

'Ask the people.'

A murmur went out among the crowd and the answers, when they came back, were many: 'Beyond the Sinking Plains!' 'On top of the Mountains of Despair!' 'Near the Cliff Perilous!'

Aude bent to the marble that had dropped from the statue's eye and gave a little cry.

'Dow, look!'

He peered at the little orb but saw only its shifting colours of fire and blood.

'Press your eye to it!' she said.

He did as he was bid and he too cried out.

It was as if he looked through a crack in a wall. He saw a vast plain leading up to a city of brass. The city burst with greenery, leafy trees and bushes, the reds and golds of nameless flowers, but all around it a vast army of devils was camped, besieging it. From the top tower of the city shone a light of such beauty and perfection that Dow felt tears come to his eyes. A delicate prism of colours spread out over the land and he saw that no devil could approach within leagues of the city wall. The devils had built great shields or piled rocks into high mounds and dwelt in their shadows.

'Dis!' he said. 'Lucifer's stronghold in Hell. The free city of Dis!'

'What does it mean?' said Aude.

Dow looked back at his huge, useless army.

'This is not the fourth key, nor even the fourth gate. This . . .' He pointed to the marble, 'This is the fourth layer of Hell. It's within this glass.'

A scream arose from the army of the dead.

'The bridge across the Lake of Fire has fallen!' Far off he saw a wall of fire spring up from the lake, high into the sky, never ending, stretching up into invisibility.

Dow made the three-fingered sign of Lucifer on his chest.

Satan had trapped them. There was no way forward or back.

'We need the fourth key,' said Dow.

'So where is it?'

'Lucifer has communicated through the walls before,' he said. 'Let me try. He might tell us.'

He pressed his eye again to the marble, as if to a lens. He saw the great city rising green from the red plain, the vast armies of devils around it and the light that shone from the highest tower – the light of a winter dawn.

'Lucifer,' he said. 'Friend and guide.'

He saw the devil armies stir. Could they tell he was watching them?

'Lucifer. You once were free. Tell me how to free you again.'

The light shone from the stone like a sunbeam through a crack in a door and images and sounds poured into Dow's mind.

Dow saw how Lucifer had once before got free. He had shone through the fourth gate of Hell, through the marble in the statue's eye, to talk to Satan, to tell him to open the gate and let him free, so that Lucifer might bend the knee to God, call Him Father and Lord if only He would forgive the sins of the world and release all the damned souls from Hell, take them to Heaven where they might dwell for ever. And Satan, who hated Hell himself, who longed to be free, had agreed and used the key to the fourth gate to allow Lucifer to be free, to travel as a beam of light to the upper world of men where he might be born as a man. Dow saw the key: it was an alchemist's athanor – a furnace. Satan put the marble within and heated it until it was white-hot. Then the beam of light that was Lucifer shone forth into the world.

But Lucifer would not remove the sword he had stuck in God when first cast into Hell, not until all the sins of man were forgiven. God – in His bitterness and spite – would rather suffer Himself than release the sinners, so He tricked Lucifer and nailed him to a tree, demanding his death and return to Hell for the forgiveness of sins.

Dow saw the beam of light return to Hell and he heard God laugh, though the laughter caused Him to clutch at the sword in His side. He sealed the fourth gate and took up the athanor, the oven which baked the marble until the gate of Hell opened.

'Here,' He said to Satan. 'So you might be more careful in the use of this fine oven in future, I set it where you will take good care of it.' And God pushed the oven into Satan's heart. 'Pluck it out and die yourself. No longer the warder of Hell but its inmate. I shall set those you have tormented here as your guards. Guard this good oven carefully.'

Dow withdrew his eye from the stone.

'We need to kill Satan,' he said. 'The Evertere will transport the army of the righteous dead!'

He offered the tail of the serpent to a tall bowman, his face still swollen by Plague. He reached out his hand to touch it but, as he did so, he evaporated like a ball of water on a hot plate, a red mist swept away in the heat of Hell.

'The damned cannot touch it,' said Aude.

Dow made the sign of the fork on his chest. It seemed his army was eternally stuck behind the Lake of Fire.

'What do we do?' said Aude.

But Dow had no answers.

17

Throughout the night before the battle, Isabella prayed to her angels, asking them to respect the will of God, to allow men to settle the battle themselves, to prove their valour before Heaven. They towered above the camp in fantastic shapes – great warriors riding burning chariots, winged swans twisting their necks in seeming ecstasy, rainbows and snowfields – but they said nothing. Might they even be persuaded to join in on the English side? Too late for that, she thought, they would not even speak to her now. Did they sense what was coming through from Hell? Did they know that the final days were about to unfold, Heaven open, and she to see her Mortimer again? They towered above her and she tried not to hate them. With a gesture they could spill the blood of the French king, burst his whole huge family like berries upon the ground of Poitiers. But they would not.

Things, creation, should learn to serve, she thought. If God had gone, if he would not return, then should it not be she – who had been raised to rule since her earliest days, in whose blood flowed the ancient blood of the kings of France – should it not be she who sat in judgement and command over creation?

Did she stand here in the garb of a nun, only the Crown of Light to mark her status, for nothing, no more than a few ladies-in-waiting and the guard John had given her to accompany her, abased and in all humility? She moved among the men, watched as the priests blessed sword and lance, arrow and mace for the coming fight. Far off, in the English camp, devils chattered and squabbled. Songs in accents so thick that they may as well have been the songs of the Saracens floated across the night. She came eventually to the banner of Orléans – the royal fleur-de-lys marked with chads of red. The Duke, when she encountered him, was pissing outside his tent.

He saw her, pulled up his hose and reset his codpiece – an elaborate thing in the shape of the elephant of myth, complete with that savage beast's blood-red tusks. Isabella had often noted that the way of nature seemed to be that more elaborate the cod-piece, the more disappointing what it covered.

'Ma'am,' he said. 'Forgive me, I have been all of a piss this evening. Too much wine, I wager. I can never sleep on the eve of a battle, too keen to . . .' He smacked his fist into his hand. 'Get to it!'

'Indeed, My Lord. May I drink a cup with you?'

'I would be enchanted.' Isabella noted that her ability to bewitch the more common men did not extend to the Duke of Orléans. Was he, like her dead husband, one of those who preferred men? Or was it the protection of his royal blood? Or both?

She stepped inside his tent. A few listless boys sat about the place, one sharpening a sword.

'Gilles,' said the duke, 'you'll wear that to nothing. Enough of sharpening, you could split a boar's thistle with that now.' The boy did as he was bid.

Isabella smiled. A boy pulled back a chair for her and she sat. She was pleased that the duke at least did not indulge the military affectation for camp stools and the like, but had transported a full set of decent furniture with him. She had been offered the best chair – high backed, carved with the images of tumbling swallows.

'A rare day we face tomorrow, Lady.'

She crossed herself. 'Indeed. Boys, leave us, I wish to speak to the duke in private.'

The boys looked a little shocked, which told Isabella they had little experience of queens. Orléans waved his hand and they vacated. She didn't like that. They should have left immediately without waiting for his instruction. *These are the days in which we live, it seems, all deference and propriety gone.*

'Ma'am.'

'I come to you, Duke, in order to speak most secretly.'

'I'm not sure I'm the right one for secrets. You know I am no statesman. Nor warrior neither, if truth be told.'

'Yet you lead a division tomorrow.'

He paled. 'I do. The reserve. To sway the direction of the battle once the mess of fighting's done. I should think your good angels will have settled it by then, anyhow. What?'

'I think not. The angels seem rather inclined to my grandson,' she lied. Having already paled there was little paler the duke could get, but he managed it.

'You have told the king?'

'Yes, but he seems not to care. He forbade me or any other from mentioning it. This is why I come to you. To steel you, sir, to bolster your resolve. Tomorrow, though the fight may be savage and the killing great, you must do your duty by your king and God.'

Orléans put his hand to his chest. 'Lady, I shall . . .' He seemed unable to finish the sentence. There were tears in his eyes.

'Tell me.'

He swayed from side to side, his head downcast. After a period of silence, she said again. 'Tell me.'

'I come from a great line of warriors.'

'Your brother John is a lion. Your family the pride of France.'

He gave a little mew, and pawed at the air with his hand.

'I am not of such stuff,' he said. 'And my only virtue is that I know it.'

'You are too hard on yourself, sir. You do well enough in the lists.'

He laughed. 'Do you know how many great knights have been forced to make idiots of themselves with lance and sword before me, just because of who I am? And still half the time it's all I can do to win.'

'So what happens tomorrow?' Isabella had thought to put the fear of God into Orléans, shake his resolve, but she saw there was no need for that.

'I go out and I . . .' He waved his arm around in imitation of sword swipes. 'I have to lead. I have to go first. The English have said they will give no quarter.'

'That's probably bluster before the battle. Who could ignore the chance to ransom you? You know when my husband left me to the Scots, it was their bickering over me that gave me the chance to get away. They started fighting each other, so rich a prize was I. You are no different. If I, a lady, can escape . . .'

He picked up his lyre.

'You are more of a man than I,' he said. 'Did you not lead your army at Orwell, when outnumbered twenty to one by your husband's forces? Did you not vanquish those forces and set yourself and your son upon the throne?'

Isabella let his words sink in. The walls of the tent seemed to breathe in the hot September night.

'I did.' She put her hand on his arm. 'Would you like me to ride alongside you? I wear the Crown of Light. They are my angels. I'm sure you will be protected. I will take the charge, if you like, I have done it before. I rather enjoy it.'

He bowed his head.

'I could not ask . . .'

'You are not asking. I am offering. I will ride beside you and pray that the angels watch over you.'

'Why are you doing this for me?'

She stood and smiled. 'Because I wish to see France prosper on the field. We cannot lose for lack of purpose.'

So it was that Isabella sat with Orléans's division at the back of the field on that sweet September morning, a coat of boy's mail about her, a borrowed sword at her side. In front of her was the meat of the battle, the ones who needed most to fall – the king's battle, his banners like a field of golden lilies. In front of that, wide and deep, was the battle of the Dauphin, a sea of leaping dolphin fish, men-at-arms to the front, horses behind. They would not make the mistake of Crécy. The footmen would advance, invulnerable in their armour, and slaughter the archers before the cavalry engaged.

The English line was thin by comparison – their trenches dug, their stakes positioned, their archers set. The devils rose in columns behind them, a thick smoke of winged worms, stone skins, blasted crows, the buzzing fly men and the writhing snakes of the air.

Orléans crossed himself.

'Cousin,' she said, 'this is France. Those devils cannot move a step forward until the ground is won by the men who travel with them. If my grandson cannot make this England, he cannot fight upon it with those unholy creatures. And see how our angels tower!'

At five points around the field, though distant from it, columns of light shone – sunset red.

'I say, they're running away!' said Orléans.

At the back of the English lines, the baggage train was moving, that was all. Would the French fall for it? They would not. 'Hold! Hold!' came the cry from the front. She'd see about that. She spurred her horse forward, through the king's lines, to the ranks of knights in the Dauphin's division, up to the Dauphin himself.

'Cousin, the English are in retreat. Press your advantage!'

'It's a trick, Lady. They want us to repeat our old errors.'

'You have no valour! The angels will not engage for cowards!'

She turned to the knights behind us.

'The English are slipping away! With me! With me!'

She spurred her horse forward through the footmen. Three knights followed her, eager for glory, then six followed them, then twelve them.

'Hold! Hold!' cried the Dauphin but he could not make himself heard. His footmen broke order to allow the cavalry through, but not quick enough. Some fell beneath the hooves of their own horsemen; some just fell. Isabella pulled down the visor on her helm and spurred her horse forward. She heard her own breath sawing, felt her heart racing as the horse took off. A sound like rain, a thump in the chest. Her horse had sprouted an arrow but it kept going, its thick caparison protecting it well. Another thump, and another. Her horse was resembling a hedgehog but still it kept on. An enormous jolt, a cry of animal pain and she was flying. But Isabella had been falling off horses since she was four years old and she rolled out of the collapse, coming up to standing. She drew her sword.

Around her was chaos. The English had dug little pits to trip the charging horses and now mounds of men and animals were piling in front of the hedges. Two more thumps – two more arrows shattering against her mail. She was calm. Now she had to make her way back to Orléans, but that would not prove easy. The charge of the French horse went on and on, and she hid behind the body of a fallen destrier to stop herself being trampled.

The angels were taking shape. No longer columns of light but huge creatures, two female, three male, pointing swords and spears to the battle field. Beside her Étampes sat down. He did not recognise her; his eyes were vacant, his helm half torn off. Étampes, in line to the throne one day given a lucky series of calamities. She took out her misericord.

'Satan!' she said. 'I call you. I call you. The last day is here. Come to the earth!'

She stabbed Étampes hard in the throat, driving the dagger between his jaw and his gorget. He turned to look at her, an expression of mild surprise on his face. Then he died. Footmen were pouring in now but the arrow fire was immense. She felt a nick as a lucky shot got through her mail and gambeson.

The French threw themselves like devils at the English hedges. Not all the horses had fallen by any means and knights hacked away, trying to find a way through the thicket of staves and briars. She looked back. King John was readying his charge. The archers in front of her ceased fire and she took her cue, mounting a loose horse, its caparison all quilled with arrows, and turning for her own lines.

The English foot were advancing over the tumble of men and horses. A charge now might be decisive. She was done, though, shouldering her horse back to where Orléans was. He was trembling, white.

'I thought you had deserted me,' he said.

'Never.'

'You are brave, madam.'

'I am of France.'

A great shout and the second wave of horse went to it, but now it was carnage. They headed for the English foot but the archers had flanked them. No longer were they aiming for the thick armour on the horses' fronts, but at the less protected sides and even the rears. A storm of arrows hit the charge and the animals screamed in torment, bucking their riders from their seats, falling, tripping others, the tripped falling and tripping still more. It was as if a wave hit a harbour wall.

'Satan, Satan,' she said under her breath. 'Our God is a god of blood and pain, of the blood of the martyrs, of Christ's blood on the Cross, of the wars of Cross and Crescent! The blood royal calls you to earth. These are the last days. Come forth and play your part as the prophets have foretold.'

John, magnificent King John, vessel of such holy blood, a living holy grail, lowered his visor and spurred his horse to the fray. The arrows were almost done, no more firing, the bowmen pouring into the battle from the sides. Now the Black Prince's ostrich banners bobbed into the fray. The English were all committed and the battle was in balance.

'Now?' said Orléans, his voice shaking. 'Now? Lady? Now?'

The great angels towered enacting movements of striking and killing. Were they ready to join the battle on the side of France?

'My Lord,' said Isabella, 'I fear the day is done. The angels have cursed me and told me that we anger God with what we do today. They will engage for the enemy.'

'What to do? What to do?'

'Why, die, My Lord, die, most certainly, and face the wrath of God eternal, for our loyalty to our king says we must.'

'No. If he is gone, then who is to rule? I mean, the Dauphin is down there, all his sons. There's only me. I am too valuable. I must. We must retreat.'

'Yes!' said Isabella. 'Retreat and find our way back to God's pleasure. Defer to the angels. Yes.'

Orléans nodded.

'God is against us!' he cried to his men. 'Withdraw, withdraw. Save yourselves!'

The great mass of the French reserve wheeled its horses, its footmen dropping their spears and bills as they scrambled to retreat.

Banners went down. She saw Tancarville's standard, and Étampes' and Marche's and Bourbon's, fall. So much royal blood. Just kill the king. Why don't you kill the king, you useless idiot, Edward? The fleur-de-lys was now locked against the ostrich feather, the fighting so loud and intense.

A party of English bowmen skirted the action, a hundred yards away. They nocked. No need to worry about them at such a distance.

Isabella looked to the skies. Something was coming towards her. A knight, in all the colours of a stained glass window, a knight so rich in colour it was as if the light of the sun itself flowed in his veins.

A tear came into her eye.

'Mortimer!' she said. 'You have come from Heaven.'

He stood before her, as radiant as the dawn.

'My love,' he said, 'you have worked mightily to release me. I am so near to regaining the world, from stepping through the gate of Heaven.'

'I have missed you for so long. But you are not yet here? Then how can I see you?' She wiped her eye and when she tried to remove her hand, she could not. An arrow fixed it in place, its head deep in the socket and she, to her surprise, was almost dead. Time slowed but she could feel her life running out.

'Will I go to Heaven?' she said. But there was no reply.

Would she go to Hell? Perhaps, but if she did then its king would not be there to torment her.

'Satan,' she said, 'come.'

She fell from her horse, and the English horse overran her, trampling her royal blood into the soil of Poitiers field.

18

In times of plague, in times of war, in times of turmoil and uncertainty, when grief strikes like a viper at the heart and love seems gone from the world, there remains, as always the problem of how to make a living.

Osbert, drunk in the streets of Paris for so long after Gilette's departure thought to return to the court, concoct some story about why he had been away but, by the time his months of drinking had come to an end – all his money gone – there was no court to return to. When he tried to enter the palace of the Louvre, he found it shut up, along with all the grand buildings in the middle of Paris.

There was not even anyone to ask. John had ridden south to face the English, five angels leading the way. That had been a month ago. People scuttled from place to place; they did not walk with any confidence, as if at any second expecting an arrow to strike them or maybe a bolt from the sky.

Things were falling apart.

October was warm but blowy in Paris and he took himself to the royal woods at Vincennes to look at a tree – the last greenery in the city itself having been burnt some time before the Romans got there, he guessed. *Oh Gilette, how could you? I gave you my heart and you traded it for what? The liberation of the poor, a dream. You took a key from me but left me in irons.* Such melancholy and self-pitying thoughts bred like street rats in his head.

He saw his first dead man on the corner of the Hôpital de la Trinité. He was not in good shape, having clearly been in the ground a while by his state of decomposition. But he stood looking around, gazing up at the great edifice of the hospital.

'I am free,' he said. 'But it is a strange freedom. I do not know what to do.'

Osbert, who preferred to limit his conversations with the dead, went to hurry past but he saw another dead man there, pulling himself from the earth of the hospital cemetery. Now a family emerged, a dead and rotted mother helping a dead and rotted child from the grave. All around the ground seemed to boil, as the dead rose up.

'Oh, shit, it's the last days, isn't it?' said Osbert. 'God, I repent. Fully, without condition. I repent. Judge me as you will but know that whatever I did, I was made in your image. By you. So whatever I've done, you are partly to blame.'

More dead people arose all around him.

'Are you all right?' said Osbert to a young girl, half her face eaten by worms.

'They prodded me with pins. For ever. It is wonderful to be free of them.'

She sat down on the ground and looked around her. He made the sign of the cross.

'God bless you,' he said.

'He did not do that. He cursed me. The torment was terrible. I lied and said I was too sick to go to mass. They burnt my tongue eternally for it.'

You knew the rules! Osbert was tempted to say, but did not.

He walked the streets. All around the dead were rising, looking around in confusion, hugging each other for comfort. The ordinary folk ran for the churches and their homes. He, who had harrowed Hell, was less easily spooked.

For the sake of God, the boy did it, thought Osbert. *He broke the walls of Hell.* But where was Lucifer? Where was the bright one they had been promised? Or where was God, to judge, to condemn and bless and tidy these stinking corpses from the streets? This half-hearted end of the world was good for no one.

He ran to the Louvre. He would need to consult all the wise people he could, to use holy relics to . . . To what? He didn't know what to do. The king would know, surely the king would know. But where was the king?

His hangover was hot in his veins and the city was suffocating him. He ran for the walls. No guards, but only more of the dead

412

wandering around in confusion. He walked for he didn't know how long, until he came to the royal wood at Vincennes.

But when he arrived, he could not believe what he saw – common men roasting the king's deer on fires they had made of the king's wood, a nervous guard around the château, its portcullis firmly shut. The dead were not here – or at least not yet.

Osbert reined in his mild outrage – he had been in the court too long to feel that a commoner feasting on venison was something that could ever be right – in favour of trying to cadge a meal. No luck there.

'God's shit,' said the man at the fire, 'it took me all day to bag this. I'll not part from it cheaply.'

Osbert's stomach kicked. He had done nothing but drink for so long.

'Why are you so bold, to hunt in the king's forest?' Through his hangover, another more important thought occurred to him. 'Why am I here, talking to you? If we're discovered, I'll be tarred with the same brush as you.'

'What king?' said the man. 'Haven't you heard?'

'No,' said Osbert. 'I've been pretty much rolling around in the street, drunk as an owl, recently.'

'The king is captured. Satan has come to earth, struck a pact with the English and carried him off to London.'

'Well, that is a surprise,' said Osbert, feeling that he might collapse.

'Hell is open, and God is nowhere,' said the man. 'We're all dead. All of us. The damned are spilling from Hell in a great army – murderers, thieves, all reborn and swarming all over the land. They won't follow even Satan.'

'If Hell is open, won't we just pop back out again if we're dead?'

'Don't ask me. My brother came up from the south, he says there's a great army of them, all falling to bits. I wouldn't want to come back like that.'

'I have seen them,' Osbert said. 'The cemeteries are emptying. They are walking the streets. Are these the last days, do you think? Is God on His way?'

'I wish He'd hurry up. Satan has come, that is sure.'

'Who told you?'

'I don't know. Everyone says so.'

'How did we lose?'

'Orléans ran for it and the angels scarpered.'

'They ran?'

'Disappeared to contemplate their own arseholes. One of them – one – could stop this tide of dead, but do they? Do they my fat bollocks!'

'Are all the royals captured?'

'Who am I? Herald? I don't know. John is taken to London, Satan with him.'

Osbert thought. Satan must still be banned from France or the English would be marching on Paris with him at the head. So John was alive and maintaining the ban. Or his son was king, or one of his sons. But the damned, the dead, were traitors to God, not His servants. They could not be commanded. But they might be led. Satan was free. That meant he had fulfilled the bargain, however indirectly, that Simon Pastus had struck with him. He was free from Hell for ever. But so were the rotting dead all around him. Was that his destiny? Such, he thought, were the bargains of devils.

He looked about him, the trees of the wood falling, fires in the streets of Paris, anarchy. When the great army of the damned arrived, he feared for the people. At that moment the dead seemed quite harmless, but who knew what might happen if they were allowed to roam ungoverned? The thought surprised him. He had habitually thought only of himself but he was beginning to see that his own prosperity and calm of mind depended rather on that of others – under the order of a king, of course; he was no Luciferian.

His head was raw. What he needed was a ruler and an angel. As far as he recalled, there was one of each in Paris at that moment.

He ran back into the city, to the first church he could find – a little chapel with one small blue glass window showing the mother Mary and the infant Jesus. The dead surrounded it, sitting among the burst graves, hugging and holding each other, looking around at a world free of fire and devils.

The door of the church was locked but he hammered on it, calling out to be admitted, saying he was a living man come to return the dead to their graves. The door opened a crack and a timorous, pale priest looked out.

'Who are you?'

'Osbert of Everywhere,' he said. 'Sorcerer to the king. Come to end this plague. Let me in.'

The man, who could see that – whatever Osbert's dilapidated state – he was at least alive, opened the door and Osbert slid within.

Already the inside of the church was lit with candles, the fish stink almost unbearable. Ten or so people knelt before the altar in prayer.

'What is happening?' a woman said.

'The Devil has come to earth,' said Osbert. 'The dead are walking the streets, the king is captured, the Dauphin is I know not where and all the angels are fled.'

A great wail went up.

'Let us not despair!' said Osbert. 'There may still be a way. Empty the font. Bring me the holy water. Any jewellery you have, pile it on the altar.'

'You are a thief!'

'I am your salvation!'

Such was their terror that people did as he said. Of course, before they had fled to the church, the people had taken up their most valuable things and a good pile of rings and necklaces was deposited on the altar, along with a jewelled communion cup.

'What are you trying to do?'

'Call an angel.'

'Only kings can do that!'

'Not if it's already here,' said Osbert.

He made a magic circle on the floor, inscribing it with the most secret names of God in the sacred alphabet of the Hebrews, delivered by God, sprinkling the circumference with holy water and holy oil.

'Have you better candles than these?' he asked the priest.

'Only for the most special occasions.'

'Well, what in the name of Christ's hot spunk is this?'

The priest, his hair fairly ruffled by Osbert's outburst, went to a side cupboard and produced two tall honeycomb candles. Osbert lit them in his circle and began his invocation.

'First angel of God, Iao, and you, Michael, who rule Heaven's realm, hear me, archangels of Olympus, Abraxas delighting in the dawn, hear me, gracious ones who view sunset from the dawn.'

'By the fire and the water.' He rattled the jug of holy water. 'By the air and the earth, I command you. By God who is called by His ineffable name, Adonai El Elyom, who is Jah, Yod, He, Waw, He. Speak to your sister Asbeel and let her attend us here.'

Osbert felt sick and desperate. He had slept, drunk, for more than a month and in that time the world had fallen further than he imagined possible. He felt oddly responsible. Should he not have clung on to the keys? If Hell was open, then it was his fault.

He repeated the words, uttered the nonsense phrases he had learned when a captive of the mad Edwin, phrases incomprehensible to the sorcerer but heard by angels. Hour after hour he kept going, his voice hoarse. A woman called him a fraud and told him to stop but another woman asked what other hope they had.

The candles burned low and the church was full of smoke, the dead scraping at the door, Osbert imagined, for something to do.

'Asbeel, angel who was trapped in Hell when the bright one fell. Asbeel, who inhabits the body of Blanche of Navarre, Abseel, who . . .' He was running out of things that he knew this angel did.

The light. The light in the jewels was brightening. Though most of what was on the altar was cheap stuff, the communion cup sparkled with rubies and now they lit up bright as fires on a dark hill.

'By the secret names of God, by the . . .'

The light in the church was bright now, lit by a powerful glow behind the church door that streamed through its cracks, around and beneath it.

'Open it!' said Osbert.

The door was opened and there she was – Blanche of Navarre, the light shining from her.

'Lady, angel,' he said, 'I have called you to save creation.'

'You killed a king,' she said.

'And now I intend to make one in atonement. We will need to find your brother.'

19

Charles of Navarre had not been attended by his jailers for a number of days and was beginning to wonder why. Starving the king to death was hardly an option. A man with the capacity to catch and eat – and at least half enjoy – mice and rats could banquet himself well anywhere. Water was not a problem either, as there had been an amount of rain and he could lean out to one of Le Châtelet's stone gargoyles to catch a good mouthful from its spout. In his former shape, of course, escape would have been no problem at all. He would have shinned out of the window and climbed over the roof of the prison to go down to the ground.

Now, however, only one half of his body was nimble and lithe. The other half, human, hardly co-ordinated with it at all. He was sure he would fall if he tried to climb.

After a week or two, however, the attraction of throwing his shit out of the window began to wane and he considered at least trying to escape. He craned his head out of the window. Above him was a ledge. If he just shuffled out then he was sure he could pull himself up onto it. Then half of him could leap . . . No, there was a problem with that. He gazed out over the courtyard of Le Châtelet.

A number of people were sitting around doing nothing much in particular. They looked like paupers – ragged clothes – but he was too far away to see much more about them.

'Hey!' he shouted. 'Hey!'

Some of them looked up, others just stared ahead.

'I am the king of Navarre. What is happening here?'

No reply.

'Hello! Answer me! I will give you a coin!'

He had only three left – sous, of little worth. He had been cut off from his men, his nobles, everyone, and had to pay all he had on him just to obtain a cell fit for no more than an earl.

'I need no coins, sir.' A voice came up, wet and rattly.

'Well, what would you like?'

'I don't know.'

That was an answer Charles had never expected. Everyone knew what they wanted. Peasants, bread; everyone else, power and gold.

'What do you mean, you don't know?'

'My needs have been few since I have been dead.'

'You are dead?'

'Yes. And newly returned from Hell with Satan.'

Well, thought Charles, *there is a development indeed.*

'Would you come and release me from this tower?'

'No.'

'Why not?'

'If a king is in a tower, he is there because God wants him to be. I do not want to sit in this rotten body for ever. I want a way back to God. Out of Hell is not the same as in Heaven.'

This, Charles said to himself, *was the peasant attitude entire. You give and you give and you give more and still they want and want and want. Out of Hell not good enough.* He lifted up his filthy tunic and looked at the stitches running up the middle of him. He poked his head back out of the window.

'We've all got rotten bodies! Some of us don't use it as an excuse for sitting on our arses expecting the world to hand them a living!'

'I was a busy merchant,' said the man. 'But I loaned money to another at interest. For that they cut off my grasping hands and sewed them into my mouth every day and every night for ever.'

'They should have left them there, you prattling dogscock!'

He went back inside. Hell open, all law in Paris gone, no guards, the dead in the street. John had lost, he could see that. But had Edward really won? If so, where was he?

All he had to do was to get out of the most secure jail in the kingdom.

There was a knock at his door.

'I am at prayer!' he said. The last thing he wanted to look was desperate.

'My Lord, it is me.'

'Who?'

'Osbert, who sewed you up.'

Charles put his human hand to his face, where the angel's blood had burned him. His cat's paw snicked out its claws.

'What do you want?'

'I have a deal for you! Just open the door and I will give you the details.'

'It's a prison, you shit-brained tit! I can't open the door. If I could, you would be drowning in your own blood.'

'Gentle, My Lord, I pray you,' said Osbert. 'I will open this door and I have brought you a rare gift.'

'I'll give you a rare gift as soon as this is open,' said Charles under his breath.

'Stand back, My Lord.'

Osbert did so. At the crack of the door a strong white light shone. It was torture to his cat's eye and painful enough to his human one. He ducked down, fearing an explosion or the entrance of some sort of battering ram. Instead the door just blackened and glowed like a log in a fire, then it turned ash white and fell away to nothing. Before him stood his sister, radiant as the dawn; behind her, the cursed sorcerer. Charles went for him, claws drawn, but it was as if he hit another wall, just beyond the door.

'Calm, good lord, calm,' Osbert said. 'I had anticipated such a reaction and so have used some of this good angel's blood to form a circle. I would strike a bargain with you. A traditional, binding bargain between devil and sorcerer. Or rather a bargain with half of you. The other half can do what it likes.'

Blanche stood smiling at him.

'Sister, strike him,' he said.

'I cannot. He has called me and bound me by the names of God. He has offered me a return to the light.'

'He can't offer that!'

'You can,' said Osbert. 'I want you to restore order to this world. Command the dead – let them live at peace with the living. Find a way to return them to God.'

'How do I do that?'

'Satan is in England, most sacrilegiously free from Hell. Return him, My Lord, or oppose and destroy him, thereby calling in the final days. Restore God and order to the land.'

'Don't tell me what to do, you miserable goat-headed, pig-dicked poltroon! I'll rip out your guts and tie a bow around your neck with them!'

'Then I will leave you here, devil.' Osbert held up his hand. 'I bind thee. In the name of God who made the world, in the name of Jehovah and in the presence of this angel, I bind thee.'

Charles felt very strange indeed. His head spun and he wanted to be sick.

'I bind thee by all the angels of the earth, by the holy blood of the martyrs, by the three names of God that are . . .'

Osbert's voice became indistinct.

'This is an outrage,' said Charles. 'You cannot bind a king!'

'But I can a cat!' said Osbert.

Blanche shone, beautiful and bright, the light of the summer sunset pouring over Charles.

'Done?' said Osbert.

'Done,' said Blanche.

Osbert rubbed out the circle he had drawn by the door. Charles sprang at him, or at least his human hand did. His cat's paw, however, came across to slash at it, forcing him to withdraw.

Osbert smiled and bowed.

'King of Navarre!' he said. 'Lord of the living and of the dead, let me escort you to your new kingdom.'

He went out of the prison, up a flight of stairs.

Charles followed him, fighting himself as he tried to punch the sorcerer. Blanche walked up beside, divine, floating almost.

Osbert leant across the parapet of Le Châtelet, looking out over Paris.

'See?' he said. 'See how the vast nations of the masterless dead await your command?'

Charles peered out. The streets were teeming but the way that people walked was odd, purposeless. Some sat down for no good reason, others stood for no good reason.

'This is your angel,' said Osbert. 'Yours to command as you will. Well, through me after I have bound her like I bound half of you with subtle magics and the names of God.'

Charles looked at his sister.

'How has she not enchanted you?' he said.

'My Lord, I don't know. I knew one such half-angel before. She too liked me well enough, but did not enspell me. Use her to address your people.'

Charles ran his tongue across the split in his lip.

'Do you have the magic to renew me?'

'I might. When you are king of France, you can command what you will. Saints' bones, angels' tears. We will find a way.'

'Say what you must,' said Charles to Blanche.

She stood on top of a crenellation, perfectly balanced, her arms spread wide over the city far below her, and she shone, her light pouring out over the city like a dawn, like enormous wings that spread out to embrace the whole world. When she spoke her voice was quiet but it sounded close by Charles's ear.

'Nation of the dead. Delivered from Hell and seeking God, know that a king has risen up, blessed of God and ready to lead you to him. Free from Hell, we will lead you to the Lord your master.'

From all over the town they came, from all over the countryside too, running in on good legs, limping in on bad, bones rattling, flesh dripping: dead mothers carrying dead children, dead warriors clutching sharp spears, dead knights and priests and farmers, all coming to heed the angel's call.

Charles and Osbert watched them coming for a day. When they were assembled, packing the Île de la Cité in mighty array, Charles turned to Osbert.

'This return to God. It can take as long as I like?'

'The last days go on for thousands of years according to the Bible.'

'Good. Because in the meantime . . .'

Osbert bowed indulgently. 'You have a rare army at your disposal.'

'There is none other in the land?'

'Not that I know of.'

Charles went to the parapet.

'I am king of France!' he said. 'King of the Dead! King of the Dead!' The mighty host saluted him, bathed in the angel light.

'I've won!' said Charles. 'I'm last man standing, I've won! Carry me to the Palace of the Louvre. I will make my enemies quake!'

Osbert bowed, though it was a different sort of bow to the one he would normally have offered to a king. This was not that of a low subject, but more the kind of indulgent bow you might offer to a child to humour it.

'Make way for the King of the Dead!' shouted Osbert. Somehow he could not but help feel he was talking about himself.

20

Philippa made the church at Gâtinais under the heavy guard of thirty knights. No devil could accompany her, still excluded by the banishment of the king of France. The lands here had paid a terrible price for the blue sickness and the years of English looting. They were empty of people, empty of livestock, returning to how the earth must have looked when new and only Adam and Eve stood upon it.

It was late summer and should have been harvest time, but the fields were overgrown with poppies, red among the barley like the flames of Hell spouting up through the fields. Even the roads were difficult going, the pilgrim ways having fallen into disuse – too many bandits, too few people left to travel them.

Would the earth ever recover? Would one day a noble sit beneath the shade of his castle, watching his sons tilt, hearing Mass sung from his chapel, watching his peasants collect the harvest, all as it should be, under God?

She flew the Three Lions of England, along with the Cross of St George, but she would not allow the whip banner. The first two insignia were enough to terrify anyone who might stand in their way; she needed no more.

Through broken villages, through fields of hives thick with bees fat on their own honey. Some of her men smoked out and split a hive and they dined well on honey that night, but the land seemed alien and strange to her. This is what war does, this is what pestilence does. Even at the height of the Plague there was still human noise in such places – church bells, funeral drums, lamentation, drunkenness, even. Here, nothing. The buzz of the bee in the meadow, the song of the thrush and, at night, the chirping of numberless insects.

They followed the River Loing and, having passed through many deserted villages, they came to one that they thought must be Gâtinais. They were wrong. The church records showed it to be the village of Moret. Death had hollowed this place out, Philippa could see by the number of dead, and it had never regenerated. From the burnt houses and the looted church she saw that routiers had come through here too.

She felt ashamed of what had been done under the name of England and put her hand on the altar of the church to vow: 'I will make this right. I will restore and heal this land.'

A few more days of fruitless searching and then they came upon the town of Grez. It had more people in it, though it quickly drew its gates to prevent access. A parley and the inhabitants directed them to Gâtinais, but not before extracting an oath that the knights would not try to break in. They followed the Loing, running its slow green course. Kingfishers flashed on the bank, a blink of orange flame that flipped blue in the flap of a wing. A hawk worked the fields above her, turning lazy circles.

At her side, the young knights knew better than to ask what they were doing.

It was nearly dusk when she came to the village – just in the crook of the river, as the townsmen of Grez had said. It had been a pretty place, once, she guessed, though now the streets were overgrown with brambles. It had escaped the attentions of the routiers, apparently, for nothing was burnt or broken in, beyond what the weather had done to the odd piece of thatch or straw-built house. The fields were alive with hare, rabbits and fowl; fig trees lined the avenues. An orchard shone with ripening apples and pears, and vines were heavy with grapes. The whole earth, waiting for man to be born, she thought.

A pretty church sat at the centre of the village. She crossed herself. This was where it was said to have begun, where the Plantagenet line's connection to the devil was first revealed. The old count of Anjou, ancestor of all the Plantagenets, had forced his wife to Mass. She had revealed herself as a devil and flown off through the church window, carrying her children with her.

The sun dipped low over the golden fields that shone like a rich cloth. From inside the church she heard the Vespers bells ringing.

Someone was in there. Her knights forced a way down the overgrown street towards the church and she followed. There were signs that someone had come and gone from the church, at least occasionally – a track through the deep grass, the bones of animals and birds at the door, a burnt patch with an improvised spit next to it.

The bells stopped ringing and a knight led her into the church. The man gasped as he stepped inside. So did she.

At the opposite end was the most magnificent window she had ever seen, lit by the falling sun. The altar was at the wrong end, she thought – the west. What kind of odd place was this? They had never had such a thing in England nor in Hainault.

The window showed a knight rendered in the most vibrant colours of stained glass. He held his sword aloft, his other hand pointing to Heaven to show from where he took his authority and inspiration. His face was dark and handsome and, as she recognised it, she crossed herself.

'Mortimer!' she said.

Once he would have been her hated enemy. He had killed old King Edward and tried to use her husband, his son, as a puppet ruler. She would have called him usurper, overthrower, tyrant. Now. No. Had she but known it, he was trying to save her.

A noise from her left. From the bell tower came a low man, his beard and hair long, nearly naked. He started when he saw her, his eyes like a deer's that hears a sound in the wood.

The knight beside her pecked towards the floor with his finger to indicate the man should bow. He did, hesitantly.

'Go,' said Philippa to her men.

'Lady, this is a wild man. I cannot guarantee your safety.'

Philippa said nothing, just allowed a royal brow to rise. The man deferred, and the retinue left the church.

'You have been restoring this window?'

He said nothing, just looked at the floor.

'I think you have made a different picture to the one that was there before.'

He tried to speak, stammering, but either could not shape the words or was too afraid to be able to speak them.

Philippa approached the window. The colours were so deep, she had never seen anything like them. Each shade suggested something

424

so much more – the blue was the blue of a summer night and it recalled the spangled stars, the brilliant moon, the hoot of owl and the song of the nightingale. The red was the colour of rubies, of throne rooms and blood. She recalled her husband, Edward, in his might, splitting heads at Crécy, she nervous on the hill.

Yellow recalled the corn fields, the wheat bowed by the winds, alive and thrusting in the rain. Purple the robes of royalty, her first day in England and the robe they brought her. Green was Windsor, the trees and the pond in the sunlight, a frog on a lily that she could not recall if she had seen or imagined.

The idiot, the low man, touched her. She almost leapt. Such an imposition was so unthinkable she hardly knew what to do. But when he held out his hand, she knew what he wanted.

She reached within her purse and dug out the fragment of glass. The idiot crossed himself, knelt, extended his hand. In the window's brilliant colours there was one chink of pinky white sunlight, a tiny imperfection in the blue of the knight's eye. The blue fragment itself was bright now, as if lit from within by its own sunset, otherworldly and unseen. She dropped it into the idiot's hand.

He took it, stood and ascended the scaffold. Philippa watched as he took the glowing blue shard and placed it in the knight's eye.

The colours of the window burned so bright she had to look away. The scaffolding fell away and the idiot cried out as he fell with it. The window shattered, falling to shards about her feet.

He stood before her, just as he had been in the window, a thing made of colour, a stained glass image come to life but real, moving. He laid his sword across his hands and presented it to her.

'I am Mortimer, scourge of the Plantagenets, enemy of devils, come back to earth to re-establish the kingdom of God. I am your servant.'

The sword before her was the silver of a lake's surface, its colours swimming and shining. He was as bright as the dawn.

She touched the sword. It was cold, and a tingle shot through her.

'England must be cleansed,' she said.

'And France, from the sea to the mountains. This is God's will.'

'God will cleanse France Himself. My son will be dead on Poitiers field by now.'

'Not so, Lady. Isabella fell at Poitiers.'

'Is Satan here on earth?'

'I cannot tell. God granted me only the moment of her death with her.'

Philippa swallowed. *What had happened at Poitiers?*

Her men were in the church, bending their knees before Mortimer, thinking perhaps he was an angel. With Edward entranced the Black Prince was the ruler – all the men of England at his side, the might of Hell too.

She had thirty loyal men and Mortimer to cleanse all of England, perhaps even France too, if the battle at Poitiers had gone to the English. A terrible thought rose up in her, terrible but irresistible. God's will, for sure. With Edward under her command, she would be ruler of England, banisher of devils, establisher of a true line. She looked at Mortimer, the perfect, radiant knight. If he were to kill her husband no one could say God did not wish it so. She must have one more child in her, she thought, that would descend from the line God had chosen, a half-angel to rule, not the half-devils she had served like a brood mare.

A noise above the church.

She went outside with her men, Mortimer beside her.

Every one of her knights fell to kneeling, crossing themselves for protection.

The sky above was black with devils, flying north-west on wings of leather, skin and stone. Flying to Calais? Flying perhaps even to England. She had never seen so many. The sun itself disappeared beneath the flapping mass.

'These are the last days!' said a knight.

'Then rejoice,' said Philippa. 'For we are on God's side. To Calais and to England. Death to devils! Let us herald the kingdom of God.'

But even as she spoke, her words were drowned by the sound of the beating wings.

> *Now the Son of the Night, his tale is done*
> *He is king and France his dominion*
> *But here lies not the end of our story*
> *For Lucifer comes on clouds of glory*

ABOUT GOLLANCZ

Gollancz is the oldest SF publishing imprint in the world. Since being founded in 1927 Gollancz has continued to publish a focused selection of bestselling and award-winning authors. The front-list includes **Ben Aaronovitch**, **Joe Abercrombie**, **Charlaine Harris**, **Joanne Harris**, **Joe Hill**, **Alastair Reynolds**, **Patrick Rothfuss**, **Nalini Singh** and **Brandon Sanderson**.

As one of the largest Science Fiction and Fantasy imprints in the UK it is no surprise we have one of the most extensive backlists in the world. Find high-quality SF on Gateway written by such authors as **Philip K. Dick**, **Ursula Le Guin**, **Connie Willis**, **Sir Arthur C. Clarke**, **Pat Cadigan**, **Michael Moorcock** and **George R.R. Martin**.

We also have a strand of publishing in translation, which includes French, Polish and Russian authors. Gollancz is home to more award-winning authors than any other imprint, with names including **Aliette de Bodard**, **M. John Harrison**, **Paul McAuley**, **Sarah Pinborough**, **Pierre Pevel**, **Justina Robson** and many more.

The SF Gateway
More than 3,000 classic, rare and previously out-of-print SF novels at your fingertips.
www.sfgateway.com

The Gollancz Blog
Bringing you news from our worlds to yours. Stories, interviews, articles and exclusive extracts just for you!
www.gollancz.co.uk

GOLLANCZ
LONDON